The Bronze Drums

ALL WHO KNOW AND LOVE SOUTH-EAST ASIA WILL RECAPTURE in this splendid novel of adventure—by France's great best-selling writer—the distinctive smell of the jungle in the dry season, the cries of beasts at night, and all the disturbing and sensuous charm of a paradise on earth. For this is Laos, in the second half of the twentieth century, the ideological meeting ground of Communism and Western democracy. The bronze drums are symbolic of war that is not war, for according to legend they were used centuries earlier to make the hill people think from the noise they made that there were troops in the valley.

It is against this background that the author weaves his fascinating plot. A key figure is Gibelin, a hero of the resistance against the Japanese, and later a smuggler, trafficker in opium and despoiler of temples; but the story really concerns the merciless struggle in which two secret agents are involved—the American colonel Tibbet, and the little, shy Frenchman Ricq, who is largely responsible for inventing the policy of neutralism, and for whom the only realities are his friend, the priest, in his faded soutane; his lovely Siamese mistress Ven; and his twenty years of life in the country.

By the same author

THE CENTURIANS

THE PRETORIANS

YELLOW FEVER

The Bronze Drums

JEAN LARTÉGUY

translated
by
XAN FIELDING
from the French

W. H. ALLEN
LONDON
1967

LES TAMBOURS DE BRONZE

Printed and bound in Great Britain by
C. Tinling & Co. Ltd.,
Prescot and London
for the publishers
W. H. Allen & Company,
Essex Street, London W.C.2.

6-11-09

Contents

Principal Characters

François Ricq	*a French agent*
Dan Ricq	*his brother*
Ven	*his Laotian mistress, or* phousao
Antoine Gibelin	*a lumberman, an old friend of* Ricq
Xavier Pinsolle	*Ambassador of France*
Father Maurel	*a missionary*
Paul Cléach	*a journalist*
Captain Meynadier	*an officer in the French Military Mission*
Pierre Prestelot	*Consul of France*
General Dubozel	*head of French Special Services*
Colonel Cosgrove Tibbet	*an American agent*
The Blue Prince Sisang	*leader of the Neutralist faction*
Captain Chanda	*commander of the Neutralist army*
Lieutenant Pierre Thon	*second-in-command to Chanda*
The White Prince Sanakon	*head of the right-wing faction*
General Si Mong	*Minister of War and head of Coordination*
Soumboun; Khammay	*two Coordination captains*
The Red Prince Lam Sammay	*head of the pro-Communist faction, the Pathet Lao*
Loan	*his Vietnamese wife*
Luong Me	*Pathet Lao secretary-general*
Le Maha Som	*chief of the Vientiane bonzes*
Flore	*a Franco-Vietnamese halfcaste*
Pamphone	*Minister of National Defence*

TO VICTORIA

Introduction

BRONZE drums are to be found in Laos, Burma and Tonkin, wherever there are still tribes descended from the original inhabitants of South-East Asia, such as the Mois or the Khas, the Karens or the Kachins. They are huge cauldrons which, on being struck, produce a noise like thunder. The flat surface of these drums is ornamented in the centre with a star, the circumference with copulating frogs.

According to one legend, General Ma Yuan, who lived in the first century of the Christian era, under the Han dynasty, had been made responsible for the defence of the southern marches of China. But since he had been given no soldiers, he had had the idea of installing bronze drums in all the cascades near the places where the credulous mountainfolk lived. The water falling on to these drums made the metal resound so loudly that the mountainfolk thought they were hearing the innumerable armies of the Son of Heaven. They remained for many long years in their highlands without daring to descend into the valleys.

Anyone who has lived in Laos finds in this legend the key to the incomprehensible incidents that have occurred there recently.

Twenty centuries after General Ma Yuan, the Chinese and Vietnamese Communists installed bronze drums in every cascade in Laos, this time to decoy the Whites, those brave and gullible barbarians. They convinced the French, then the Americans, that they were going to conquer this country. From north to south they engineered several minor incidents, skirmishes that resulted in a handful of casualties. They seized villages which no one ever dreamt of defending. With a great song and dance they created a pro-Communist movement, the Pathet Lao, which owed its existence solely to their support. Each time a couple of Laotian soldiers turned tail, the world press announced there was a Vietminh regiment or Chinese division on their heels.

Obsessed by the roll of the drums, the Whites came to the rescue of Laos to fight against an army which did not exist. They exhausted themselves in their attempts to find it. Having thus diverted their attention, the Communists, working secretly underground and sapping all resistance, were able to infiltrate South-Vietnam, Cambodia, Burma, Indonesia, Malaya, Singapore . . .

This book aims at recording the history of this gigantic and dextrous deception by which so many men and so many countries allowed themselves to be caught. But it is above all a novel, whose imaginary characters live in the Never-never land of Laos, a country sufficiently legendary to be known as the Kingdom of the Million Elephants and White Umbrella.

For the last ten years Laos has lived under the sign of a rather special tripartism. She has three capitals—Luang-Prabang in the north, Vientiane in the centre, and Savannakhet in the south—and three political factions whose leaders are three princes of royal blood, cousins of one another and also cousins of the king.

Each of these princes relies on an army and on foreign support, and for most of the time they act as mere standard-bearers or figureheads.

An American journalist called Johannes Milestone realized, a week after his arrival, that he would never be able to explain the complexity of the situation to his readers and so decided to allot a colour to each of the princes. The Blue Prince was Sisang, the head of the "Neutralist" faction which was supported by the troops of Captain Chanda, a strange character who had suddenly made his mark as a result of a *putsch*. He was backed by the French and the British, and, recently, also by the Russians after the latter had fallen out with the Chinese. Prince Sisang modelled himself on Gandhi. But this apostle of non-violence was a full-blooded and quick-tempered character. He had a weakness for strong tobacco, neat whisky, women and big-game hunting. A Public Works engineer and down-to-earth peasant, he was a different person altogether when he thought of his fields or expounded his views.

The White Prince was Phoum Sonakon. A former captain in the Foreign Legion and descended from the kings of the South, he was more at home in a guardroom than in a drawing-room, in a brothel or bar than in a palace. His little court consisted of a crowd of pimps, procuresses and libertines. He took no interest in politics but regretted having abandoned his crown under French pressure. He would rather have abandoned it of his own accord. Without knowing it, this loud-mouthed, courageous and coarse-grained character symbolized tradition. General Si Mong, a Thai halfcaste, was the real head of this faction. Quick-witted, scheming and grasping, a graduate of French military academies, he had none of a general's qualities and all those of a racketeer. The Americans furnished aid to the White Prince and General Si Mong, but not without suffering a few twinges of conscience.

His Highness Tiao* Lam Sammay became the Red Prince. Officially at least, he was the leader of the Pathet Lao, a National Front movement modelled on the Vietminh. Lam Sammay, who had studied at the School of Palaeography, dreamt of living like those romantic revolutionaries conceived by Malraux. He had displayed every quality that displeased true Communists: ostentation, gallantry and knight-errantry, and a sense of humour. So, although he was treated with consideration, he had become a mere tool in the hands of the Vietnamese Communists who directed his guerrillas and his party. The Chinese and North-Vietnamese were unreservedly behind this movement.

Milestone had drunk a lot of Pernod one day and got the

* A prince of royal blood.

princes and their colours mixed up when filing his copy. Neither the editor of his paper nor his readers noticed anything was amiss, which seemed to prove that Laos was not a matter of great interest even though it was considered necessary to mention it frequently in the press.

The king lived at Luang-Prabang in an uncomfortable palace from which he never emerged. A disciple of Jean-Jacques Rousseau, he personally tended a little vegetable plot in which he grew lettuces. An odd, confused character, he believed in spiritualism and table-turning and played the clarinet.

Antoine Gibelin, a few days before being assassinated, described how he had come upon the king one evening marching up and down the huge deserted halls in the palace blowing his clarinet. He was preceded by a servant carrying an oil lamp and followed by Ricq, the ethnologist, dressed in his old bush shirt and baggy trousers.

The king listened solemnly to the suggestions and recommendations he was given, but refused to take any decision for fear of unnecessarily jeopardizing the authority he had long since lost.

His court whiled away the time playing cards. Money would pass from the Grand Chamberlain's pocket to the Queen Mother's and end up in that of the king's brother.

At the period with which we are concerned, Laos had about one million five hundred thousand inhabitants belonging to a number of different races.* The Communists were in control of two thirds of the country, and the rainy season, the Nham Fon, had started a month before.

* Forty-two, to be precise, according to François Ricq's article in the *Bulletin of the French School of Far-Eastern Studies*: seventeen tribes of the Kha or Proto-Indochinese group, a small Khmer group, eleven races of Thai extraction, of whom the Laotians are only a small branch, five sorts of Meos and Yaos and five tribes of Sino-Tibetan origin like the Hos. And even apart from these, Ricq added with his usual modesty, the whole of the north of the country is still hardly known at all.

[1]

Xien Nip Camp

BETWEEN one and four o'clock in the morning of Sunday, 17 July 1964, a most mysterious coup d'état took place in Vientiane, the administrative capital of Laos. It did nothing to change the situation of the country and caused not a single casualty. It was the seventh or eighth that had occurred since independence and, had it not been for its utter pointlessness, no one would have paid more attention to it than it deserved. Never had anyone seen such lack of organization, such a chaotic operation, so few men and such little material engaged in order to capture a town. The "specialists" who had congregated at nine o'clock in the morning on the terrace of the Constellation tried in vain to find a motive or a purpose for this *putsch*. Yet these men were either journalists who were by no means lacking in imagination, secret agents who were even more fully endowed with it, or opium "carriers", procurers and police informers who had plenty of secret information. The total outcome of the coup d'état boiled down to the arrest of the President, His Highness Tiao Sisang Vang, of several Neutralist officers closely connected with him and of a certain François Ricq, an affable, unobtrusive man who had been sent out by the French School of Far-Eastern Studies to investigate the tribes and dialects of Laos.

Ricq had lived in Vientiane for twenty years and was therefore by now no more conspicuous than the flamboyants in the gardens or the saffron-coloured robes of the bonzes in the streets.

Paul Cléach, the local correspondent of Agence France Presse, put forward an explanation, however. According to him, the "Coordination" officers who had carried out the *putsch* were sozzling in the Bijou Bar at midnight. Always law-abiding when he saw there was nothing to be gained by not being so, Eugène Battesti, the proprietor of the night-club, hustled these revellers out at curfew time. Not knowing where to go and not wishing to break up the party, the worthy warriors decided to go and wake up Sisang, the Prime Minister, who lived nearby. Instead of offering them a drink, Tiao Sisang had shown he was anything but pleased to see them. From insults they came to blows. In their frenzy the roisterers brought out their revolvers, bundled the prince into a jeep and drove him to their barracks in Xien Nip Camp. After sobering up they were panic-stricken by the gravity of their offence and went off and dragged their leader, General Si Mong, out of bed to ask him to straighten things out. Si Mong informed them they had just carried out a coup d'état, which apparently had not occurred to them. At first he refused their request but finally, to get them out of the mess they were in and save the country, he agreed to take command of the *putsch* and at the same time assume power.

Needless to say, none of the "specialists" agreed with this interpretation—not that it was over-fanciful but because it came from Cléach who had been in Laos only a year.

At ten o'clock in the morning Father Olivier Maurel of the Foreign Missions celebrated High Mass before a scanty congregation. The absentees from his usual flock were a number of officers from the French Military Mission, most of the members of the French and Italian embassies, and the three Canadians from the International Control Commission who were all kept back in their offices as a result of the new coup d'état. They had to draft a report on the incident and try to disentangle its causes and effects. But in this coup d'état everything was incomprehensible, and nothing takes longer to explain than the inexplicable.

After the Gospel, Father Olivier Maurel turned towards the congregation. A sparse, nicotine-stained beard sprouted from the end of his pointed chin. The hem of his sun-bleached cassock was splashed with red mud. His eyes were set deeply in their sockets and his nose jutted out exaggeratedly above lips that curled back from a toothless jaw.

Forty years of Asia, tropical sun, wars, revolutions and acts of treason had tanned his skin and tarnished his illusions. He was now a tolerant sceptic, closely akin to the Buddhist monks whose religion he had come out here to oppose.

Having always lived in the bush, Father Maurel felt ill at ease as Curé of Vientiane. He refused to wear false teeth and when he preached he had an impediment in his speech:

"Blethlen, let us play. Flesh incidents have once again endangered peace in this countly. Play for those among us who are sufferling, for those who are experliencing plison, tolture and death. Play for them even if they have sown the wind and are now leaping the storm."

Pauline Helbronn, better known as Muguette, raised her head. She realized the priest was alluding to the incidents that had occurred during the night. Muguette was nearly seventy years old. Twenty-five of these she had spent at the girls' school where she taught good manners—those of the last century—the piano, sewing and needlework and how to lay a table properly. She was always to be seen in the same flat shoes, the same suit of ecru linen, the same incongruous straw hat adorned with a bunch of lilies of the valley. Pious and unassuming, Muguette was part and parcel of Vientiane; like the Breton mechanic who ran the airport garage; the three Corsican thugs who dealt in arms, drugs, gold and kindred commodities; Desnoyers, nicknamed Nutcracker, the pilot of the Junkers of Laos Air Transport, more commonly known as Air-Opium; Monsieur Moreau who did absolutely nothing; Ricq who did any amount of things; and Troussier, the former civil servant, who from habit and although pensioned off long ago still turned up every day at the Customs

House which had become the Ministry of Foreign Affairs. The Laotians, a conservative people, cherished Muguette like one of their own traditions and gently made fun of her little weakness: Muguette would occasionally get plastered on horrible sickly liqueurs. On these occasions her pale cheeks would flush, her hat would sit askew on her thick white hair. She would mumble to herself about her late husband, Monsieur Helbronn, a Treasury employee, whom the Japanese had executed in 1945. Monsieur Helbronn had been mistaken for a resistance leader and had paid with his life for a bit of harmless bragging.

Muguette pondered on the priest's words. Father Maurel's allusion to those men who had sown the wind and were reaping what they deserved could not apply to good Prince Sisang, the man of peace, and still less to Ricq. To whom, then?

Muguette made the collection, which amounted to a hundred and seventeen kips—not a very large sum. Madame de Saint-Urcize produced her usual twenty-kip note folded in four, and Madame Marcellin, the wife of the manager of the Indochina Brewery, one kip. Muguette made a mental note to mention this in her next letter to Juliette.

Every Monday since she had been out in Vientiane, Muguette wrote to her sister Juliette Marayet, who ran a stationery shop at 82 rue Claude-Decaen, Paris, XII, describing in minute detail the political news that came to her ears and the gossip of the French colony.

Muguette went back to her pew, pursing her lips, carrying the velvet offertory bag which was almost empty. She reflected: "People can say what they like about Monsieur Ricq, but at least when he came to church he wasn't tight-fisted. He would fish a note out of his pocket and put it on the plate without even looking. It was usually fifty or a hundred kips. On one occasion it was even five hundred kips, which doubled the rest of the collection. At other times he gave nothing at all, for his pockets were empty. He would then smile and make an apologetic gesture. Unfortunately, ever since he had been living with that young Laotian girl, he was no longer to be seen."

Madame Antoinette de Saint-Urcize, the wife of the Councillor at the French Embassy, was furious. Muguette realized this from the way she was fidgeting in her pew. This Sunday happened to be the day she was receiving the better-class ladies of Vientiane. She had had some cup-cakes sent from Bangkok by diplomatic bag. But Edouard, her husband, had asked her to cancel this annual reception because of the situation. What was she going to do with all those cup-cakes?

In the eyes of her women friends Antoinette was looked upon as thrifty, in anyone else's eyes she was regarded as a skinflint who "skimped" on her entertainment allowance. She looked like a big thoroughbred mare. "There's madness in Antoinette's family," Madame Marcellin always said. Muguette, who was better informed, knew what Antoinette took such pains to conceal. Edouard de Saint-Urcize had met her in the little scent-shop she ran at Moulins. He was looking for some socks and had come to the wrong store. The councillor was as lean and lanky as his wife. Gibelin, a queer sort of rogue who had come to the sticky end he deserved, had christened the couple the Hackney Ponies.

Antoinette was too much of a snob to dare to hold His Highness Prince Sisang responsible for all this inconvenience. In return, she spent the remainder of the service mentally inveighing against François Ricq who had been arrested by the "Coordination" police for some reason or other and whom the whole embassy was doggedly striving to get released. The wretched fellow, who lived like a native with a coloured woman and almost certainly slept on the floor, would not have found it a great hardship to spend a day or two longer in prison. It was the ambassador who had thought of this feeble excuse to make Antoinette cancel her reception. Glaring critically at Father Maurel as the service came to an end, the councillor's wife reflected it would be more suitable for him to be in a pensioners' home, or at a pinch in one of those jungle villages from which he came. In Vientiane he cut a poor figure. She made a mental note to discuss the matter with the bishop.

All of them had a good lunch—Pinsolle, the French Ambassador, in spite of his worries; Madame de Saint-Urcize, even though she was vexed; Muguette, because she paid special attention to her cooking on Sundays; Cléach and his mistress, Flore, because they were lunching in a Vietnamese restaurant. Then they all had a siesta.

At four o'clock in the afternoon Xien Nip Camp with its dilapidated hutments and marshy parade-ground was still plunged, like the rest of the town, in a sluggish torpor which only the first evening showers would dispel.

After being used as a training centre for the Laotian army, then as living quarters for the refugees from the Thai districts, Xien Nip had recently become the headquarters of the "Coordination" special forces. It had since acquired its sinister reputation. Here, it was said, was where they brought all the people whom General Si Mong's thugs discreetly abducted, either to hold them to ransom or because they were his political enemies.

Xien Nip lay five miles south of Vientiane on the edge of the forest, on the banks of the Mekong, on the Siamese border. This position made it a secure and convenient place. The reddish waters of the river served as a burial ground for anyone whom the Coordination soldiers failed to render amenable. The fishermen occasionally came across their waterlogged corpses but were careful not to retrieve them to avoid any fuss.

Prince Sisang and the ethnologist Ricq had been locked up in a large empty room which served as a guardroom in the days when the Colonial Infantry still occupied the camp. The two windows looking out on to the courtyard were equipped with iron bars. The wooden bunks and rifle racks had been used as firewood. The only remaining furniture consisted of an old bedstead with broken springs and, in one corner, a latrine bucket which stank to heaven and attracted the flies.

During the first few hours of his detention Ricq had applied himself to deciphering the graffiti on the walls which were thinly covered in brown plaster. They consisted mostly of lists of names —Faye, Lieutard, Orcelle—accompanied by the most elementary declarations of love, such as "To Phim for life"; warnings like "All the tarts at Mother Dok's are poxy", boastful claims such as

"My girl's hot stuff"; declarations of principle, "Down with respectibility, long live crime!" and further lists of names, sometimes accompanied by regimental numbers: "13227 Rifleman Le Roux Gérard; 17664 Rifleman Autron Léon . . ." All that remained Ricq reflected, of the hundreds of French soldiers who had been locked up in this room for being late on parade, brawling in a bar or forgetting to salute a superior, all that remained of them apart from the little bastards they had hastily sired and who could be seen toddling around bare-arsed in the market place.

What would remain of Ricq in a few hours, in a few days? A little bastard growing in Ven's womb, which he would not even have time to acknowledge; a name in the secret files of certain departments; a few articles he had published in the *Bulletin of the French School of Far-Eastern Studies* on the minorities of Laos—scarcely more than the Colonial Army soldiers had left.

Heavy raindrops started pattering down in the courtyard outside, filling the air with the stench of humus, rotting vegetation, quagmire and decay, which is the smell of the rainy season in Vientiane.

Prince Sisang sat on the rusty bedstead, with both hands laid flat on his stubby little legs, sucking at an empty pipe. He had received a punch on the jaw, and a large bruise varying in hue from purple to yellow gave him the grotesque face of a clown whose make-up has melted in the rain. The lapel of his white jacket was torn and hung limply like a shred of skin.

"They were Thais who struck me," he said in that slow, measured voice of his which seemed to swallow every word. He waited for Ricq to say something in reply, then went on more firmly:

"No Laotian would have dared. I am not only the head of a government which has been recognized by all the great powers: America, Russia, China . . . I am also a royal prince and a cousin of the King of Luang-Prabang."

Each time he mentioned the king, Tiao Sisang never omitted to add that he was only the king of a little province, a minor monarch whose authority over the whole of Laos could not be acknowledged by anyone in his right mind.

Ricq, with his old bush shirt hanging unbuttoned over his skinny torso, sat on the floor hugging his knees.

He realized the prince was asking, yet again, to be told lies because he needed these lies in order not to lose face and to recover his disarming optimism. Of course there were Thai agents and officers in the Coordination, but none of them had taken part in his arrest. Ricq had proof of this: he was still alive.

He drew his hand across his face. He had been arrested before being able to have a shower and a shave and to change his clothes. He had not even been allowed to put on his shoes.

Sisang was getting restless. Out of lassitude Ricq acquiesced:

"Yes, they were probably Thais." But out of honesty he corrected himself: "There were also some Laotians with them."

"Men who've been led astray, Ricq. This coup d'état is nonsense, just when I was about to reconcile the various factions by an international agreement. Have you any tobacco on you?"

Ricq got up and handed him his pouch. Short, but well-proportioned, he moved with a slightly rolling gait. He had a youthful figure, but his face with its grey stubble made him look like an old man with the body of an adolescent.

"How old is he really?" Sisang wondered.

He had met Ricq for the first time in December 1944, or January 1945, he could not remember exactly. In those days Sisang was a member of the Resident's staff and bore the pompous title of "Chargé de Mission". It was a very fashionable term in the administrative phraseology of Marshal Pétain in France and Admiral Decoux in Indo-China.

The Resident had asked him to establish contact with some Gaullist officers who were reported to have been parachuted from India into the region of Paksane.

His job was to persuade them not to provoke the Japanese by any spectacular or bloodthirsty operation. In return, it might be arranged for a blind eye to be turned on their activity and, if needs be, for assistance to be given them.

"How am I going to find them?" Sisang had asked. "They haven't left cards on the Administrator of Paksane."

The Resident had sighed and shaken his head:

"Come along, my dear chap, use your brains. Antoine Gibelin has some lumber camps in that region, and Father Maurel with his usual firm grip administers a dozen Catholic villages there. If these agents exist you'll find them either with the one or the other—with Gibelin because he can't stand the Vichy régime, or any other régime for that matter, or with Father Maurel because he's a refuge for anyone in hiding and because he has a weakness for conspiracy and war."

Father Maurel had arranged a meeting between Sisang, Ricq and Gibelin. In those days Ricq could have been no older than twenty-two and looked like a girl. He and his radio operator, a French warrant officer, passed themselves off as Public Works surveyors. They had all the tools of the trade, plane-tables, levels, measuring chains, etc. Sisang, himself an engineer, had been astonished to see that Ricq knew how to use these instruments, that this little wisp of a man already left nothing to chance and had built up a perfect "cover story".

Gibelin had been as foul-mouthed as ever, calling the Resident and these "bloody little Chargés de Mission" every name under the sun. Ricq had proved amenable. They had come to an agreement: so long as the Japanese did not attack the French, the resistance groups would confine themselves to receiving parachute drops, storing arms and, if necessary, training guerrillas.

On 9 March 1945 the Japanese attacked all the French garrisons in Indo-China. Sisang had fled to China with most of the senior French and Laotian officials in Vientiane.

After the reconquest of Laos by Leclerc's French troops, Ricq, Gibelin and a few others had tried to form a Laotian government from the former members of the anti-Japanese resistance movement. They had appointed the worthy legionary Sanakon as its head. They had even created the "Lao Renovation Party". In less than a year they had met with total failure. With the exception of Prince Sanakon, this government did not include a single member of the great Laotian families who control the country through their connections. The "Renovation Party" had melted away. Ricq, once more a civilian and already engaged on delicate missions on behalf of his own government, had gone to fetch Sisang from Bangkok where the prince was playing the part of a moderate nationalist and man of reason. Sisang had agreed to become president and had governed Laos after a fashion up to the defeat of the French at Dien Bien Phu. After this there had been various incidents, the Americans had arrived in force at Vientiane, and the prince had resigned and returned to France.

Once again Ricq had gone to fetch him back from Paris. This was last year, in May 1963. Sisang still remembered the skinny, ridiculously clad figure he had seen coming into the lobby of the Hotel Raphael where he was waiting for him. Ricq had greeted him in the Laotian manner, pressing the palms of his hands together, and said:

"All the Laotians are waiting for you now that you're the only one capable of restoring peace."

To hide his emotions, Sisang had almost snubbed him: "You'd better get yourself another suit. The one you're wearing dates from the last war. Everyone's looking at you as though you were a ghost."

Ricq knew he would be held in prison for a long time, that he might never come out of it alive, whereas Sisang would be released tomorrow night or the day after. He watched the prince filling his pipe, trying to cram as much tobacco into it as possible, even scattering some on the floor in the process.

No one had wanted to overthrow the government, they had only tried to frighten him. But, as in every improvised affair, some blunders had been committed.

Sisang would shortly be back with his big jar of strong tobacco, his whisky, his villa, his servants, whereas Ricq would have nothing but an ounce or two of shag left to withstand hunger, fear and, what was even harder to bear than torture, the conception he had of it. Would he be able to hold out? Would he behave like his brother? But what could he give away? In Laos there were no secrets.

"Ricq?"

"Yes, Your Highness."

"Ricq, we might perhaps forget some . . . how can I put it . . . some of our differences of opinion?"

The prince spoke a French full of ready-made phrases and clichés, weighing his words like a provincial politician elected for the first time to the Palais Bourbon.

"This senseless . . . coup d'état . . . leads me . . . to believe . . . you are not entirely . . . wrong . . ."

Ricq felt like blocking his ears. He controlled himself and came and sat next to Sisang. Then he spoke in the composed and melancholy tone that people generally use to evoke the distant memory of someone dead.

"Your Highness, it's not only differences of opinion that separate us. For the last six months we haven't seen eye to eye on anything. You've let General Si Mong combine all the police departments in a single organization, the Coordination. You've allowed the Coordination officers to be sent on training courses in Thailand, you've believed in the American assurances, but you've let down Captain Chanda and his Neutralists who brought you to power because you didn't like Chanda, because you were irritated at being indebted to a little paratroop officer. Chanda is a brave man but simple-minded and credulous and above all he can't bear not being popular. When he realized you were fed up with him, he began to lend an ear to what the Communists told him. He has given you the slip . . ."

"He has given you the slip as well. Yet it was you who created him. In any case one can't run a country by relying on a sentimental savage and an army that no longer obeys anyone."

"Nor on a racketeer like Si Mong, who can't even keep his gangs under control."

The rain drove from the courtyard the two Coordination soldiers in paratroop uniform who were mounting guard outside the window. Clutching their sub-machine-guns, they ran off to take cover in a doorway.

"They're frightened of the rain," Ricq went on gently, jerking his head in their direction. "They're as frail and timorous as children, but if they're ordered to shoot us they'll do it."

"What do you know about them?"

"I've taught many children of that sort how to handle a weapon and kill. It was for what I believed to be a good cause. Now these children no longer believe in anything and they kill for the sake of the leaders they follow because those leaders keep the specific promises they've made. General Si Mong has no aim, no political ideal, no programme to put forward to his men. No one gives a damn about anti-Communism in Laos. But he has given them money, girls, the right to beat up any poor wretch they come across, permission to extort, racketeer, steal and make money on the side. Those are tangible benefits. As long as they last, as long as the police, the bodyguards and shock troops are not required to maintain a certain standard of discipline, as long as they are not required to fight against soldiers as well armed as themselves, they will never abandon their leader."

Irritated, as he always was when anyone failed to share his opinion or criticized his policy, the prince cut Ricq short:

"They surrounded my residence at one o'clock in the morning. Two sections, no more. Without a word of warning, they opened up with a bazooka . . . The first shell smashed the roof, the second failed to detonate, the third went through the wall of my office. Then they started spraying the front of the house with machine-guns. A senseless fusillade. My guards were playing *phay-thong** in the kitchen. Two of them were wounded and the others took to their heels through the garden. I was left all by myself, with the electricity cut off. I dressed in the dark and forgot my tobacco. Two Coordination officers burst into the room flashing their torches. I saw at once that they'd been drinking. They could hardly speak properly. One of them at least was a Thai. I protested . . . I tried to make them see reason, to show them the folly of what they were doing . . . It was then the Thai struck me in the face. If I ever find that fellow, Ricq, I'll make him pay for it. Jabbing a sub-machine-gun into my back, they made me get into a jeep and brought me here. The drunkest of them kept saying I was a traitor to Laos. How dare he!"—at this point the prince embarked on another verbal flourish—"when I have sacrificed everything for Laos, when I could be living quietly in France, when I have renounced my rights to the throne so as to bring peace to the country . . ."

"The man who struck you," said Ricq, "is called Sounboum. Captain Sounboum. The other man's name is Khammay. He's

* A Laotian game, played with 120 narrow, rectangular Chinese cards.

also a captain. Both of them were trained at the Police College in Bangkok. They were the same men who came and arrested me and they hauled me off in the same jeep as you. To carry out the coup d'état, they had only one jeep."

"You're joking."

"Only one jeep, Your Highness, and as for troops, only one battalion. Khammay told me all this after preventing Sounboum from shooting me. Luckily he was with me in the maquis in 1945. I had actually helped him to get into the police."

"And what of Sao* Ven?" Sisang politely enquired, although he did not give a damn about her.

To him she was just an insignificant little *phousao** who is taken on as a servant or concubine when a legal wife grows old and ugly and no longer wants to make love. Yet Ven was considered pretty. She was Captain Chanda's niece. Like him, she probably had Kha blood, the blood of the savage and the slave.

"In my house the soldiers battered the doors down with their rifle butts," Ricq replied. "Khammay called Ven a whore because she was living with a Frenchman, and a Communist because she was Chanda's niece. But he prevented Sounboum from laying a finger on her. A little later, in the jeep, just as we were driving out of Vientiane, when Sounboum produced his revolver, Khammay once again stopped him. Perhaps, in his own way, Khammay is quite fond of me; or maybe his first trip with you had sobered him up."

"I'll get you out of here, and you'll be entitled to damages."

"The surprising thing," Ricq went on, as though he had not heard, "the surprising thing is what the Coordination people hold against me: giving you bad advice, although for months you've always done the opposite of what I've told you."

Prince Sisang grunted and jumped down from the bedstead.

"Ricq, Laos wants peace. There's only one way of making peace: getting everyone to agree and uniting all the factions to form a government."

* A girl of humble background as opposed to Nang, or Miss, which designates an unmarried woman of the middle classes or aristocracy.

† Young girl.

"That would be like uniting under a single roof an earthenware pot and an iron pot, a tiger, a fox, a lamb and a wild boar."

"It was Colonel Cosgrove Tibbet who engineered this coup d'état, wasn't it?"

"I don't think so. Cos would never have done anything so foolish. He knows the country too well. And the proof is, they say the same about him as they do about me: that he's been undermined by Laos, girls and opium. I've never set foot in an opium den. Nor has Cos. As for girls, I hardly bothered about them at all until I met Ven, and Cos is said to be anything but demanding in that respect."

"You've become great friends, haven't you?"

"Friends is hardly the word. We've been working against each other for so long that we've come to know each other inside out and sometimes have the same point of view."

"What is France going to do?"

"Protest, Your Highness."

"And England?"

"The same. The Americans are also going to protest, but not so forcefully. Then they'll wait and see. They weren't able to prevent the coup d'état, which put your government against them. They can't afford to have Si Mong and his Coordination against them as well."

"What about the Communists?"

"Fighting will break out again in the Plain of Jars. It's too good an excuse to miss. It was with your government they signed the cease-fire agreements, which in any case they never had any intention of honouring. Now you've been thrown into prison by 'a handful of adventurers and Fascists'—that's what they called Si Mong and his police even before. So they're no longer bound by any agreements. What have they facing them in the Plain of Jars? Chanda's Neutralists—and all the Neutralist officers who were in Vientiane have just been arrested together with their families. The Neutralists are already demoralized, they won't fight any more.

"You know, Your Highness, this coup d'état is so idiotic that I can't help wondering whether Si Mong himself didn't have a hand in it."

In point of fact Ricq could not imagine the general, who was head of the Coordination and Vice-President, an utter scoundrel and racketeer, but as wily as a Chinese merchant, being involved in such a risky business.

With his fists thrust into the pockets of his tattered trousers, His Highness Tiao Sisang strode up and down the cell. His pace increased as his anger mounted at the thought of all this muddle and disturbance.

"Then who?"

When he was worked up, Sisang could become as violent and vicious as a buffalo. He was then capable of charging without feeling the blows, insulting without weighing his words. But he quickly reverted to his true character, that of a peaceful ruminant champing high-falutin' phrases about Neutrality, the United Nations, the Third World, fundamental principles, international pledges and self-determination. Ricq wondered whether Sisang was going to react or acquiesce, whether his anger was merely a flash in the pan or would be sustained.

"Our friend Sisang," Pinsolle, the French Ambassador, always said, "is the myth of Antaeus in reverse. The giant Antaeus in his combat with Hercules recovered his strength on touching the ground. Sisang loses his on returning to his native land. He only begins to exist when he sets foot on foreign soil. Sisang is an excellent prime minister when he's living in Paris."

It had stopped raining and a sentry had just reappeared outside the window. He was whistling through his teeth a popular song imported from Bangkok.

"It's not the same man as the one before," Ricq observed.

"What difference does that make?"

"I'm going to try and have a word with him. We might get some news."

Sisang leaned forward to see what would happen. He still did not understand how Ricq managed to collect so much information and maintain so many contacts in every class of society, in every race. The Americans and Thais spent fortunes and received nothing but tittle-tattle in exchange, whereas this Frenchman without money or any other means knew practically everything that was going on, every scheme and plot afoot, from the Chinese border to the flooded districts of Champassac and Sithandone.

Ricq went over to the window and in a a low voice started whistling the same tune as the soldier. The latter turned round to reveal a big round head with a tiny beret perched on it.

"What's your name?" Ricq asked him in Laotian.

Surprised at finding a *Phalang*, a Frenchman, who could converse in his own language, the soldier replied:

"Pheng."

Pheng had been ordered not to speak to the prisoners, to prevent them even from coming up to the window. But guard duty was so boring that one had to make the most of what distractions were offered.

"Stand back there," he said to Ricq, to assert his authority. "You've no right to approach the window."

Ricq did not budge and went on:

"Pheng, you're from Savannakhet, aren't you?"

There was every chance he might be since most of the Coordination men had been recruited in the south of the country, General Si Mong's stamping-ground. The soldier nodded his head: yes, he was from Savannakhet all right.

Growing more and more interested, he rested his rifle against the window-sill and drew close to the bars. Like all Laotians, he was extremely curious. In his turn he enquired: "Is it true the little fellow in there with you is Tiao Sisang?"

From him Ricq learnt that Captain Chanda, the head of the Neutralist troops, had fought back when they tried to arrest him. With his personal bodyguard, he had been able to take to the bush.

"In any case they would never have been able to kill him," said Pheng. "You can't kill someone invulnerable except with a silver bullet which has been cast while certain incantations are pronounced over it."

The soldier suddenly turned round and snatched up his rifle. An officer was coming into the courtyard.

Ricq commented on the news:

"I suppose a small Coordination unit tried to capture Chanda at home. To scare him, they fired on his villa; Chanda and his men returned the fire. Whereupon the special troops took to their heels and Chanda calmly set off down the Luang-Prabang road, maybe even by truck. Chanda's invulnerability is first and foremost his courage."

"No," said the prince.

"You believe in this legend?"

"The others believe in it and so does Chanda. That's all that matters. Invulnerability is a secret of your friends the Khas; Chanda is a Kha on his mother's side, a Thai-Neua on his father's. He hasn't a drop of Lao blood in his veins."

The prince relapsed into his stolid silence.

He too was invulnerable, but he had been taught in France not to believe in such nonsense.

In his family, that of the "kings of the front" of Luang-Prabang,* it was a tradition for one of the sons to be sent secretly to an old sorcerer at Attopeu. It was he, Sisang, who was chosen, because he was about to go to France and was therefore exposed to danger.

He was thirteen at the time; he was now sixty. It was a long journey. He still remembered his trip down the Mekong in a pirogue with two servants who were well acquainted with the rapids, the whirlpools, the sharp rocks on which the hull might be smashed.

Since they made no sound as they drifted down stream, the animals

* In the ancient kingdom of Luang-Prabang there used to be five kings: the king of the centre, or King Luang, who was the religious leader and dealt with nothing else; the king of the front, a sort of palace marshal who was in charge of the administration of the kingdom; the king of the right who ran the treasury; the king of the left who was responsible for agriculture and fishery; the king of the rear who was the court minister. Antoine Gibelin, true to his inveterate antimilitarism, maintained that the king of the rear, the one who saw nothing, must have been the head of the army.

Already in the days of Pavie there existed no more than two kings of Luang-Prabang.

Occupied by the Siamese, devastated by the black, yellow or red flags, the kingdom had been reduced to its most elementary expression. The French Republic, very punctilious about anything bearing on royalty and protocol, wanted only one king. They therefore chose King Luang, the king of the centre, made a viceroy of the king of the front and court ministers of the others.

were not scared away and at dusk Sisang could see them all at close quarters as they came down to the river to drink: elephants, stags, wild buffaloes, tigers, macaws, gibbons, langur monkeys . . .

How lovely the jungle was on the banks of the King River! Nowadays one could only leave Vientiane by air. The few roads and tracks that had not been destroyed were in the hands of the Communists, who had also set up machine-guns above some of the gorges overlooking the Mekong.

He, Sisang Vang, the head of this country, who adored the jungle, who used to dream about it when he was at school in France, who had hunting in his blood—he too had to travel by plane like any white man.

He was seized with fury. He gave the bedstead a kick and hurt his foot. Ricq looked at him in astonishment.

At the end of the voyage, at the end of the river, young Sisang was taken to the sorcerer's tall-roofed hut. This hut was also the guest house.

The sorcerer paid hardly any attention to him. He fed him on game and stodgy rice and made him drink brews made from bitter plants. Sisang used to tremble with fright when a branch scraped the roof in the dark, or a rustling sound came from the nearby forest. The *phis* were on the prowl. Was it the herbs that made him nervy and on edge or else plunged him into a sleep akin to torpor? At any rate, on several occasions, he fancied he saw or heard those evil spirits that come and devour a man's brain.

Young Sisang, who was about to be educated in France, witnessed the ritual sacrifice of a buffalo tied to its stake and watched naked men daubing themselves in its blood. On several occasions, and always at night, the sorcerer led him up to a tree in the forest. He made him recite certain phrases which he did not understand, then pricked him with the point of an arrow and mixed his blood with the earth. On the last day he said to him in his broken Laotian:

"You are now invulnerable to bullets, daggers and the diseases which the *phis* of the forest inflict. But I cannot do anything in respect of arrows and poison. So never get on bad terms with a Kha."

Three months later Sisang entered the Alsatian School in Paris. One day, to overawe his French schoolfriends, he had revealed that he was invulnerable.

"Is that so?" said a scruffy little ginger-headed lad. "Well, we'll see."

And he had punched him in the face.

The ginger boy's fist, mathematics, chemistry and other subjects had made him forget the *phis*. But deep down inside him, in those innermost recesses in which all the mysteries of a man's race lie hidden, there remained a vague belief in this invulnerability. This was perhaps the key to his courage and the explanation of his good fortune. Twice over he had almost been caught by the Japanese, on another occasion by the Vietminh, and on yet another by the Thais in the service of the Americans. A year ago, when he had landed at Bangkok, the hired killers of Marshal Aprasith, General Si Mong's uncle, had made an attempt to abduct him.

Ricq sat down on the floor again, hugging his knees.

"Si Mong is a coward," the prince said suddenly. "He wouldn't mind being invulnerable. Did you know, Ricq, that this graduate of the French Military Academy is frightened of the forest and the *phis*? Nothing will induce him to go into the forest except when he has to cross it to go and collect his opium from the Meos up on the mountains. But Si Mong is so rapacious, he's so fond of money that he forgets his fear, a fear which makes him physically ill. I've seen him. But the Khas are the only people who can make a man invulnerable and they don't like Si Mong."

"The Khas, Your Highness, don't like anyone. I've lived with them. They tolerated me. Today I wouldn't take the same risk. They're riddled with Vietminhs. The missionaries have hardly any success with them, but the Communists, by dint of patience, by respecting their gods, their customs and their women, have managed to foist themselves on the tribes. The Khas now have rifles and machine-guns. It's not only sambar, buffalo and wild boar they hunt these days, but men as well. They no longer need to believe in the *phis*."

"Ricq, you're like those little leeches that drop from the trees and have to be burnt before they'll lose hold. We don't know what's going to happen to us, we don't know who's behind this plot, we don't know if that sentry who's so good at whistling Thai songs isn't going to come in here and empty his sub-machine-gun into our bellies, yet you just sit there ruminating over old grievances."

"There are five hundred thousand Khas in Laos, Your Highness, a third of the population, and they're now against us and on the side of the Communists."

"That's not my fault. I realize all the blunders that have been committed against the Khas, against the Meos . . . It's the army."

"Your Highness, you've done nothing."

"I can't do everything. Lieutenant-Colonel Ricq, of the French Special Forces, you were put at my disposal to help me and also to keep an eye on me, weren't you? But all you think of is criticizing me. I was the one who got you promoted in Paris."

"I'd rather you hadn't lost the Khas."

"You helped all right as long as you agreed with me . . . But that was before you met that girl Ven and sided whole-heartedly with Captain Chanda's party. What's going on in Vientiane, what are Chanda's partisans up to?"

"Nothing, Your Highness. Maybe they're going to reassemble in the bush or just drop every thing.

"The women in Vientiane are preparing their rice; the Co-ordination men are swilling their beer; the journalists are having a drink on the terrace of the Continental and cursing this bloody country where something always crops up just when they're about to return to Hong Kong. In Hong Kong the hotels are air-conditioned and everyone speaks English.

"The *sambos* are pedalling their cycle-rickshaws along the streets, looking to right and left in search of a customer. The ambassadors are conferring. General Si Mong has summoned his accomplices to your office and they're sharing out the loot—you get the rice import licence, Bong Pha; Phim Pho, you get the gold; I'm hanging on to the opium."

"What about the people?"

"Your Highness, the people don't give a damn. This is the seventh coup d'état in three years and they always see you come back, promising them that this time you'll make peace. Only once did they take a stand, but it was in favour of Chanda. They were punished by being shelled for three days by artillery and mortars from the Thai bank. In the bush, in the villages, in the isolated valleys, the peasants don't hear the news until six months later. More often than not it's the Communists who put them in the picture. Naturally they give their own version."

"I've never seen you so pessimistic."

"Laos is lost, you know it as well as I do. Today it needs only one jeep and two hundred men to overthrow a government. It's not serious for you, Your Highness, you have another country . . . yes indeed, France . . . a wife and children who are French, an apartment in Paris and a fine estate in the Dordogne, an estate on which you dote as though you were a French peasant. I once caught you looking at some seed catalogues—seeds that don't grow in Laos. I have no other country but this, no garden in which to plant seeds, and only this woman Ven who's twenty-five years younger than myself."

"I love Laos as much as you do."

"Not Laos, but your own conception of Laos: a sensible country that resembles France."

Sisang felt renewed affection for Ricq.

"Do you want to borrow my jacket?" he asked. "You could roll it up and use it as a pillow."

"Don't bother."

"Are you frightened?"

"Yes, of being murdered like Gibelin before completing what I still have to do."

Red and black clouds formed overhead, filling the squares of sky outlined by the windows. The Mekong was quite close and Sisang strained his ears to hear the lapping of the water, the noise of big fat fish leaping from the river and falling back with the deep resounding splash of a stone dropped down a well.

Stout and greedy, His Excellency Pinsolle had just finished his usual cup of chocolate with the rich cream pastries specially made for him by Fernande, his cook, whom he had sent for from Pilles, her native village in the Drôme.

After wiping the froth of chocolate from his lips, he heaved a sigh of content, then went over to the window looking out on to the statue of Auguste Pavie* and stood there waiting for the rain to stop. Zavier Pinsolle did not like going out in the wet. As soon as the shower was over, he would leap into his car and, pennant flying, make a round of the embassies and ministries where he would cajole and threaten with his usual mixture of volubility and adroitness, cracking jokes but pursuing his own ends, single-minded and determined but never appearing to be so.

He had to obtain the immediate release of Prince Sisang and Ricq and see that this coup d'état was presented to the world as an unimportant incident, a misunderstanding, an outburst of temper on the part of a handful of young officers. Yet Sisang had been a great disappointment to Pinsolle. The ambassador had hoped, thanks to him, to use Laos as a spring-board for a policy of neutralism which would then be extended to embrace the whole Indo-Chinese peninsula. It was Ricq who had put this idea into his head and Pinsolle had got it accepted at the Quai d'Orsay. Since then they had been brought closer together by this scheme. Three days before the coup d'état, Pinsolle had invited Ricq to dinner and for the first time had given vent to his feelings.

"Sisang is no longer in Laos," he had said. "He's already in France. If he's staying on, it's only because he wants to polish up

* Auguste Pavie, born at Dinan in 1847, started out as a telegraph agent and eventually became a consul and minister plenipotentiary. He marched for thousands of miles over the tracks of Laos and gave this country to France without firing a shot. With that perfidy which was second nature to him, Pinsolle once said to his councillor, Monsieur de Saint-Urcize, whose only point to him was being well bred:

"Luckily, my dear fellow, in 1964 there's no longer any danger of trouble-makers like Auguste Pavie getting into the service. Do you realize, he travelled on foot, spoke all sorts of dialects, slept on the floor, was adored by the locals and, I believe, hadn't even passed school certificate."

"Yes, very luckily," the councillor had agreed. "In our profession people with too much personality and too little education cause nothing but disasters."

"Why, yes, my dear fellow. These days all that's asked of anyone is a modicum of manners."

his statement for the few French papers that are interested in his story. He can't bank on any other nag, it's the only one that still has four legs even though the rest of it's in pretty poor shape."

For all his faults, Sisang was nevertheless courageous and honest in his own way. He even represented an exception in this Far-East Asia where whole countries were at the mercy of gangsters, racketeers and military leaders who were either arrogant and circumscribed or else young, inexperienced, insensible and jealous of one another—in which case they were inclined to cause even greater havoc than the racketeers. This was what was happening in Saigon.

When he had been appointed to Vientiane, Pinsolle had shown certain reservations. He was not at all fond of countries with an uncertain existence, where politics are conducted by secret agents, whom he regarded indiscriminately as chatterboxes, muddlers and braggarts.

General Durozel, head of the S.D.E.C.E.* had called on him at the Quai d'Orsay to tell him that Ricq, the agent in question, was not at all what Pinsolle imagined. He had explained:

"He's a shrewd, sharp-witted, unassuming man who knows everything about Laos, all its dialects and intrigues, the past of every man and woman living there. He would never allow himself to encroach on your prerogatives; he's our best agent in South-East Asia. Furthermore, I look upon Ricq as a personal friend."

Such glowing references were uncharacteristic of Durozel, a cold, withdrawn person who was far from lavish in his praise.

And in Ricq Pinsolle did indeed find a valuable collaborator, a man of few words, though he always answered any question clearly, and with a keen sense of social and hierarchic distinctions —somewhat too keen for the ambassador's liking.

He was not the sort of person who could be a close friend. Ricq was evasive, secretive, so much a prisoner of his own little

* *Service de documentation, études et contre-espionage*, the French Intelligence organization previously known as D.G.E.R. (*Direction générale des études et recherches*) and during the war in Free France as B.C.R.A. (*Bureau central de recherche et action*).

world that he could only talk shop. He was the exact opposite of the exuberant and colourful character that Antoine Gibelin had been.

Pinsolle had come to Luang-Prabang to present his credentials to the king and had spent a week there, staying with his councillor, Baron de Saint-Urcize, in the former residence of the French governors. The river flowed past it, a red ribbon in the midst of the dark encircling mountains. An old gendarme and his Laotian wife did the cooking, combining Oriental spices with French sauces. The gendarme used to drive them round the royal city in a jeep. The jeep was old and often broke down. Monsieur de Saint-Urcize and Pinsolle, the former cursing and swearing, the latter having the time of his life, had to help the gendarme push it to the top of a slope. They would return from these drives covered in mud, but Pinsolle used to bring back lengths of silk embroidered in silver or gold, little brass buddhas and photographs of clear rivers with lovely girls bathing in them. Monsieur de Saint-Urcize concentrated on landscapes and monuments, Pinsolle on the smiling faces and bodies of the *phousaos*.

Gibelin spent six months of the year in Luang-Prabang. A friend of the former king, he had remained a familiar figure in palace circles after the monarch's death and was said to be having an affair with one of the princesses.

Gibelin, who as usual appeared to have nothing to do, took Pinsolle and his councillor by pirogue to visit Pakou, the gateway to Luang-Prabang, a gorge which the river had pierced through the limestone mountains. On the right bank there were some caves below high-water level. They had been converted into temples and were adorned with buddhas carved out of the solid rock. The water dripping down the walls was collected in stone basins and used by the priests at the coronation ceremony of the kings. On their way back, at dusk, after passing the rapids, they came out into the wide loop of the Mekong which encircled Luang-Prabang. Here they encountered another vessel paddled by four young boatmen. A young girl, with her hair hanging loose, her thighs and legs uncovered and a damp shawl stretched across her breasts and stomach, sat in the prow singing. She gave a long-drawn throaty cry which reverberated over the motionless water. The boatmen took up the cry after her, but modulating its savage tone so as to harness it to the rhythm of their paddle strokes.

What was originally just the call of an animal in love became a song which already followed a melodic theme. The girl repeated her cry and the men once again transformed it into music and rhythm. The pirogue went past them, while the *phousao* waved to them with a gesture that was imbued with grace, distinction and all the freedom in the world.

Gibelin sprinkled some water over his gaunt, hatchet-face, swept back a grey lock and confessed to Pinsole:

"That's why I love this country: because of certain encounters that have something miraculous about them, like this encounter on the river, like others I have had in the forest, in the distant isolated valleys, in the blue highlands of the Meos when the whole of the Tran Ninh is one vast flower-bed. I've come across men in their pure state, living in natural surroundings that haven't yet been spoiled. It's difficult to explain, but I now feel almost inflated with gratitude towards this country which has given me so much delight. Did you know that in Pavie's time, about 1887, the coins of Luang-Prabang had the shape of a male organ and those of Xieng Mai of a female organ?"*

"Do you know of any other country in the world where you can buy rice, meat and cloth in exchange for this pagan symbol, the sexual organ, which gives not only delight but life? That's why a fellow as different from me as little Ricq is devoted to Laos. Sometimes I feel as though we're the last two angels defending this doomed paradise against annihilation, Ricq the black angel, myself the white."

"Why do you call him Little Ricq?" Pinsolle had asked.

"I knew him in Paris when he was fifteen years old. I came across him again in the maquis; he was twenty-three. There are

* Pavie writes: "Narrow, elongated and flat, one side (of the coins) is adorned with what appears to be wild flowers. This design is produced by drops of ant juice being dabbed on to the heated metal by means of a straw. Crown-shaped blisters are thereby formed and this pattern is preserved when the metal cools, as proof that the coin is not merely silver plated.

still two of us who call him Little Ricq—Father Maurel and myself, the sole French survivors of our resistance group."

Pinsolle had then asked:

"I'd very much like to know if the operation you've just attempted with Ricq and Prince Sisang—which is why I'm here—doesn't derive its origin, like a certain form of Gaullism in France, from the myth of the Resistance? It's with the help of the memories and men that you knew at that time, with whom you fought, that you've created this Neutralist movement. But since the Japanese occupation, twenty years have elapsed. Sisang, Chanda, his second-in-command Thon, the officers, the police, the deputies who are backing this movement, are only bound together by this slender thread, some twenty-year-old memories. It seems rather insufficient to me."

Gibelin had burst out laughing:

"Of course, but there's always the question of personal gain. I don't mean merely money. Like the Gaullists, these men have known a very brief moment of glory; they still feel the urge to be applauded again, to make another appearance on stage. They still think that just because they constituted a chosen few who went on fighting when the others gave in, they are entitled to certain rights over the country until their dying day."

"That doesn't explain why you embarked on Laotian Neutralism."

"I don't like people and things changing too much round me. I had conceived a particular picture of Laos and I'm sticking to it. I don't want it daubed with red or blue, or parcelled out, or made into a concentration camp between the Chinese, Thais and Vietnamese. Laos can't be saved, I know. How can you save a nation that doesn't exist, a people that won't fight? Ricq is labouring under many a delusion on that score. All I want is for Laos to survive long enough to enable me, Antoine Gibelin, to be happy here for my last remaining years . . . happy, that's to say, to my way of thinking. The only possibility of survival for this country was Neutralism.

"You see, Your Excellency, I'm a selfish man. I need Laos, I need my long trips in the forest or on the river, my hunting, my encounters with a past that seems to have been kept on ice. Of course, there are also the girls, the money I make without any effort, life on a grand scale, my friends. Ricq loves this country because of everything he has given it. Ricq is generous and charitable. Father Maurel is right, he's a genuine Christian. It's funny, Westerners always seem to be seeking excuses for being happy and enjoying life: Ricq wants to help the Laotians, Father Maurel to convert the pagans. It's false, Maurel merely loves Laos and doesn't even try any longer to make Christians of these people to whom Buddhism is infinitely better suited. Ricq is like a goldfish that's used to its bowl. If he came out of it, he'd die."

For a moment Pinsolle believed he had found the special partner and friend that he felt he needed every time he came to a new country. In Venezuela it had been Ramon Da Silva; in Bolivia, Helmuth Herrendorf; in Norway, Inge Olafson. In Laos was it going to be Antoine Gibelin?

But Gibelin could not resist playing one of his usual little jokes on the ambassador. He showed him round the most beautiful pagodas of Luang-Prabang: the Vat Sen, the Vat Xien Tong, the Vat Chum Kong, all made of perishable materials such as wood, brick and dried mud and which, being destroyed over and over again, were rebuilt each time more flimsily.

He convinced Pinsolle and Saint-Urcize that they had to take off their shoes before entering the sanctuaries and behave as though they were in a mosque. To the utter astonishment of the priests and the local population, the Ambassador of France and his little escort were seen to untie their shoe-laces and tramp along the cold flagstones and worm-eaten wooden floors in dark purple (Pinsolle) and red-and-black striped (Monsieur de Saint-Urcize) socks. The joke lasted until, on entering the Vat Chum Kong, Pinsolle perceived that the Laotian builders who were restoring the woodwork there were all shod in heavy jungle boots.

He steered clear of the lumberman from then on and this was why in Laos his special friend and partner was not Antoine Gibelin.

Still standing by the window, Pinsolle tried desperately to fathom who was behind the *putsch*. According to the latest information he had received, Si Mong had recovered control of his officers. But it was not he who had launched the operation. He had merely jumped on to the train after it had started, thereby enabling himself also to appear as the saviour of law and order.

Night fell abruptly, bringing with it, after a few minutes' silence, the sound of fluttering wings, a rustling and scuffling that seemed to emanate from the stones, while the huge lizard known as the *tokkee* gave its almost human cry: "Tok . . . kee". Pinsolle began thinking about that odd little fellow named Ricq.

The military attaché, Lt.-Col. Andelot, came rushing into the room with a telegram in his hand.

"You've got ants in your pants, Colonel?" said Pinsolle who enjoyed using coarse language on occasion.

"Your Excellency . . ."

"Take a deep breath. Has China just declared war on the United States, or what?"

"Almost, Your Excellency, almost. Fighting has broken out again in the Plain of Jars. I've just had a signal from our military mission."

"Andelot, you've been here a year now, and during that year you've rushed in here at least three times a week to tell me . . . guess what? . . . that fighting has broken out again in the Plain of Jars. What's happening to that gang of colonels and generals, captains and sergeants, who call themselves . . . what is it now? . . . something to do with renovation . . ."

"The Military Committee for the Renovation of Laos. General Si Mong is head of the movement. I have the honour to know him extremely well. He graduated from the Ecole de Guerre the same year as myself. Placed very high."

Pinsolle cut him short:

"What about Ricq?"

Andelot scratched his neck:

"It's extremely difficult for me to intervene with the Coordination officers, as General Molliergues pointed out himself. Officially, Monsieur Ricq is just a member of the French School of Far-Eastern Studies. His rank of lieutenant-colonel is purely honorary."

Pinsolle produced a sheet of typewritten paper from his pocket.

"Read this, it's a translation from a Laotian newspaper, the one that finances that rogue Si Mong."

"The spy has been unmasked.

"François Ricq, who for several years has passed himself off in Vientiane as an ethnologist attached to the French School of Far-Eastern Studies has just been unmasked and arrested by the Coordination forces of General Si Mong. This person in the service of the Communist powers was in regular contact with Hanoi and the rebel government of Sam Neua. He had access to the Prime Minister, Prince Sisang, and controlled a vast network of agents on his payroll in the army as well as the civil administration. Further arrests are expected, particularly in the Prime Minister's circle. The Laotians, who are an affable but proud people, cannot tolerate such abuse of their hospitality. According to a statement from Coordination Headquarters, François Ricq will shortly be indicted before a court-martial to answer the charge of espionage on behalf of enemies of the kingdom."

Colonel Andelot raised his head:

"Monsieur Ricq will never be charged. He'll be expelled."

"You're right. Ricq won't be charged. What have they got against him apart from advising the President, Prince Sisang? But he might well be found floating in the Mekong, like Gibelin, with a knife in his back or a bullet in his head. Beforehand he will have been tortured to make him talk. Fighting has broken out again in the Plain of Jars! You can't stand Ricq, I know. It annoys you that this fellow who's never seen at a cocktail party or in an embassy knows everything that's going on, even among the Communists . . . and that he's actually senior in rank to you because you're only a sham colonel."

"His liaison with that . . . Laotian woman . . ."

"I'd love to have a liaison with such a pretty girl who's also the niece of the head of the Neutralist army."

"His sympathy towards the Communists . . . at least towards the pro-Communist Neutralists . . ."

"The real Communists, those of Hanoi, have tried to bump him off. The last time, they made a mistake. They killed that poor wretch Espèredieu instead."

"The Neutralists don't amount to much any more. My American colleague, Colonel Edwards, was just telling me . . ."

"France is banking on Prince Sisang and Neutralism in Laos. Furthermore, Andelot, I'm fed up with your prevarication and knowing airs. You go straight off to General Si Mong and do your utmost to get Ricq released. Promise them the moon, which we haven't got, and threaten them with sanctions, which we haven't the means to apply. Ricq's release is also a matter of personal concern to me because, however odd and exasperating he may be with that governessy manner of his, I care about him."

Half an hour later, not daring to confront the ambassador in person, Colonel Andelot rang up from his office. General Si Mong had refused to see him.

In the former guardroom where Sisang and Ricq were under arrest, the naked bulb hanging from the ceiling flickered on as the electric generator, after an erratic start, began turning over. It, too, dated from the French. It was somewhat the worse for wear and kept running down every four or five minutes. When this happened, the light from the bulb was reduced to a glowing filament.

Still sitting on his bedstead, the prince growled:

"Vientiane had become an absolute cesspool. Opium dens on every street corner . . . Racketeering and prostitution . . . The American Ambassador gave me to understand that his government couldn't disregard such immorality any longer. What would we do without American aid? The Russians give us nothing but arms and the French nothing but advice. Communist propaganda was becoming too easy. That was when I took the decision to clean up Vientiane, establish strict control over gold, rice and opium, and assign you to this particular task. Not officially of course; you would have approached your old friend Chanda for the officers I needed."

"As usual, there was a lot of careless talk among your circle and this time it didn't even get as far as Si Mong. As soon as they heard it, the Coordination officers acted on their own initiative to protect their rackets. They got drunk in order to give themselves

Dutch courage and then pressed on. Did you think they were going to let themselves be stripped just to gratify American susceptibility? No, it wasn't a coup d'état at all. It was just the automatic reaction of a crowd of petty gangsters. At least, Your Highness, if I'm murdered I'll know why."

Since Ricq was yet again presenting the incidents in a light with which he did not agree, Sisang grew sulky. Scowling, he watched a house-lizard scuttle across the wall. Then he carefully re-tied his shoe-laces to impress upon Ricq that he did not want to hear any more from him.

There was a sound of footsteps in the corridor outside, a clatter of rifle butts on the flagstones.

Ricq got up and Sisang put his torn jacket on again after smoothing it down with the palm of his hand.

"Now what are they after?" Sisang asked. "Are they going to kill us? What can we do?"

"I have nothing but a penknife, Your Highness, and your dignity forbids you to seize a leg of the bed and hit them over the head. I think they're coming to release you."

"I shan't go without you."

"You'll be more useful to me outside than in this prison."

"I'll get you released. You'll spend a few months in France. Then you'll come back and I shall again be obliged to support you. I couldn't do anything else but promise the American Ambassador to clean up the town."

"The ambassador would have done better to ask General Si Mong direct. He's on his pay-roll."

Three Coordination officers came in carrying electric torches: Deng, a colonel who was related to Si Mong, a major who was well known as a Thai agent, and a captain.

Sisang stood with his arms crossed and a set expression on his face. Deng came up to him. He looked no older than twenty-five.

"Your Excellency . . ."

"Your Highness," the Tiao tersely corrected him.

"The Military Committee for the Renovation of Laos . . ."

"What committee? There is only one legal government in Laos and that's mine. In what bar or brothel was this committee born?"

The colonel looked overawed and snapped to attention. He stammered:

"My uncle, General Si Mong, sends you his apologies for this morning's incident. Uncontrolled elements, soldiers who had misunderstood . . . They had only received orders to protect you. The officer who struck you has been severely punished. We're going to take you back to your villa where we shall continue to ensure your protection until the situation becomes calmer."

Colonel Deng did not know what else to say. His uncle had stated quite clearly:

"Now we've got to repair the damage done by those drunken sods. Take Sisang back to his villa first of all. He's a ninny. I want him to be seen in his own car being driven by his own chauffeur. Apologize to him, tell him any lies you like.

"Get a move on, Deng. It wasn't for nothing I got you promoted from major to colonel,"—he counted on his fingers—"in five months. The ambassadors were here just now. They kicked up a bit of a fuss, especially the French Ambassador. What a piercing voice he has! He wanted me to hand over Ricq as well. I'll hand him over one day, but dead. I wasn't the one who had him arrested. I can prove it. The American Ambassador was with them. He threatened to stop all aid if Sisang was not released. One never knows what to do with these Americans. With one hand they urge you on, with the other they hold you back. Get a move on, Deng."

It was all very well to say "Get a move on, Deng", but it was not so easy when one was confronted with the Tiao who in his prison looked anything but a ninny.

Ricq realized that Sisang, in his eagerness to get home, was going to accept every lie he was told, even the clumsiest, every promise he was given, even if it could not be kept.

Afterwards he would wait for the suitable moment to take his revenge. If the opportunity did not arise, he would leave Laos. The blow he had received in the face had estranged him for ever from the country in which he had been born, and cast him towards the one in which he had been brought up and in which he had chosen to end his days.

Out of a remnant of friendship, mingled with a slight feeling of pity, Ricq forced the prince to put up a semblance of resistance. He asked in Laotian:

"What punishment was Captain Sounboum given for striking the Tiao who is also the President and Regent Designate of the kingdom?"

Reluctantly, Sisang in his turn asked: "Yes, what punishment?"

"I don't know," the colonel replied. "The general himself is dealing with the matter. Meanwhile he has placed Sounboum under close arrest until . . . until . . ."

Deng racked his brains, not knowing how to finish the sentence. Captain Sounboum had been given a fifty-thousand kip bonus for his display of moral fibre. He had received it from the hands of Si Mong himself, who had merely asked him to keep out of the limelight. When Uncle Si Mong was unable to give orders, he resorted to bribery. It was as good a way as any other of exacting obedience . . . provided of course there was always enough money.

But here was this Frenchman once again meddling in matters that were none of his business! He was doing his best to spur on the prince! But he wouldn't be able to do so much longer. He would be taken care of this evening. His *phousao*, Ven, was one of the prettiest girls in Vientiane. It would be interesting to look after her. Frenchmen teach Laotian women plenty of tricks in bed.

"Until what?" the prince repeated.

Deng at last thought of a suitable answer.:

"Until we have your decision, Your Highness."

He had won the day; he could feel it. With a respectful bow he added: "We have brought you your car and chauffeur."

"And the pennant?"

"What pennant?"

Sisang flared up, but now he was merely acting: "Idiot, the Laotian pennant which is meant to fly on the car of the head of state."

"It's there, Your Highness, it's there."

"I'm taking this man with me," Sisang went on, nodding towards Ricq. Colonel Deng bowed more deeply.

"That's not possible at the moment. Monsieur Ricq will be released tomorrow. General Si Mong would like to see him first. Oh, it's nothing, Your Highness; he doesn't even contemplate expelling him . . . he just wants to ask him to stop sticking his nose into Laotian affairs."

"I have your word that he'll be released tomorrow?"

"You have, Your Highness, and also my uncle's word. We're going to transfer Monsieur Ricq to a more comfortable room in the Central Police Station."

"As soon as he's released, I want him brought to my residence."

Sisang turned to Ricq.

"I think all these misunderstandings are going to be cleared up very soon. We'll talk about all this tomorrow. As you see, you're in no danger."

The prince shook hands with Ricq, who reflected: "If Pontius Pilate lived today, he would not confine himself to washing his hands. He would actually shake hands with Christ before handing him over to the executioner."

Sisang walked towards the door and Colonel Deng stood aside to let him pass.

The door clanged behind them, the bolts grinded, and Ricq felt a shiver go down his spine. He had frequently risked his life but he had never had occasion to ponder on all the problems that death presented. He had had specific action to take: an explosive charge to set, a detonator to insert, a mine to lay, men to lead, physical tasks to carry out.

This time he found himself alone with this wild beast clawing at his guts. Like Antoine Gibelin, like his brother Dan, he had to master this beast.

His fear was accompanied by a great anxiety for Ven and the incipient creature growing in her womb. The halfcaste child she was carrying would be all that remained to him of Laos after spending twenty years trying to consolidate this unstable country. But it had slipped out of his hands, leaving only a trace of sand and mud. He felt too weary, too sick at heart, even to pray. For the last few months his God had bleached and faded, like holy pictures forgotten in an attic.

He even had no more tobacco left. Sisang had smoked it all. He felt hungry. Since his arrest he had been given nothing but a cup of tea which tasted of mildew.

The light went out and his solitude became unbearable.

Outside the window the darkness was as intense as inside the prison. The guards had gone off duty.

"I must do something," Ricq said to himself, "anything, even something silly."

He went up to the bars and tried to prise one loose, but it held fast. The wall, however, sounded hollow.

Ricq began scraping away at the mortar, but the blade of his penknife snapped back between his fingers.

Again there was a sound of footsteps in the corridor outside. A man came in, masking the light from his torch with his hand. It was Khammay. He addressed Ricq by the rank he had held in the maquis.

"Captain . . . Captain . . . you won't ever reach the Central Police Station . . . because on the way you're going to be finished off. You'll be *tay*, you'll be dead."

And he went through the motion of slitting his throat.

"The soldiers who are on guard here are from my company; they won't do anything to you. The Americans are just round the corner. You must shout as loud as you can when they come to take you away; the Americans will hear you. Then they might perhaps intervene. General Si Mong wants you to be killed, like Gibelin, but he also wants to be able to say you were shot while trying to escape from the jeep. If you refuse to get into the jeep while the Americans are watching, it won't be possible to kill you."

"Why does Si Mong want to have me killed?"

"Sounboum wants it, so as to take over your *phousao* and your house. As for Si Mong, I don't know."

Ricq reacted quickly. Khammay's idea was a good one. The Americans alone could prevent him from being transferred. In fact this was his only chance.

He asked Khammay:

"You know the American Colonel Cosgrove Tibbet, the one

who's at Camp Kennedy? Go and see him and tell him what you've just told me. Don't speak to him on the telephone. Also tell Ven to send word to Chanda and Captain Meynadier in the Plain of Jars."

"Anything else, Captain?"

"I'd like something to eat. Get some rice, *padek** and tea sent in to me. Thanks, Khammay."

As he went out, the captain repeated:

"Whatever you do, don't leave Xien Nip or you're *tay*."

Since the maquis days Khammay had put on weight and his belt was stretched tight over his stomach. He had become a racketeer. He put the squeeze on here and there and dealt in contraband rice with Thailand. Though only a captain, he had built himself a villa with a swimming-pool a hundred feet long and lit by projectors. The house and the pool had cost twenty million kips, whereas his pay was only twelve thousand kips a month.

But it was this same Khammay, then as lean and supple as an eel, who used to creep into Paksane in the dark to find out what the Japanese or Chinese were up to, although he had a price on his head. He it was who had executed the Japanese major responsible for the massacre at Thakhek.

Khammay the pimp, the crook, the thief, was proving more loyal than the prince. He did not shake hands with Ricq, but gave a slight bow and closed the door gently behind him.

At the wheel of the old two-horsepower Citroen from which the paint was peeling away in strips, Paul Cléach drove through the gateway of Camp Kennedy after a cursory explanation in French to the American sentry who asked him for his papers:

"I'm going to see that old rogue, Colonel Cosgrove Tibbet."

Having been given a name, the sentry inscribed it in a book. Then he popped another stick of chewing-gum into his mouth, paying no more attention to this flashy fellow and his tin-lizzie which he must have constructed with his own hands out of empty

* The basic Laotian condiment, made of salted fish and bran.

tins. In the evening the colonel received all sorts of people, and sometimes Frenchmen. The sentry felt that all the Frenchmen who lived in Laos, and wore their shirts hanging out of their trousers, were a lot of tramps.

Camp Kennedy stood on the outskirts of Vientiane, opposite a horrible monument in black cement that General Si Mong had erected to celebrate his victory over the Communists. But his valorous troops had known nothing but defeat. It was after a pointless and gory bombardment that Si Mong and his army had succeeded in driving out of Vientiane the thirty-five paratroopers whom Chanda, the Neutralist leader, had left as a rear-guard. For the occasion these thirty-five men had become "Communist battalions".

Camp Kennedy consisted of white bungalows, green lawns, flags, equipment stores, a P.X., a cinema, an officer's mess, clean-clad men with crew-cuts, a whole world of self-assurance, comfort and cleanliness extending over fifty acres in the midst of the seething misery and disorder of a country in the process of disintegration.

Each time he entered this club, which required nothing from its members save American nationality, Cléach felt furious.

After filling in a form beneath a portrait of President Johnson flanked by a flag, he was shown into a sort of air-conditioned waiting-room where he again encountered Johnson with an expression of entreaty in his eyes, as though begging for a vote. Living examples of self-assurance went hurrying by carrying files, running into others with aerial photographs and chinagraph paper under their arms. From time to time they went up to a fountain for a drink of iced water, handing round cigarettes and glancing with mild astonishment at Cléach slumped in an armchair. All of them had flashing teeth, well-polished boots, called one another by their Christian names and wore the happy smiles of tycoons whose business was prospering.

These same smiles were to be seen in the magazines spread out on the table, in the photographs of generals hanging on the wall on either side of that of the President. Confronted with this elegance, this neatness, this radiant health of the American officers and men, it was all very well for Cléach to say to himself, "They don't stand up to heat, rain or adversity," he still could not overcome a sensation of discomfort and poverty, the complex of the "small European". He hitched up his baggy drill trousers, he buttoned his jacket which was too narrow at the shoulders and too wide in the waist. It made no difference to his appearance. He was still the hefty lout with hands like paddles, blurred features and abrupt gestures, whom no tailor would ever be able to make elegant and who, in fury or confusion, clumsily collided with everything and everyone. His darting Celtic eyes were hazel-coloured when he was happy or amused but turned yellow when he was vexed. At Camp Kennedy, Cléach's eyes were always yellow.

Twenty-six years old, he sometimes looked thirty, at other times eighteen, according to his shifting moods. Cléach would tell anyone who was willing to listen that Laos was the most "stinking awful" country in the world and the Laotians a nation of ne'er-do-wells, liars, thieves and racketeers. But he admitted they were not hypocrites, were always affable, had no sexual or racial complexes and that, in spite of war and disorder, Laos was still one of the last remaining earthly paradises for people like himself.

Cléach pictured yet again the speech he planned to make one day to the most self-sufficient, the most high-and-mighty, the most loathsome of all these Americans in South-East Asia, that fellow Cosgrove Tibbet who had stretched snobbery to the point of assuming his mother's maiden name as his own Christian name. He would say to him:

"You sorry specimen of a colonel, perhaps one day, when you were not completely absorbed in admiration of Cosgrove Tibbet, you might have wondered why the Americans as a whole and you in particular were utterly detested in Laos. Yet the people here really love everyone provided it costs them no effort.

"I also suppose it has never occurred to you to put yourself in the position of a Laotian and to see Camp Kennedy and its inmates through his eyes? You dole them out dollars which they don't know what to do with, accompanied by nice trustful smiles.

But you remain perched up there on your platform like a headmaster at prize-giving. You stroke the heads of a few brats while giving them some tins of powdered milk, you shake hands with a few ministers or generals who are on your pay-roll and whom you despise because at the same time you consider them dishonest. Then off you go, back to Camp Kennedy, to scrub yourselves from head to foot.

"But Christ Almighty, stop smiling and patting yourself on the back and telling yourself everything's going well! It's high time you wore an expression to suit the occasion, the convulsed expression of fellows who are repeatedly taking a thrashing in Asia as well as South America. This isn't the moment to display your lovely teeth but to clench them, to show a little humility and keep out of the limelight . . ."

An officer touching him on the shoulder put an end to Cléach's fine imaginary speech.

"The colonel will see you now," he said.

Cléach followed him. This time he would once again keep silent. He needed some information and still hoped to visit one of those Meo maquis bands organized by the American special services in the region of Xieng Khouang. This dirty swine Cos was the only one who could give him a permit. He also wanted to help that worthy blockhead Ricq who, doubtless from sheer absent-mindedness, had once more got involved in some impossible affair! For this, again, he needed the colonel.

Cosgrove Tibbet sat at a desk in a cream-coloured uniform without badges of rank or regimental insignia, dictating a series of orders to one of his assistants. As usual, he did not even look up. Cléach strained his ears but the orders merely concerned the installation of a repairs workshop.

Officially, Colonel "Chicken" Cos was merely a M.A.A.G.* advisor and dealt in particular with the transport of the Royal Laotian Army.

Of medium height, he had greyish close-cropped hair revealing two finely-chiselled ears—the ears of a woman, Cléach opined—sharp, dark eyes and a pasty complexion. He chewed inces-

* Military Assistance Aid Group.

santly at a long cigarette-holder gripped between his teeth which had gaps in them like a child's. His body was lean and sinewy, he had small feet and fleshy lips.

"He's a pansy," Cléach said to himself, "one of the nastiest kind, the kind that doesn't give into his instincts, a lousy fanatic and racialist, probably a member of the John Birch Society because the inordinate sexuality of Negroes attracts and repels him at the same time."

Having dismissed his subordinates, Cos rose from his table and walked over to the journalist whom he greeted with a curt nod.

"Excuse me," he finally said, "a few details to attend to . . ."

His excuses always sounded like an affront, on account of his stiff, toneless voice.

Cos went on in excellent French:

"To what do I owe . . . I shan't say the pleasure . . . but the occasion of this visit?"

"Ricq, the fellow in the French School of Far-Eastern Studies has just been arrested. He's accused of being a Communist agent. I believe you know him fairly well. What do you think of him?"

"Officially? This affair is none of my business. I provide the Laotian army with vehicles, which incidentally it puts to the worst possible use, and that's all. The Laotians are entitled to arrest anyone they please. Unofficially—because it's an unofficial conversation we're having, isn't it?—I don't believe Ricq is a Communist agent."

"I wish you'd say so to General Si Mong."

"I'm not on close terms with the general. The only thing we have in common is our liking for poker. When he doesn't cheat, I win."

"Were you, as usual, involved in this coup d'état?"

"My dear fellow, you're out of your mind. An over-vivid imagination leads you to provide me with a rôle I don't have. Colonel Cosgrove Tibbet, Contractor of Coup d'États! Come on now, be serious. What's more, this one is particularly unwelcome. Needless to say, that again is a strictly personal opinion."

"That gives me something to go on with," Cléach immediately reflected. "The C.I.A. isn't behind it. But in that case who is? All the same, this bloody swine Cos doesn't want to get involved for the sake of Ricq."

An officer came in to tell the colonel he was wanted on the telephone in another office.

Major Harry Bart was calling him from Xien Nip Camp. Cos considered his second-in-command, who was attached as adviser to the Coordination troops, one of the stupidest people he had ever had to command. But Bart had guts. He was devoid of imagination, so nothing ever surprised him; he was convinced he belonged to a superior race, so he never lost his self-assurance.

On the other end of the line, the major sounded in a state of great excitement.

"Hullo, sir. Some of Si Mong's officers have just come to fetch Prince Sisang. They made him get into his car and drove him home. The old ape looked in pretty poor shape. A black eye, his suit torn . . . but that's all."

"What about Ricq?"

"They're holding him. There's talk of moving him shortly to the Central Police Station."

"I know, Harry. One of his Laotian friends, a certain Captain Khammay, came to see me a short while ago."

He sniggered:

"Quite an interesting lad, our Ricq. They intend to bump him off on the way . . . The usual grounds, attempting to escape."

"What can we do about it, sir? After all, Ricq with his choir-boy's manner has played us enough dirty tricks."

"Now listen to me, Harry. At all costs you mustn't allow Ricq to be transferred tonight. You and your men will have to manage it somehow. Mount guard in turn outside his door. If that doesn't work, call me up straight away."

"You don't think we're exceeding our duties?"

"I'm the only judge of that and I take full responsibility."

"Right. I'll go and see what can be done."

The colonel rejoined Cléach who was looking at the maps and propaganda posters pinned to the wall. The colonel had deliberately left a couple of unimportant files lying on his desk. They had been moved slightly from their original position, Cléach had dipped into them. This amused the colonel who had a soft spot for the journalist which he was careful to conceal. He was always afraid of a sign of humanity, in other words weakness, being spotted in him.

Cos felt that only men like Cléach ought to be employed in secret services. Tenacious and efficient, they loved the country in which they lived. They were not burdened with silly prejudices against the local food or the native women, and stood up well to the climate. For several years he had been furnished with Harvard or Princeton graduates, athletic types with a rudimentary knowledge of the languages and customs of South-East Asia, but totally unsuited to the sort of activity required of them since they were still at the textbook stage.

Cos put the files back in place without Cléach showing the least embarrassment. Incapable of making him realize he was only amused, the colonel went on in the same biting tone:

"My dear fellow, I wouldn't like you to have come all the way here for nothing. I just happen to have heard some news. Prince Sisang has been driven back to his residence in his own car."

"He's free?"

"Not exactly, not yet."

"Si Mong's losing his nerve?"

"Not exactly, either. He's trying to repair the damage done by his men."

"What about Ricq?"

"Your compatriot is still in Xien Nip Camp. His situation seems rather more tricky. The disappearance of a little ethnologist who is made out to be pro-Communist is a mere incident; the arrest of a prince of the royal blood, the president, is a revolution. I believe—and this is just my personal opinion—that none of the great powers interested in the fate of Laos, including Russia, can tolerate further disorder in this part of South-East Asia. What with Vietnam, Indonesia, Malaya and Korea, there's quite enough as it is."

"It's Ricq I'm interested in, Colonel. When Sisang is flung out through the door he comes in again through the window, which enables him to hold two press conferences on the same day, one on his way out and the other on his way in."

"I've told you I can't do anything for your friend. It's up to your ambassador, not me. I deal with technical aid."

"To the Meo maquis of Xieng Khouang?"

"You'd better go off and file your copy; you're going to be pipped at the post by your competitors. You might also add—and it would be doing him a favour—that there are grounds for extreme anxiety about the fate of an ethnologist attached to the French School of Far-Eastern Studies."

His tone became ironical:

"A peaceful lad who has lived in Laos for twenty years, just as I have; who speaks all the dialects, better than I do; who disappears into the bush for three or four months at a time, which I can't do any longer; who goes off, when he feels like a jaunt, in search of some manuscript of *The Ramayana** proving something or other about Hindu influences, just as I deal with the repairs workshop of the Laotian Army."

"What do you mean by all that?"

"I thought you were more quick-witted, Cléach. I'm merely saying that my opposite number in the French secret service, Lieutenant-Colonel Ricq, appointed by France as adviser to Prince Sisang, has been blown. Everyone now knows his real activity. His cover story is no better than mine. So long, Cléach, and mind you don't forget this conversation of ours has been confidential."

Cléach climbed back into his Citroen in a daze. He had always thought that Ricq, who had been parachuted into the maquis during the resistance against the Japanese, and who knew the country backwards, was bound every now and then to provide the "whiskers"† of the embassy with information. But, that he was the head "whisker", he would never have believed.

* One of the great epic poems of India, 24,000 verses long, which describes the adventures of the noble and great-hearted warrior Rama and his wife Sita, a model of feminine virtue.

"The most monumentally boring work in the whole of Eastern and Far-Eastern literature," according to Antoine Gibelin, who of course had never attempted to read it . . .

† Meaning "false whiskers", the name given to the agents and secret services operating abroad. Since the Algerian troubles the term *barbouze* has generally assumed a pejorative connotation and is no longer used.

Cléach went back to his shack in the Vietnamese quarter which served him both as an office and living quarters. It was built partly of planks, partly of dried mud. The rickety wooden balcony looked on to a garden where flowers bloomed among pools of water and refuse.

A long-bladed fan whirred round in the ceiling but it did not succeed in stirring the heavy air or in removing the smell of rotting vegetation, quagmire and dried fish.

Cléach loved his shack and this quarter of the town.

"When you live in a country," he said one day to his colleague Radzienkov of the Tass Agency, "you must wallow in the midst of the girls, the stinks, the noise, and not cheat with the climate. My hut is the ideal, an absolute sieve. I live out in the street. Three houses further down, there's the opium den of Uncle Yong, a former Chinese Kuomintang general who sells the best dope in the whole of the Far East. One of those astonishing characters you come across only in Asia. When I have time I'll write a book about him. Two doors further down still, there's a little Vietnamese restaurant run by some Tonkinese which has the best *pho** in town. Next door is the brothel of Ma Dok, a cynical, jovial old procuress. On the other side of the street you have the Chinese shops, where you can get claret, lacquered pork, noodles, Fly-tox and unlimited credit."

"That's a lot of romantic nonsense," Radzienkov had asserted, exaggerating his Slav accent.

Radzienkov would live only in an air-conditioned room.

Cléach swept the table clean with the back of his hand, put his typewriter on it and started to type. "Further sensational developments in the Laotian crisis . . . Prince Sisang was released at eight o'clock in the evening by the coup d'état *junta* . . ." But he was unable to concentrate. He was thinking of the powers of deception that Ricq had shown in leading the life of a seedy little

* A Tonkinese dish of Chinese origin. Flore, Cléach's halfcaste mistress who knew nothing except how to make love and *pho*, prepared it as she had been taught by her mother who was from Nam Dinh, with thin slices of beef in its own gravy, noodles, herbs, ginger and red pepper.

scholar and simultaneously controlling networks and drafting policies. As a result of his activity, people died, others survived, coups d'état failed or succeeded, and even the fate of the world could be changed. But Ricq kept quiet. Methodical, discreet and unassuming, he derived no profit, no glory from his role. What prompted him, then, to assume it? Loyalty? Ideals? Love of his own country or of Laos, with whom he had been living in sin for twenty years? Maybe also monstrous pride, which he kept well concealed?

Flore, with her long black hair hanging loose to her waist, came into the room and pottered about, exuding her warm provocative smell of vanilla and youthful animal sweat.

"She's been smoking opium again," Cléach reflected. "She must have pinched some money from my wallet. When she comes back from Uncle Yong's, she always wants a roll in the hay."

He called for Kham, the houseboy, who arrived giggling and unsteady on his feet. While Flore was smoking, he had finished off the bottles of beer in the refrigerator. That capped everything! Cléach sent him off to take his cable to the post, then caught hold of Flore by her hair.

"You've been smoking again?"

"A little," she said, swaying her hips and drawing in her stomach to excite him. "Only five pipes."

Her silky voice sometimes went hoarse and croaky. It disturbed Cléach even more than her long legs, her girlish breasts, her ivory-smooth skin, her sauciness and lack of modesty. As he released her he gave her a slap, not too hard.

"I told you: only once a week, on Saturdays, and with me."

She snivelled:

"I was so bored, you're never here."

"If you think, my girl, that with a coup d'état going on I have nothing better to do than deal with your trivial little problems!"

Cléach felt sublime in his indignation but Flore merely considered he was taking a long time to start making love, the only thing she wanted at the moment. Flore lived in the present, had no difficulty in forgetting the past and never worried about the future.

Letting her skirt fall to her feet, she stepped out of it and brazenly sat astride him.

Cléach swore at her:

"If I still believed all the nonsense I was taught by the priests in Rennes, you would be the personification of sin to me. Sin can only have your lovely face, your smell and your sort of deliciously croaky voice."

"Paul, you're always saying things I don't understand. You're like Gibelin, it's just to make fun of me."

Flore led him towards the bed, having recovered all her self-assurance, for bed was her profession, her speciality, her end-all and be-all. A little later Cléach asked her:

"What do you think of Ricq?"

"He's very nice."

"Well, he's fooled us all, has nice little Ricq! He must even have had a good laugh at my simple-mindedness and pretensions. To think I used to explain Laotian politics to him and it seemed to interest him!"

After Flore had gone to sleep, Cléach went out to the Constellation for a drink. Radzienkov sat slumped in an armchair drinking a gin to which he had added a few cubes of ice. The Russian correspondent had narrow shoulders, a pot belly and short fair hair revealing a pink skull. Loud-voiced and sentimental, he wore his heart on his sleeve after sunset. As soon as he caught sight of Cléach he bellowed:

"Come and have a drink, you bloody old French bugger. I'd like to hear your distorted bourgeois version of this coup d'état which everyone was taking seriously until a short while ago . . . and which seems to be a lot of balls . . . since Sisang has gone back home."

Cléach came and sat down beside him. Radzienkov wrinkled his nose.

"You've just been making love and didn't have a shower afterwards. You stink of woman."

"You've been boozing and haven't cleaned your teeth. You stink of gin. Tell me, Igor, you're not a spy, as well, are you, you're not working for the M.V.D. or N.K.V.D. or anything like that? You're not a colonel by any chance, are you?"

"You must be even drunker than I am."

"This evening I see spies everywhere. Vientiane is choc-a-bloc of them and they've fooled me completely. Maybe it was you who arranged for Flore to shack me up with me so as to photostat my cables with a tiny little machine concealed in an ear-ring?"

"I swear, Frenchy, if I could have managed it, Flore would be in my bed, not in yours."

"Who engineered last night's coup d'état, Colonel Radzienkov?"

"The Chinese," the Russian declared, delighted with his quip. "They're the only ones who'd be silly enough."

Ven's slender figure appeared on the pavement outside in the garish neon lighting; she was soaked to the skin by the rain and her dress clung to her girlish body. The heavy chignon she wore on the left side of her head was coming undone and her face was devoid of all expression but fear. She caught sight of Cléach, looked relieved and gave him a diffident smile.

"Who's that woman?" the Russian enquired. "She looks like a pretty doll who's been dropped in the gutter."

"The *phousao* of Ricq, the French ethnologist who was arrested at the same time as Sisang. They now say he was a Communist."

"On whose side? Was he working for the Chinese?"

"That's true, nowadays one can no longer be simply a Communist, just as at the time of the Wars of Religion one couldn't be simply a Christian. One had to choose between Catholic and Protestant, just as today one has to choose between pro-Russian and pro-Chinese, White and Yellow. . . . At least the colour of one's skin didn't come into it in the days of the Guises and Colignys."

"Of course not, everyone was white . . ."

"At one time I was tempted by your Marxist nonsense. It was an attractive proposition, a religion that was at the same time an economic and political system and could work for the entire world, the Whites, the Negroes, the Yellow races . . . Communism is the same as everything else. It doesn't prevent one from being fooled."

"You haven't answered my question. Who was Ricq working for?"

"Ricq wasn't a Communist. I believe he was even extremely right-wing. So long, Popoff. Look, there are some Yanks coming in. You'd better go and have a word with them. They're your future allies."

Radzienkov angrily dipped his nose into his glass. He too had believed that Communism was a universal movement which could be applied without modification to every nation. Eight months in China, six months in Guinea had taught him the contrary. Now he once more considered himself a white man among other white men. He felt slightly ill at ease, as though guilty of treachery, and at the same time relieved at recovering his place among his own people. Cléach was still young. One day he would understand.

Cléach went out and put his hand on Ven's shoulder. She was trembling. He saw she was utterly distraught. He reflected somewhat bitterly that if he ever found himself in trouble like Ricq, Flore would immediately pinch everything she could find in the shack and go and set up house with that swine Nate Hart who had been leering at her for months.

"Ricq's been arrested," said Ven in her hesitant French.

"Yes, I know."

"Maybe they're going to kill him. A Coordination captain came to see me a short while ago."

"To ask you for money? The usual racket."

"No, not this one. He was with Ricq during the war. You see, Ricq knows lots of Laotians who come and see him even at night time. Ricq had sent me word to contact Chanda—but I don't know where he is—and one of his friends, a French captain, who's at the Plain of Jars, Meynadier. Do you know him?"

"Do I know him! To get in touch with him, you'll have to approach the French Military Mission. Anything else?"

Ven spoke rapidly, without punctuating her phrases, and her shrill, high-pitched voice sounded like an old gramophone record revolving at too high a speed.

"The councillor at the embassy, Monsieur de Saint-Urcize, also came a short while ago to see if Ricq had left any papers lying about. But the soldiers had removed everything. He gave me some money and told me if I needed any more I could have it. If there was any trouble, he would get me over the border into Thailand. I'm frightened."

"You'd better sleep in my place tonight," Cléach suggested.

"Flore doesn't like me."

"Flore's like a cat. She's even jealous of the walls and floor of the house. She'll have to get used to it. She puts on airs in order to share the first saucer of milk. Then she doesn't think any more about it."

The Little Citroen went bumping over the furrowed streets, splashing through the mud, pitching and swaying from side to side.

Forced to halt by a military convoy passing through, Cléach asked the young Laotian girl:

"No news of Chanda?"

"He's gone."

"Yes, but where?"

"Don't know. Xien Khouang perhaps."

As they drove past the white bungalow where Prince Sisang lived, Cléach saw some lights. He drew up and asked Ven to wait for him. The wall round the garden was guarded by Coordination sentries, except for the main gate which was wide open.

On the balcony, Sisang, in shirt sleeves, stood leaning against the wooden balustrade, puffing at his pipe. Below him His Excellency Pinsolle formed a gesticulating group with Sir Thomas Wyne, the British Ambassador, Nicolas Ordinsky, the Russian, and Hugh de Vandemalle, the American.

The milky light filtering through the clouds transformed the scene into an amateur dramatic society's production of a bad musical comedy.

Cléach passed through the gateway without any trouble.

"What's going on?" he asked.

Pinsolle stopped gesticulating.

"Oh, there you are. I've been looking for you all evening. An absolute circus show, my dear fellow, and it's still going on. Isn't it, Sir Thomas?"

Sir Thomas, who was prevented by an attack of dysentery from fully appreciating the situation, nodded his head. The American was holding the Russian by the arm and speaking to him in an undertone. He was trying to explain that he had nothing to do with this *putsch*, but the Russian wore the inscrutable expression of a judge. In fact he was not listening to Vandemalle at all and had composed his features in this way just in order to day-dream in peace. In a few weeks' time he was going to leave this damned country, where he sweated through three shirts a day, and rediscover the bracing air of Moscow. He might subsequently be sent to a proper country, in Europe or America, among adults. He had had enough of all these disconcerting childish nations.

"This is the situation," Pinsolle went on in his shrill voice. "His Highness Prince Sisang is a prisoner in his own residence. There's a soldier guarding the front door but no one has bothered about the garden or the gate. Sisang is able to come out on to the balcony and speak to us. No orders have been given to his guards, so they let him do this with that fine Laotian indifference towards anything that has ceased to interest them. But Sisang is as stubborn as an Aragonese mule . . ."

Pinsolle called out:

"Your Highness, your Highness."

Exasperated, Sisang leant a little further over the balustrade.

"What is it, Your Excellency? I can't say anything, I can't do anything, I'm a prisoner. Once I'm released I'll make a statement, I'll hold a press conference."

Pinsolle pushed the journalist forward.

"He'll transmit your statement."

The prince had had frequent disagreements with Cléach who reproached him for mistaking his dreams and hopes for information. He snapped:

"Cléach writes whatever he chooses. He'll only misquote me again."

"I assure you I'll check everything he says. In any case the post office is closed and Si Mong's men are guarding it. We'll transmit your statement over the embassy radio."

"But what do you want me to say—that I was arrested in my own house in the middle of the night, that I was struck and flung into prison as a result of a *putsch* engineered by my vice-president and supported by elements alien to the country? The whole world knows it and is indignant about it."

"Nobody gives a damn about it," Cléach grunted. "This farce has been going on too long—it's the old story of the boy who cried 'Wolf!' just for fun. When the wolf did come no one believed him and His Highness Tiao Sisang was gobbled up."

Feeling he had sulked long enough, Sisang embarked on one of his usual high-falutin' speeches.

"A lengthy task of reconciliation reduced to nought... Since my country does not appreciate my efforts . . . I shall go into exile . . ."

"Your Highness, may I ask you a question?" said Cléach. "If General Si Mong apologises to you and you are granted complete liberty, would you agree to continue governing the country?"

"I don't know. Anyway, what are you doing here? This is a meeting of ambassadors."

Cléach apologised:

"Since the gate was wide open . . . Your Highness, what about Ricq?

This time Sisang turned nasty. He did not like being bothered by details just when he was about to launch into higher politics from his balcony.

"Ricq? That concerns the French Ambassador exclusively. But since I've known him for a long time, and he has done a lot for Laos . . . from the scientific point of view . . . I have personally looked into his case. Before I left Xien Nip Camp, General Si Mong gave me his word that he would be released tomorrow morning."

The ambassadors' conference was getting out of control.

"The king . . ." Sir Thomas interjected, partly from habit, partly just for something to say.

Pinsolle pounced on the word.

"The king . . . yes, of course, the king. According to the terms of the constitution, it's up to him to decide the question."

Everyone agreed on this point, even though the king was bound to decide nothing but would simply take pleasure in seeing Sisang, whom he could not abide, in a difficult position. This move would at least provide a breathing space, even perhaps clarify the situation, at least furnish an excuse for sending the various Foreign Ministries concerned those long signals in cipher on which successful careers are founded.

Pinsolle seized Cléach by his short sleeve.

"Come and have a drink at the embassy . . . We'll draft that statement together."

"I've got Ven, Ricq's girl friend, with me in the car."

"Bring her along. Why didn't that idiot Saint-Urcize take her to his house?"

"His wife has principles, so has he . . ."

"The world is badly divided. Either I come across someone like you, who hasn't any principles and behaves in an unforgivably off-hand manner towards a president, or else solemn idiots like the Saint-Urcizes, who have too many. What a show, Cléach, eh! That act of Uncle Sisang's out on the balcony! He might have asked us up and given us a drink. The sentry wouldn't have said anything. Only Sisang wanted to play the part of a prisoner. There was only one thing which could dislodge him . . ."

"An international conference?"

"No, running out of tobacco . . . in which case the whole Coordination army wouldn't be able to hold him. I'm worried about Ricq. I went to see Si Mong. He was adamant. Did you know at least who Ricq was?"

"It's an open secret tonight. Lieutenant-Colonel Ricq, head of the French special forces!"

"An irreplaceable colleague!"

"France has a complex about irreplaceable people: MacMahon, Pétain, de Gaulle . . . The graveyards are full of irreplaceable men who have been easily replaced."

"You think Ricq was useless?"

"Not at all. I think, on the contrary, that he was very well suited to this country where old men remain children. He didn't grow old either. He was always sixteen, and surrounded by people who were always eleven. Everything was working out nicely. But then the adults arrived: Viets and Americans, Chinese and Thais. How old are you, Your Excellency?"

"On some days sixteen, like Ricq."

"Why are you doing an old man's job, then?"

"I graduated from the Normale Supérieure in 1935. The hazards of war, the boredom of teaching and a liking for luxury travel turned me into a diplomat. Are those reasons enough for you, Mr. Public Prosecutor, who plead in the name of the rights of youth alone?"

Pinsolle accompanied Cléach to his Citroen; he took Ven's hand and kissed it. From his past life as a free man he had retained a liking for gallant gestures.

Tiao Sanakon, the Prince of the South and Inspector General of the Kingdom, was on to his second bottle of whisky. He was not drunk, only more uncouth than usual.

Stripped to the waist, clad in nothing but a sarong which revealed his flabby breasts, the "White" prince sat with his legs wide apart—he was so fat, he could no longer bring them together—listening irritably to what General Si Mong had to say.

"Your Highness, you must assume the leadership of the government. Your name, your prestige . . ."

"No," he replied in French, to be all the more insulting towards this former colonial service clerk. "You've got yourself into a mess, or others have got you into it, and you want to get me into it as well. Why did you have to back this coup d'état and this morning assume responsibility for it? You have your army, which does bugger-all, you have the police, the opium, gold and rice. They even say you've recently got hold of a number of other rackets. You're scraping the barrel all right. You put part of the American aid into your own pocket. You're even a general and Vice-President. What more do you want?"

"Your Highness, to maintain the police and the army, I had to cover that gang of young idiots who arrested your cousin Prince Sisang. Subsequently I heard Sisang had decided to clean up Vientiane, inaugurate a reign of virtue, combat peculation and send me off to some boring embassy in London or Bonn, not even Paris. I'm not a prince, I need money if I want to have men behind me."

"Everything has changed since the Americans arrived. Even

princes need money now. Before they turned up with their dollars, I wouldn't have stolen a cent. I've had to start stealing.

"They also arrested Ricq. I'm very fond of Ricq. He has never put a penny in his pocket. He still believes in the Laotian nation. I also did, mind you. Why do you hate the French so much, Si Mong?"

"They're colonialists . . . They occupied our country . . ."

"Balls, they made our country what it is."

The prince picked up the whisky bottle, poured himself out a glass, then reluctantly filled Si Mong's.

The general screwed up his eyes and with exaggerated politeness said:

"Your Highness, let me remind you that had it not been for my troops the Communists would have seized your estates. I had to send several regiments to drive them out."

"And now your regiments are occupying my estates instead. They smash everything, they steal, they rape the girls. For the sake of my peasants I have become your ally. I was happier when I was a mere captain in the Foreign Legion. My pals didn't call me Your Highness, but Toto . . ."

"The French did you down. They made you abandon your throne in favour of the little king of Luang-Prabang, on the pretext of unifying Laos. But the French only like those who betray them. The others, they despise and abandon. Look at Algeria. The Americans would be able to give you back your throne."

"It's too late. I'm sixty-five and I have liver trouble. I have to take drugs in order to make love to girls, and pills when I drink too much."

"I've had Prince Sisang released."

"See how clever you are."

"But this time I'll appoint my own men to advise him. They'll give him what information I choose, and the French Embassy will no longer manage the affairs of this country."

"It's easy, expel Ricq."

"I'll think it over, Your Highness. I only hope my officers haven't put paid to him in a fit of temper."

"So do I. I wouldn't want that to happen."

Si Mong bade farewell, pressing the palms of his hands together —was he not in civilian clothes?—and went out ruminating his grievances against the haughty drunkard. His escort was waiting for him in front of the door of the prince's hideous villa. He looked at his watch. Midnight. Ricq must have been executed.

The Prince of the South poured himself out another drink, but his hand was shaking. One day he would pack up and move to France. He and his old friend, Major Lerot, had bought a villa on the Côte d'Azur near Saint-Raphael. It stood in a grove of pine-trees, with the sea visible just beyond.

Like two old pensioners, they would end their days playing bowls, arguing and citing the names of contemporaries killed in action, locked up in prison, or laid low by alcohol and illness. They would get dead drunk on the anniversary of the Battle of Camerone and would go on drinking peacefully the other days, until death intervened.

Tiao Sanakon would be buried in an ordinary grave on French soil instead of being burnt like a king, on a pyre, in a sandalwood coffin in front of the temple of Vat Phu.

Barefoot and clad in a light white *yuccata** embroidered on one shoulder with a blue bird, Colonel Cosgrove Tibbet lay flat on his back on a straw mat with his knees drawn up. He was trying to listen to a record he had just been sent by Mitzi Mayberry—Handel's *Four Sonatas for Flute and Harpsichord.* Knowing Mitzi's taste for anything strange and unusual in music, painting or literature, for the "really stunning" sect, clan or place off the beaten track, he pictured her gazing at the shop assistant with her gentle short-sighted eyes and asking:

"Are you really sure this little work of Handel's isn't just a little bit hackneyed? They haven't made a jazz arrangement of it? It hasn't become the theme song for a toothpaste advertisement? Really?"

No one could resist Mitzi's over-detailed questioning.

* Summer kimono.

But this evening Handel's music with its ponderous, mannered charm could not find its place in this atmosphere of an air-conditioned prison-cell. It clashed with the walls and was drowned by the irregular buzzing of the air-conditioning system. Above all, it was unable to surmount the obstacle represented by the worry and remorse that devoured Cos.

In despair at the poor quality of the officers he had been sent to organize the partisan groups and Meo maquis, he had made a flying trip to the School of Subversive Warfare at Fort Knox. He found the training there had no bearing on the activity and living conditions which these men were to encounter. He had applied for an interview with General Walpish, who was nicknamed Dolly on account of his child-like features and schoolgirl complexion. He was the most merciless, narrow-minded brute in the whole American army.

Cos had tried to explain to him that he needed men who were not only physically tough but also mentally vicious, the sort of brawlers who are more likely to be found among the underprivileged—ugly, runtish, rebellious men, the sons of emigrants or emigrants themselves, whose characters had not yet been softened and whose blood had not yet been thinned by comfort and good food. There was no point in a man being able to march eighty miles in one day unless he was also able to march thirty or forty miles every day for weeks and months on end. It was not a question of breaking records. They had to be taught how to survive in the jungle, to stand up to intense heat and strange food, to adapt themselves to the customs of the races among whom they would have to live, and to know at least the rudiments of their language.

The general had abruptly cut him short:

"What you want are saints who are at the same time capable of behaving like gangsters and are also welfare workers or university professors. We don't have anyone like that. I myself drew up the training programme and I know the sort of men I can turn out. You'll have to be content with what you get. You've stayed too long in that country out there. It might be a good thing if you came back to the States."

By his clumsiness Cos had made a powerful enemy for himself. Walpish, that brazen bluffer who knew absolutely nothing about South-East Asia, its races, its history, its problems, was today the most highly regarded adviser to the Pentagon on Indo-Chinese affairs. A disaster!

Cos arranged to meet Mitzi in New York.

She had taken him to the Bon Soir, a "really" sensational night-club in Greenwich Village.

No one danced there. It was much too common, but Felicia Sanders crooned sophisticated songs. For the rest of the time two pianos played blues or old Western tunes. Cos would have preferred to be in bed with Mitzi, to make love to her with all the concentration that ought to be devoted to the celebration of this rite, and then talk about his only interest in life: the great upheaval in Asia and the rest of the world.

Mitzi remembered only the little anecdotes, the slivers of coloured glass that she could use again as topics of conversation. After drinking a bottle of mediocre French champagne at eighteen dollars, Cos had had to be content with a swift embrace and taking the young girl home to her father.

Mitzi had generous impulses in which she draped herself as in those lengths of multicoloured Thai silk that Cos used to send her. But she would quickly pack the impulses and silks away in a chest and continue to lead her agitated life—a charming, selfish, superficial little monster, born for pleasure and happiness, protected by her selfishness against pain and suffering and against anyone who was liable to inflict it.

Harry had still not called up from Xien Nip Camp. So nothing could have happened to Ricq. Maybe General Si Mong had recoiled from this fresh murder. Yet he had had Gibelin executed.

The Thai halfcaste must have wavered for some time: executing Ricq meant alienating the French, at least for a certain length of time. But in any case the French were so unsettled, they had had to take so many knocks, that the killing of one of their agents would be of little importance. Cos pictured the fat general counting up on his fingers.

"The French . . . they still have some friends in Laos but they're the sort that can't bother me: former civil servants, intellectuals, a few army men. There are the Neutralists, of course, but I'm already up against them. Money! The French sometimes promise but never give any. Ricq's men? Those belonging to his network, former members of the anti-Japanese resistance. They follow him as a person and do so out of friendship. Ricq is only a man, not a cause. Once the man is dead there'll be nothing left."

"If I were in Si Mong's place," Cos reflected, "I shouldn't hesitate for a moment. I'd have Ricq executed. How silly not to have bumped him off when they came to arrest him! On the night of a coup d'état one can set so many things down to disorder and the disastrous initiative of subordinates. If I were in Si Mong's place! But I could only put myself in his place if I was still convinced that the death of a man can make any difference to the outcome of events. All the same, I'm going to try to save Ricq. He's a first-rate technician and a shrewd, disinterested man, in spite of that innocent expression of his which he assumes even when he has just played someone a dirty trick. The policy he is defending is maybe the only possible one, even though it may lead after two or three years' interval to the same result as our disastrous enterprise: the Communization and Vietnamization of the whole of Laos.

"The die is cast. The die is cast in Laos and throughout the world. All the numbers are coming up except our own. We're passing the deal. In the last twenty years how many men have died without having been able to change the final result? And what of the millions of dollars that have been spent, the troops that have been lost, by an over-prodigal America? What's the point of continuing to respect normal secret service regulations and allowing Ricq to be murdered?"

Cos tried to remember all the men he had met in Thailand, Laos and Vietnam since that morning in January 1945 when he had touched down in the Gulf of Siam in an old Catalina. A customs launch had come out to fetch him and taken him to Bangkok to see the head of the anti-Japanese resistance movement who had the code name of Ruth. This was Luang Pradit who, after the Japanese capitulation, was to become head of the Thai government. Luang Pradit was now in Peking, completely in the hands of the Communists and leader of a shadow Pan-Thai movement which the Chinese would one day produce out of their pockets when they needed it. And what remained of all the others? Faceless characters, names he could only dimly remember. Coup d'état colonels and generals, puppets who performed their little turn, went off stage, then came on again the same as ever. They had put on weight, and owned Mercedes cars, villas and concubines.

Rapacious bonzes, politicians so crafty that they seemed downright stupid! And all the gang leaders and sect leaders whose colourful characters were all that prevented them from being utterly odious. They too performed their little turn and went off stage, but they did not come back again because they had been murdered, hanged or shot, because one of their lieutenants had betrayed them or a woman had given them away for a handful of bank-notes.

Pirates, whores, racketeers, warlords, prophets and mad bonzes in a spicy, decaying continent! But for the last few months one particular face had emerged—the face of Lieutenant Marc de Belza as he was dying. There were drops of sweat running down his cheeks like tears, others beading the hair on his chest. And that voice of his! . . . Belza was already almost unable to speak, but he managed to murmur in that off-hand manner peculiar to regular officers:

"Cos, I'd like to tell you you're the filthiest swine I've ever known."

As he wiped the dying man's face, Ports, the Englishman, had said in the same off-hand tone:

"It's a disgrace, Captain Cosgrove, that you should be wearing the badges of rank of an officer of an allied army. Didn't they ever teach you honour at West Point? You've failed in your duty."

Cos had not failed. He was years in advance of these officers who belonged to the past. He had been right. But now he had ceased to be right, and so he was going to do his utmost to save Ricq. Lieutenant de Belza and Major Ports were now the ones who were right, with their old-fashioned notions of honour, maybe because there was nothing else left.

It was in September 1945. The Japanese had just surrendered and, in Laos, they had very politely enquired to whom they were to hand over their weapons: to the English, the Americans, the French, the Chinese or the local resistance movements? They even seemed grieved that all these people against whom they had fought were apparently unable to agree among themselves.

The Americans, abiding by the terms of the Potsdam Treaty, informed them that, north of the 16th parallel, they were to hand over their weapons to Chiang-Kai-shek's Chinese divisions and, south of it, to the British. The French had no business there, even though their guerrillas had occupied a number of rural districts and towns.

Cos remembered the O.S.S. conference that was held at Bangkok between one lot of officers who had arrived from China and came directly under General Wedemeyer, and another lot from Washington who took their orders from Wild Bill Donovan. At certain moments it looked almost like a social gathering—the cream of Fifth Avenue deciding the fate of Asia—comprising a few military figures, but mostly Wall Street bankers, lawyers and university professors, who were more interested in this sort of warfare than in landings and hand-to-hand fighting.

It was these people who were responsible for O.S.S. being regarded as a snobbish outfit, a mixture of club and welfare organization. Under Roosevelt's impetus, the organization had adopted as its aim the liberation of the people who were still colonized and the eviction of the former colonizers from the territories they still occupied.

"There's just one little difficulty," Patrick Amadian, who represented the Washington staff, had observed. "These former colonizers are now our allies—the British, the French and the Dutch. Since they have no wish to be pushed around, they have joined forces together. To confront us, they have created an organization with opposite aims, Force 136.

"The United States must become the leader of South-East Asia and earn the gratitude of the people by ridding them of colonialism and its effects. The task of O.S.S. in these regions will be to help our country to fulfil this role. We shall thus find ourselves at grips with this Force 136 which we shall have to try to eliminate."

Major Reeves had remarked:

"We've only just stepped into the shoes of the Japanese and here we are repeating their propaganda slogans: the liberation of Asia and the expulsion of the Whites. Their enemies become our enemies after having been our allies. But we remain Whites all the same. For a regular officer this is hard to understand, and even more so to act on it."

"A little tact's all that's needed, my dear Reeves. The necessities of power politics, the right of nations to self-determination, the Atlantic Charter . . ."

Amadian had then turned to Cos:

"You at least will only have the French to deal with, which will spare you the scruples Reeves has towards his British friends. The French in Indo-China collaborated with the Japanese forces of occupation from 1940 to 1945. So there's no point in using tact."

Colonel Harrisson, a member of Wedemeyer's team, had broken into a loud guffaw.

"Mustn't go too far, Pat. When, in 1940, the Frenchies asked us to help them against the Japs, we were not yet at war and we sent them off with a flea in their ear. On 9 March 1945, when the Japs turned nasty, they again asked for our help. But Wedemeyer, who couldn't stand the Frogs, told them: 'Not so much as a grain of rice, not a single pin.' That's the truth."

Amadian had continued:

"Cos, I want you to help the anti-French resistance movements in Laos, even though they're rather Communist, and make use of the Chinese, Japanese and Vietnamese to force them to scram. Don't ever forget that Laos became independent the very day the Japanese surrendered and the French no longer have any business there."

Cos put another record on, turning down the volume. He could not but appreciate the irony of fate. Pat Amadian was now living in France. He had been in trouble with the Committee of Anti-American Activities. His sister Mitzi Mayberry, who had kept the name of her first husband, had become Cos's mistress and his off-hand and demanding tyrant.

In September 1945 Cos was stationed at Nakon-Phanom, in Thailand, on the opposite side of the Mekong to the RC13, the "Colonial Road" linking Luang-Prabang and Vientiane to Cambodia. He was officially engaged in controlling the application of the armistice terms. But his actual rôle was to keep an eye on French and British activity on both sides of the river and to report on all the parachute drops of arms, food and medical supplies that were made from India by the Force 136 Liberators.

Cos was to help the Laotian "resistance forces" to defend the independence of their country against the French. But in Laos these forces happened to be Vietnamese Communists, a fact on which he had been asked not to lay too much stress. Thus it was that he had to make sure that the Japanese handed over part of their arms direct to the Vietnamese without waiting for the arrival of the Chinese.

To the north of Thakhek there was a French maquis group which was seriously frustrating the plans of the O.S.S. Commanded by a Force 136 officer, François Ricq, it had found supporters among the racial minorities, the Laotian civil servants, the former military men, the Catholic missionaries and their flocks, and was firmly established over a huge territory of forests and savannah. Barefoot, ragged, poorly armed, living on the country, Ricq's men would infiltrate into the towns and villages, disappear at the slightest alarm and come back immediately afterwards, having accomplices and information agents everywhere. O.S.S. Headquarters at Bangkok was anxious to have done with these people before the imminent arrival of the 93rd Chinese Division which was to occupy the sector.

Thus it was that Cos had been advised to make use of the Vietminhs for this task. The Viets, it was then thought, did not constitute a serious danger for the future.

Lieutenant Marc de Belza considered his compatriots' conduct disgraceful.

"We are perfectly entitled to reoccupy our former possessions," he said, "but we ought to do so according to the rules of warfare, that's to say officially. Why does Ricq have to behave like Kipling's Kim, wear neither badges of rank nor uniform, and oblige all his men, even the Whites, to march barefoot?"

Major Edward Ports found the strange behaviour of Ricq's bands rather interesting. In every pipe-smoking, cricket-playing Englishman there lurks a romantic child and boy-scout in disguise. Belza was naif. He believed in law and order, which could only be French law and order, in the civilizing mission of his country in her colonies, in the gratitude of worthy savages and in the Geneva Convention in wartime. Cos liked him because of the way he kissed a lady's hand, behaved at table and got drunk without ever being uncouth and also for his worship of America, the fatherland of Franklin, Washington and the great democratic principles.

Belza's America had no gangsters or crooked politicians or corrupt policemen or tramps or unemployed or hotels forbidden to Jews or clubs open only to millionaires. The Negroes, the Cubans, the Mexicans were not exploited there. The women did not make the men's lives impossible, they did not control the country through their leagues but made huge apple pies according to the recipe of their ancestors who had disembarked from the *Mayflower* at Plymouth chanting hymns.

On 16 September a Laotian village headman who had crossed the river in a pirogue reported that a band of Viets and Japanese deserters from Thakhek were burning the villages that refused to join them and executing the notables. Major Ports decided to go and see what was happening and asked Belza and Cos to accompany him. Cos would not very well refuse, because of the deserters. But in the night he sent word to the Vietminhs to make sure there were no Japanese visible in their ranks. Next morning a motor launch deposited them on the other side of the Mekong. A couple of dozen Viets in old Japanese uniforms were waiting for them, their weapons at the ready. Their leader's name was Nguyen van Tho. On several occasions Cos had met him on the Thai or Laotian bank of the river and had issued him with arms. Naturally Nguyen always presented himself as a member of the National Liberation Front and claimed not to be a Communist.

He was a fascinating character, compounded of petrified hatred. He had murdered the director of the plantation whom he had served as a right-hand man throughout the war. Nguyen considered the Laotians idle ne'er-do-wells, heedless and incapable of organization, and he felt the rich land they occupied ought to revert to the Vietnamese. He envisaged a large-scale deportation into Thailand of these *khene**-players who thought only of feast days, dances and courts of love. When Cos told him America wanted to come to the assistance of the oppressed nations, he nodded and spat out these words:

"You Americans are also white, like the French, and in your heart of hearts you're on their side. They're your allies."

"One can be allies in Europe and not in Asia or Africa."

"I'd like to believe you, but I want proof."

That day Cos had furnished him with proof.

Nguyen advanced towards the officers across the strip of red mud on which they had landed.

"The French," he said, "have attacked independent Vietnam. We are therefore at war with France. I request you to hand over this enemy officer."

He indicated Belza.

Ports claimed there could be no question of this and that in any case Belza was on Laotian territory, where the presence of a Vietnamese unit could not be accounted for. He requested the Vietminh leader to withdraw at once to let them pass. Thereupon Nguyen turned to Cos and with a glance asked him for his proof of "good faith".

Cos stiffened, for what he had to do was difficult.

"I believe I'm a neutral," he finally said, "and this affair is no business of mine."

Then he withdrew ten paces or so to the rear.

The Vietminhs trained their rifles on Belza. Ports placed himself in front of him so that they could not fire without hitting him. Seeing that the Viets refused to be intimidated, he suggested getting back to the boat and pushing off; But Nguyen insisted on

* Pan-pipes made of different lengths of bamboo. This instrument is capable of a great range. It exists in three varieties: with six, fourteen and sixteen holes, respectively, some of them all white, the others dappled with brown patches.

having his prisoner. Once again he looked at Cos standing motionless in the sun with his feet in the red mud. One of the Viets slipped behind Belza and Ports to cut them off from the boat. Cos wanted to cry out to warn them but did not do so; he had to give proof of his "neutrality". Nguyen gave a signal and the Viet fired two shots from his revolver into Belza's back. As Ports turned round, the Frenchman fell into his arms.

The Viets and their leaders then rushed off, leaving the three of them together.

Cos would have liked to say:

"I'm terribly sorry, but I couldn't do otherwise. I too have my orders and my mission."

But one can't give these reasons, however good they may be, to a colleague whom one has allowed to be murdered.

It was then Belza and Ports spoke one after the other. Shortly afterwards Belza died on the strip of red mud. Cos had to come back in the same boat with the lieutenant's body covered by a tarpaulin. Ports had not spoken another word to him; he had merely said on landing that he did not even have the excuse of being a coward.

Cos got dead drunk and moved next day to another sector. Nguyen van Tho was now in command of the Vietcong guerrillas of Western Cochin-China near Tay Ninh, where over a hundred American "advisers" had already been killed, taken prisoner and sometimes tortured.

As the record came to an end, the telephone rang. Harry was on the other end of the line, still as excited as ever.

"Hullo, sir. I think you'd better come over. There's a helluva balls-up at Xien Nip! A crowd of Coordination guys came to fetch Ricq to give him the third degree. But there's another crowd that wants to keep him here. They're bawling each other out in their lingo, jabbing pistols and burp-guns into each other's stomachs. There's only one point on which they agree: no one gives a damn what I say."

"I'll be over right away. Hang on."

Cos quickly donned his uniform, jumped into his car and drove out along the road skirting the Mekong. Ripping the clouds away like bandages, the moon cast its reflection in the black waters.

On the outskirts of the town there was a Coordination guard-post blocking the road. Cos showed his pass, but the sentry, who was illiterate, kept turning it this way and that. Cos had difficulty in controlling himself. Finally, with a shrug of the shoulders, the sentry lifted the barrier. The officer in command of the post, who might have been able to read, had gone off to see his wife or get drunk with some girls. He could not make this American, who seemed to be in a great hurry, wait until the morning. White men were always in a great hurry, as though they were afraid of not having enough time to live.

At the entrance of Xien Nip Camp, Cos came up against Pheng, the sentry who had guarded Ricq and Prince Sisang during the afternoon. This soldier could not read either. Cos told him in Loatian who he was and what he was doing.

First there had been that *Phalang*, and now there was this *Amelikain*, who spoke Lao. Pheng was astounded to find that Laotian was a universal language.

In the corridor, outside the door of the guardroom, there was a fine shindy going on. Ricq, still barefoot, had been hauled from his cell: a couple of dozen soldiers and two captains were tugging him to and fro. One of them must have just got out of bed for he was wearing a sarong instead of trousers. Harry and three of his officers were bellowing at the tops of their voices, delivering punches at random and receiving punches in return, in the erratic light from the electric generator. Cos heard the sound of a machine-gun being cocked. The situation was getting out of hand.

He flung himself on Ricq who was being held by a couple of screaming men, jammed him up against the wall and stood in front of him, spreading his arms. Then he shouted in Laotian:

"I'm Colonel Cosgrove Tibbet. Go and bring General Si Mong to me at once. Who's in command here anyway?"

The soldiers stopped brawling and Soumboun shuffled up like a gorilla, thrusting forward his ugly mug which was more black than yellow.

"I'm Captain Soumboun, sir. I have orders to take the prisoner to the Central Police Station."

"At one o'clock in the morning?"

The other captain, Khammay, who was wearing a sarong instead of trousers, dashed up furiously:

"Sir, there's a stamp on the order, but it isn't signed. I'm the one responsible for the prisoner."

"Thank you," Ricq gently murmured behind Cos. "I thought you'd arrive too late. Khammay was beginning to waver."

"This is what I ought to have done," Cos reflected, "stood with my arms outstretched in front of Marc de Belza and sent Nguyen packing. The Viet didn't give a damn about my proof; he didn't believe in it, he was too much of a realist. He simply took pleasure in seeing me betray my own people. Out of hatred for the Whites. But how could I have known!"

Ricq was still speaking behind him.

"Tell them to put me back in the cell. Presently, when you get through to Si Mong, tell him, to account for your presence here, that you were called by your officers because, while attempting to separate the Laotians who were fighting among themselves, they got beaten up. Be indignant about it . . ."

"You're almost at death's door, yet you haven't lost your nerve."

"I'd lost it a short while ago; now things are going better."

Ricq was taken back into the guardroom. But it was impossible to get through to General Si Mong. His telephone seemed to be out of order.

An agreement was eventually reached, however, after lengthy negotiations punctuated by shouts, threats, insults, even bursts of laughter, with everyone brandishing weapons, rushing off and rushing back again in the best *commedia dell'arte* style.

Khammay was to put one of his men on guard outside the door Soumboun one of his, and an American would do the rounds every hour.

Major Harry Bart accompanied Cos back to his car.

"To think," he said, "that a crowd of idiots in the Pentagon imagined they could make this country and musical-comedy army into a bulwark against Communism!"

He broke off, then went on:

"I'd like to know, sir, the reasons you had for saving that fellow's life."

Cos climbed into his car without answering and drove off abruptly. He was furious with Bart, with himself, and reproached himself for that romantic and out-of-place gesture; standing with arms outstretched in front of Ricq to protect him. He had presented the ridiculous spectacle of a man putting on a solitary tragic act in the midst of a burlesque show.

Standing behind him, Ricq had given him advice as to how to deal with Si Mong, just as a good cook might hand over a recipe to another.

"I thought you'd arrive too late, Cos." So Ricq knew he would be coming. Life was amazingly simple for the little Frenchman. He had appealed to Cos, who naturally had the same sense of right and wrong as himself. Cos could not but answer the appeal, although he was on the opposite side. As in a game of football at school, when a player is injured, it's always the fellows on the other side who carry him to the infirmary. But, God Almighty, when were all these people going to grow up, when was the world going to become adult?

By the time he arrived back at Camp Kennedy, the colonel had already thought of the means of "professionally" justifying his gesture. Ricq for the time being was eliminated, so why not steal a march on him by taking over his networks and personnel: the Neutralists? The key man of the situation, apart from Prince Sisang, was still little Captain Chanda who was at the moment trotting about the bush with a handful of paratroopers. Some people said he was finished, but on several occasions he had managed to get out of disastrous situations into which he had been led by his simplicity, his carelessness, his refusal to submit to discipline, his incapability of obtaining a semblance of order from his officers and men. Chanda was a djinn; he had the small stature and instability of one. He was cut out to command a company, at the most a battalion, but chance, Ricq, Captain Meynadier and a few others had transformed him into an army commander.

If Chanda did not arrive in time in the Plain of Jars, his troops, who were already sufficiently swayed by Communist propaganda, were liable to change sides completely as a result of this disastrous *putsch*. Cos had had detailed information: the report on the morale of the troops, which Maynadier had just drafted for the Ministry of War in Paris. He had got hold of a copy of it by slipping a Laotian liaison officer a few thousand kips.

This report, although coming from one of Chanda's staunchest supporters, revealed the total disintegration of the command, the senseless proliferation of officers and the ineffable lack of order.

The only units still holding out were the two paratroop battalions. But they were under the orders of Colonel Thom, who for the last few weeks had been lending a willing ear to Vietnamese propaganda. To avoid total disaster, Chanda would have to return as soon as possible to his command post at Luong Pha in the Plain of Jars. Only this time it would be the American services who would handle him, and not the French. It would be the C.I.A. who would go and retrieve him out of the bush. Cos would explain to Chanda that it was the Americans who had made the *putsch* fail and liberated Sisang, and that even Ricq owed his life to them. Cos would offer to undertake to equip his troops. He would have to act fast before they disbanded! It was easy since he had at his disposal a transport unit which was already supplying the Meo maquis, some of whom were on the heights overlooking the Plain of Jars.

Cos imagined what was going to happen in the next few days: a great reconciliation which would turn out to be a short-lived, makeshift peace. Sisang, on his return from Luang-Prabang, would resume his duties as Prime Minister, but General Si Mong would be pulling the strings. The few Neutralist troops would constitute no more than a thin defensive screen. They would nevertheless be worth more than the entire royal army combined.

Behind Chanda there would no longer be Ricq and the French Military Mission, but Colonel Cosgrove and M.A.A.G. A fine trick to play, Cos reflected, but only for his personal satisfaction. The Neutralists were done for, whatever happened; so were the others. Laos, this country in ruins, would have to keep going until the American presidential elections. Laos, like the whole of South-East Asia, was doomed to the terrifying and inhuman

Chinese form of Communism. Even if the French, the British, the Americans and everyone else to whom this form of Communism meant the end of the world, even if the Russians came to the rescue, nothing could be done to prevent it.

Instead of going back to his quarters, Cos went to his office. He sent the duty officer off to instruct two Piper Cub pilots to be ready to take off at dawn and two Banana* crews to stand by on the airfield. They would probably have to pick up a couple of dozen men from a clearing north of Vientiane and fly them to the Plain of Jars, so they had better fill their fuel tanks.

To Harry's question, Cos would now have been able to reply: "I saved Ricq in order to steal Chanda from him. Chanda would never have been able to get rid of Ricq. His death would have bound him even more closely to the French clan. Now that Ricq's alive, he is free."

But Cos knew he was cheating only for Harry's benefit. He had simply behaved like a primitive, trying to exorcise a dead man at the cost of the blood of a living one. Cos, the civilized man, was not much better than little Captain Chanda who believed in spirits, in lost souls, in the *phis* of the mountains and the rivers, and who steeped himself in the blood of a buffalo to recover his virility.

The Red Prince, Tiao Lam Sammy, dressed in boots, riding-breeches and bush-shirt, stood waiting to be fetched from his tent, his "forward command post" as it was pompously called by the journalists from the brother-nations, that's to say the Chinese and Vietnamese. The Russians no longer belonged to this group and for the last six months had been backing the Neutralists.

Of short stature, with a lean face, thick, close-cropped hair, finely-etched features and barely slanting eyes, he sported a superb moustache. At one time it used to droop like Stalin's, but he had clipped it after the dictator's death. All that remained of it now was a thin line above his lip which made him look like

* Heavy helicopters, so named because their fuselage is vaguely banana-shaped.

Charlie Chaplin's 'Dictator', but a worn-out sceptical dictator who no longer had anyone in his command. Since it was cold at night on the Tran Ninh Plateau, he wore an old tweed jacket round his shoulders and stamped up and down to keep himself warm. Accustomed to their hot damp deltas, the little group of Vietnamese "advisers" who formed his escort sat huddled in padded smocks.

Along some rough tracks traced out by the artillery, he was to be driven up to the heights overlooking Muong Tham. He might have been left to sleep in peace, but the Communists were punctilious about matters of representation. It was with him, the official head of the Pathet Lao, that the two Neutralist battalions and their commander Colonel Thom were to throw in their lot. This defection had been negotiated two months previously, but the Vientiane coup d'état was going to allow the operation to have far greater consequences. There would be newsreel cameramen from Hanoi and Peking, in uniform, the acclamations from the soldiers and the crowd, orchestrated by cheer-leaders, and a speech. He had the text in his pocket. Then he would go back to Sam Neua. Luong Me would give him a "friendly" reprimand for sounding half-hearted or forgetting a few phrases, a few gestures of Marxist ritual.

His wife Loan would perhaps come from Hanoi to see him. She never stayed longer than two or three days at Sam Neua, for it bored her there, and only came to deliver the latest instructions from the Party. In the capital of North Vietnam he was considered sometimes too soft, at other times too excitable, never perfectly attuned to the secret and oppressive rhythm to which the apparatus and its committees were geared. Nowadays only Chinese music was tolerated. The worst offence was to recall, as he had done, that there were still Communists in Russia and that Lenin had seen the light of day neither in Peking nor Canton.

In her breathless, sibilant voice Loan would again say to him:

"Whatever you do, you remain an aristocrat. To you, revolution and civil war have never been anything but an adventure or an aesthete's distraction. Out of pride, you refuse to assume the demeanour which the Party demands from its leaders. Out of tradition, you continue to attach importance to a certain outworn form of Laotian or even Thai nationalism. Sometimes I wonder if you haven't more in common with harmful, anachronistic characters like that dirty spy Ricq or that American colonel to whom you think you owe your life."

Loan had known Ricq for a long time since she had been in the same section of the School of Oriental Studies. She vented on him a vigilant hatred that could not be explained by mere political conviction. She it was who at Vientiane had urged Luong Me to have him eliminated. Loan was cold-blooded and hard-headed; she thought of nothing but the cause, which she confused with her race and her country, Vietnam. How tedious everything had become these last few years—so tedious that he had even lent an ear to a suggestion dear old Ricq had put to him a little over a year ago! Chance, the semi-failure of the French plans, the distrust which Loan had awakened in him when she had repeated that old resistance story, had decreed otherwise. Chance! The Communists had found another word for it when it served their ends—"historical evolution". Revolutionary wars are only fascinating as long as they remain uncodified and the band has not yet been replaced by the battalion. The defection of the two Neutralist battalions was going to enable the combined forces of the Pathet Lao and the Vietnamese "advisers" to seize Luong Pham. After that the whole of the Plain of Jars would fall into their hands, and also the airfield. But even now it was used only by the International Commission aircraft. The Americans had long since built some airstrips higher up in order to supply the Meo maquis. Colonel Cosgrove was not the sort of man to let himself be caught unawares.

It was by signal from Hanoi that Prince Lam Sammay had heard about the coup d'état, the arrest of Sisang and also of Ricq, who was described all of a sudden as "a highly regarded scholar and friend of the Laotian people."

Luong Me's killers had missed Ricq, Si Mong's would perhaps undertake the task. The coup d'état was of course depicted as "a provocation of American imperialism".

The Central Committee had passed a motion, which meant

nothing, but given orders forthwith for the artillery to pound the positions of "the right-wing Neutralists". The right-wing Neutralists were Chanda's troops who were not prepared to follow Colonel Thom's example.

Prince Sammay lit a cigarette, which made him cough. He smoked only French army issue cigarettes and his supply was beginning to run out. Colonel Cosgrove, who was then only a major, had said to him in that hospital in Bangkok where he often came to visit him:

"In Asia it's always the same men or the same sort of men who engineer incidents. The mob follows them. These men may change sides, parties or opinions, but they're impelled by one motive: self-interest, which is not always monetary but more often the fear of being bored. You're one of those men. So don't feel you're bound to any one party."

Cos had arrived too late: Lam Sammay was already bound to the Vietminh. When Ricq, his other crony, had come to give him other reasons for leaving the Communists eighteen years later, it was too soon. He was not yet sufficiently bored by them.

It was Cos who had saved his life by coming to fetch him in a pirogue under fire when, wounded and losing blood, he had dragged himself into a tuft of reeds.

It was Ricq who had wounded him. He had heard him passing close by with his pack of tatterdemalion partisans. Yes, it was always the same men who were to be seen coming on stage or being toppled off it. It was Si Mong who had betrayed him and sold him to Ricq.

An American jeep flying the red and blue pennant of the Pathet Lao and some snub-nosed Russian trucks drove up, water splashing through the puddles.

At one time operations used to cease in the rainy season. It was the great truce of the skies and the waters. The Communists had broken this truce. Prince Sammay suddenly found himself thinking of the Communists as though he was no longer one of them and was already outside the Party.

The convoy climbed up towards the heights with all lights extinguished. They had had to take these precautions ever since

Captain Meynadier's French "advisers" had taken over the Neutralist artillery and directed the firing. Chanda's men were far too idle to come out of their tents or fox-holes and lob a few shells on some trucks moving with their lights on.

Sammay had tried for years to shake his people from their sloth, but without result. "*Bo penhang*" the Laotians would reply, "everything will turn out all right in the end." No sooner were they recruited and he believed them to be converted than they would go off to rejoin their families or girl friends. At the time of the opium harvest they would club together in groups of ten and a couple of them would go up and buy the stuff from the Meos to resell in the valley. He had had these petty racketeers shot, whereupon entire companies had deserted.

Nowadays his army was composed of white Thais, black Thais, Pouthais, varicoloured Meos, Lolos, Kha Phoutengs but above all "Vietnamese advisers". His army! Today it belonged to Singvilay, just as his party belonged to Luong Me. Neither of them had a drop of Lao blood in his veins.

The convoy halted near the big jars carved out of the rock, jars now half-shattered and eaten away by moss which were once used as funerary urns. Their origin dated back to the ancient people, long since disappeared, who once inhabited the Tran Ninh. Day was beginning to break. There was a faint glow on the horizon which nibbled away the deep blue of the sky and revealed the outline of steep crags. Their bare slopes were thrown into relief by others, dark and wooded. The Meos had "devoured" whole areas of the forests, burning them down to make firewood and *rays* in which to plant their rice.

The huge basin was filled with thick white mist like milk. The smells, at 4,500 feet, were the smells of early morning in France: the sweet scent of pine resin which the sun had not yet heated and turned sour, the smell of grass and moss. Smoke rose above the ridges. Prince Sammay was reminded of those happy arduous days when he had been both hunter and hunted and wild dreams used to gallop through his head. Like Boudienny's horsemen, those dreams carried huge red flags attached to their lances.

Colonel Singvilay, Chief of Staff of the Popular Army, emerged from a path, followed by several men. He walked like the Vietminhs, or rather glided along like them, swinging his skinny arms, agile and silent in canvas boots. Like them he saluted Sammay, his bent arm not quite touching his helmet. Curling his lip, he did his best to smile, since it was advisable for a leader always to appear confident and happy.

"The idiots," he said. "They let Chanda escape. We'll soon have him up against us."

Sammay shrugged his shoulders.

"If he feels like coming all the way on foot from Vientiane!"

"The French or their American accomplices will provide him with a plane or a helicopter. On the same night in Vientiane, they also released your cousin Prince Sisang. Radio Peking, relayed from Hanoi, announced it a short while ago. The *putsch* is collapsing. The imperialists won't have anything to do with it. But they've assassinated Ricq."

The prince did not turn a hair.

"At least there's every reason to believe he's been shot. Colonel Thon will be sorry about it. It will prevent his being tempted to change sides yet again. Colonel Thon was very fond of Monsieur Ricq. He fought under him against the Japanese and afterwards against us.

"Another thing, Your Highness"—he laid stress on the title—"during the defection ceremony tomorrow morning our troops are going to attack Chanda's command post. The ceremony must therefore last as long as possible."

"Why did Thon decide to come over to us, Comrade Singvilay?"

"Jealousy. Thon had had enough of playing second fiddle to Chanda, watching Chanda preening himself in front of the cameras, Chanda holding press conferences, Chanda being received at Moscow, being invited to Peking, while he was left behind to fight on his own in the mountains and plateaux. Besides, Thon was a colonel. It was maddening for him to take orders from a mere captain who refused to be promoted. Thon has spent a long time among the French, they have contaminated him with their . . . their . . ."

"Cartesianism . . . as they have also contaminated me with their romanticism. Isn't that what you mean, Singvilay?"

In his cell Ricq struggled painfully to his feet. The air all round him had grown thicker and it was difficult to breathe. It was an effort for him to move. His joints ached and his head throbbed painfully: all the symptoms of a severe attack of malaria.

By giving the door a few kicks he roused the two soldiers on guard. He asked for a blanket, some quinine and some tea. A soldier from Khammay's detachment went off to the infirmary and came back with four tablets wrapped in a piece of newspaper. Not to be outdone, his opposite number produced a blanket and some lukewarm tea in a rusty mess-tin.

Ricq swallowed the tablets, rolled himself up in the blanket and tried to decipher the piece of newspaper: an advertisement in Anglo-French jargon of an Indian merchant who had received from Calcutta some "sumptuous material for a select clientèle at prices to suit every pocket".

"We'll go out to India and trade in spices," his brother Daniel used to say. He already wanted everyone to call him Dan because he thought Daniel was a cissy name, the name of "a chap who let himself be eaten alive in a cage full of lions".

Ricq had stayed three months in Calcutta, at the end of which he no longer noticed the poverty in the streets, the stench of garbage and excrement, the beggars covered in sores, the children blinded by trachoma, and the little prostitutes on sale in their booths.

Dan who had dreamed for so long of voyaging to the lands of gold, silk and spices, the bazaars of Central Asia and the caravan-serais of China, had never travelled beyond the gates of ancient Europe. His body lay rotting somewhere there; no one even knew where he was buried. His name was merely inscribed on an ossuary.

[2]

An Agent's "First Blood"

"WE'LL go out to India," Dan used to say at the age of fourteen, "and trade in spices . . ."

Dan would produce an atlas from under the table, an atlas he had probably stolen from Gilbert's in the Boulevard Saint-Michel, "where pinching was child's play, even for an absolute duffer." But he might equally well have bought it with the money he had "lifted" from the Brasserie till. Dan insisted on everything he did, both good and bad, being fraught with mystery, which enabled him to twist the facts to suit himself.

The Ricq family ran a little bar-cum-tobacconist's shop in the Rue du Petit Musc, in the Marais, which Eugène Ricq had christened the Brasserie because three or four times a month he used to serve tinned choucroute or cassoulet.

On the first floor there were four dark rooms connected with the Brasserie by a narrow staircase which came out by the lavatory: a bedroom for the boys, another for the parents, a damp kitchen and a dining-room cluttered with cases of apéritifs and spirits. These were the supplies that had not been declared at the excise office. Eugène Ricq had two obsessions: the excise office and war. In anticipation of war he stockpiled drinks and tinned food which he carefully concealed from the tax inspector.

"I'm a man of foresight," he would declare with self-satisfaction. "But there are always silly fools who laugh at people with foresight. Afterwards, when 'things become difficult', they think nothing of coming round and begging."

Dan and François shared a big bed with broken springs, but they often slept on a mat instead, to harden themselves for "adventure".

On the wall hung a print of a three-masted schooner in a storm, with birds skimming above it. The light was kept on all day, dim light dispensed by a lamp in fake Breton style.

Dan would open the atlas and with his finger map out an imaginary route following the contours of the Indian peninula.

"We'll go to Jodhpur, Bombay, Hyderabad, Mysore, Madras, up into the Himalayas as far as Katmandu. We'll stop off in Calcutta. We'll fill a truck with spices, pepper and cinnamon, nutmeg, ginger and cloves. We'll come back to France wearing silk robes and turbans. We'll make the spices up into small packets and, disguised as Indians, sell them on the street-corner at a high price because of our disguise. We'll make a fortune . . ."

Dan had a square jaw and forehead, a small mouth, an almost straight, finely chiselled nose and thick curly hair like the hair of the Greek gods in the sculptures in the Louvre.

"Daniel's a good-looking boy," his mother Hortense used to say, "but a guttersnipe. He talks like one and behaves like one. Fortunately François will make good if he doesn't come under his brother's bad influence."

François Ricq was short and skinny, but always had first-rate school reports. Dan was wayward. Some weeks, he came top of the class, but more often than not he was near the bottom, which infuriated Eugène Ricq more than if he had been an incorrigible dunce.

"When he comes top, it's just to annoy me," he would say to his "regulars".

His "regulars" consisted of four or five people for whom Eugène had a certain amount of respect: the baker Picut, who had fought at Le Chemin des Dames; Beaufret, who owned three greengrocer's shops; Cimmare, who was the dogsbody, in other words the secretary, of the local commissaire; Rougier, an old professor of classics; and Faustin, the printer.

A disturbing and non-conformist character, Faustin professed pro-anarchist tendencies. He even said he was in favour of free love. He was a good bridge player, whereas Cimmare was too absent-minded, Rougier too cautious, and Picut made bids that were against the most elementary rules of contract. Faustin was the only partner worthy of Eugène Ricq. For this reason he was forgiven his political views.

Eugène Ricq excelled at bridge. A dull-minded unimaginative man, he became, with cards in his hand, an Alexander the Great through the audacity of his finesses, a Napoleon through the lucidity with which he could assess a hand, an Odysseus through the wiliness of his discards.

Every evening the regulars would discuss the deeds and misdeeds of the two boys.

Picut, the baker of the Chemin des Dames, and Cimmare, the dogsbody, had decided once and for all that François would be a credit to his parents and that Dan was liable to cause them quite a few surprises.

The term "surprises", when used by these defenders of tradition and established privileges, was intended of course in a strictly pejorative sence. Eugène could not but share their view. Had he not tried all his life to anticipate the surprises of war and the tax inspector?

François resented this meddling of the "regulars" in his private life, whereas Dan reconciled himself to it.

At an early age Dan displayed the disillusioned wisdom and distant tolerance that children have towards adults. At fifteen he blossomed out into a dazzling adolescent, whereas François, who was fourteen months younger, was afflicted with pimples and lassitude.

Dan's thickset frame grew finer, his arms and legs developed, his features became more pronounced and his eyes slightly more heavy-lidded and a deeper shade of blue. His cheeks flushed at the slightest emotion, while the two dimples near his mouth disappeared.

François was clumsy and prone to fits of melancholia. He read the romantic poets and stopped growing. Dan had abandoned the spice trade, ivory hunting and filibustering in favour of other projects.

"We must have a shack," he now said, "in a country with plenty of sunshine, sea and mountains. But no one must be able to come and bother us there. No old fogies around us. Out of bounds to the regulars. We'll pinch the whole of Eugène's supply of tinned food."

It required almost nothing more than a picture glimpsed in a magazine, a herd of elephants, a bridge of lianas, a curly-roofed pagoda in a Japanese park, a name with a foreign ring to it—Kabul, Bali, Bokhara—for Dan to let his imagination run riot. But François was conscientious even in his day-dreams. Should Dan mention a name, he would forthwith look up where the island of Bali was situated, what the history of Bokhara was and why the Afghan brigands at Kabul used to massacre foreigners so easily. When he brought the question up again with Dan, his brother would already have forgotten that on the previous day he was astride an Arab stallion in the narrow lanes of the bazaar at Bokhara with a Balinese dancer riding pillion behind him, escorted by a bodyguard of Afghan brigands.

One morning, spring cast her net over Paris and Dan started leaping and twisting like a fish out of water. Every Thursday and Sunday the Ricq boys used to go to the youth club. There they would kick a ball about in a dusty yard, strain their eyes over old serial films and pick up a few snatches of religion. Dan decided all of a sudden to "give the priests a miss" and as soon as the first chestnut blossom appeared in the Place des Vosges he dragged his brother off with him on long walks. Each week he would choose a different quarter of Paris, which he described to his brother in his own poetic jargon: "This time we'll go and get a load of the Seine near La Rapée. Just imagine: the Métro above, the barges below, masses of tramps swigging away and blinking with surprise at the sun's reappearance . . ."

François did not dare tell his brother how far the reality fell short of his promises. The tramps on the Rapée embankment never looked up at the sky but quarrelled among themselves, insulted one another and counted their lice. The barges were full of coal, and the Métro made a dismal rumble as it crossed the meccano bridges. For all his good will, François was unable to follow Dan on these picturesque flights of fancy.

Hortense Ricq sat in state at the cash-desk, happy as a canary in a beam of sunshine. She would dispense cigarettes, cheroots, tobacco and stamps.

"That'll be all, Monsieur?"—then she would count out the change in an arch and jaunty manner—"three francs twenty-five, three francs fifty, four, and one makes five. Thank you, Monsieur."

Hortense would find her sons exhausted on their return—Dan pale and thin with a feverish glint in his eye, quivering all over like a bloodhound about to set out in pursuit, and François dragging his feet, with dark circles under his eyes. She would cut them two big sausage sandwiches and, if Eugène could not see from the far end of the room, pour them out half-pints of beer which she drew herself from the barrel.

Hortense dreamt of a happy old age when, rid of her husband's nagging tyranny, she would be able to go to the cinema and read romantic novels to her heart's content—pastimes which he forbade her on the pretext that the cinema and novelettes disturbed a woman's brain.

Her son François would have a good job—a schoolmaster, for instance—and Dan, who would be at the other end of the world, would send her letters with "exotic" stamps. "Exotic" was a word she had discovered in a film magazine and which for her symbolized the South Seas, the veiled women of Africa, Trader Horn's adventures, and also aeroplanes, liners, "creatures" who smoked, lived by themselves and wore trousers like that hussy Ira Guibert who had a studio near the Place Monge but who came to the Brasserie to buy American cigarettes by the carton. She failed to realize, poor woman, that she was mentally condemning her husband to a speedy death and her son, who was guilty of being too handsome, to a life of exile, women who smoked and the Foreign Legion.

Dan, when his mother's head was turned for a moment, would purloin a packet of English cigarettes and ask:

"Where are we going for our holidays?"

"Go on with you, Dan, as though you didn't know. To Aunt Marcelle's in Ardèche. She's very lonely now that poor Uncle Robert is dead."

"Aunt Marcelle's the biggest bore in the world! High Mass and Vespers on Sunday, and the rest of the week you have to listen to her telling her beads or extolling the merits of poor Robert, who was all the seven plagues of Egypt combined in one man: he was stingy, his breath stank, he drank like a fish . . ."

"We're not rich, Daniel."

"Dan, mother."

"We can't afford a holiday in a seaside hotel. We're in debt; we still haven't paid off the Brasserie bills . . ."

"You're working yourself to the bone to send us to the lycée, everyone knows that. Later on we may become postmasters or chemists. I don't mind sweating it out for three months at Aunt Marcelle's, but couldn't you at least buy us a bike each so that we can get away now and then? We could cycle to Rochemaure. We could go off with a haversack on our carriers, sleep in haystacks, drink water from the springs."

"You're out of your mind! What about your father?"

"We could always ask him."

Eugène Ricq naturally refused to countenance this "idiotic suggestion." But he hinted that if Dan passed his school certificate the following year—which was not very likely—and if François continued to behave himself, he might buy them their bikes.

Dan forgot this project, but François spent weeks mapping out a detailed itinerary, calculated in forty-mile stages, in which nothing was left to chance: compulsory stops at certain monuments mentioned in the guidebooks, places where they could bathe, the hotels where they would stay and their prices.

The following year was 1935. Dan Ricq started going out with friends older than himself, which obliged him to control his unbridled imagination. His new companions were not such a good audience as his brother. Dan became hero of his street and of his class at school, but he was not aware of this. He had the strange gift that is granted to certain children or certain adolescents of crystallizing round themselves the dreams, the devotion, the homage, the confused and sensual yearning of their comrades.

François learned to live in the shadow of his brilliant brother. He nurtured himself on his success, his encounters, his discoveries, while already developing his own personality, that of a secretive, easy-going figure who avoided the limelight and kept his desires and dreams to himself.

One evening in May, when the air was full of the honey-like scent of young shoots, Dan disappeared and did not come back all night. Since his school certificate exams were one month off, he said he had gone and mugged up his "physics" with a friend who lived on the other side of Paris. Having sat up too late, he had missed the last Métro and had therefore been obliged to spend the night at his friend's place. His parents believed him, for the Ricqs never took a taxi except to go to hospital or fetch supplies of clandestine spirits from the Quai de Bercy.

When Dan slipped into bed at dawn, he exuded a smell that was new to François. Dan burst out laughing.

"Well, old boy, I've done it. I've slept with a girl."

François felt as though he had just lost his brother. The mysterious world of women repelled him. They were, he believed, many-sided creatures: young girls in the gardens who flaunted their dresses in the sunshine, prostitutes in dark alleys who stood with their hands on their hips and a tight jersey over their breasts calling out to men. They were Isolde and Messalina. Dan was done for. For him there would be no Asia, no silks or spices, no big house between the mountains and the sea, no Bokhara or Samarkand. François suspected women of depriving men not only of their virility but also of their dreams and chaining them to everyday routine. In a trembling voice he asked him:

"The real thing? It was the real thing?"

"And how! It was with Ira, that painter woman who smokes two packets of fags a day. You ought to see her place! From the bed there's a view of the Jardin des Plantes. On the bed there's a fur, some South American animal or other. She's been pestering me for ages to go and pose for her. Why do you suppose she came so far to buy her cigarettes?"

"You never told me."

"Ira wanted me to come alone. She showed me her books on Italy, Spain and China."

"What did she do to you?"

"Ira! She's dotty, if you ask me. She must be rolling in dough! The studio's bigger than the Brasserie, the front room and the parlour combined."

"Go on."

"A thousand francs, she told me the other day, a thousand francs if you pose for a portrait. I'm cushy, naturally. We fix a date and I make up the story about swotting for my exams."

"Ira's an old woman."

"She's thirty. Her husband lives in Indo-China. She was born out there. She liked the country all right, but not her old man."

"What did you do with her?"

"I turn up at 17, rue Buffon. I peep in at the concierge's. 'If it's for the painter lady,' she says, 'third floor, left-hand door, and knock hard; she's usually wool-gathering.' Ira comes and opens up, dressed in a white smock covered with paint. We talk a bit about school, the weather, and she offers me a cigarette, then some sherry, a very dry wine from Spain. How she knocks it back! She buys it by the case. The Brasserie doesn't stock it. It's no booze for paupers. She produces a new canvas, sets it up on the easel and sits me down in a chair.

" 'Dan, hold that pose,' she says. 'Dan, don't move, don't pick your nose, don't scratch your thigh.'

"After half an hour she says:

" 'It's no good, take off your shirt so that you neck shows more.'

"A moment later my pants were off and we were on the fur rug.

"The first time, it made me sick. You'll know what it's like one day. You feel like soaking yourself in a clear stream for a whole day and rubbing yourself all over with a scouring brush. But Ira understood. She was very kind. When we got down to it again it was much better. I wasn't frightened any more. We lay in bed together looking at reproductions of paintings, books illustrated with stark naked women. Ira specializes in book illustration. She even writes poetry.

"If you could only see her bathroom, with all sorts of bottles and scents, but not like the barber's, when he pours some muck on your head as a sort of bonus because you're a customer here, or the public baths which smells of dirty water. You put bath-salts into the tub before getting in, and there's a thick warm robe for when you get out. No one to shout 'You've been soaking in there for half an hour. There are others waiting.' It was like heaven! Ira showed me the photo of Perseus which is in Florence—it seems I look like him. Another one of Apollo which is at the museum in Rome—that's meant to be me too."

Dan stretched as he lay in bed.

"I feel sleepy. I'm going to give the lycée a miss this morning. Tell them I'm ill . . . But I'm not at all ill, little brother"—how condescending this "little brother" sounded—"I now have a skin made to measure, I've been to the tailor's. Beforehand, I didn't feel comfortable. It's so much better to make love to a woman instead of spurting all over the sheets by oneself . . . This morning I was woken by the sun and not that vile dim bulb, by the cries of the animals in the Jardin des Plantes and not the noise of dustbins being emptied. I've been a million miles from Paris."

Ricq turned over on his palliasse. The fever made his recollections incoherent. He now recalled that poem inspired by Lorca which Ira had sent him in Laos. It was illustrated with a pen-and-ink drawing of Dan in shirt sleeves, his shirt collar unbuttoned. With a beaming expression on his face he was walking along a dark street, the Rue du Petit Musc, crowded with stray cats and dustbins.

Had the poem been accepted on account of the drawing? Ira's poetry had never been very original; but her drawings, which betrayed the subtle influence and brushwork of the great Chinese masters, were remarkably competent.

"*A sergeant-major in a steel helmet*
And with dark circles under his eyes
Raised his arm
And a dozen bullets killed Dan Ricq.

His body fastened to the stake
Slowly slumped.
The soldiers marched off
To eat a meal of bread and dripping . . ."

At the time there was a lot of talk about renaming the little street in which he was born the Rue Dan Ricq. But the protectors of old Paris were against it, and so were certain resistance groups.

Dan Ricq, during his lifetime and even after his death, had remained the same disarming and complex character, so difficult to define that now no one could tell if he had been a hero, a weakling or a liar.

François Ricq, Little Ricq as Ira had straight away called him, had discovered Asia in the Rue Buffon studio. It was a baroque paradise perched above the trees of the Jardin des Plantes, an untidy paradise cluttered with cushions and hangings, stone buddhas purloined from Angkor, Korean marriage chests in dark lacquer, cream-coloured Chinese carpets patterned in blue, others from Persia which looked like gardens of crushed flowers. If ever some essential was lacking, if the refrigerator was empty, there were still baskets of exotic fruit and flowers to be found there, curiously shaped bottles of wine and spirits. And in the midst of this bric-à-brac there was Ira—Ira with her little triangular face, her short hair, her bare feet, her long legs, her thighs clad in tight velvet trousers, her flat boyish breasts, her long neck and strong, blue-veined, mannish hands.

There were no fixed times for eating or sleeping at Ira's, where slender Annamites who were studying mathematics turned up with short-haired Chinese girls studying medieval art at the Sorbonne. Beefy white men who had businesses in Shanghai or rubber plantations in Cochin-China were also to be seen there, consorting with archaeologists who were battling against the Cambodian forest to preserve the decaying serpent-haunted temples. The white men, as Dan pointed out, were free from many complexes, specially those bearing on love, whereas the yellow men tended to be puritanical, as though the urge to free themselves from the West obliged them to don other chains.

Little Ricq, lolling on a divan, would listen eagerly to the confused and glowing tales of all these travellers who would pay a brief call on Ira, then set sail again, arranging to meet at Chungking, Peking, Hanoi or Bangkok.

One warm evening in June, Dan arrived at Ira's after completing the first part of his school certificate exam. To celebrate his success —for he was sure he was going to pass—he got drunk and flung himself on the bed. Mathematics, in which he had always refused to take an interest, was the only subject in which he might have failed. But he had cribbed from his neighbour, who wore the sort of gig-lamps that would get him straight into the Polytechnic. As she walked by, Ira kissed him on the small of the back, and this tender shameless kiss disturbed François. He was trying to read *The Temptation of the East* by Malraux.

But, since the kiss, he was unable to take any more interest in the splendid resonant imagery which reminded him at times of Heredia. A man came in with his jacket slung over his shoulders, pushing a pretty halfcaste girl in front of him. He was lean and hatchet-faced, with a shock of tow-coloured hair. His small black eyes sparkled; from his wide mouth, which drooped sadly at the corners, came a deep bass voice:

"Hello, Ira. This is Geneviève, my half-sister. My father sired her on a Thai woman from Phong Saly while Maman Gibelin was back in Paris knitting bust-bodices for the little Chinese. The old man asked me to see what she was doing with the pittance he gives her as an allowance. She isn't doing anything but she manages to live."

He seized Ira by the waist, gave her a kiss, then went over to the bed where Dan still lay fast asleep and whistled through his teeth:

"What a fine little leopard you've bagged there! Why aren't you interested in men? They're less cruel!"

He nodded at François.

"Who's this lad?"

"It's Little Ricq, the leopard's brother."

"Must be from another litter."

Gibelin took the book out of François's hands.

"*The Temptation of the East*. Sheer pathos! You'd better read

Malraux's other books: *The Conquerors, The Royal Road, The Human Condition.* You'll get a magnificent and utterly false idea of Asia. You'll long to bugger off and join the revolutionaries, but they exist only on this side of the Seine. Good old Malraux!

"I was at his trial in Saigon. Luckily he was later reprieved.

"What had he done? Merely pinched some old stones, in which no one was interested. It was nothing, but he had also transgressed the unwritten laws of Asia, which was more serious."

Antoine Gibelin sat down beside Little Ricq. It was at this moment their long friendship began.

"I've pinched some bas-reliefs myself—dancers, *apsaras, devatas* and buddhas. The ones in this studio came from Angkor. Never had any trouble about them. All these stones were falling apart in the midst of the lianas and had taken on the greenish tinge of mildew. They belonged to whoever saved them. I didn't go off, like Malraux, and ask for an excavation permit or an official appointment. In Asia, as soon as you find yourself in the world of the written word, all freedom ends and hypocrisy begins. No Chinese merchant would think of asking his debtors for an I.O.U. They'll never sign any paper, but on the whole they keep their word."

Antoine Gibelin had just arrived from Northern Laos, where his father ran a teak business. Since Ira asked after him, he thundered in reply:

"The old man doesn't suffer from the temptation of the West. Impossible to make him come home; opium, *phousaos* . . . I can understand him. I've been in France eight days and I'm already bored. How can you live here, Ira? You can find just as many leopards in Indo-China. In Saigon, at the Sporting Club, I've come across some splendid specimens . . . At the age of fifteen these sons of schoolmasters from Marvejols or tax inspectors from Barcelonnette are as bitchy and cruel as the Chinese procuresses of Cholon."

Ira tried to calm him down:

"Let my young animal sleep in peace. He's digesting, he's just stolen the first part of his school certificate. Talk to Little Ricq; all he thinks about is Asia."

"It would suit you out there," said Antoine, lowering his voice. "The men are even shorter than you are. The women not only have a taste for young leopards but for anyone who gives them what's most important in a country where people fight over a bowl of rice—face, in other words power, wealth, security. Since they're honest, they pay cash down. They don't give love—that doesn't exist for them—but a certain fidelity, a certain devotion, smooth graceful bodies, the eroticism of the gourmet which is the opposite of that of the glutton.

"If you get bored with the women, you can always resort to opium, to help you believe you're not frightened of life or of death or of others.

"It's a good place for men like myself who are ugly but have guts, or those like you who are small and feel they have to assert themselves against the big fellows and the leopards . . ."

"What's Laos like?" Little Ricq enquired.

"Paradise. It's as hot as hell in the narrow valleys; icy cold on the plateaux. The rains wash away the roads, the Laotians refuse to work; the leeches drop from the trees. You catch malaria and dysentery and, in the towns, pox and clap. But it's paradise all the same. The women's amber bodies clad in gold and silver cloth! The *khene* music! The girls bathing stark naked in the red rivers, the feast days, the courts of love, the bonzes, the Meos up in their blue highlands and the Thais on the banks of the clear-running rivers!"

Little Ricq looked at him with eager, burning eyes:

"I'm going to go to Laos, Monsieur, I'm going to live in Asia."

"And what'll you do out there, Little Ricq?"

"I don't yet know whether I'll pinch statues or make war or do business or write books or organize revolutions, but I'll do something out there."

Dan woke up, glanced at the halfcaste girl and appeared, rather too obviously, to disregard her. Ira kept a curious and at the same time anxious eye on him.

The Ricq brothers said good-bye to Gibelin, his half-sister and Ira, who were going to dine in a Vietnamese restaurant, and went home to the Brasserie.

"I know what I'm going to do," François declared. "I'm going out to the Far East."

"I'm not quite sure myself," Dan replied, "but I shan't stay in France either. If you could have seen how silly they were, those students ragging in public, shouting obscenities in chorus down the Boulevard Saint-Michael and nipping up side-streets as soon as the police appeared. Either you leave the police alone or else you take a pot shot at them. All the rest is a lot of nonsense."

"What about your school certificate?" Eugène enquired as Dan came in.

"It's in the bag."

"I'd be surprised, you haven't done a stroke of work."

"I was well placed."

"Well placed?"

"Yes, papa, in the examination hall."

"You dirty little beast, you've got lipstick all over your shirt."

"It's a tradition to kiss a girl when you pass your school cert."

"In my days . . ."

Eugène went back into the parlour where the inevitable game of bridge was in progress. It was Cimmare's deal and he was getting impatient.

When the two brothers climbed up to their dimly lit room, in which they were allowed to switch on only two of the six bulbs of the Breton chandelier, Dan burst out:

"I'm fed to the teeth with this dump which smells like a cellar; I'm fed up with dim lighting, with that old bugger Eugène bleeding himself white to give us an education, with the 'regulars' who are probably now discussing our case. Give us some air, God Almighty, some air, wide open spaces and a free rein! Did you notice that girl who came to Ira's?"

Dan passed the first part of his school certificate with distinction. He proved brilliant in the oral even though the history examiner was surprised to find the Wars of Religion depicted as a large-scale settlement of old scores between foul-mouthed libertines and debauchees.

François attended his brother's examination and was astounded at his self-assurance and quick-wittedness. Dan had repeatedly finessed and indulged more often in practical experiments in eroticism with Ira than in theoretical physics and natural science. Dan was given his bike, and so was Little Ricq. Eugène was proud of this first certificate to be bestowed on a family that had been doomed for generations to petty Parisian trade.

On 26 June the brothers put their bikes on to the train at the Gare de Lyon and travelled down to Clermont Ferrand. From there they were to make for Ardèche, where Aunt Marcelle awaited them with her Paternosters and quince jelly. But the Ricq brothers were firmly resolved to do the tour de France first of all. Little Ricq felt the same urge to escape as his brother. Though less exuberant in word and deed, he had made lengthy preparations and provided himself with maps, compasses, guide-books and jack-knives.

Their mother had given them enough food for a week, advice to last a lifetime and sweaters suitable for Arctic weather.

Ira had set off on the previous day in a second-hand Rosengart convertible. She had piled in her paint-box, canvasses, easel, and also a tent and some sleeping-bags for which François Ricq had gone shopping with her at the Bazar de l'Hotel de Ville.

He had astonished the salesmen with his expert knowledge.

Ira had arranged to meet them at an inn on the outskirts of Clermont where, she said, you could drink pink Limagne wine accompanied by Saint-Nectaire cheeses as yellow and runny as butter.

In his prison in Xien Nip, Ricq recalled the highly-coloured or faded memories of that bicycle trip in Puy-de-Dôme and Ardèche—dusty roads with hens pecking about in the ditches, mountain streams full of trout, huge forests, banks of moss, springs, cool star-studded nights. Smiling peasants would give them wine to drink. It was often sour but they protested when François added water to his. What were the roads in France like in 1964? No longer dusty, but black and asphalted and jammed with cars, as he had been told by everyone who had recently been there. The peasants no longer offered their wine but carefully bottled it and gave it some trade name or other.

Subsequently Dan took to going off on his own.

François and Ira were his twin havens. Every time he returned from one of his "jaunts" he made straight for Ira with her paint-brushes or for François with his books. Hortense, that clucking hen of a mother, was unhappy at first to have given birth to this wild duck. Then she fell madly in love with Dan, as only a mother can. For his sake she used to pinch money from the till and it was François, the dutiful son, whom she could no longer abide.

Ricq woke up, then relapsed again into a feverish sleep, a sleep that at one moment was as burning-hot as the Sahara, the next moment as damp and clammy as a cheap Turkish bath.

The memory of Dan kept haunting him. This time it was Dan on his return from the draft board. White in the face, he had gulped down a glass of brandy and turned to Ira:

"They don't want to have me. There's something wrong with my heart—a cardiac anomaly, they called it. I'm exempted for life. There's no getting round the rules. The French army doesn't want physiological cases like mine. On the other hand, mental cases are perfectly all right. The main thing is not to have flat feet."

Ira did her best to comfort him:

"I thought you hated the prospect of military service and wasting two years of your life."

"I needed to waste those two years. On my return from military service everything would have been clear. I could have started a new life."

He added spitefully:

"Without you, Ira, without a woman-guardian, a woman-teacher, a woman-haven."

He went over and stood by his brother, his mouth set in a thin line, his features strained:

"It would have suited you, wouldn't it, François, to avoid the army. To be able to continue peacefully with your course in Papuan, Patagonian or Chinese. You've always been frightened of other men. Can you see yourself sharing a barrack-room with chaps whose feet stink, who bawl out idiotic marching songs, compare the length of their cocks, and go off in a group to the Grand 13, the garrison brothel. You have a maidenly modesty; I haven't.

"Ira, could you let me have some dough? I'm going out to get drunk. It's a tradition: the draft is something to be celebrated . . . even if they turn you down."

He went out, slamming the door behind him.

Little Ricq felt miserable; his brother had hurt him with the dexterity he always showed when being unpleasant. But he was not displeased to discover his hero's Achilles heel.

After the final part of his school certificate, François Ricq had told his astonished parents that he was going to study at the School of Oriental Languages and read for a diploma in ethnography at the Sorbonne.

"Will it help you at least to earn a living?" Eugène had asked with a solemn, absorbed air.

"With an Oriental Languages diploma I could always get into the Foreign Office, become a consul or even Secretary of State for Far Eastern Affairs."

Reassured by these brilliant prospects, which were guaranteed by a pension at the end of the career, Eugène Ricq acquiesced to his son. François was firmly resolved not to become a consul or end up on a pension. He was dreaming rather of looting temples and living among the unknown tribes on the Chinese border by selling them arms and buying opium from them.

"What's your brother doing?" Eugène would ask him from time to time. "Still living on that old hag?"

"Ira's only thirty."

"And Dan's eighteen. To him, she is an old hag; and he's a gigolo."

Little Ricq was quite glad of this opportunity to stick up for his brother:

"Dan isn't a gigolo; Ira often doesn't have a penny; Dan is working. He spent two months in a sawmill, then he went in for breeding Roquefort sheep, and trout on the Spanish frontier . . . Once or twice he was able to go and see what was happening in Barcelona."

"This Spanish affair is no business of ours," Eugène solemnly declared. "We have enough on our hands already with our own problems, without going and meddling in other people's."

"It was only to make you see, Papa, that Dan is interested in other things besides his own pleasure. This war has given him food for thought."

"It has also put prices up. Needless to say, he was with the Reds!"

"I think he was with the Reds because it was easier to cross the border that way. He came back with a Rolleiflex."

"He stole it!"

"No, a German gave it him. Dan took some first-rate photos. I was amazed when I saw them. I assure you, Papa, Dan's going to surprise us all."

But Eugène Ricq shook his head despondently:

"That ne'er-do-well brother of yours is having a bad influence on you."

"Dan's not a ne'er-do-well, Papa, any more than he's a gigolo. He wants his freedom and doesn't bother about what people think of him."

"That's just what I hold against him. Your ne'er-do-well brother is having a bad influence on you and you're sticking up for him."

One day Ira had said to Little Ricq:

"You know, you're not so very different from Dan. Like him, you're curious about the way other people live. You also have the same gift of being able to be at your ease anywhere, like a woman. But Dan is immediately conspicuous on account of his beauty, his elegance which is so out of keeping with the coarse language he delights in using. He inspires affection but also distrust. You, you're a chameleon. You assume other people's colour without the slightest effort. Dan is too eager and restless to be happy. But you, Little Ricq, you're perfectly happy because you don't dream of any exceptional destiny."

This gift of mimicry which Ira had noticed in François was accompanied by that of languages. His teachers were astonished at the ease with which he assimilated dialects as different as, for instance, Annamite and Thai. He managed to reproduce perfectly the tones and accents that are most difficult to grasp for a Western ear. Without ever having set foot in England, he could pass for an Englishman and assume at will a Scotch, Welsh or even Cockney accent. He had achieved this merely by listening in to the B.B.C. for a couple of months.

Little Ricq shared Dan's taste for a vagabond life. But he remained for the most part anchored in Paris, where he was certain of finding a square meal and a warm room at the Brasserie in the Rue du Petit Musc.

"François can't imagine adventure except with a safety-net stretched below him," Dan used to say.

François Ricq passed his exams in foreign languages and ethnography at the first attempt. In his second year he started to read for another diploma.

One day he ran into Geneviève, Antoine Gibelin's Laotian half-sister, who had come to fetch a friend of hers from the School of Oriental Languages. Gibelin, disgusted with Paris, had left for good.

Asia had closed down on him.

Little Ricq greeted her with a few lines of Laotian verse from the ancient epic of Sin Xay. As his teacher, Marcel Odelin, used to say: "Only a blasted little prodigy like that could recite a text in any dialect after a single reading. Primitive people often have that sort of memory—the Bandiaguara Negroes of Africa, for instance . . ."

Pressing the palms of his hands together, François recited:

> "*So I shall see your face no more*
> *Except in dreams*
> *Your adorable face*
> *Indelibly engraved on my heart* . . ."

Geneviève, whose knowledge of Laotian was limited to stock phrases and swear-words, was astonished. Whenever she failed to understand, she was captivated. Straight away she invited him to come and have dinner one evening in her room, promising to cook him a Laotian meal.

"Bring your brother along with you," she said. "I've only seen him asleep. My girl friend will be there too. Won't you, Loan?"

Loan was short, ugly and intelligent. She was a Tonkinese and came from Vinh—the revolutionary town, she would proudly explain, the town from which the movement against the colonialists would be launched.

On the day arranged for the dinner, Geneviève had no food ready. She was in a bad mood because the skies were grey and she was bored and displeased with her appearance. But Loan, mousy, tiny and efficient, put some rice on to boil, fried some *nemes* and even unearthed some *ngoc-mam* and red peppers. The Laotian dinner turned into a Vietnamese one.

Dan lay on a dilapidated sofa, smoking in silence without making the slightest attempt at conversation. Geneviève was like the back wall of a squash-court made of felt, which deadened every ball driven against it. She was not exactly stupid, but took no interest in anything but her little world of frills and petting parties. Dan's indifference had straight away restored her beauty and vivacity, as though an electric current was running through her listless body, making the blood rush to her cheeks and bringing a sparkle to her eye.

As her hair brushed against him, Dan stroked her thigh.

"We must leave them alone together," Loan said to Little Ricq.

In the manner of the Vietnamese, she spat out each word.

"They're going to make love," she went on. "Let's go out for a walk. Geneviève and your brother are incapable of thinking of anything else. It's up to us, little weeds like you and ugly ducklings like me, to tackle the most important task: the reconstruction of the world by means of revolution."

François Ricq remembered, as though in a nightmare, that endless walk along icy streets with that Tonkinese girl trotting along beside him and talking about the revolt of the oppressed nations. Loan wanted the war between the Whites to break out quickly so that they could cut one another's throats. Then their slaves would rebel and drive them out. In the Rue des Ecoles she suggested:

"It's cold. We're not far from where I live. Come up to my room. I'll make you some tea."

Her voice became sibilant and she suddenly blurted out: "If you like, we could also make love."

François Ricq was surprised and shocked by this suggestion, for which he was not prepared. Loan had not even once taken his arm. Her invitation was brazen, cold-blooded, so devoid of any trace of artifice as to reduce love to mere copulation.

He had conceived a very different idea of it, poetic and at the same time indistinct. He imagined lengthy preliminaries, endearments, caresses, whispered words, trysts, disappointments, misunderstandings and finally, long afterwards, that intoxicating crowning action.

Loan was an ugly girl. Everything about her displeased him: her didactic quality, her spirit of rebellion which derived largely from resentment, her aggressive realism. But he was tired and under the spell of this wilful little ugly duckling.

They climbed up to an attic room as cold and denuded as a monk's cell. On the wall there were two photographs: a stout man with a goatee, Loan's father, who had been imprisoned by the French on Poulo-Condor Island; and Karl Marx, with his beard and a heavy watch chain stretched across his waistcoat. Both of them looked like average, decent middle-class citizens. The furniture consisted of a deal table, two chairs, a bed, and a wash-basin and water-jug standing on a packing-case. Loan lit the gas fire which emitted more fumes than heat.

"Get into bed," she said to François, addressing him by the familiar "*tu*". "You'll be warmer there. I'm going to make the tea."

François lay down half-dressed between the damp sheets. He was shuddering with cold. The tea warmed him up a little.

Loan slipped out of her clothes, revealing the body of a young boy or immature girl: scarcely noticeable breasts, flat stomach, small waist, narrow hips, and exceptionally slender wrists and ankles.

"Women in my country are extremely reserved," she said. "The teaching of Confucius. They are slave-women. None of them would ever dare behave like this with a man, especially a white man. Not even a whore. Communism has freed me from those secular chains. You're the best student in our class. One day you'll speak our language perfectly. You mustn't get to know us in our ancient aspect but in our new one."

Loan got into bed beside him, unbuttoned his shirt and adroitly but dispassionately removed the rest of his clothes.

François Ricq acquiesced, surprised all of a sudden to feel the blood throbbing in his veins and thundering in his ears. Loan's skin was soft, her nails were sharp as claws.

She crouched over him, a slender youthful body of exceptional beauty surmounted by that ghastly mask of a face with its pug nose, jutting cheekbones and prominent teeth.

At the moment of climax she jerked away from him, and the cold air on his damp body made him shiver.

"Another time I'll take the necessary precautions," she said. "I'm shocking you, I can see, but I like to speak frankly about anything connected with sex and the sexual act."

François longed to rush away but did not feel up to it. In order to avoid seeing Loan again, he kept away from the school for a week. When he came back, the Laotian girl gave him a quizzical look. But she never spoke to him again and Little Ricq realized she regarded him as a lamentable scrap of French petty bourgeoisie, who was incapable of facing up to his destiny and physical constitution. He was to run into Loan again ten years later.

In July 1939, Little Ricq passed his second-year exams at the School of Oriental Languages. He obtained his additional diploma with distinction. His professor, Marcel Odelin, invited him for a two weeks' holiday to the villa he rented every year at Tréport.

"You're working too hard," he told him. "You look like a piece of chewed string. The sea air will do you good. I'll show you some Pali manuscripts, you can help me decipher them."

Marcel Odelin already regarded François Ricq as his future assistant, maybe even his successor. He also had three daughters to marry off, none of whom was very pretty.

The professor, his wife and daughters lived in a big uncomfortable building corroded by the salt-laden air. The food was poor, the conversation was highbrow. François Ricq accompanied the Odelin girls to Mass, and went bathing and played tennis with them. He carried the rackets and towels, and was bored to tears.

The sea, either green or grey, full of algae and smelling of iodine, the huge beaches under an invariably grey sky, the sea-gulls uttering their forlorn cries, dispirited and depressed him.

He could easily picture what his life would be as the husband of one of the Odelin daughters, the son-in-law of Professor Odelin, doomed to years of sterile research into the origin of the Thai branch of languages. A congress, a controversy or the discovery in a manuscript of some new root would occasionally stimulate this studious and monotonous existence with a semblance of ferment and excitement.

One evening he found a bunch of flowers in his bedroom but made no attempt to find out which of the girls had put it there.

Dan, meanwhile, had become a journalist. In a bar in the Rue du Croissant he had come across Maurice Paget, a reporter on a daily paper who was only three or four years older than himself. Paget had extolled the joys of his profession—the personal freedom, the incessantly renewed interest, the prestige it bestowed in the eyes of women—to such an extent that Dan decided to "have a go at it". With extreme condescension, Paget offered to take him on an assignment as his assistant. A year later he could be heard declaring at the top of his voice in the editorial office:

"I hatched a viper. If I had to paint a portrait of a 1939 Rastignac, I'd choose Dan Ricq as my model. His background is very, very . . . humble. One might almost say he comes from nowhere. He has no political views and even fewer principles. He'd do anything for money and position. He accepts presents from women, and only a vague prejudice prevents him from accepting them from old gentlemen as well. His pet subject is war with Germany, because that gives the readers a thrill.

"But although he's in perfect health, he managed to get himself exempted from military service. Rastignac can't afford to waste two years in the service of his country. He can't write for toffee, but gets his articles 'vetted' by an elderly mistress or a discreet younger brother at the university. If I were you, I wouldn't touch him with a barge-pole. Mark my words, he's going to come to a sticky end."

For two weeks Dan had run errands for Paget and taken photographs for him. Subsequently he was sent out on assignments of his own, doing the rounds of the police stations where his breezy hail-fellow-well-met attitude stood him in good stead.

One fine morning he had leaped on to the front page with a story of some political and at the same time sexy scandal. A disillusioned old news editor had taken him under his wing. He had found it amusing to make a political correspondent out of this young hooligan who was so quick on the uptake and at the age of twenty seemed more cynical than an octogenarian. He had packed Dan off to Germany, where his personality and handsome Aryan features had opened all doors to him.

On 3 August, a telegram from Dan snatched François Ricq from his gloomy research. "Return to Paris. War Imminent."

"My mother's seriously ill," said Little Ricq, who promptly packed his bags and took the first train home.

Six months earlier he had been passed fit for military service, but, like all students, had been granted a deferment. In wartime deferments would be rescinded. Was he going to find himself toting a haversack and rifle?

In the papers he bought to read in the train, there were some big photographs of the Maginot Line and a statement by General Weygand:

"The French Army is more powerful today than at any time in its history; it possesses first-rate material, first-rate fortifications, excellent morale and an exceptional high command. No one in this country wants war, but if we are forced to fight we shall be victorious."

Once again Dan must have been carried away by his over-vivid imagination.

He was waiting for him at Ira's, with his bags all packed and ready.

"I'm taking you with me to Poland," he said. "I've got your visa for you. Things are hotting up there."

"How do I come into it?" asked Little Ricq.

"Don't worry. I told my editor you spoke Polish, and he at

once coughed up your fare as well. You work yourself to death at the University and, as though that wasn't enough, you go off on holiday with your prof!"

"I don't know a word of Polish."

"The only Poles that matter will speak French, German or English. The rest are bumpkins. We're taking the Orient Express. We'll be travelling through countries that are all a-flutter, in big silent coaches crammed with beautiful spies and pimply terrorists."

It was difficult to resist Dan's high spirits. François acquiesced. He even agreed not to show up at the Brasserie, so as to avoid complications and delays. Dan spent the night with Ira, whom he had dropped for several months.

From the next room Little Ricq heard her long moans of pleasure. Her young lover had come back to her at last.

"Ira makes too much noise in bed," Dan told him next day on the train. "It's amazing, the pleasure women get out of it. When there's nothing left but force of habit, it's just like any other job. But you, at least, don't bother your head too much about girls. I think about them all the time. I'm always scared of missing the essential girl, the girl who'll send me into raptures. So I try them all out."

At Berlin, Dan bought some newspapers. They all denounced the brazen Polish provocations.

Dan shrugged his shoulders.

At the German-Polish frontier there were lengthy police formalities. One of the German customs officials asked Dan with a grin:

"Tell me, is it true the French all want to die for Danzig?"

"They don't want to die for anyone," Dan grunted in reply. "But there's a limit to what they can stand. They might recover their taste for dying."

In Warsaw, Dan was able to meet one or two generals in Marshal Rydz-Smigly's set-up. They paraphrased Marshal Weygand's statement:

"The Polish Army is more powerful today than at any time in its history . . ."

But one of the French assistant military attachés, Captain Durozel, did not share this optimistic view.

A graduate of the Polytechnic, lean-faced, hard-working and ascetic, whose only vice was tobacco, in which he over-indulged, Captain Durozel had a passion for information and organization, a horror of romanticism. He laboured under no delusion as to the result of his arduous toil. One day Dan had asked him:

"What difference is there between a spy and a journalist?"

The captain had replied with a smile:

"Thousands of readers, my dear fellow, read what a journalist writes and, though they say, 'He can't fool me,' they nevertheless believe him. A spy, an agent or an intelligence officer drafts confidential reports which he sends to other specialists who chuck them into the waste-paper basket because they think they know more about the subject than he does."

Durozel asked Dan and his brother to a Spartan dinner in his small bachelor apartment near the Church of the Visitation.

He endeavoured to give them an idea of the complexity of the Polish problem. Little Ricq bore in mind that the large number of Jews in Poland tended to be pro-Russian, while certain elements of the army admired the Nazis.

As they left Durozel's, he said to his brother:

"I think you ought to look into the question of the Jews and those pro-German elements in the army."

Dan shrugged his shoulders:

"That's a spy's job, not a journalist's. Leave that to Durozel. In any case war and peace are matters that are thrashed out above the heads of the people."

"What about revolution, isn't it the people who are responsible? Look at the Russians of yesterday, the Chinese of today."

"I might have expected you to bring in those precious Chinese of yours. The Russian Revolution was organized by specialists in charge of an army that had mutinied and kept its arms. I don't know about the Chinese. All the Poles want is to kill off the Huns."

François persisted:

"You might at least make contact with certain Poles, students, intellectuals, local doctors. They could then write to you . . ."

"What a mania you have for information! You ought to get a job in Durozel's outfit. You expect me to set up an intelligence network. I haven't the time. It's too dangerous. One needs money, one has to know the language and have a cover story."

"It's fun having a cover story. A language is easy to learn."

François did not press the matter any further, but on several occasions he went off by himself to bathe in the Vistula. All those white bodies stretched out beside him set him thinking. What did these men do when they went back home? Most of them naturally believed what they read in the newspapers. The newspapers said what the government wanted. But what of the others?

How would these people react to war and defeat? In two weeks his practised ear had already grasped several words and expressions. One day he lost his way in the Warsaw ghetto and a young Jew who spoke French walked back with him to the hotel.

He invited him to meet "some friends". Ricq realized he had made contact with a pro-Communist. It was easier than Dan thought.

He even had an adventure with a waitress in a restaurant. She had rosy cheeks, came from Silesia, spoke German and hated the Jews. So there were Germans in Poland. But ever since the night he had spent with Laon, François had a sort of horror of women. He went for a walk with the girl one afternoon and when she gently suggested he came back to her place he took to his heels.

The Ricq brothers left Warsaw for Cracow. It was on arriving in that ancient city, which was shrouded in blue mist, that they heard of the signing of the Russo-German pact. The two dictators, the red and the brown, had carved up Poland between them. All that remained was to help themselves.

Dan and François got back to Paris as the Panzer divisions were sweeping across the rich plains of Silesia.

A month later François Ricq was called up. He was allowed to choose his branch of the service "provided it was in the infantry". France seemed to be short of cannon-fodder.

He opted for the Colonial Infantry, hoping to be sent overseas. The fighting in the mud of Flanders and the forests of the

Ardennes had always struck him as repellant. The stories of the baker Picut, who had cleaned up whole trenches with a knife, were partly responsible for this.

Promoted a cadet officer in 1940, Little Ricq was given ten days' leave before rejoining his unit "somewhere in the front line", in other words at Chalons-sur-Marne. He ran into Dan who was wearing the uniform of a war correspondent. Having at last found a regular job and "a livery which was in fashion", he had healed the breach with his parents. Dan had discovered a new dodge: each time he came back from an assignment, he made up some fantastic stories for the benefit of the "regulars". It was a sort of testing-bench.

Cadet Officer François Ricq found himself slapped on the back and stood rounds of drinks although he never touched alcohol. But he realized yet again that Dan was the hero, not he. The window-panes had been painted blue "because of the air raids", and entering the Brasserie was like plunging into a pool of water tinged with litmus.

Eugène Ricq was happy. He had been right to lay in supplies and now waited with secret delight for the ration cards which everyone was talking about but which had not yet been issued. He already rationed his own customers, telling them, for instance, that he was short of Pernod although his cellars were crammed full of it. To anyone who protested, he tersely replied: "Don't you know there's a war on?" For fear of being suspected of defeatism, his victims would order Byrrh, St-Raphael or Noilly.

Ira, who dreaded air raids and all forms of patriotic hysteria, had taken refuge in the South. There were no air raids or hysteria in Paris, only gloom and apprehension. Dan lived alone in the studio overlooking the Jardin des Plantes. One evening he asked his brother out to a Russian restaurant in the Champs-Elysées.

There was vodka, smoked salmon, shashlik and gypsy violins. Pretty girls smiled at Dan. But in the last few months he had altered. He no longer told lies except to overawe the regulars. It was therefore about lying he spoke first of all. As he raised his glass to little Ricq, he gave this toast:

"Here's to lying, little brother, to the lie that surrounds us and in which we're wallowing, to the curtain of lies that's going to be torn apart tomorrow. You know what we'll see when that happens—an army taking to its heels, a country taking to its heels, with a few armoured cars up its arse. And the clown of Berlin and Nuremburg, with his hands on his hips, laughing his dirty little head off.

"Mark my words, François. When you regulars and conscripts have lost your war, it will be our turn to fight—we the unregimented, the useless, the bolshy-minded. Maybe we'll win. I drink, little brother, to your war that's coming to an end and to my war which is about to begin. Now I'm going to take you to a brothel. I'm beginning to get fed up with girls who don't do it for money."

"I'd rather go home."

"Good old Little Ricq! So you want to go off to the wars a virgin, with your rosary round your wrist. Do you know at least how you'll react under fire?"

"I'll certainly be frightened. But I'd never allow myself to run away. Everyone would laugh at the sight of me taking to my heels. Like all small men, I don't like being laughed at."

François Ricq was never to see his brother again. On his arrival at the Nth Colonial Infantry Regiment, he was posted to the Congo where instructors were needed to transform semi-savages straight out of the bush into valiant riflemen in hobnailed boots who were to be packed off to defend justice and civilization in a temperature ten degrees below freezing point. The colonel had considered Cadet Officer Ricq too weedy, too feeble, too small "to make a good soldier, damn it all."

Like Frederick of Prussia, the colonel cared only for giants. If he had been given his way, he would have pinched them from other units. It was on the boat, off Dakar, that Ricq heard of the German offensive in the Ardennes. The captain in command of the detachment stood drinks all round in the bar.

"The Huns are going to get a good licking," he proclaimed as he raised his glass.

But Cadet Officer Ricq remembered Dan likewise raising his glass and drinking to the big lie, Dan predicting defeat and a whole army, a whole country, taking to its heels.

On landing at Pointe-Noire, Cadet Officer Ricq was sent to Brazzaville and from there posted with two other cadet officers to Maugin Camp. This camp, which did not yet exist, was to serve as a training centre for Equatorial African troops. It consisted of a few straw-huts and a little landing-strip covered in yellow grass.

Wireless communications with Brazzaville were poor and the only occupation of the officers and handful of European N.C.O.'s was hunting game in the savannah or on the banks of the two neighbouring rivers, the Sangha and the Lionala. The rest of the time was spent chatting together, playing cards and drinking Pernod, while waiting for the Adrian hutments and equipment which never arrived.

The captain in Command of Maugin Camp, Marcel Creyssel, was a French Colonial Office administrator. He had spent the whole of his professional life in Equatorial Africa, systematically choosing the least privileged districts and the most backward tribes. He had been seen in the Tibesti, among the Goranes, and with the naked savages of Oubangui-Chari. Short and thickset, dark and hirsute, looking ill at ease in uniform, he was alternately familiar, voluble, sarcastic, haughty and sharp towards his subordinates. With him one never knew what line to take. He had nicknamed Ricq the "Chinaman" and seemed to prefer the company of the other officer cadets to his. But on the evening of 17 June, while everyone was confidently awaiting the new miracle of the Marne, Captain Creyssel asked Ricq to come back to his quarters with him after dinner. He poured him out a tumbler of brandy. Insects fluttered round the lampstand, sizzling as they burnt their wings. Somewhere outside, a rifleman was singing a song, beating time on a mess-tin.

"I know," said Creyssel, clearing his throat at regular intervals, "that you're not in the habit of drinking. Bad for a Colonial Army man. But knock that back. You'll need it. I've just received a signal from Brazzaville. Marshal Pétain has asked for an armistice. The roads of France are cluttered with refugees fleeing with nothing but their bedding. The French Army has ceased to exist. The British have re-embarked at Dunkirk."

Ricq took a gulp and choked.

"I can't stand people like you," said Creyssel, "university graduates, chairborne ethnologists who believe in the worthy Negroes without having ever lived among them. You're the weediest of the bunch. Yet on hunting expeditions you show the most stamina. Even when you're exhausted, you're a good shot. I've also noticed you never lie. When you're thirsty you don't drain your water-bottle. When a native tells you his endless stories, you listen to him with patience. You never behave irritably or roughly with your riflemen. Instinctively you treat them like human beings who happen to be younger than yourself. That's what made me have second thoughts about you. You're the only one here who can understand me. Since I don't often unburden my soul, I'm liable to take a long time over it."

Captain Creyssel spoke all night. He told Ricq what he knew about the Blacks of the Congo, of their immoderate respect for power, of their simple-mindedness and cruelty.

According to him, they belonged to the oldest and most under-privileged race in the world. But they had petrified round their taboos, their customs and strange gods, like insects which, without knowing why, continue eternally to make the same gestures, take the same paths, build their ant-hills or nests in the same manner.

"The Blacks won't understand our defeat," Creyssel asserted. "If they hear we've ceased to be powerful, they'll reject us. Therefore I don't agree with this armistice, because I'm fond of the Blacks, knowing what they are—the oldest children in the world—and because no one in Africa can replace us for the time being.

"Are you with me, Ricq? Good."

"Now all we have to do is wait for the first opportunity and meanwhile keep our traps shut. Defeat always gives rise to cowardice, waywardness and treachery. But I'm going to continue the war for the sake of my Blacks. What about you?"

Ricq screwed up his eyes.

"Look how small I am, Captain—5 foot 4—and weedy. I weigh 110 pounds. I need to assert myself. There's nothing like a defeat to which everyone else consents."

"Are you trying to be funny?"

"I'm not only trying to be funny. I have a brother back in

France. He's tall and strong and handsome. But he was turned down for a malformation of the heart. He too must be thinking this defeat is going to enable him to take his revenge."

"Against whom?"

"Against what he calls 'the old boys, the regimented and fit for military service', those who prepared for this war inadequately and those who were incapable of waging it properly."

"He's an anarchist."

"Worse than that, Captain. After lying all his life, he now dreams of truth. After being amoral, he dreams of purity; after being idle, he dreams of effort. I came across a passage in a book which he had underlined with his thumb-nail:

" 'Pray God that men reading the story will not, for love of the glamour of strangeness, go out to prostitute themselves and their talents in serving another race . . .' "*

Captain Creyssel continued the quotation:

" 'A man who gives himself to be a possession of aliens leads a Yahoo life, having bartered his soul to a brute-master. He is not of them . . .' Believe me, Ricq, I've often thought of that sentence in connection with my Negroes. A white man can never melt into Africa or Asia without degrading himself. I've had to struggle against this temptation . . . in the first place because . . ."

The captain lowered his eyes:

"I love African women, their smell, their skin, their warm, soft, contractile sexual organs, their splendid lack of modesty, like Eve at the dawn of time. Eve was a black woman. Did you know that?

"Presently, Ricq, I want you to fall in the riflemen, the orderlies, the boys, all the N.C.O's. for a ceremonial saluting of the colours. You will parade the detachment. An idiotic ritual, but we're going to need every bit of ritual we have, however out of date it may be."

General de Gaulle's appeal was not made known in Camp Maugin until the end of June. It met with a mixed reception. This unknown general did not carry sufficient weight compared to the victor of Verdun. Captain Creyssel considered de Gaulle had one merit that was greater than all the rest: he wanted to continue the war. What did it matter, then, if he was a regular soldier, brought

* *Seven Pillars of Wisdom*, by T. E. Lawrence.

up by the Jesuits, a follower of Maurras, and even born north of the Loire? In July the captain crossed the river several times to attend some mysterious conferences being held in the Belgian Congo.

"Things are moving," he merely said to Ricq. "I've seen some men who came from London. Be ready when the time comes."

On 27 August, Captain Creyssel left for Brazzaville without permission and appointed Ricq commander of the detachment even though he was the youngest. The two other cadet officers were furious at being passed over and consequently refused to join the Croix de Lorraine when, on the following day, the Gaullists seized the capital of Equatorial Africa.

Ricq found himself a second-lieutenant in the Free French Forces without having done anything except listen sympathetically one evening to the sexual and patriotic ramblings of Captain Creyssel. A week later Ricq was summoned to Brazzaville, the camp was wound up and Creyssel, now a major, took him on in the Political Department of Government House. It was merely an intelligence organization in disguise. Creyssel avoided the office and encouraged Ricq to do likewise. He promised to initiate him into what he called "applied ethnology", in other words intelligence activity in African surroundings.

He took Ricq to the Etoile du Soir, a night-club in Poto-Poto. It was a squalid dive consisting of a few tables of planks nailed down on piles, some wooden stools and a roof made of several layers of palms piled one on top of the other. The rain came through but no one seemed to mind. Beer and wine were available, and also a horrid local drink called *bangui* which gave one a splitting head-ache.

Oil or carbide lamps lent a touch of mystery and glamour to this wretched joint swarming with flies and naked children, their stomachs swollen by manioc.

A group of women in long gold or mahogany-coloured robes, with scarves round their heads and with their finger and toe-nails varnished bright red, sat huddled round a fatter, older woman who was telling a story. They punctuated each of her sentences with sycophantic giggles.

Hungry-looking men prowled around, clad in pale pink or rosewood-coloured suits, some of them wearing crocodile or snakeshin shoes, clumsily trying to assume the manner of Place Pigalle pimps.

Everyone greeted the major, even the sham pimps, whose haughty and distant faces split all of a sudden into wide grins. He embraced the women, fondled their rumps and ordered beer all round. Then he sat down at a separate table with Ricq.

"They're all tarts," he said, "and they make quite a packet."

"For the pimps."

"Not at all. These girls don't have pimps. Those oddly-dressed fellows are sweating blood to pass themselves off as such. The fat woman who was talking when we arrived, she's the *mama-mozouki*. Her name is Epiphanie. She's got her head screwed on the right way! She's the one who rakes in the dough and handles the accounts. When there's enough cash in the kitty, these girls throw a big party. One day Epiphanie, who doesn't know where to draw the line, even invited the Governor. The invitation fell into my hands and I came along. The wine was served in old tins. The girls were dolled up to the eyes. Epiphanie has about fifty girls on her pay-roll, all of them the same tribe as herself. Some of them occasionally get into trouble with the small-time pimps who'd like them to work for them, with the police who demand 'protection' money, with the health authorities since they catch diseases.

"I handle all that. I give the over-ambitious lad a spell of stone-breaking, I have the policeman removed, and I tell the doctor to give the girl a clean bill of health and leave her in peace in future. In exchange, Epiphanie provides me with information. Through her network of girls she knows all that's going on in Poto-Poto.

"I use Epiphanie, but I'm also fond of her, even though she'd sell her eight-year old daughter to any old bastard if he gave her a good enough price."

Epiphanie waddled up to their table with a cigarette in her mouth. Her robes were stretched tight over her well-upholstered frame which rolled and wobbled at every step. Her face was flat, her eyes small and sharp.

"Will you stand me a beer, Dudule?" she asked as she sat down.

"How's the war going? Do you think N'Gol's* going to win?"

The band started up and the strutting peacocks in their pastel-coloured suits asked the girls to dance. They shuffled round the floor with a glazed expression, as though performing an unpleasant duty.

Creyssel gave the fat procuress a slap on the thigh.

"Epiphanie, old girl, I shan't be coming to see you any more, in future you'll be dealing with Lieutenant Ricq here. He'll be able to do you the same favours. I'm beginning to get a little too well known in Poto-Poto. Is that clear? From now on you'll tell the lieutenant what's going on, what people are thinking and what they're saying."

"Try and get some information on what the Laris are saying about Matswa†, Pitain and N'Gol."

Ricq and the major came back from the native city along a dirt track littered with refuse and full of pot-holes across which some rickety planks had been laid. At certain points they had to light their way with a torch and the glow would send figures scattering into the shadows: some dogs or famished children fighting over the garbage. The various stenches were dominated by the more pungent small of charred grass.

"They smoke hemp round here," said Creyssel. "It sends them

* De Gaulle. They even made a fetish of him in Poto-Poto. It had two faces, like Janus, but painted lemon-yellow and culminating in a handle.

† A strange figure who emerged from the African darkness. Starting off as a catechist, he worked in the customs, then as an officer's houseboy, and finally joined the Colonial Infantry. As a rifleman he took part in the Rif campaign, on the strength of which he was engaged after demobilization as a runner at the Colonial Ministry in Paris. He stole some official note-paper and wrote in the name of the Minister to his tribesmen, the Laris, promising them his protection in exchange for certain sums of money. Matswa's swindle was discovered and he was hauled before the courts at Brazzaville. But on the day of his trial the Laris tried to batter down the door of the law court. Matswa was sentenced to five years' prison and deported to the Chad with five hundred of his followers. While working as the houseboy of the prison governor, back in the Congo he became a god. The Laris engineered his escape. He landed in Marseille on the day of general mobilization. The police caught up with the god Matswa in a blockhouse in the Maginot Line and sent him back to Brazzaville, where this time he was given a life sentence.

mad, especially those who believe in the black Christ, Matswa. André Matswa was born in a shack in Poto-Poto, not far from here, about forty years ago. Some missionaries picked him up in the street, where he had been abandoned stark naked by his parents, like those kids you saw just now fighting with the dogs over the garbage. Do you believe in God, Ricq?"

"On certain days, Major."

"Why only on certain days?"

"Because I don't always feel in need of Him. I'm often amazed at the way men manage on their own. Then I see them sink, struggle, cry for help and die, clamouring for an explanation. I believe God may be that explanation."

"Unlike Asia, Ricq, Africa wallows in godliness because everyone here is sinking and eternally crying out for help."

In one week Major Creyssel introduced Ricq to all his agents: a Houssa Muslim, who from time to time needed the help of the administration to get his debts collected; a Dahomey quack, who was only a medical orderly and anxious not to draw too much attention to some of his activities; a bar proprietor who served adulterated liquor; a Cameroun truck-driver who carried other things besides the groundnuts for which his licence was valid.

"What about the missionaries?" Ricq asked.

"As a last resort, as the last resort of all. They'll only help us if the situation becomes dangerous for their flocks."

"They refuse to serve France?"

"Don't forget that today there are two Frances, Pétain's and de Gaulle's. The missionaries don't want to let down the Africans by betraying their secrets or to get on the wrong side of the Pétainists. The paternalism of the National Revolution suits them. What else have they done here for the last fifty years except drive the slogan 'Work, Family, Country' into the Negroes' thick skulls?"

Ricq made a habit of going on his rounds every evening. The Blacks looked upon him as a sort of white maniac, a missionary without a religion to sell, a soldier who did no soldiering.

One morning Creyssel summoned his assistant to Government House and showed him a hand-written document, soiled and tattered by all the fingers that had touched it:

"*War is close at hand. At the start of the rainy season perhaps . . . We have emerged to announce these good tidings to the whole world. Those who belong to our church are ordered not to speak to anyone connected with the Government and the Missions or anyone who has remained in the background. The time for bloodshed has arrived . . . Those who return from the dead will enter the glory of the victorious kingdom.*"

"It's getting serious," said the major. "In the bush this leaflet has stirred up a certain amount of agitation, as usual among those damned Laris. They might decline military service, which would be the last straw in war-time. It would be playing into the hands of the Vichy people who still hold Gabon but are frightened Free France might attempt to seize it. Come back and see me when you have something to report."

"How do I go about it?"

"I haven't the faintest idea. Put pressure on your sources one way or another. Make them more frightened of you than of those bloody Matswanists. Get in touch with the police commissioner of the native city. He knows his job and he's used to this sort of thing."

Four of Epiphanie's girls were put in quarantine in the hospital. The daughters of six others took legal action and asked for their daughters back. The Etoile du Soir was closed three nights running on account of the brawling there. Then the dive was put out of bounds. The truck-driver had a cargo of tinned food confiscated which he had smuggled across the river. The Dahomey 'doctor' was threatened with prosecution for an abortion that had turned out badly. The Houssa was expelled from the colony; his papers were out of order. He was given eight days to pack up and leave.

Grieved at having to play this game but convinced that it was necessary, Ricq went and saw all his agents one after the other, commiserating over the misfortunes of all these colourful rogues. They knew perfectly well what he wanted: one name. But either they did not know it or else were afraid to give it.

One evening a young native boy as unctuous as an archdeacon came to Ricq with a message from Father Froment of the Lazarist Mission. The priest wanted him to come to a little evening ceremony in honour of the Virgin.

He was a tall, gaunt old man who ruled his little church with a rod of iron. Normally he steered clear of the lieutenant, even though the latter was a regular member of his congregation. Ricq was therefore surprised but accepted the invitation.

In the clear equatorial night he attended a service punctuated by hymns, and was moved by the innocence and touching faith of the worshippers. A hundred all told, they had put on their Sunday best and each held a candle in his hand, so that only their heads were illuminated—their heads and their red lips opening like flowers in their faces.

Afterwards the priest took Ricq into his little shack and gave him some lukewarm water mixed with orangeade. Without any preamble he went straight to the point.

"I know you're looking for someone and I can give you his name. But before I do I must have your word as an officer and a Christian that you won't do him any harm. Expel him, and that's all. He's just a crazy wretch whose head has been turned to make use of him. Give me your word, otherwise I'll tell you nothing."

"I give you my word, Father. All we want is to get rid of this fellow . . ."

"His name is Honoré Batéga. He lives near the goods station and has been in Poto-Poto for two months. He's not short of money and he's sufficiently conversant with religion to make people believe he was once a sacristan."

"Thank you, Father, but . . ."

"I'm not doing this for your sake, Lieutenant Ricq, or for your blasted General de Gaulle. I was at Verdun, and Pétain was in command there. De Gaulle was a prisoner at the time.

"Several members of my flock have been beaten up. One of my choirgirls has been abducted. No doubt she'll end up as a tart at your friend Epiphanie's. Three others have joined the religion of Matswa."

"You're eliminating all competition, Father?"

"No, I'm protecting my flock and I know how weak they are. Good-bye, my son, no one must ever know it was I who gave you this information, least of all that dirty Freemason Creyssel. To think of him being made a major! It's disgraceful!"

As soon as Ricq was able to provide a name, tongues began to loosen. Batéga, Epiphanie told him, was an old man with a beard "who knew the Bible by heart and many other books and also the secret of poisons that kill from afar". He was an "absolute saint". He went around saying that the white men's war was their own affair and the Laris and Bakongos ought not to fight for them. When all the Whites were killed, then the Negroes would be free and God Matswa would return in a white aircraft.

The Batéké truck-driver confirmed that Batéga was often in the bush and that he had driven him on several occasions. Batéga would spend a week or two near a military camp and talk to the soldiers. Afterwards there would be palavers.

The Houssa, like a good Moslem, despised the Negroes even though he himself was coal-black. But he wore a flowing white robe. He was interested in the financial aspect of the man.

He made a gesture of counting out money.

"He has any amount . . . He says Pitain gave it him to liberate the poor Negroes, that Pitain and Matswa are the same thing . . ."

Ricq longed to go and see what this strange character was like, but was afraid of alerting him and so went off to report to the major, stressing the fact that he had obtained his information only by giving his word.

Creyssel congratulated him:

"Good show. Anyway, it's not this fellow Batéga we're after but the people behind him. Now I'll take over. Go and have a few days' leave in Leo. It's full of buxom Flemish girls pedalling about on bicycles with packets of sandwiches strapped on to the carriers. You might find your heart's desire there since you seem so scared of black women."

Ricq spent three days in the Belgian Congo, found it boring and so came back. On his return he asked Creyssel:

"What about our 'absolute saint'?"

Creyssel pointed to the sky:

"He's up in heaven."

"What!"

"Poisoned. Batéga must have taken some herb or noxious brew which our Dahomey friend made up for him to cure a stomach-ache."

"You mean . . ."

"Do you suppose we have time to waste over fellows of that sort, Ricq?"

"I gave my word of honour . . ."

"To Father Froment, wasn't it? Out here Froment is something like the Deuxième Bureau of the Church. In our job we make lots of promises. Sometimes we keep them, when it's in our interest to do so. But even so, these promises had to sound sincere for Father Froment to be willing to talk. They could only be made by the sort of man who was liable to keep them. You, for instance. That bloody priest would never have believed me. He can't stand me because I sleep with Negresses and pervert the black race. As though it wasn't already perverted! He's also convinced, poor fellow, that I'm a Freemason.

"I dangled you before him as a bait. You were a nice quiet lad, you knew how to serve at Mass."

"You might have told me, Major."

"If I had told you, you wouldn't have played your part so well. Father Froment is an old fox. He too compromises with his conscience. If he didn't give the information to me personally it was because he knew I'd put paid to the fellow. It was in you he confided. But he knew perfectly well that you would come and report to me and that I would therefore liquidate Batéga just the same."

"Father Froment isn't such a tortuous character as you think."

"Let's act as if he were. You can't get out of it now, Ricq. You're made for this fascinating dirty work which is half way between a policeman's and a spy's. Try and appease your scruples by setting yourself a principle which is so demanding that it forces you to overcome them, or a purpose that makes every sacrifice worthwhile."

"Thanks to you, I'm an accessory to a murder and also guilty of a lie."

"Your first blood. In the old days German university students used to duel with sabres. They were muffled from head to foot in protective clothing which left only their faces exposed. The only wound they risked was a cut on the cheek or the chin. The duels were fought till blood was drawn for the third or fourth time.

"Let's call the Batéga affair your first blood, Ricq, but at least you didn't shed it for the sake of some vague point of honour. It was to serve your country."

"I want to be posted to a fighting unit."

"Don't be silly. In this war men of your sort are more important than platoon or company commanders. You can put in an application, but we shan't let you go. There are no more than a handful of us to drive the Germans out of France, the Italians out of Tunisia, the Pétainists out of French Equatorial Africa, the Japanese out of Indo-China. We'll never have enough men, or enough material or money. So I'll be forced to fight with secret agents. Your brother was right. We . . ."

"Who do you mean by 'we'?"

"The B.C.R.A., the Bureau Central de Recherches et d'Action—the Free French Intelligence Service, if you prefer. An organization to which I've belonged ever since I crossed the river after the armistice to attend a certain meeting, a conglomeration of the best and the worst. You're going to be attached to this organization."

"I don't want to be."

"There's a war on. No one's asking your opinion. At the moment the B.C.R.A. is looking for specialists in South-East Asia, to be sent out to India on a course with a curious unit which is known only by a number: Force 136. You have a smattering of Laotian and Annamese, a knowledge of ethnology and other qualifications. Furthermore, your English is excellent. You're not cut out for regular warfare."

"No, I'm too small and weedy . . ."

"But for another form of warfare which is infinitely harder, because it demands courage, stamina and strength of character, since you're mainly on your own.

"You'll be engaged in this form of warfare in Asia. You'll have the good fortune to fight in a country where you already know you'll be at home although you haven't yet set foot in it. I felt the same about Africa. Major Durozel, one of the B.C.R.A. chiefs, wants to have a word with you. He's passing through Brazzaville."

"Durozel? Wasn't he in Poland in 1939?"

"That's right. He was captured by the Germans but escaped in December that year, bringing with him some valuable information on the Wehrmacht's use of tanks and support planes. He was sent away with a flea in his ear and given command of a territorial company. He has just spent six months in occupied France setting up some intelligence networks. Durozel remembers you well, and also your brother Dan—handsome Dan Ricq, as he calls him. It would amuse him to have both brothers working for him."

"Why both?"

"Dan Ricq is running one of our initial networks in Paris. Durozel stayed in his flat."

"Near the Jardin des Plantes?"

"I think so. We're lunching together tomorrow. Come and join us—wearing your new badges of rank."

"What badges of rank?"

"You've been promoted to lieutenant, the reward for your first blood."

A few days later the native boy who looked like an archdeacon came and called on Ricq. He intoned:

"Father Froment says that if you come to the mission he'll bash your face in, because you're a . . . a . . . filthy swine and a murderer. Good-bye, Monsieur. Thank you, Monsieur."

Ricq was grieved. But it was too late; he was caught up in the machine.

Major Durozel still looked like an austere Spanish priest, with his thin lips and forbidding manner. But it was in a tone of admiration that he said:

"Dan Ricq frightens me. He's our best agent at the moment and I wouldn't like to lose him. Incidentally, we promoted him to captain and he seemed quite pleased. That rather surprised me."

In October 1943 Lieutenant Ricq went up through the Chad, crossed Tripolitania, flew over the carcasses of Rommel's tanks in the desert and landed one afternoon at Maison-Blanche aerodrome.

The town of Algiers was full of drunken, loud-mouthed American soldiers, quiet but still drunker English soldiers, and Frenchmen wearing shabby 1940 uniforms. The French were divided into Giraudists and Gaullists. The Giraudists, upholders of tradition and the regular army, were by far the more numerous.

A staff car that had seen better days drove Ricq to the Palais d'Eté where the B.C.R.A. headquarters were installed.

With his kitbag on his knees, he waited in an anti-chamber with a marble floor and tiled walls. The kitbag served him as a briefcase and contained a number of folders that Creyssel had asked him to hand over direct to Durozel who had just been promoted lieutenant-colonel.

"Watch your step up there," he had told him. "There are heaven knows how many chiefs, each one trying to recruit his own personnel, and all of them at daggers drawn. A real feudal set-up! Durozel's the only technician who keeps his head in the midst of that crowd of madmen."

Durozel himself came to fetch Ricq and showed him into a completely empty office where there was not even a telephone. He shook hands and even patted him on the shoulder, which was utterly unlike his usual distant manner. His ashtray, as in Warsaw, was full of stubs.

"You're a soldier," said Durozel, "and we're at war, so I shan't beat about the bush. Your brother Dan has just been shot by the Germans. His network is completely blown. There were thirty-seven arrests."

Ricq felt as though he was going to faint. The only link that still bound him to France was his brother. Dan was one of those people it was impossible to imagine dead, so self-assured and uninhibited was their manner of life. With Dan deceased, a whole slice of his past went down the drain.

"That's not all," Durozel went on, "your brother was horribly tortured by the Gestapo."

Ricq now understood why he had been shown into this office. The colonel was going to ask him to give up the idea of India and the Far East and take his brother's place in France. Otherwise why was he being forced to picture a disfigured and mutilated Dan who had had to be dragged to his execution because he was no longer able to walk? It was horrible. Like Creyssel, like the rest of them, Durozel could think of nothing but the efficiency of his service. Was he going to be used as bait again, as he had been in Poto-Poto? A pawn which would be moved about on the huge map of France hanging on the wall? But the pawn was a human being who risked being tortured and shot.

"I'm ready to go to France," said Ricq. "I'll take Dan's place."

"No question of that, old boy. It's even impossible."

Durozel rose from his armchair, looked at the map, then turned round to Ricq:

"Your brother failed to hold out; he gave away his network, his safe houses, his letterboxes, his contacts, everything, with one exception—myself. I had been sent into occupied France to tidy things up a little, because you can't imagine the mess there. Your brother had found me a hiding-place; he didn't give it away."

"And why not? I'll tell you. It wasn't Dan who talked but another member of the network who knew as much as he did except for your safe house. It's obvious, sir. If he had given everything away, you would have been caught."

"I've given the matter a great deal of thought, as you can imagine. I even conducted the court of enquiry myself. I find it unpleasant to accuse a man who saved my life of being . . . let's not say a traitor, but a weakling who overestimated his strength. I haven't been able to account for it. Maybe the Germans tortured him so much that after spilling the beans little by little he was incapable of talking any more by the time they came to the most important point: where the envoy from London was hiding. I prefer to think he finally had the courage to pull himself together. Like all our agents, Dan had instructions to hold out for twenty-four hours so as to enable us to break contact with the network once it was blown. If he felt he was incapable of doing so, he should have swallowed his cyanide pill. But Dan never carried this pill on him. He had a horror of it, like some people who can't bear being anywhere near invalids or corpses. He was captured because of his lack of security and caution, and thereby destroyed my network, the best of the lot because it had infiltrated collaborationist circles. It had been created by him, I admit. The men who were arrested—journalists, politicians, professors—almost all belonged to the extreme left wing.

"You understand now why I don't want to drop you into France?"

"Because I would give way as well?"

"No. But if you were known to be Dan's brother, certain elements might distrust you. Some left-wing groups have spread the rumour that Dan, in agreement with the B.C.R.A., had orders to get rid of certain agents whom London and Algiers considered undesirable because they were working with the Communists. As proof of this, they point out that I never had any trouble. That's tantamount to calling your brother a double agent. When clandestine warfare is complicated by political rivalries it often becomes ignoble."

"I had conceived a different picture of the Resistance."

"We're working with human beings and in every human being there's a mixture of good and bad. We have to eliminate certain competition. I may find myself one day impelled to do what my service is already accused of doing, in the name of some interest or other that I consider to be higher."

"I can't understand it . . . Men are dying for their country."

"We're on stage. But in the wings everyone makes use of the living as well as the dead, according to his needs. We don't all love our country in the same way, we don't all picture it with the same political régime. In the Resistance there are already the seeds of what we shall have to fight against later."

"I don't want to have anything to do with it."

"You'll see; one gets used to it. In three days' time you leave for Calcutta. You're attached to Force 136. You'll go through an extremely arduous but, I hope, intensive course of training. We need to get some agents into Indo-China as soon as possible. There's a lot of work to be done there."

"In Indo-China the fighting will be simpler than in France."

"Not at all. You'll have to work against other Frenchmen, those who back Admiral Dacoux, and who are not completely wrong or completely right; against our American allies, whose soldiers are going to be killed in thousands to liberate France but who don't want to see us back in our former colonies; against the British, who are helping us but who want to take the lion's share. You can always count on me. I was very fond of your brother even though he was only an amateur. Even in Poland I already felt you were of quite a different calibre, that this work of ours was in your blood. Your strolls through Warsaw and that young Jew in the ghetto, you remember? He was one of my agents. I had instructed him to follow you. He contacted you but you never mentioned this to anyone, not even to me when I made a point of seeing you again next day. You already knew how to bide your time. An excellent reaction. Captain Dan Ricq has been posthumously awarded the Légion d'Honneur for his resistance activity. The citation was published yesterday. I consider he deserved it. And besides, it was also necessary to put a stop to certain rumours."

"What am I supposed to do?"

"Keep your ears open, learn what you can, train yourself to live as the poor do, without means. The vanquished ex-colonialist returns to Indo-China in rags. His former protégés have turned against him. They have gone over to the stronger side, the Japanese. You will therefore have to rely on the least privileged elements in the country: the racial minorities, the lower classes and all the young ragamuffins who may be captivated by the prospect of adventure. To my mind, you have one great advantage: you already have the rudiments of the local dialects. You are therefore six months ahead of anyone else I would have to train. Does that suit you?"

"Yes, of course, Colonel. I want to leave Algiers, start a new life . . . if possible under a different name."

"No one in Asia will know about Dan Ricq and his story. One of my assistants will make you out a movement order. Good luck and good hunting."

Durozel got up and showed Ricq out, still with his hand on his shoulder, as though he was henceforth promising him his protection.

Ricq embarked on the *Empress of Australia* which had been converted into an auxiliary cruiser. She was equipped with two guns, a false funnel and anti-submarine devices. The voyage lasted forty-seven days, the ship putting in at every port on the way to embark or disembark more troops.

Ricq retained a confused memory of that crossing. He recalled the noisy binges in the bar, the brawls between Australians and New Zealanders, the constantly repeated air raid drills, the prohibition to smoke after dark on deck, and the ports of call where all the soldiers rushed off to find themselves women, get drunk or else buy horrible local "curios".

Thirteen months later Lieutenant Ricq was dropped by parachute into Laos, in the vicinity of Paksane.

The Liberator was flying over Burma at a height of twenty-five thousand feet. The eight members of the crew and the ten passengers all wore oxygen masks which turned their faces into pig-like snouts. On an aerial map the pilot had shown Ricq and Sydney the route they were going to take. In order to avoid the Japanese fighters and anti-aircraft defences, they would pass north of Mandalay. They would swing round above Lashio and come back towards the four frontiers, where China, Thailand, Laos and Burma touched. Captain Sydney's stick would jump with all its material to the east of Taunggyi, the capital of the Shan States. It would then be 1945 hours. The plane would afterwards head due south as far as the Mekong. At 2200 hours Ricq and his wireless operator, Sergeant Meynadier, would in their turn drop into a clearing half a dozen miles north of Paksane. The weather was fine, the sky sufficiently overcast for the operation not to entail too many risks.

Through the perspex porthole, Ricq tried in vain to get his bearings. The ground was barely visible. In the rays of the setting sun the clouds looked as though they were on fire. Then they went black at the edges like burnt newspaper.

Sydney, in a blue padded flying suit, came and sat down beside him on the metal bench. He tapped him on the shoulder and pointed out a stretch of river the colour of tarnished pewter:

"The Irrawaddy."

His men were already beginning to get ready. In a few minutes' time they would launch themselves through the trap and float down suspended from their rigging lines. Some friends would be waiting for them down below, or else some Japanese who would shoot them on the wing like game-birds. The only risk Ricq and Meynadier ran was getting caught up in the branch of a tree, twisting an ankle or breaking a leg. In front of their colleagues they felt shamefaced, as though they were cheating.

Lieutenant François Ricq was completing his training in Calcutta by learning how to print leaflets on lavatory paper when, on 3 December 1944, at eight o'clock in the morning, he and Captain Sydney had been ordered to report to Commodore Fayne, who was in charge of Force 136 operations. Major Durupt, the French liaison officer, was already there. Spread out on a table, opposite a big bay window giving onto a lawn on which monkeys scampered about, was a map of South-East Asia covered with red and blue pencil marks. The few patches of white indicated the areas that were still unknown.

"In good form, both of you?" the commodore enquired, as he sized up Sydney's athletic frame and Ricq's small stature.

He was a handsome, jovial man who always had a cigarette stuck in his mouth. A regular officer in the Royal Navy, he had been attached to this "crowd of visionaries and maniacs" and seemed to enjoy going as far as he could to disconcert his trainees. His diabolical imagination invented the most incredible situations from which the students had to extricate themselves by showing even more imagination, invariably playing the same unpleasant role of the hunted beast. He would then send them off to some country in South-East Asia with instructions "to get a move on and start the ball rolling".

Ricq and Sydney looked at each other, wondering what sort of scheme Fayne had thought up for them this time: to leave them for a month in the jungle without any food or weapons, with one knife between the two of them, a handful of salt each and a coil of wire with which to make traps; or else to abandon them in a Calcutta suburb without any money or identity papers and set the Indian police on their heels by depicting them as Axis spies. But this had all been done already and they had acquitted themselves with honour in these tests.

Whereas the commodore always showed supreme indifference towards the men he commanded and the events he unleashed, he now appeared, judging by the way he coughed more than usual, to be slightly embarrassed.

"Gentlemen," he went on, "I think we are at last going to have a bash. Come and have a look at this map."

With a commando knife he indicated Burma, Northern Siam and Laos.

"We're going to strike here. But this time it won't be a hit-and-run affair like the Chindit raid. We're going to hang on to the territory we seize. The High Command has decided to launch a big offensive in January 1945, which should reach the Mekong and French Indo-China by June.

"All along the route the regular troops will be taking, we shall set up clandestine camps for training guerrillas and secret depots for storing arms supplies. Meanwhile groups of partisans will keep the Japanese troops under observation. When the time comes, they will also carry out a number of demolitions and act as guides.

"This is the task for which we have been training you for the last ten months."

The commodore then took Captain Sydney by the shoulder and as jovially as ever broke the bad news to him:

"My dear fellow, according to all the instructors, you're in command of the best team on the course. Let me take this opportunity to congratulate you. You were to have been dropped in to the Karens, who are loyal friends of England, Christians, courageous and reliable. Unfortunately we've taken a bad knock in the Shan States north-east of Burma. Major Edwards has been caught by the Japs. We believe he was betrayed. Now, it's absolutely vital for us to control this region and establish communications with it. Out of the whole Edwards organization, there's nothing left but a small group with one transmitter. You're going in to join it. But the Japanese may possibly be using this group to lure you into a trap and you may find them waiting for you when you get there. The Shans have never been models of loyalty. In fact they're a lot of bloody bastards. As far as we know, Edwards died a painful death. One word of advice: if you see you have no chance of coming out of it alive, defend yourself to the utmost and keep the last round for yourself. I'm sorry to send you into such a beastly mess, Sydney, but you're the only one who might be able to get out of it."

Then he turned to Ricq:

"Lieutenant, you're going to have the honour of being the first French officer to be parachuted into Indo-China. Since we're pressed for time, we consider you've completed your training. The interior resistance movement is agreed for once on our choice. This movement exists above all on paper. It seems in a hopeless muddle to me. But so far at least there are no Japanese in Laos apart from an intelligence organization disguised as a mineralogical mission."

He pointed to a black dot on the map.

"You're dropping into Paksane, so you're not liable to have any serious trouble, and you, Sydney, here, north of Taunggyi. The Liberator in which you'll both be travelling takes off at three o'clock this afternoon."

"But two members of my team, Cadet Jusso and Sergeant-Major Perrier, are on leave," Ricq announced in despair.

"Never mind. You're only taking a wireless operator with you. Sydney alone will be jumping with a full team. Good luck to you both, good luck and good hunting. I can't do anything about the luck. As for the hunting, what you've been taught here ought to stand you in good stead. In so far as we can, we'll keep in radio contact with you and drop you anything that's absolutely necessary. Any questions, Sydney?"

Sydney snapped to attention.

"No, sir, except I'd like a bottle of Irish whiskey to be dropped to me for Christmas."

"Irish? Well, there's no accounting for tastes. What about you, Ricq?"

"I'd like to choose my wireless operator."

"Very well."

"I'll take Sergeant Meynadier with me."

Ricq had chosen Meynadier in spite of his spirit of independence and lack of enthusiasm for endurance tests, assault courses and anything else in the nature of "boy-scout business". But on the jungle course he had proved to be handy with a trap and endowed with an animal sense of direction and enormous stamina. Instinctively, he knew how to live in the jungle. He freely admitted to being a pacifist, an anarchist, a syndicalist, an antimilitarist. But he never managed to conceal how much he loved this form of warfare, in which a man's worth is judged by his natural capacities rather than by his rank or military experience.

With a smile or two, a couple of jokes and a knowing wink, Ricq had made a friend and accomplice of him.

Major Durupt was the Calcutta representative of the B.C.R.A., which had just changed its name to the D.C.E.R. He was a taciturn, red-faced man who smoked a pipe and held his tongue.

Durupt took Ricq into his office and filled his pipe while casting penetrating glances at him which were meant to impress him.

"My dear fellow, it was London that chose you for this assignment, Colonel Durozel himself. I had no idea you knew each other. We've notified our man in Laos, Antoine Gibelin, who seems delighted with this choice. Personally, I should have preferred this initial contact with the Resistance in Indo-China to be established through Captain Puyseguin. Not that I doubt your capacities, but Antoine Gibelin is a captain himself. It seemed more sensible to send him an officer of equivalent rank.

"You see, this fellow Gibelin knows the country backwards and he has collected a gang of colourful rogues round him. But we have another contact in Paksane, a man I consider more serious and efficient: Father Maurel, who controls a number of Catholic villages. Gibelin and Maurel can't stand each other and are always at loggerheads. You'll have to fix that for me. Just be tactful, that's all. I believe you already know Gibelin?"

Ricq recalled with pleasure the great lump of a man who had burst into Ira's studio. He barely had time to say good-bye to the Frenchmen in his group. Captain Puyseguin seemed resentful:

"Well, Ricq, still the blue-eyed boy of the British, eh? They seem to have complete confidence in you. As far as I'm concerned, the British will always be foreigners, today our allies, tomorrow perhaps our enemies. I'll never trust them. Mers-el-Kebir, Syria."

"You forget Dunkirk, Fachoda, Waterloo and the Hundred Years War, Captain."

"Good luck all the same, Ricq. I hope the leeches and mosquitoes won't have eaten you up by the time we arrive."

Puyseguin had sauntered off to his quarters, swinging his shoulders. But Lieutenant Masson had shaken hands with Ricq and said:

"I wish I were going with you. Where are you going to be dropped?"

"Into Laos."

"That's where we're going to be dropped too; at least there's a rumour to that effect."

Meynadier merely observed in his drawling voice, spiced with a strong Southern accent:

"It's a good thing I'm going off on this show with my lieutenant. I was beginning to get a bit fed up here. I can't stand these Indians."

"Why not?"

"They're filthy dirty and they're dying of hunger . . . and they're resigned to being filthy dirty and dying of hunger."

They piled their gear into a truck and drove out to Jessore airfield, twenty-five miles from Calcutta. They were made to put on padded flying suits, in which they stifled. The big bomber, bristling with machine-guns and painted in green and yellow camouflage colours, rose ponderously from the strips of sheet metal that served as a runway.

After flying for five hours at a hundred and twenty miles an hour, the Liberator began to lose height. The morse on the wireless stopped. They were passing close to some Japanese airfields. The roar of the engines grew irregular as the aircraft bounced about in the air pockets. A sergeant handed round slices of cake and tea in enamel mugs.

"Only another quarter of an hour for stick No. 1," the skipper of the aircraft announced on the intercom. His distorted voice increased the apprehension that reigned in the cabin.

Ricq was amazed by the youthfulness of the crew. The pilots, gunners and observers were all between twenty and twenty-five. It had required the war, the failure of all military regulations and all the old fogies on the staff who abided by them, for these ancient Western countries to risk entrusting a bomber to a lad of twenty-one and to tolerate an organization like Force 136.

"I'm scared stiff," Sydney said to Ricq. "My stomach's heaving, I can't even get this tea down. Mustn't let the men see. What do you think the Japs did to Edwards? It seems they have Korean executioners attached to them.

"Here we are sitting side by side, weighed down by our harness. Our muscles are working perfectly, our hearts are beating regularly. And all of a sudden a trap opens, a minute goes by and a dirty little bandy-legged Jap in spectacles puts an end to all one's hopes and dreams by squeezing a trigger."

Sydney seized Ricq by the arm:

"I'd like to tell you, old man, I've not always behaved as I should. There was that vicar's daughter in Poona. I promised to marry her, just to get her to sleep with me. After a couple of weeks I couldn't stand the sight of her. I'd found another girl I liked much better. To get rid of her, I told her I was already married. Lisbeth said God would punish me. I've also occasionally cheated at cards. The fellows playing against me were blind drunk. I've always been able to hold my drink."

Ricq realized Sydney was making his confession. Yet he could hardly give him absolution for these pecadilloes, play the part of the priest and order him as a penance to kill a dozen Japs and blow up a couple of bridges.

Meynadier shifted closer up and produced a brandy-flask from his flying-suit. He handed it to Sydney.

"One for the road, sir."

Sydney took a gulp and thanked him.

"Any moment now."

"Only five more minutes," the skipper announced.

The aircraft was still losing height. The trap was unbolted and warm damp air flowed into the cabin. The warning light came on. Sydney stamped his cigarette out on the floor and, having recovered his composure, swung his legs into the aperture after fastening the static line of his parachute to the bar above him. He smiled at Ricq and gave him the thumbs-up sign. The light switched to red.

"Go!" yelled the dispatcher.

Sydney jumped, followed by the seven men in his stick. The aircraft made another run, during which a dozen containers were dropped, then climbed abruptly. The pilot came into the cabin:

"I think it went off all right," he announced. "The dropping zone was correctly lit. All the same, it must be an odd sensation to jump into the dark without knowing what's going on down there. Nine months ago we dropped an extraordinary character called Edwards in the same area. He took his Malay boy with him wherever he went. In the middle of the jungle his boy would put on white gloves and serve him his tin of bully-beef or bowl of rice on a silver dish. Came to grief in the end, poor fellow.

"You have another two hours to go; try and get some sleep."

Ricq was witnessing the birth of a legend, the legend of Edwards, the man who went off to the wars with his native servant. He remembered how, ten months earlier, the major had greeted the new trainees of Force 136 who had just landed at Delhi. There were twenty of them all told, from every country and from every army, who listened to him in a variety of attitudes and uniforms. Some of them, like Ricq and Puyseguin, wore the American drill of the African Army; others, British tropical kit with rolled up sleeves; still others, shorts and singlets without badges of rank or regimental insignia. Some lay back in their armchairs craning their necks so as to inhale the air from the big fans in the ceiling. Others sat round a table shuffling their feet. Two Dutchmen from Indonesia, with ash-blond hair and brick-coloured complexions, stood leaning against a wall, each with a beer-mug in his hand. Captain Puyseguin sat stiffly at a table, with his elbows tucked in, his legs pressed close together and a notebook lying open in front of him.

Major Edwards had a bony face, a prominent nose, carefully brushed fair hair and stooping shoulders. He wore spectacles and was not yet thirty. A product of Eton and Cambridge, he spoke with an affected drawl which he enjoyed exaggerating, for the same reasons that he enjoyed making himself unbearable wherever he went.

His opening words were:

"Gentlemen, in a few months we hope to turn you into bad soldiers but first-rate guerrilla leaders. We shall be forced to teach you the opposite of what staff officers call the art of warfare. None of you is a regular officer. Our job will therefore be all the easier. By rejecting the humiliation of being mere regimental numbers buried in some vast unit, you have insisted on maintaining your dignity as individuals. That's a privilege beyond price."

He had raised his glass of whisky:

"I welcome you to Force 136."

Edwards drained his glass in one gulp and hoisted himself up on the bar.

"We offer you a conception of warfare based on experiments recently carried out by people like us, civilians. But whereas the regular soldier pig-headedly continues to apply the same old methods, even though they've been proved useless, the civilian tries to adapt himself by inventing new tactics.

"In December 1941 the Japanese invaded the Malay Peninsula. The British regular forces insisted on fighting a classic engagement; they were crushed. Our commanders reasoned, stupidly, as follows: since the Japanese are yellow men, and since they're Asians, they must be expert at jungle and guerrilla warfare. Let's fight on our own ground, in our own way, with artillery and tanks. So no one went into the jungle, least of all the Japanese. The Japanese, gentlemen, will soon be your opponents. They are a sort of white race who live in a cold or temperate climate. They don't take kindly to heat; they are afraid of venturing into anything unfamiliar like the jungle. There were a few of us who took the risk of moving off the beaten tracks. The convoys of enemy trucks used to go past a few yards away, within hand-grenade range. They sped along without taking the slightest precautions. I could hear the angry parrot-like cries of the officers of the Mikado. The Japanese advanced down both sides of the road, wheeling their bicycles. They went by in long columns, in the most amazing rig, heavily clothed and heavily laden. 1914-18 infantrymen encumbered with out-of-date equipment! My colleagues and I drafted a report entitled *The Jungle is Neutral.* We were given the brush-off and, by way of punishment, were sent to dig slit trenches to defend Singapore. Singapore fell. Thousands of men allowed themselves to be taken prisoner and turned into coolies. Not us. Our little group had already taken to the jungle. When we turned up in India in relatively good shape, we were asked what our secret was. We produced our report. We are now going to subject you to the same experimental conditions as ourselves and we'll see how you manage once you've learnt the tricks of the trade. Afterwards your own adventure will begin, without any wet-nurses to tell you how to cook your rice, throttle a sentry, booby-trap a trench or tend your sores. Once your training is over, you will have become the most expensive soldiers in the world, for we're going to spend a fortune teaching your how to live like primitives. Success or failure, survival or death will depend above everything on your intelligence, your endurance and all the little tricks you will have learnt from us. This will be my first and last period of instruction. In a few hours' time I shall be dropped somewhere in Burma. There's quite a lot to be done over there; I've got to persuade people, who are none too keen, to fight on our side and give them a good reason for doing so. Soon it will be your turn. It's a good thing I'm leaving you; I'm a rotten instructor."

Major Edwards jumped down, gave a little wave and marched out.

Captain Puyseguin came up to Ricq. He had close-cropped hair, a sturdy yet supple body and a strictly military demeanour. Cut out to be a soldier, chance had made an agricultural engineer of him. Luckily the war had set things to rights.

"Well, old boy," he asked, "what do you think of Major Edwards' act? I hope our instructors are going to be more serious than that degenerate, affected fellow. He's so well-bred he barks rather than talks."

Ricq could not stand this typically French attitude of Puyseguin, who never stopped criticizing foreigners, their mode of life, their cooking, their method of fighting, the way they smoked a pipe or their attitude to women. The captain's exaggeratedly martial air was equally repugnant to him, so he made no attempt to conceal his feelings:

"On the contrary, I hope the other instructors are all like Edwards. He tries to turn warfare into a sport and de-mystify it by removing all its awsome and sacred attributes. The major lived for six months in the jungle near the Chin and Naga Hills, where there are still head-hunters."

"He was accompanied by his houseboy who carried his haversack for him. At least, that's what I was told in the mess this morning."

"I had breakfast at the same time as you, but at another table. I was told that for the last month Major Edwards carried his servant, who was exhausted. He was given the D.S.O., which of course he doesn't wear, out of snobbery. In a few hours' time he's going to drop into Japanese-occupied Burma."

"What's so wonderful about that? One day we'll also be dropping, but without making such a fuss about it. I'd like things to be clear between us. I, Charles Puyseguin, like war and I don't like sport. I like wine and I don't like tea or whisky. Sessions like that disgust me. War's too serious a thing to joke about or de-mystify. I agree that during training we should obey our instructors, if only to show these bloody English that we're every bit as good as they are. But off duty, we are entitled to behave and amuse ourselves according to our own temperament, that's to say like fighting men, not alcoholic old maids. This evening we've organized a jaunt down to the out-of-bounds brothels in Delhi. Are you coming along?"

"No, Captain. We're in British command. Since those brothels are out of bounds to officers, I feel it's only right we shouldn't go there."

"We're Frenchmen, not Englishmen. We've come to India on a training course. As for the rest, it's no business of the Anglo-Saxons. Are you afraid of women?"

"Who knows? . . ."

"Were you in a seminary before the war? Setting a good

example, with a rosary in your pocket? Run along, then, and have tea with your little pals. We'll see which yields the best results, first of all on the course and then on active service afterwards: tea or wine, brothels or rosaries."

Tea and wine both yielded good results.

Camp F., to which the trainees of Force 136 were posted, lay ten miles or so away from the big garrison town of Poona, on the edge of a flooded valley which served as a water reservoir. The Western Gates, with their dilapidated old Mogul forts, rose three hundred feet above the plain. But the days of Kipling were over. Camp F turned out men whose main role was to destroy what other white men had built: dams, bridges, roads. They were instructed, in the first place, in the art of silent killing. One of the weapons they were taught to use was the edge of the hand, which had to be hardened. It served to strangle, break shoulder-blades or wind a man with a blow in the liver. Another was the knife. They were shown how to grip it and thrust it in, aiming at a point where bones and equipment did not impede penetration. At the end of the course the trainee had to hold his own against half a dozen others. The assault course, dotted with obstacles, catwalks and tunnels, and booby-trapped with plastic charges, served to eliminate anyone lacking in resolution. Thirty per cent of the trainees were returned to their units. Several times a week there were night marches—thirty miles on a compass bearing—through an area infested by tigers, with each man carrying a seventy-pound pack. To defend himself or hack his way through the undergrowth, he was equipped only with a knife. Then there was instinctive firing with every sort of weapon, especially Japanese, more marching, firing on the march, firing at the end of a march when fatigue made one's hands shake, and still more marching—marching for a whole week, with tea, salt and prunes as one's only food, and hooks and lines with which to catch fish in the rivers.

The trainees were also taken on to the lake, where the British had collected every type of pirogue existing in South-East Asia: Laotian and Burmese pirogues, Malay pirogues with outriggers, Vietnamese sampans and Indian junks.

From seven in the morning till noon, from four in the afternoon till seven in the evening, they were taught to use every kind of oar and paddle, while Major Skinney kept telling them again and again:

"South-East Asia is a mass of water, a few strips of dry land surrounded by water. It's more useful to know how to handle one of these damned contraptions than a camel in the desert. Heave-ho, my lads. I want your hands to become as hard as cricket bats."

The French were divided into two teams of eight men each, the first commanded by Captain Puyseguin, the other by Lieutenant Ricq. The rivalry between the two officers, their different conception of human relations, had quickly set them one against the other.

Puyseguin was out to break records and tried to inspire his men with the competitive spirit. He insisted on taking them with him on his binges in Poona. He would get them drunk, then drag them off completely sozzled on a difficult exercise, a dangerous assault course or an exhausting march. He despised the weak and the irresolute, was only too ready to lash out against his subordinates but always showed exaggerated respect for the instructors.

Ricq, on the contrary, encouraged his men and in spite of his short stature showed exceptional endurance. He was considerate, and respected the whims and independence of each of them. But once the exercise was over, the elusive Lieutenant Ricq would take refuge in his quarters. He had found some excellent works on the ethnography of South-East Asia in the camp library.

The instructors' respective opinions of these two French officers reflected their own temperament and background. To Major Skinney, who was a rubber planter, Puyseguin had all the attributes of the Prussian officer, whereas Ricq fitted in perfectly to Force 136 in which civilian qualifications ought to outweigh those of a soldier. The colonel in command of the camp belonged to the Indian Army. He considered that Ricq lacked moral fibre and was a mere civilian in disguise, whereas Puyseguin seemed to be a born leader.

The commando course lasted two months. It was followed by the marine course. On the coast, near Bombay, they learnt how to land in pitch darkness among enemy sentries, how to handle a sail and what precautions to take when organizing a rendezvous with a submarine out at sea. At Rawalpindi, in the foothills of Kashmir, they went through their practice jumps and marked out dropping-zones. In a game reserve in the Mahratta Forest, which had not been hunted over for a century, the foresters taught them how to use snares, build a bamboo hut, find their bearings, conceal themselves, march barefoot, take shelter from the rain and cook their rice.

In Calcutta they were taught all the secrets of clandestine propaganda and the subjects that were liable to carry weight with primitive people. They learnt how to organize a resistance movement and how to turn to their own advantage the gross errors committed by the Japanese in regard to the people they had conquered.

One evening Ricq had let himself be dragged along unwillingly by Puyseguin and a few other trainees to a bar called The Cat. There were two American officers there, dead drunk. They came from Lousiana and spoke perfect French. Puyseguin asked them to have a drink and the conversation turned to Indo-China.

"We'll get there before you," said one of the Americans. "By the time you arrive the place will be taken. At least, that's what that goddam snob Captain Cosgrove Tibbet told us."

Ricq managed to keep Puyseguin calm—the captain was always ready to start a brawl, "to keep up appearances"—and feigned astonishment, which unleashed a flood of boastful confidences from the two drunks. It was thus he learnt that the American clandestine organization, O.S.S., was combing the United States and even the theatres of operations for officers, warrant officers, N.C.O.s and privates who spoke French and knew the South-East. They were given intensive training in China. But it was from India they were dropped, disguised as engineers, doctors or pastors. They had orders to evict the former colonizers by playing on local national feeling. In India, to get their hand in, they openly indulged in violent anti-British propaganda.

Ricq mentioned this next day to his instructors. One of them replied:

"What do you expect us to do about it? It's the Yanks who hold the purse-strings. They're the ones who provide the arms, the aircraft, the ships. We can't very well expel them from India. We'll soon be faced with the painful but only solution: stealing a march on them. Immediately after the war we shall grant independence to this caste-ridden country which is incapable of surviving. You'll also have trouble in Indo-China. You'll be forced, like us, to grant independence to people who aren't yet ready for it. The Americans are fighting against the Japanese in the Pacific Isles, but in India and the Far East they're doing the same job as them: inciting Asia against the white man."

Once again the Liberator started losing height. Ricq's ears were buzzing.

"You jump in ten minutes," the skipper announced. "Get ready, you Frogs. May God and the devil help you."

The green light came on.

Ricq was sitting on the edge of the aperture which contained a sort of slide, with Meynadier behind him. The only equipment he carried was a revolver, a folding spade to bury his parachute and flying-suit, a compass, a map, a movement order from the French delegation and a wad of Banque d'Indochine piastres. The rest was stowed away in the containers which would be dropped after them. The sergeant despatcher checked the parachutes, the static lines and helmets. The light switched to red.

"Go!"

Ricq turned round and saw Meynadier giving the thumbs-up sign. He launched himself through the aperture and was happy to find he felt neither fear nor regret. The air that lashed his face was as sharp and invigorating as the first breath inhaled by a prisoner who has just escaped.

The rigging-lines of the parachute jerked tight. Below him he could see some light flashing.

[3]

The Ho Track

ON Monday 18 July, the day after the coup d'état, Muguette went to the Vientiane post office early in the morning to mail her sister a letter in which she gave her own muddled version of the incidents that had just taken place.

"Bao, it's for my letter."

Bao was in a bad mood. He had been to a *boun* the night before and drunk some raw rice spirit which had given him a splitting headache.

"A hundred kips," he said, as he took the letter.

"But Bao, you must be mad! That's much too much."

"Sixty kips."

"At least weigh my letter."

Almost prostrate from his hangover, Bao suggested:

"Thirty kips, will that do you?"

Muguette left the post-office in amazement. She had seen all sorts of things in Laos but had never yet bargained over a postage stamp.

With difficulty Bao looked for the stamps. They had run out. At the bottom of a drawer he found some old sheets issued before independence and surcharged "Union Francaise". He affixed them to Muguette's letter and all the other letters that were posted during the morning. Then, when there were no more stamps left, he locked up and went home to sleep in peace.

As they arrived for work, the entire staff of the Ministry for Foreign Affairs, from the runner to the Chef de Protocole, were mobilized, but in vain, to look for the text of the Franco-Laotian agreements of 19 July 1949.

The French Ambassador had rung up about some additional protocol concerning the export of stick-lacquer which was not being put into effect. The Secretary General then sent out for Koutsoulat, an elderly clerk who had worked all his life in the colonial service and whose administrative competence was for that reason undisputed. After an hour's search he was found at the Chinaman's where he had breakfast every day and read the morning paper.

"Where are the agreements with France?" the Secretary General asked him.

"*Bo mi.** Monsieur Troussier put them away before going off on leave."

"Where did he put them away?"

"*Bo hou.* I don't know."

Monsieur Troussier, although pensioned off, had retained his mania for official documents and wax seals. Appalled by the disorder that reigned in the Ministry, he had one day started sorting out the archives. Since he knew what the Laotians were like, he had locked them up when he had left for France to collect a small inheritance.

"When is Monsieur Troussier coming back?" the Secretary General enquired.

"In two months, maybe three. *Bo hou.*"

"Very well. As soon as he's back, remind me we need those agreements."

* Literally, "there aren't any". The phrase denotes ignorance combined with lassitude.

"What about the French Embassy?"

"Ring up the Councillor and tell him we have to study certain legal aspects . . . that it's liable to take some time."

"Couldn't we ask the Minister about it?"

"No one knows where he is, no one knows if he's still a minister, not even himself. What do you think of all these incidents, Koutsoulat?"

"Nothing so far, Monsieur le Secrétaire Général."

"Did you see, they even arrested Ricq. Are they going to release him?"

"Provided he's not found in the Mekong, like Gibelin. Did you listen to Radio Hanoi?"

"A Coordination officer has just moved in next door. I daren't listen to that station any longer. What about you?"

"They said Monsieur Ricq was a friend of the Laotian people."

"The Laotian people have far too many foreign friends looking after them."

Half an hour later Monsieur de Saint-Urcize burst in on Xavier Pinsolle and announced in consternation:

"The Laotians are now questioning the 1949 agreements."

"That's all we needed!"

"What do we do about it, sir?"

"As usual, we wait and see. We wait for them to forget about questioning those agreements, we wait for the men in power to swap ministries, we wait for the dry season to replace the rainy season . . . We'll have to send a coded signal to the Quai, all the same. Draft it for me. I've other things to worry about. Is there any news of Ricq?"

Jacob Flayelle, a Protestant from La Rochelle, an agronomical engineer by profession and a humourless, conscientious man by nature, was one of the best European rice experts in the world. U.N.E.S.C.O. had therefore sent him to Laos a year earlier to improve the cultivation of this cereal. Jacob Flayelle had a secret—a certain species of rice that had just been discovered by some Japanese scientists. Without requiring additional attention, it yielded an output three times greater than the ordinary cereal. The expert had been told that the Laotians were idle, but this made him all the more resolved to improve their lot. Jacob Flayelle belonged to the tribe of Bible readers who rush all over the world educating people, rescuing them from destitution and introducing them to the blessings of science, on condition they are officially catalogued as under-developed.

No sooner had he arrived at Vientiane than he selected some candidates for instruction. He put them through a course and taught them how to grow the Japanese rice. Then he sent them home to their villages. No sooner were the instructors back in the bosom of their families than they forgot the famous secret or, better still, refused to divulge it. To make sure it was not discovered, they even allowed the seed they had been given to rot without planting it. But do-gooders like Jacob are generally pig-headedly intent on doing good. He mounted a shaggy pony and rode from village to village, a new missionary of Japanese rice, planting the paddy-fields with his own hands and thus showing the peasants how to set about it. He caught dysentery and malaria, and on several occasions went so far as to infringe the laws of Our Lord with some merry *phousaos*.

Despite these ups and downs Jacob was finally victorious, for he managed thereby to demonstrate the outstanding qualities of his rice. During the next season these peasants, who by now were reasonably well instructed, made use of the miraculous seed . . . and planted three times less rice than usual. They had seen no point in producing more than was needed for their own requirements.

Jacob Flayelle sat bent over his typewriter in his room in the bungalow. The report he had started drafting for U.N.E.S.C.O. opened with the following sentence:

"The Laotians, for all their good qualities, are still a disconcerting people who are difficult to instruct . . ."

On the bed, with its mosquito-net drawn back, a little prostitute from the Viengrathry sat polishing her nails. Jacob Flayelle was no longer exclusively intent on doing good.

The rate of exchange of the kip, the national currency which was secured on nothing except the goodwill of the Laotians and a few foreign powers, had dropped hour by hour on Sunday, when the coup d'état became known. The dollar went from three hundred kips to five hundred and sixty. The news of the release of Prince Sisang and of the conference that was due to be held at the royal palace in Luang-Prabang brought the dollar back to four hundred and eighty kips, and the franc to one hundred.

Ven had left Cléach's shack at dawn. She was frightened of being left alone with Flore and did not wish to miss the collection for the bonzes. Back in her own house, she told her servant Phila to make up a basket of stodgy rice and another of fruit decorated with banana leaves and frangipani flowers. She put on a purple sarong with a broad gold fringe and wrapped a shawl of the same colour round her white bodice.

Ricq did not like her going out with bare shoulders and this morning Ven wanted to behave as he would have liked her to behave always. She would not play with Phila, who was the same age as herself; she would not go round all the haberdasheries in the market or saunter along responding to the sometimes uncouth, sometimes tender compliments from the *phoubaos*.* How pleasant it was, however, to know that one was pretty and to hear men say what they would do to one if one were less hard hearted.

Since becoming Ricq's mistress, that night the guns were firing and bullets kept whistling through the thin partitions of the house, she was no longer afraid of men. Even at the time of his arrest she had not been seized by the tremor that used to paralyse her and deprive her of all defence. She was cured.

The mirror had been shattered with a rifle-butt. Phila came and squatted in front of Ven, holding a sliver of looking-glass up for her while she tugged and twisted her thick black hair into a bun.

She wound a necklace of hollow gold round the bun and fixed it in place with a large pin. That was how it was worn by the girls

* Young man, as opposed to *phousao* or young girl.

up north, at Phong Saly, which the Chinese were reported to have occupied recently.

Phila was more of a friend than a servant but Ven, enobled by the drama through which she was living, miserable at having lost Ricq and at the same time happy to have such a fuss made over her, felt an urge to put her in her place:

"Phila," she said, "hold the mirror higher, no lower, and stop pulling a face. Get to work on the food for the master. I want him to have everything he likes most: stuffed fish cooked in banana-tree bark and some *khao-poun*.* Make sure the coconut milk is fresh and the vegetables finely chopped. You'll have to go out and buy some noodles. Not at the market. You loiter too long there. Are you listening, you little goose?"

Phila replied crossly: "He'll burst. Besides, he's in prison."

"Phila, you ought to know that when a meal is sent in for a prisoner there must be enough food for the guards as well. Otherwise they keep it all for themselves."

"So far I've never known anyone who's gone to prison."

But Phila, who was very fond of Ricq and her mistress, was ashamed of what she had said. She apologized to Ven and offered to go with her to Xien Nip, despite the fear she felt at the very name of the camp.

Ven declined. Clèach was going to drive her there. One evening she had come upon Phila and the journalist embracing against a pillar in the shack. Clèach was stroking her waist, her

* Here is the recipe for *khao-poun*, which Muguette sent to her sister, and which her sister never once used. She was narrow-minded, in culinary matters at least, and would not countenance mixing meat with fish. Spices burnt her tongue and upset her stomach. Finally, she mistrusted anything her sister told her:

"Take 1 kilo of lean pork and 1 kilo of fish. Cut the pork into small cubes and simmer in salted water together with garlic and onions. Plunge the fish into this broth, withdraw it to remove the bones and put it back to boil.

"Reduce the broth and add 1 cupful of coconut milk per person, crushed dried peppers, fresh red peppers, two cupfuls of crushed roast peanuts.

"Boil for 45 to 60 minutes so that the fish and meat are thoroughly combined, thus producing a thick grey sauce to which is added some tomato purée to turn it red.

"This sauce is served with rice vermicelli."

hair, her breasts, and kissing her neck, where the smell emanating from a woman's body is more warm and disturbing than in any other part. The little hussy was giggling and letting him have his way. While she was at the prison talking to the guards, Clèach would come and fondle Phila again. One fine morning the girl would wake up, as she herself had, with a white baby growing in her belly. But Cléach would not want it and would give her a few kips to pay for an abortion. He was in love with that harlot Flore. Ricq, because he loved Ven, had naturally wanted her to keep the child. He had even promised to marry her.

Ricq was not like a foreigner; he had been her father's friend. Everyone knew him in the village of Nouei-Phou Lak, even the Meos in the highlands who grew poppies and cultivated opium. Ven was very fond of Ricq, as though he had taken the place of her father. When he was by her side, she knew she could come to no harm. But she never felt like laughing or singing. When she put on her finery, it was not for his benefit. Did he even notice her dresses and artfully draped shawls? Ricq lived on another planet, where men thought only of politics, war and conspiracies. One evening, when he had come back utterly exhausted from one of his mysterious trips, he had told her he had to do what he was doing in order to protect Laos against her enemies. When peace was restored, he sometimes promised, he would lead a calm and tranquil life with her. Maybe they would go back together to Nouei-Phou Lak?

But Ven knew that white men like Ricq can never lead a tranquil life, that they die of boredom in peaceful villages. Or else they bring with them war, suffering, disorder, soldiers looting the huts and raping the women. Chanda, who likewise wanted peace, was the same sort of man as Ricq.

More than money or jewels, more than love itself, Ven wanted a tranquil life, geared to the rhythm of the seasons, punctuated by feast days and bathing parties, singing and music—everything Koumane would have given her if he had married her. She recalled the sound of his laughter, his jokes and his particular way of dancing, with a grave expression on his face as though he was praying. Koumane was young and handsome and when he went bathing up stream from the girls, all the *phousaos* used to hide in the bushes to watch him. But the child Ven was carrying, this child which had not yet begun to move but only made her feel sick in the mornings, bound her for ever to Ricq, that gentle little elderly white man. Ricq had brought her to Vientiane, to this town she hated, where she knew no one of her own race. He had given her clothes, jewels and a servant. But there was nothing for her to do to while away the time except buy more clothes and more jewels.

"You're nothing but a whore because you sleep with a *Phalang*," she had been told by Soumboun, the tubby Coordination captain who had come and arrested Ricq.

She had been able to see the lust glinting in the eyes of that fat pig. Ricq was under arrest, Chanda was on the run, but everyone was still frightened of them both. Khammay, the other captain, had intervened because he secretly belonged to Ricq, like many other men who indulged in war and politics in Laos. She knew Soumboun would come back, that he would try to possess her by force, like the soldiers last year. But the friends of Ricq and Chanda would protect her. Once again there would be an outburst of disorder and violence.

Everyone now kept saying Ricq was an important man. Even the Communist radio had spoken about him. Ven had always hoped to become the wife of someone unknown who would spend long hours lying beside her instead of rushing about the jungle or organizing plots and revolutions. Yet she liked it when Ricq, after making love, went limp on top of her, weak and defenceless as a child. She was so grateful to him for restoring her enjoyment of life. But Ven could never forget Koumane's smooth brown body, his thick black hair, his sturdy powerful thighs when he went out stark-naked in a pirogue or emerged laughing from the water, playfully splashing the girls and the other boys.

Several times this month she had dreamt it was Koumane who had made love to her, who had given her pleasure. But on waking in the morning she found herself beside her *Phalang,* who exuded that slightly sour smell of sweat which white men never manage to shed.

Hearing the gongs that announced the collection for the bonzes, Ven picked up the two baskets and made her way to the little tree-lined square in front of the Vat Sisaket pagoda. She lined up with the other women. The bonzes, with their shaven pates and saffron-coloured robes, strolled past disdainfully and, as they helped themselves to the food and put it in their begging-bowls, she pressed the palms of her hands together and bowed her head.

The Maha Son appeared, preceded by a pair of slender little acolytes. People said the Maha enjoyed the company of beautiful boys. Antoine Gibelin, who was his friend, used to call him Socrates. But Ven did not know who Socrates was—probably a scholarly bonze from the far side of the ocean who likewise spoke the language of Buddha, Pali.

Ricq often visited the Maha Son in the Vat Sisaket library, where there were piles of holy books written on palm leaves with a hard etching-needle. But Ven knew Ricq and the priest did not confine their conversation to Buddha and his exemplary life. Other men coming from the north or south would join them there, taking care not to be seen. Why did Ricq's friends always have to take care not to be seen?

The Maha Son had long skinny legs and hunched shoulders, which made him look like a heron. He was always protected by a black umbrella and wore cheap sun-glasses which concealed his sharp little eyes. On several occasions General Si Mong had wanted to have him arrested. But he was afraid the population of Vientiane might rise in revolt, so great was the prestige of this wise and holy bonze among these ignorant lunatics.

The Maha Son had placed his aggressiveness, the influence he had over countless monasteries and countless pagodas, at the disposal of Chanda's and Prince Sisang's Neutralist cause. Disregarding the rules of "Moderation and Impartiality", he had engaged in political agitation. His intelligence network covered the entire capital and extended into the countryside. No incident could occur without his hearing about it even more rapidly than the Coordination men with all their wireless transmitters.

As he drew level with Ven squatting on her heels, he bent down, put a handful of rice in his basket and said:

"Nothing will happen to Ricq now. You can go back to your house. No one will come and harm you there. We are keeping watch on it. Place your trust in us."

Strutting along on his heron-like legs, followed by his little disciples and accompanied by deep bows from all the women, he entered the pagoda.

Ven would have liked to hold His Reverence back by the hem of his robe and ask him if it would not be better for her to go back to Nouei-Phou Lak and wait for Ricq there. But she did not dare. How could the Maha Son have understood? He too had forgotten that thousands of Laotians belonging to every race longed only for the end of the war and for everything to be the same as before.

Ven picked up her baskets and went home. Phila, in a state of great agitation, told her she had seen a *samlo* prowling round the house with his bicycle-rickshaw empty. He had refused several customers. Everyone in Vientiane knew that the *samlos* were controlled by the Coordination and acted as spies and informers. Ven felt an urge to collect her few possessions, knot them in a handkerchief and rush away from Vientiane, from the war, the soldiers and the policemen, away from Ricq who needed her.

At eleven in the morning everyone took the plane to go and see the king at Luang-Prabang: Prince Sisang, who was far from delighted at the prospect of confronting his cousin; General Si Mong, whose hooded eyes revealed no emotion of any sort; the White Prince, Phoum Sanakon, who was suffering from a hangover; two or three ministers, who did not yet know if they still held their posts or not; a couple of Coordination colonels, looking rather sheepish; the British Ambassador, Sir Thomas, who happened to be responsible for this expedition and was already beginning to pride himself on it; His Excellency Pinsolle, clad all in white and puffing his chest out like a pigeon; Nicolas Ordinsky, in a muck sweat and no longer even surprised at finding himself, a former collectivist farmer, involved in a musical-comedy royal court; and finally, Hugh B. Vandemalle, representing the United

States, who had no idea what was going on but hoped the king would make him a gift of one of those little gilded wooden buddhas on which his young wife Barbara doted.

The news of the desertion of two Neutralist battalions in the Plain of Jars had caused consternation. The Communist artillery was now pounding Muong Pham, the command post of those Neutralists who had remained loyal, and no one knew where Chanda was.

At Xien Nip Camp, Captain Khammay's and Captain Soumboun's men were still on guard, two by two, outside the door of Ricq's prison. But, no longer bearing any animosity towards one another, no longer even remembering why they had ever felt any, they now sat on the floor together playing dice.

Sergeant J. D. MacMallay of the Rangers, who had a passion for craps, wandered over every now and then to watch them. He did not understand their game at all and was left with the impression that the loser always pocketed the stakes. This was typical of Laos, where everything was contrary to commonsense. The sergeant was conscientiously learning French, the rudiments of Laotian and even a few words of a strange language which he had been told was of Sino-Tibetan origin. He still hoped to be posted "up there", to Colonel Cosgrove's Meo maquis, which was said to be a modern replica of the old-time Far West. The men wore silver collars round their necks, the women gold jewels with their rags. The Meos cultivated opium in the highlands and rode shaggy little ponies. At night they would go off with their American advisers to lay mines and set ambushes along the tracks used by Uncle Ho-Chi-Minh's dirty little bastards.

It meant war, adventure, treble pay. What did it feel like for a boy of twenty-two to become a petty king on a mountain peak?

Will Dupont appeared at the end of the corridor, his hat pulled down over his pasty face, wearing a tie and a grey suit with the sleeve of his missing arm tucked into a pocket. He had lost it ten years earlier in a car accident. But everyone nowadays was convinced it was in action, while tending some wounded. His personal prestige had thereby been considerably enhanced. An officer in paratroop uniform and a shabbily-dressed police commissioner tried to hold him back.

But Will Dupont, on the strength of his infirmity, refused to acquiesce. He was Swiss, a nationality that did not tally with his pugnacious nature but which was useful to him in his position as a Red Cross delegate. He lost his temper:

"Gentlemen, in accordance with the International Geneva Conventions, to which Laos adheres, I demand to see in what conditions Monsieur François Ricq is being held. I have General Si Mong's consent . . ."

Will Dupont had been notified in the middle of the night through the good offices of the French Ambassador at Pnom-Penh. He had taken the first plane and, on landing at Vientiane, had immediately had a talk with Pinsolle. The ambassador had asked him to share what he modestly called "pot luck": chicken in aspic with tarragon, duck pâté and a spread of French cheeses, washed down with claret. He explained he was going to Luang-Prabang and was taking his precautions. The king, who had become a vegetarian, was bound to ask him to lunch and he would have a poor meal.

"Go to Xien Nip straight away," he added, "and try to see Ricq. If necessary, say you have Si Mong's permission. That old rogue will be in the same plane as myself on his way to Luang-Prabang; he won't be able to contradict. Draft a report which we can use to prove that Ricq is officially detained by the Coordination. After that, they won't be able to put him out of the way. That's our main worry. I'm counting on you, as usual. I've laid on a car for you."

The police commissioner and the Special Forces lieutenant, who were more and more impressed by the delegate's self-assurance, signalled to the soldiers to get to their feet and to the guard to open the door.

"Particularly revolting conditions," Dupont observed as he entered the police guardroom.

Ricq lay stretched out on the palliasse that Khammay had had brought in, delousing himself with the conscientiousness of an old lag. He still had fever and the blood was drumming in his head. He tried to get up and said:

"Oh, hello, Will. Don't touch me or you'll be covered in vermin. The palliasse is crawling with bugs. Since you have only one hand, it will be difficult for you to scratch."

Dupont did not mind people joking about his disability. He turned towards the police commissioner, the lieutenant, the two soldiers and the American sergeant who had followed him:

"Insufferable, isn't it, gentlemen? François Ricq is a political prisoner. He is being held, I'm told, because of a difference of opinion. He's being treated like a common thief or murderer."

He went up to the latrine bucket and held his nose:

"I demand he be moved from here and given a clean bed with a mosquito-net, a table, a chair, writing materials, be allowed to have food sent in from his own house or a restaurant of his choice, and to be visited by his consul and lawyer. He is also entitled to take exercise in the open twice a day."

"Good old Will," Ricq cried out in astonishment. "If I'm entitled to all that, they may as well allow me to go home."

"I forgot to add," the Swiss went on, "that his wife can visit him. Make a note of it, Commissioner, make a note of it . . ."

"Will," Ricq pleaded in an undertone, "get me some tobacco, shaving-kit and quinine, because I've got a touch of malaria, and let me stay here."

"Why?"

"It's the only place in which I'm safe."

Two hours later, together with the meal Ven had prepared for him, Ricq was brought another latrine bucket, which this time had a lid, an exercise-book and a pencil, a jug of water, a cake of soap and some cigarettes.

"We haven't been able to find you a lawyer," said the guard, squinting at the food. "There aren't any more French lawyers. The Laotians are either scared or else they're too busy. But if you have any kips, I can go and buy you some beer or even some *choum*. The doctor will be coming shortly."

Ricq rinsed his face, tore off a few shreds of fish with his fingers, left the tasty *khao-poun* untouched and finished off with three mouthfuls of rice.

Utterly exhausted, he fell asleep, holding the exercise book and pencil, tortured by the thought that he might lose Ven or that something might happen to her.

She was all he had left; she was more precious to him than life itself. She was his only reward for twenty years' self-sacrifice and effort.

The first evening showers roused Ricq from his sluggish torpor. The sweat was streaming down his chest, his throat was parched. In his hand he still held the exercise-book and pencil.

He wanted to write a letter to reassure Ven. But she had difficulty in reading Laotian, even great difficulty in reading French, and he could not think of the simple words to suit her. The letter had little chance of ever reaching her. Khammay was willing to deliver any oral message, but a sheet of paper would scare him.

Khammay came in, followed by some soldiers carrying a trestle table stained with rifle oil, a chair, an old hospital bed—there were still traces of white paint on the frame—a dusty grey mosquito-net which looked like a spider's web, and a parcel of clothing.

He was accompanied by a Filipino medical officer in American uniform. Dr. Ramon Sanchez was as plump and fidgety as a quail. He examined Ricq from every angle and declared in English that he could not give an opinion without a blood and urine test, which of course could only be made at the Camp Kennedy hospital. He spoke airily of sedimentation rates, globular numeration and haematuria, then, having come to the end of his trained chimpanzee act, produced a couple of cigars from his pocket and offered them to Ricq and Khammay. Ricq refused his, so Khammay took both.

Ricq wanted to shave. But his hand was shaking. Khammay sat him down on a chair, took a dirty handkerchief from his pocket, wound it round his neck and went to work with the masterly skill of a professional barber. In fact this was his former profession, before Ricq had recruited him to slit throats instead of passing a razor over them.

Over the bloodstained mattress, an old army "biscuit" had been laid which still bore the stamp of the 3rd Colonial Infantry Regiment. Ricq lay down for, with the coming of evening, the fever had returned more violently than ever.

Some Japanese, then some Vietminhs, were chasing him along a path which was suddenly blocked by a torrent in spate. Dan stood on the other side holding on to a tree and stretching his arm out towards him, while Gibelin brought out his black notebook and recited an incomprehensible poem in honour of Don Quixote and his madness. Big bronze drums were beating in his head, calling to war the Khas and all the other primitive tribes of the mountains and valleys, those drums of Chinese legend which Gibelin had wanted to make the symbol of Laos, her pointless wars and futile agitation. They beat louder and louder and drops of blood splashed down on the bronze surface adorned with its copulating frogs.

A hand shaking him roused him from this feverish nightmare. It was Father Olivier Maurel, accompanied by a sentry. The light in the ceiling of the prison had been switched on and the electric generator was grinding away.

Father Maurel took hold of his wrist and brought a big steel watch out of his pocket.

"My son, you've got a raging fever. You're delirious. You were talking out loud to your brother, the one who was shot by the Germans. Your temperature's over 104; Dupont asked for you to be transferred to the infirmary. Seems it's impossible."

"I'm thirsty."

The missionary turned to the sentry and said in Laotian:

"Go and get some tea. You can see for yourself, your prisoner isn't going to escape; he can't stand upright."

Creaking in every joint, Father Maurel lowered himself on to the edge of the bed.

"You've played with fire too long, Little Ricq. I told you so."

Father Maurel held his hand under Ricq's head so that he could drink the tea.

"The Laotians don't want to have anything more to do with us, even the ones who are fond of us. I'm bringing you the succour of religion—you're liable to need it—some pipe tobacco, which you must be missing most of all, some quinacrine, two tablets every three hours . . . and some bad news if you can bear to hear it.

"Your efforts to create a third Neutralist force through Sisang and Chanda have come to nothing. Everything has collapsed. Our little Thon, Pierre Thon, has gone over to the Communists with two paratroop battalions. I've just been to the French Military Mission, where I heard the news. Naturally you're being held responsible.

" 'Monsieur Ricq thought he was a Lawrence of Arabia but he was just a booby', General Molliergues said about you. Andelot, who happened to be there, was lapping it up."

"Is that all?"

"Without Thon, Chanda's done for, as you know. Without an army to support him, Prince Sisang will have to rely on Si Mong, who at least has some bands. He'll fall into the clutches of the Americans and the right wing. The Coordination officers have just brought off another successful coup. On the pretext of Colonel Thon's treachery, they filled five aircraft with all the Neutralist officers, their wives and children and landed them on the Plain of Jars. In the midst of the fighting, mind you, in the rain, the cold, the mud, among exploding shells and mortars, acts of treachery and settlements of old scores. The general called Meynadier up on the wireless in front of me and asked him what he was doing up there.

"Meynadier, as usual, was up to the mark and replied in that ghastly accent of his:

" 'I'm suckling the kids they've just sent us from Vientiane, General. After this you can't say I'm not in line with the new army in wet-nursing the babies of the Third World. On the strength of this I ought to be made a major'."

"He sounded as though he was on the verge of a nervous breakdown. Molliergues shrugged his shoulders and switched off, saying:

" 'Those paratroopers are as sentimental as schoolgirls. To think we were frightened of them!' "

"Where's Chanda, Father?"

"They say Cosgrove picked him up and he's with him somewhere in a Meo maquis. It's a total collapse. Do you want to hear any more, Little Ricq?"

"Go on."

"Pinsolle thinks he'll be able to get you out of here . . . provided you don't have an accident. There's no one in command in Vientiane any more. Even the Laotians working for you don't want to get involved. You'll soon find yourself back in Frqnce. What are you going to do with Ven?"

"Marry her."

"I should hope so. Where will you live?"

"I don't know. In Paris, but I don't know anyone there any more. My father died of boredom in his cottage in the suburbs, which I sold to pay his debts; my mother died of grief when my brother was shot. Apart from the gap of twenty years, my fate and Dan's are identical. But he died full of illusions. He didn't know the world was a barren desert, and adventure a form of masturbation. This evening I have nothing left in life. Little Ricq is at the end of his resources."

"You're mad. You've left your mark on this country . . ."

"The pitiful mark of the White Man in Asia! Neither you nor I will leave the slightest trace. Remember what Gibelin used to say: 'The yellow races have their own laws; they have their own gods and their own customs. They don't react as we do; their nervous system is utterly different from ours.'

"One fine day they revert to their own people. It's not that they're betraying us; they've simply had enough of our protective friendship. Yet they've made the effort, they've fought on our side. Some of them, like Thon, have even consented to accept our God. It's so silly, Father! We've failed because our skin was a different colour and we didn't have the same nervous system."

"Do you remember, Ricq, when you came and knocked on the mission door? You were in rags. You told me a cock-and-bull story about having lost your way and being robbed. But I noticed the revolver under your shirt. I've never since met a man who believed as much as you do in his mission in Laos."

"It took me hours, Father, to persuade you to help us and

make it up with Antoine Gibelin. Yet that was all you wanted."

"I was playing for time. I wanted to sum you up. I didn't want to launch my Christians into this adventure without knowing exactly who you were and whether you were man enough to bring Gibelin to heel and make him a little less crazy. I had asked Calcutta to send us an officer who was up to the mark and would not be impressed by Antoine's line-shooting and eccentricities. At one moment that wretched fellow Puyseguin was suggested. Luckily for him, he was posted to the Meos. My judgment of you was favourable, since I wanted Thon to be your right-hand man."

"Four months later Thon brought Chanda to my shack in Nouei-Phou Lak. Because of those two meetings, because Gibelin dreamt of dying a hero's death in Laos, and because I was obsessed by the sound of the bronze drums, ten thousand men have died."

"I must be off. You don't want to make your confession? No need to give me a list of your sins. I know them all. You've been forced to kill and get people killed, to lie and make others lie, to snatch men from their peaceful life and urge them to fight. You thought it was for their own good. Today you realize it was pointless. So you feel guilty. You have loved without benefit of marriage, but you had to love in order to escape from your little hell of intrigue and conspiracy. You will make amends by marrying Ven."

The sentry made a sign to the priest, who rose to his feet:

"I'll go and see Ven tomorrow. After all, she must learn the rudiments of catechism before marrying a Catholic. You still are a Catholic, aren't you, my son?

"Don't forget to take your quinacrine, two tablets every three hours. The box is under your bolster. If I'm allowed to, I'll come and see you again tomorrow. You think you haven't left your mark on this country, yet everyone who was with you remembers you, even that rogue Khammay. Good-bye, Little Ricq.

"I thought you were no older than sixteen and were telling a lot of lies when you informed me you really were Lieutenant Ricq of Force 136 and that you'd just been parachuted from Calcutta. To impress me, you tried to light your pipe, which made you almost choke."

Ricq had waited a month before going to call on Father Maurel at the Paksane mission. During all that time, from the moment he had dropped through the trap of the Liberator up to the night he had returned to the banks of the Mekong, he had been living in the forest and Gibelin had not left him for a moment.

As soon as he had landed on the hard ground, he had been struck by a peculiar smell, a pungent and putrid mixture of charred grass and decaying leaves, the smell of the jungle during the dry season.

Gibelin had come striding up, wearing an extraordinary Australian hat with one side turned up, with a carbine slung on his shoulder and an electric torch in his hand.

Ricq had snapped to attention in his blue flying-suit.

"Lieutenant François Ricq reporting for duty, sir."

Gibelin had burst into a loud guffaw:

"Welcome to this bloody paradise. But I say, Little Ricq, this won't do at all. I'm only a captain for the benefit of those people in London, who need to dole out labels and ranks to everyone. You're not under my orders, we're going to work together to get things moving in this country where nothing ever happens but where any amount of things are being prepared . . . Take that boiler-suit off and tell me how Ira and your brother are faring."

Every time Dan's name was mentioned, Ricq felt uncomfortable and at the same time anxious to bare his claws to defend his memory. But Gibelin did not know the circumstances in which he had died; Ricq merely told him he had been shot by the Germans.

Gibelin did not utter a word of sympathy but simply observed:

"Plenty of girls must have shed tears over the end of the handsome leopard. What about Ira?"

"When war was declared she took refuge in the south of France. She must still be there. I don't think she was in any way involved in my brother's activities."

"That surprises me. She was so keen on him that in order to keep him she put up with his infidelities and even helped him seduce the girls he found attractive. She would have been even more willing to live a dangerous life with him, carry his messages and hide people. Ira's a brave girl."

Ricq could only reply:

"If Ira had belonged to Dan's network, she would have been arrested, tortured and shot."

Gibelin calmly lit a cigarette, without masking the flame, while his men dragged the containers away under cover of the forest. He went on:

"Ira had a yearning for unhappiness. I was once in love with her, you know. We lived together for three months, in the middle of the forest, on my estates in Upper Laos. Clear streams, blue mountains, herds of elephants and wild deer. She never stopped painting them and enthusing over them. But I made her happy, and she couldn't stand that. I believe her mother was Russian. Well, we'd better be moving off."

"What about our stores?"

"We'll come back and pick them up tomorrow with some Public Works Department trucks. In any case, you mustn't deceive yourself. The Japanese will know all about this drop. There are almost two thousand Annamites living in Paksane. With very few exceptions, they're all prepared to give information to the enemy, either for a reward, or for nothing, or because they can't bear the sight of us."

"Why's that?"

"The French are preventing them from gobbling up Laos. Laos is a paradise, as I told you in Paris. Only, like paradise, Laos doesn't exist; it's a figment of the imagination of a few French administrators. The Annamites look upon it as a colony of their own."

"Let's bury the parachutes and flying-suits at least."

"The coolies will only come and dig them up to resell them. We'll burn the whole lot."

Meynadier arrived, dragging his parachute behind him. He took Ricq aside and complained indignantly:

"These bloody monkeys tried to pinch my chute to make knickers for their women. The chaps on the reception committee look an odd lot to me!"

He nodded in the direction of Gibelin:

"Who's this fellow?"

"Captain Gibelin."

Ricq heard Meynadier murmur:

"Never seen such a dirty, shabby captain before."

But Meynadier was delighted with the sloppy appearance of his new chief.

Ricq and the sergeant spent the night in the vicinity of the dropping-zone. Gibelin's men had lit some fires and, crouching round the flames, chatted together endlessly as they passed round the *choum* and little baskets of stodgy rice. Gibelin proudly listed their qualities:

"Stout fellows! They belong to every race under the sun and they've done every kind of job. Those two lean-faced chaps with striped handkerchiefs on their heads are Hos; they smuggle in the Chinese opium coming from Yunnan. Their ancestors looted and destroyed the villages of Laos. They even seized Luang Prabang. In their sacks they have little ivory scales and egg-shaped Burmese weights. The four others over there, with beards and moustaches, and stark-naked, are Khas; they're the best trackers I know. The ones just behind them are Laotians from the river district, first-rate boatmen. Throw in a couple of Phoutengs and a handful of Vietnamese I can rely on, and I have a team with whom I can take to the maquis for months on end. They know how to hunt; they know all the tracks. Father Maurel says they're a lot of brigands and that brigands make bad fighters. His men are a bunch of choirboys . . . as though choirboys are any better."

"I'd like to meet Father Maurel."

"He's a hopeless pessimist."

"The fact that he made contact with Calcutta shows he wants to carry on the war. It's men like him we're looking for."

"Like all priests, Maurel is backing both sides. He's well in with Admiral Decoux's set-up and well in with London and de Gaulle."

Ricq was unable to get anything more out of him.

They were woken at dawn by the Public Works Department trucks that had come from Paksane to pick up the containers.

An engineer and a couple of foremen, all three Europeans, were squeezed into the front seat, with a dozen coolies crammed onto the loading platforms in the back. They had brought hampers of food and bottles of beer with them, as though setting out on a picnic. For two pins they would have brought their wives and children along as well. They were big brawny fellows who clasped Ricq's and Meynadier's hands in a vice-like grip as they greeted them:

"Glad to see you here at last. Must come and dine with us one evening."

The engineer, whose name was Guérin, winked at Ricq, then took Gibelin by the arm and said:

"I say, Antoine, we notified Father Maurel on our way here. He says half the weapons and dough are for him. But he doesn't mind your keeping those 'blasted Gaullists' who were dropped as well."

"He can take a running jump at himself," Gibelin roared. "He'd better stick to those little choirboys of his. The arms are for us, and so's the money. Isn't that so, Ricq? Maurel's already financed by the Residency. He's not going to have it both ways!"

The Laos resistance movements seemed to be animated by a spirit of fantasy. Gibelin always struck out on his own, according to his moods and grievances, and paid little or no attention to the orders and instructions he was given.

The lumberman also had an odd idea of security. Out of boastfulness, or just from a sense of fun, he had let the entire population of Paksane into the secret. The three Frenchmen from the Public Works Department would go around tomorrow saying they had just collected a parachute drop. Their Vietnamese houseboys or their cook would hear them and spread the news abroad, or even report it to the Japanese.

In order not to get on the wrong side of Gibelin, Ricq told him at great length that he had been ordered to establish a number of camouflaged depots where arms explosives, food and medical supplies could be stored. These depots should not be too far from the dropping zones on which the Liberators from Calcutta would come and launch their containers, but far enough from the Mekong and the R.C.13 which ran alongside, a road that was kept under close observation since Japanese convoys used it the whole time.

"You're the head of the resistance," he finally said. "I'm just a technician entrusted with a military operation which headquarters in Calcutta is planning to launch in January or February 1945. When I've finished installing those depots, I'll come and put myself under your orders."

"This operation's a lot of balls," Gibelin replied. "Staff plans are never put into effect. The big offensives peter out or else they're postponed, either because it's raining too hard, or because it isn't raining hard enough, or because the Japanese don't do what they were expected to do. I can see it a mile off. You want to slip away and do a Robin Hood act all on your own. Out of the question. I'm not leaving you for a moment. You don't know the country and you wouldn't last a week in the Laotian jungle.

"I'm coming with you. I'll take a dozen or so of my thugs with me. We'll install your depots in the Phou-Khouay range, twenty miles further north. It's a mass of rocks, jungle and ravines where the Japanese will never venture.

"Let me tell you how I conceive resistance work—not as a mean little business of plots, contacts, conferences, meetings and rendez-vous, but a heroic enormity. A Spanish author, Miguel de Unamuno, once suggested, as an enormity, launching a new crusade, setting off in quest of the tomb of Don Quixote which, as everyone knows, doesn't exist."

Gibelin brought a black note-book from the hip pocket of his tattered drill trousers and began reading a long quotation, beating the air with his free hand, the very picture of Don Quixote, as lean and also apparently as mad:

"There are but a handful of us to liberate a country which is not even our real country and to re-establish a colonial system which can no longer endure. We need a justification. Our justification will be this quest for a tomb that does not exist, in a country that does not exist either."

Gibelin suddenly changed his tone and at the same time his expression:

"We can go our separate ways, Little Ricq, before having joined forces."

"I'll make him see reason," reflected Ricq, who had likewise come to Laos in quest of the tomb of Don Quixote, but with a plan, a compass and maps.

The containers were unpacked and buried. The stores were loaded on to the trucks, which then set off along the bumpy road leading north to Ban Ta Hua. After two hours' drive they reached the village, a few huts built on stilts on the edge of a river, the Nam Leuk. Some girls were bathing in the clear water, splashing one another and uttering shrill little cries. Their damp dresses clung to their firm breasts and graceful hips. The stores were transhipped onto some flat pirogues, which were punted upstream until the water became too shallow and the rapids too frequent to enable them to continue. Guérin, the Public Works Department engineer, and his two assistants then started back for Paksane. Their pirogues disappeared, bouncing along in the strong current, manned by stark-naked boatmen singing and shouting.

"How happy these people are," Ricq observed. "I'm ashamed of bringing war to them."

"No need for remorse," Gibelin interjected. "They've always known war. They've never stopped being invaded, except since the French conquered Laos without firing a shot. The looting, the destruction, the invasions made no difference. The Laotians are incapable of foreseeing the future and derive all their enjoyment from the present moment. The white men who live in Laos have grown to be like them.

"We'll spend the night on the bank of this river and move upstream tomorrow on foot. In Laos, the tracks are usually the beds of torrents like this one. Now all we've got to do is find some coolies."

Meynadier came up, soaked to the skin:

"My God, what lovely girls! All these people living more or less stark-naked in all innocence! After the war I'm coming to settle in Laos. I'll start a hotel, get tourists to come out. No, I shan't do anything of the sort. Tourists would spoil everything."

"Wait until you know the country and the girls a little better," Gibelin advised him, "not to mention the leeches and mosquitoes. Now try and get that box of tricks working."

"That's no way to refer to a Mark B 2, the most up-to-date transmitter in the world! What shall I tell Calcutta?"

"That you've arrived safely, that the situation is calm, that the

Japanese on the Mineralogical Mission are dead drunk because today they're celebrating the anniversary of some victory or other. You might add that we're moving up north to establish our first camp in the Phou-Khouay range. It will be Camp A. In three days, time we'll signal our new map-reference and the position of the dropping-zone."

"What's your code-name, sir? I have to send all messages in code."

"Frangipani, and Ricq's Jasmine. I keep forgetting these codes and cyphers and formalities. War is becoming a crossword puzzle competition. Sign the message with the two names, Frangipani and Jasmine—from crossword puzzles to flower shows."

"It's necessary," Ricq pointed out. "I think we're being careless as it is."

"What are the girls like?" Meynadier enquired. "Easy?"

"If they find you attractive. Tarts don't exist. Yet the Laotians spend a large part of their lives making love, the rest of the time they think about it or sing about it—extremely well, incidentally. Love to them is, above all, the joys of the body."

"You talk like a book, sir."

"You don't have to call me 'sir', call me Gibelin."

"I wouldn't dare do that with Lieutenant Ricq."

"You could always try," said Ricq with a laugh.

They pitched camp on the edge of the Nam Leuk. The reflections of the fires were like red scales shimmering in the water. The nimble little Laotians chatted merrily away as they cut down some bamboos which they made into windbreaks by tying them together with fibre. Then they covered these with palm fronds to make a roof and some litters. The sweetish smell of rice on the boil rose from the cauldrons.

Stripped to the waist and glistening with sweat, Meynadier crouched over his transmitter, trying to get through to Calcutta. As soon as it was dark thousands of mosquitoes fell upon them.

"What do I do about it?" bellowed the sergeant, as he went on fiddling with his set.

"Nothing," Gibelin replied. "Just wait until you get used to them. In a month's time you won't feel them any longer.

Have you taken your quinine? Good. That's all that matters."

Sounds could be heard coming from the forest, muffled growls and whines. All of a sudden some branches snapped and the ground shook, as though a huge herd of wild beasts was forcing its way through the bamboo thickets.

"What on earth's that?" said Ricq, who had grabbed his carbine.

Gibelin slapped his thigh:

"Elephants. They always make an infernal row. As they're inquisitive animals, they come and prowl around. If you leave them alone, they never attack. I like elephants. I've hunted them in my time. Now I only shoot the solitaries, to spare them suffering. I can't think of a worse end than an old elephant's once his tusks are worn down and his defences are cracked. The pain's unbearable. He goes mad, the herd abandons him. Then he dies of hunger, alone, for he becomes incapable of feeding himself. I do them that favour. I only hope that when my time comes a friend will do the same for me."

"Are there a lot of elephants in Laos?"

"No more than in the rest of South-East Asia, less than in Africa."

"Yet they call Laos the Country of the Million Elephants."

"You know the origin of that name? Just a phonetical error. The Chinese had called all the territory between the Mekong and Yunnan 'Lan Tsang', which the Laotians distorted into 'Lan Xuang', which means 'million elephants'. Do you like stodgy rice, Little Ricq? And what about this fish sauce that goes with it, *padek*?

Ricq followed Gibelin's example and helped himself with his fingers from the little basket of rice he had been brought.

"It's an odd taste and makes you thirsty. Can one drink the river water?"

"No, Full of bugs. It kills more surely than anything else. Nothing but tea for you."

Gibelin got up, took a billy-can, plunged it into the river, drank half the water and washed his face with the remainder. Then he turned round and said:

"I was born with bugs in my blood. They can't hurt me. When I have dysentery I chew opium and get over it."

One of the two Hos, lean-faced under his turban, came and squatted next to Gibelin. They spoke in a dialect which Ricq tried to identify. The Ho nodded and vanished into the darkness.

"A mixture of Chinese and Thai, the *lingua franca* of all the opium smugglers of Upper Laos," Gibelin explained. "I asked him to find some coolies."

"Isn't there a village near here?"

"I know of only four within a radius of two miles. But you can walk right past them without seeing them. The paths leading to them are hidden in grass or undergrowth. The jungle is a world of initiates. It's full of surprises, resources and snares. You may be sure everyone knows we're here. The bush telephone! The Ho is going to reassure them by saying we'll pay the porters. The inhabitants of these villages are fed up with working for a pittance and for the administration. Allowances in kind, they call it. One month a year to build roads which the jungle swallows up in the rainy seasons. And the taxes! Since they never have any money, they have to sell their buffalo, their pigs or their girls. How silly to muck up an entire race for ten piastres a year! You watch, the porters will be here tomorrow."

Bitten by the mosquitoes or roused with a start by the infernal din made by the elephants, Ricq and Meynadier did not sleep a wink all night. At dawn the noises stopped and the mosquitoes calmed down.

Gibelin shook Ricq, who was dropping off from exhaustion:

"On your feet, we're off."

"What about the porters?"

"They're here. The loads have been distributed, fifty lbs. a man. We've agreed on the price. What the hell are we going to do with all these tins of bully-beef and dehydrated potatoes? Everyone here eats rice."

Ricq rubbed his eyes. Gibelin was standing there stark-naked, with nothing but his Australian hat on his head, his carbine on his shoulder and, on his belt, a little leather sheath with a sliver of bamboo stuck in it.

"You'd better strip as well," the lumberman advised him. "On account of the leeches."

"But the water's low. It'll never be over our knees."

"The river leeches aren't dangerous, they're known as buffalo leeches. But the others, the ones that drop from the trees and are no bigger than a pin-head, penetrate any clothes you're wearing. Much better to be starkers."

He took the sliver of bamboo out of its sheath:

"You dip it in tobacco juice. Every time you halt, you dab it on the leeches; they drop off. I've already persuaded Meynadier to get into his birthday suit. He's very proud of showing the other lads he's as hairy as a bear and well endowed for the ladies. Modesty—yet another Western vice. In Laos there's no modesty and no vice. Take your boots off as well, you'll only slip on the pebbles."

Ricq stripped off his clothes and Gibelin peered at him:

"You're the right type, Little Ricq. Lean and well muscled. I know from personal experience, your sort have far more stamina than gymnasium athletes."

Preceded by the two scouts, the long column of naked porters with their loads strapped on their backs set off along the bed of the Nam Leuk. Ricq noticed that, unlike the Laotians, these porters had long hair, many of them were bearded, and they all smoked long clay pipes. Their sexual organs were enclosed in a bamboo sheath and dangled between their legs like a donkey's penis. They were tall, sturdy, with dark skin and sharp features like a white man's. As they filed past, each of them was issued with a small chunk of blackish substance that looked like liquorice.

"Opium," Gibelin explained. "That's all they'll eat on the march. In the evening they'll be given another ration, two grammes. Those who don't want it get a piastre in cash. But they all prefer opium. The Hos turn them into addicts so as to use them as low-priced coolies. They're Khas, the ancient inhabitants of Indo-China. Kha means slave. The Vietnamese call them Mois, or savages.

"They're good lads, but they're frightened of everything: the *phis* or evil spirits, the dead, the rain, the sun, fire or wind. They spend their time making sacrifices to all the powers of nature. A dog's life. And touchy into the bargain. No one's allowed to tamper with their filthy females."

Ricq followed in the wake of Gibelin's scrawny buttocks, long legs and knock-knees. Only yesterday he was listening to Commodore Fayne in his big office in Calcutta, guarded by Sikhs in immaculate turbans. Here he was, twenty-four hours later, in the midst of one of the most primitive and mysterious people in Asia. The porters were paid for their toil in opium, wild elephants kept one awake all night. The heat was stifling, the jungle dense. But torrents flowed between the rocks, as clear and sparkling as any in France. After a few steps Ricq followed Gibelin's example and slung his carbine on his shoulder. He felt happy. Laos was indeed the "bloody paradise" of his dreams.

They skirted a path tucked away under the trees and Ricq felt the first bites of the leeches. He had a horror of these slimy animals, which dropped from the trees in clusters, chafing his skin.

At the first halt Gibelin handed him his sheath and he set about detaching the little black tongues swollen with blood. The porters performed this function for one another, like monkeys getting rid of their fleas.

In the evening the mosquitoes returned in even greater numbers. They stuck to the men's skin in solid slabs. Bloated, dazed and deafening, they kept sizzling in the naked flame of the carbide lamps.

The trackers had killed a big sambar. The animal had been skinned and was now roasting over a fire. With their daggers, the partisans detached long strips of blood-red meat and stuffed them into their mouths, yelping with delight.

On the third day they reached the foot of the Phou-Khouay range.

This range was twenty-five miles from the Mekong as the crow flies. Eight miles broad at its base, it rose to a bare two thousand feet at its highest point. It was merely a big hill entirely covered in forest and dense, mostly impenetrable jungle.

The Phou-Khouay was inhabited by a few hundred Khas, dispersed in four villages tucked away in the clearings.

These villages of high-roofed houses built on stilts stood on both sides of the Nam Leuk, into which flowed several other smaller streams that went dry in the non-rainy season.

The tree-trunks, milky-white, black as marble or blood-red, rose like pillars to a height of a hundred and even a hundred and fifty feet in the glaucous, aquarium-like light. Their foliage formed a roof which the sun never managed to pierce. There was not a single flower in sight. The ground was covered in a thick layer of humus, while the undergrowth and slimy lianas rose to the height of a full-grown man. A path had to be hacked through these tentacles which, on being touched, exuded a thick evil-smelling sap.

Other lianas hung from the high branches, floating like algae in this greenish motionless sea, or else connected one trunk to another like rotting ropes. Rarely did the visibility exceed twenty yards.

"A rifle is useless in the jungle," Ricq diffidently explained to Gibelin, "when you come face to face with an enemy patrol. No time to take aim. All that counts is the rate of fire. The only worth-while weapon is the submachine-gun. Or else hand-grenades. We tried it out in India."

Gigelin fingered a Sten without much enthusiasm:

"What a lot you've learnt since I last saw you, Little Ricq. That gun of yours is made of odds and ends of sheet metal, and a length of old bath-pipe for a barrel. At twenty yards you couldn't hit an elephant. I've always liked accurate weapons with a long range, which kill cleanly. I hate anything that maims, anything that mangles. Gas gangrene sets in. A hideous death. Before you die you inhale the stench of your own putrescence. A filthy weapon, that Sten of yours!"

"In 1944 there's no such thing as fighting cleanly. One doesn't set out in quest of the tomb of Don Quixote on horseback, with a sword at one's side and carrying a banner embroidered in gold thread: 'I'm off to commit an heroic enormity.' The weapons of today are the knife, the hand-grenade, the Sten and the plastic charge."

The lumberman was amused:

"You've not only learnt a lot but you're a good talker."

Gibelin and Ricq established five camps in the range, two or three miles apart but linked together by tracks concealed by bushes or petering out into river beds. Each camp housed a group of eight partisans. The thatch huts were carefully camouflaged. Ricq, Meynadier and Gibelin set up their headquarters on the edge of a big clearing which had been used as a timber yard. The clearing was transformed into a dropping zone.

In one month the Liberators dropped five tons of material there: ammunition, medical supplies, food and explosives, which were stored away in some nearby caves. Dragging the cumbersome material, which had to be cleared before daybreak, over these rough tracks demanded superhuman efforts. Ricq, Gibelin and Meynadier were forced to work as coolies themselves.

A dozen Frenchmen, including Guérin and his assistants, joined them for a ten-day training course. Ricq and Meynadier instructed them in the use of the submachine-gun and the latest explosive, plastic.

But Camp A, the one by the clearing, was the only camp they saw. Ricq was anxious to keep his depots and other camps secret. This mania for security irritated Gibelin, for whom the jungle in itself was a safe enough refuge.

Mysterious and withdrawn, the two Hos, after showing an initial interest in the handling of weapons, now spent all day crouching on their haunches, without saying a word, without doing a thing, waited on by some Khas who had stayed behind with them and whom they paid in opium.

One morning they disappeared, each of them taking a weapon and some rice.

Ricq was horrified and rushed off to Gibelin:

"They're going to give us away to the Japanese. You'd better warn your friend, the *chau-mong* of Paksane, to have them arrested before they go and report to the Mineralogical Mission. We'll change the position of all the camps tonight."

Gibelin shrugged his shoulders:

"My two chaps have just gone off on a jaunt. They'll be back."

Ricq, who did not share Gibelin's confidence, made enquiries.

The two Hos had not taken any of the tracks leading down to the village and the Nam Leuk. They would have been seen. They could not have gone northwards. The impenetrable jungle and sheer cliffs barred access to the Tran Ninh plateau.

They returned a week later, as taciturn as ever. They came to see Gibelin, exchanged a few words with him, then made their way up to the camp where they were installed. It was the highest and most inaccessible of the lot.

"Where did they go?" Ricq enquired.

"I've no idea. To see what was going on elsewhere."

"And they didn't tell you?"

"I was careful not to ask them. That would have shown I mistrusted them. They would then have no further reason to remain loyal. They're Chinese. They hate and despise the Japanese. They hate them for the harm they have done to China and despise them because it was they who brought them their civilization."

Relations between the partisans and the Kha villages on the banks of the Nam Leuk were confined to an occasional exchange of goods. The Khas had been warned not to approach the camps. They had taken the warning to heart, since they had no wish to get into trouble.

Ricq and Gibelin attended one or two local feasts, at which they were obliged to imbibe enormous quantities of rice-beer fermented in jars. The women, stark-naked except for a strip of material concealing their private parts, cooked the food between the piles under the big rice stores, while the men palavered and got drunk. The Frenchmen were not only obliged to drink straight from the jars but also to consume a sort of greenish porridge with chunks of buffalo offal floating in it.

"The animals aren't de-gutted," Gibelin told Ricq. "They're stewed in their own shit. You'll have to get used to it."

Not once did the Khas ask the Frenchmen or their partisans what they were doing in the forest or why the big planes came once a week and dropped parcels fastened to parachutes which opened out like flowers. They merely traded their poultry, rice, fruit, aubergines, sometimes a black pig, against lengths of coarse cloth, tobacco and tin saucepans dropped by the Liberators. It was the witch-doctor, the "medicine-man," a shrivelled old fellow with filed teeth and a black turban, who presided over the bartering.

Inside his hut Ricq came across a bronze drum. The centre of the flat surface was adorned with a twelve-pointed star, and on the outer rim with small stylized frogs astride one another. It looked like an old cauldron.

"It's to make the rains come," said one of the Khas, who had followed them from Paksane.

The drum emitted a sound like thunder. The croaking of frogs, as everyone knows, attracts water. The twelve-pointed star represented the sun that appears after the rain.

Gibelin shrugged his shoulders:

"They'll also tell you that they're old pots which were used at ceremonials meals and turned upside down to serve as drums. They'll tell you anything, that they're the signs of investiture bestowed by the Chinese on the chiefs of the mountain tribes. I've heard yet another explanation. It's not worth any more than the others but at least it has the merit of being connected with a fine legend."

At this moment the Khas arrived with the little black pigs which the Frenchmen had come to buy. Gibelin went no further.

On Christmas Day, Gibelin and Meynadier got drunk on a couple of bottles of whisky which had been dropped by parachute at the same time as some Australian tinned turkey, red currant jelly, some Bibles, pipe tobacco and cigars.

"I always hated Christmas," Meynadier told them. "I had to help the cook at my parents' hotel and used to spend the day peeling potatoes or running round the markets in search of lobsters. To me, the festivities merely meant dishing up what the clients had ordered. By the time they came to an end, it was three in the morning. The streets of Antibes were empty and the last whores had gone off to bed.

"I'm much better off here—almost dying of heat on Christmas Day! So what? Didn't I also almost die of heat every Christmas in my parents' kitchen?"

"What persuaded you to join us?" Gibelin asked.

"I always wanted to see the world. Youth camps, to begin with, then Spanish prisons, then Morocco and India. There were always too many people around for my liking. I've never been very fond of army types, but with Ricq I hit it off straight away. So here I am, as happy as a sand-boy on this Christmas Day on which the temperature is ninety in the moonlight!

"It is true that miracles happen at Christmas? You know the miracle I'd like? For the mosquitoes to stop biting, for once."

Gibelin took a long swig of whisky.

"We could do with a few girls here," he said without much conviction.

"I don't agree," Ricq retorted. "They wouldn't contribute anything. In Paris, Dan and I used to climb up to the Eglise Saint-Etienne-du-Mont at the top of the Rue de la Montagne-Sainte-Geneviève. On our way back, in the freezing cold, we used to stop and have some oysters. What do you think the Japanese are going to do? They're losing the Pacific Isles one after the other. The B25s are bombing Tokyo."

Gibelin wiped his mouth in disgust:

"If this goes on, we shan't be needed any longer. When we talk about our war in Indo-China we'll say. 'We went camping for a couple of months in the Phou-Khouay range. It wasn't even uncomfortable. For Christmas, we had cigars, turkey and whisky.' We must get a move on, though. Tomorrow I'm going down to Paksane with Ricq. You, my poor Meynadier, will remain glued to your Mark B2. But we'll try and arrange for you to come down some other day to get all that dirty water off your chest."

"I've already seen to that, sir."

"What!"

"With a widow, in one of the villages. She's filthy-dirty but not bad-looking. One of the new recruits put me on to her. I hope I haven't done something silly?"

"No," said Gibelin, "not if she really is a widow and as ugly as I think she is."

"What'll we do in Paksane?" asked Ricq, who bore in mind that they ought to steer clear of towns.

"We'll go and stir up that sleeping ant-hill a bit. We'll recruit some more chaps to come out camping with us. You'll have the opportunity to make your devotions at Father Maurel's. Damn it all, the Japanese can't do this to us—leave us in peace until they surrender. The Samurais have become a lot of cissies. Maurel lived ten years in Japan. Maybe he'll know something about their intentions. Try and pick his brains."

Four days later Ricq knocked at the door of the Paksane Mission. The Public Works Department truck which was meant to come and fetch them at Ban Ta Hua had not turned up. It was a feast day, to which war took second place. They had had to come the whole way on foot.

Father Maurel opened the door. He was then about fifty years old and his sly peasant face was adorned with a great beaky nose. The Viets had not yet smashed all his teeth with rifle-butts.

Ricq made up some story or other to account for his torn clothes and unshaven cheeks. The missionary let him flounder in his lies, gazing all the time at the revolver which made a bulge under Ricq's grimy shirt. Then he showed him into the bare room which served as his office. A crucifix hung on one of the white-washed walls, above a map of the region marked with red dots. The furniture consisted of a big deal table, an old rocking-chair, an upright chair and a prayer-stool. There was no fan.

Father Maurel sat down in the rocking-chair, while Ricq, to give himself an air of self-assurance, brought out the pipe Gibelin had just given him and started smoking. The only result was a fit of coughing. The missionary went on rocking to and fro. Ricq looked up at the map.

"Those red dots are Catholic villages?" he asked.

"Alas, no. They're the towns and villages in which the Japanese and their agents are installed. The latter are almost always Annamites or Siamese. I take an interest in what's going on in the district. That's not forbidden, is it?"

All of a sudden he rose to his feet and thumped the table:

"Enough of this nonsense, my son. You must be Lieutenant Ricq whose arrival was reported to me. Judging by appearances, you seem just about capable of serving at Mass. I'm told, however, that you're not doing so badly at Camp A in the Phou-Khouay. I also have a map showing the positions of your other camps. You see, I'm not badly informed. You've allowed Gibelin to get his clutches on you. What nonsense has he told you, I wonder? That I'm a Pétainist, a collaborator? Idiotic. In Indo-China there can't be any collaborators among the white men. There's just a handful of us, surrounded by millions of yellow men and kept under constant observation. We have to stick together in order to survive. We've managed to do so up to now, thanks to the policy of Admiral Decoux and his team. But I'm labouring under no delusions, it can't go on like this. I feel the kettle is on the boil.

"It merely needs someone to lift the lid for disorder and revolution to break out. We're all agreed on preparing ourselves for this. I'm a bad priest; I'm not keen on being a martyr. What do you want from me?"

"Your help."

"And my Christians, because they at least won't let us down. The Laotians like the French, but they won't go so far as to die for them. My Christians are another kettle of fish. In choosing our God, they made a pact. They're committed up to the hilt on our side. Gibelin's brigands are in the game for the money. Others besides him could buy them out. I might be able to persuade a hundred of them to come to your help when the time comes.

"How?"

"By appointing them."

"They must know how to fight, Father. Could you send them in groups of twenty to go through a course in our camps? We'd teach them how to handle a rifle or a machine-gun, how to use a grenade or mine a road."

"All right, but I'll come with them. I also ought to do some training. Besides, I don't want some dirty trick to be played on me behind my back. You can tell Gibelin, I mean Captain Gibelin, that Sergeant-Major Maurel says to hell with him and invites him to dinner tomorrow evening at eight o'clock sharp. I offer him a truce until the end of the war. I agree to obey him on condition he agrees to listen to me. After that, we'll both go our own ways."

"And what if there was no fighting in Laos?"

"What on earth do you mean? Of course there's going to be fighting here. Go and have a shower; I'll get you some clean clothes. You'll share my humble dinner and sleep here tonight."

The missionary stopped all of a sudden.

"It's funny, I used the familiar '*tu*' to you straight away, Lieutenant Ricq. I always do to people I like. I can't stand fools. I also address Gibelin as '*tu*'. I've known him such a long time! He's a dirty dog, he has no religion, he has no morals, he ought to be in a padded cell. But I address him as '*tu*.' Has he shown you his hold-all?"

"What's that?"

"A sort of notebook in which he jots down his personal thoughts, his accounts—mostly debts—anything he picks up from the books that happen to pass through his hands, and dirty stories that no one but himself finds funny. Oh yes, also a list of the girls of easy virtue with whom he sleeps, together with their personal particulars. He grades them from 0 to 20, like a schoolmaster."

"How do you know all this?"

"He got tight one night, I pinched his notebook and corrected everything in red ink . . . Except for the girls, I wasn't in a position to know about them. It was full of spelling mistakes. Antoine never passed school certificate but fancied himself as a walking encyclopedia. The silly ass was terribly angry."

"Maybe he had reason to be."

"Misplaced personal pride. Antoine has always dreamt of being the hero of one of those novels he despises so much. All that reading went to his head. Now that I've flayed him alive, I'm willing to start the truce. I'm going to introduce one of my young believers to you. His name is Pierre Thon. He says he wants to be a priest. In actual fact all he thinks of is fighting, hunting and *phousaos*. You can take him with you. I think you'll find him useful."

Father Maurel clapped his hands. A young Laotian with a square intelligent face and an already massive body came in with a Sten gun in his hands. Ricq saw at once that it was cocked and equipped with a full magazine.

"What's biting you?" Father Maurel asked him.

Thon indicated Ricq with the barrel of his gun:

"I don't like the look of him, and he has a pistol under his shirt.

I saw it when he came in. Hand over your pistol, Monsieur."

"It's Lieutenant Ricq. He has come from France to fight on our side."

"Why isn't he in uniform? Why is he filthy-dirty and in rags?"

"It's the latest fashion in London to wage war in rags."

Thon struck the table with the butt of his gun:

"I don't like the look of him, Father."

"Look out," Ricq warned him. "A Sten goes off if you so much as breathe on it."

The burst riddled the ceiling and brought down a shower of plaster.

Thon was furious at his own clumsiness, but Ricq noticed he had not even jumped.

He picked up the weapon and showed it to him:

"Look, this is the safety-catch. Didn't anyone ever teach you how to use it?"

"No."

"Where did you get this gun?"

"Monsieur Guérin's houseboy sold it to me. Thirty piastres. Apparently there are a dozen more in the house. Was the price too high? There were a couple of magazines thrown in."

Ricq turned to the missionary:

"Father, you must help me establish a little order round here."

"I'll tell Captain Piétri to come tomorrow. He's in command of the Paksane garrison. I'd rather keep the administrator out of this business. He's a nice fellow but he's afraid of his own shadow, and his wife can't keep her mouth shut. On the other hand, Pamphone, the Laotian *chau-muong*, is absolutely trustworthy. We'll ask him along as well."

"Is he a friend of Gibelin's?"

"They do business together. All Laotians, even the most honest ones, whether they're princes, army officers, civil servants or bonzes, are merchants at heart. New arrivals are shocked by this."

During the meal Father Maurel talked about the Japanese:

"They're people who never feel at ease in their own skins, a half-caste breed riddled with complexes, unbearable faults, remarkable qualities, a mixture of tenderness and cruelty, nobility and vulgarity. Frugal, long-suffering, treated like dogs by their officers, the soldiers put up with any hardship and never complain. But they lack initiative and are bad shots.

"As soon as they join the army, whether as schoolboy cadets of fourteen or recruits of nineteen, they are drilled in Japanese pride. The N.C.O.'s manual starts off with this sentence:

" 'Japan is superior to every other nation in the world. Non-commissioned officers must drive this idea into their men's heads . . .'

"This pride may be taken for granted nowadays, but the Japs aren't yet prepared to admit defeat. Before they do, they'll go to any lengths. During the recent fighting on Leyte Island, in October, some Japanese pilots deliberately crashed their planes, which were loaded with bombs, on the American aircraft carrier *Franklin*.

"The Japanese have demystified the power of the white man. They have defeated him at Pearl Harbour, Singapore, the Phillipines. Before dying themselves under the American bombs, they'll succeed in exploiting the myth of the white man."

Next day's meeting at the Paksane Mission yielded few results, since everyone wanted his own way. Captain Piétri demanded that all weapons be handed over to him for storage in the military post.

He was a little Corsican of about forty who already had a bit of a paunch. He was courageous, sharp-tongued, uncompromising in matters of rules and regulations except when one of his compatriots was concerned. He would then obey other, secret laws which were buried in the very depths of his being. For all his efforts, he never managed to transgress them, even when they came into conflict with regulations or his own rudimentary conception of honour.

"No," said Piétri, puffing his chest out, "we can't let everyone wander about with a revolver in his pocket or a machine-gun and grenades in his car. One day there'll be an accident. It's a bad example for the natives. When the time comes, I'll issue the weapons. We'll draw up a list. Each man will have the number of his rifle or machine-gun opposite his name. Like that, everything will be ship-shape."

"By then it'll be too late," Ricq replied. "If the Japanese launch an attack it'll be without warning. The jungle alone can serve us as a refuge."

"Nonsense, old boy, nonsense I've had ten years' service in Indo-China; I know the country. When the Germans surrender, the Japs will follow suit. They'll come and hand over their arms. I have reliable information.

"I get it from Si Mong, a cunning little fellow who's just been commissioned. He's well in with the Japs—passes himself off as a nationalist who wants independence for his country and believes in the Co-prosperity Sphere. But he reports whatever they say or do to me."

Ricq was appalled that such a valuable agent should be identified in public out of sheer boastfulness.

"That Si Mong of yours is a dirty little sod," Gibelin broke in. "All he's after is making money and betraying everyone. Isn't that so, Pamphone?"

The *chau-muong* nodded:

"If I had to give my opinion of him, even though he's a compatriot, a native like myself, I'd say much the same as Gibelin."

Pamphone was an elegant, cheerful young man. The upper lip curling back from the teeth gave his face an ironical expression, while the square chin, candid eyes and broad brow accentuated its look of determination.

Related to all the big families in Laos but employed under French statute as a civil servant, like his cousins Prince Sisang and Prince Lam Sammay, he could afford not to be touchy and to laugh at the Corsican captain's blundering remarks. In a clear voice he pointed out that if the general situation was calm in Laos, a certain amount of unrest was nevertheless noticeable in the Annamite quarter of Paksane. The agitators, he believed, were paid by the Japanese secret service. But their orders came from a pro-Communist movement which had taken root mainly in the vicinity of Vinh and which bore the pompous and disturbing name "Unique Front of the Anti-Imperialist Indochinese Peoples," or Vietminh.

Gibelin interrupted him.

"Their programme is to oppose Japanese imperialism as well."

"Perhaps, but they don't do much about it. What on earth are the Americans up to? Some leaflets were dropped by their planes. They promise the Laotians independence, but these leaflets are printed in Vietnamese."

"Stuff and nonsense, stuff and nonsense," Captain Piétri repeated.

Since no agreement was reached, they all took their leave singing the *Marseillaise*. On the following day Guérin provided Ricq with a foreman's card, plane-table and surveyor's chain. He would thus be able to make an undisturbed reconnaissance of the R.C.13, the main thoroughfare bordering the Mekong, and carry out the orders he had received from Calcutta to provide for a number of demolitions which would block it completely when the British offensive was launched.

Ricq fell into the habit of calling on Pamphone at regular intervals. The *chau-muong* would greet him with a broad grin. He would lend him a sarong and, surrounded by boisterous children and women trying to keep them in order, they would sit together and talk about Laos, her history and customs.

Pamphone was touched by the regard the young officer showed towards him and by his discretion. But he was amused by his prudishness concerning women and the delusions under which he laboured as to the motives behind men's actions.

Pamphone felt that had it not been for France, Laos would already have been parcelled out between Thailand, Vietnam and China. He was therefore in favour of the French returning to Indo-China, while wishing immediate independence for his country within the framework of a sort of French commonwealth.

Thanks to him, Ricq was soon acquainted with all the police reports and all the information that reached him from the members of his innumerable family and the humble folk belonging to his network.

"Intelligence work in Laos," Pamphone told him, "is largely a matter of friendships. When you have a friend, it's natural to do him a favour but it's vulgar to offer him money."

It was at Pamphone's, where he came for instruction, that Ricq first met Second-Lieutenant Si Mong, who was seconded to the youth movement.

He was then about thirty, the same age as the *chau-muong*, but already worn out by anxiety and voracity.

He was of medium height, with carefully waved hair, a large mouth, a pug nose, small lively eyes darting about in an absolutely inscrutable face. He spoke French in a somewhat stilted but gentle voice. There was nothing of the soldier about him but everything of the Florentine courtesan, always ready to use a dagger or poison, and with a facile excuse on his lips if the attempt failed.

Pamphone introduced Ricq as a new assistant of Guérin's. Si Mong was not deceived by this.

When he had left, Pamphone tried to define his character:

"You see, Ricq, it's too simple to say Si Mong's a dirty dog. He's very intelligent and yet he's had a hard time making his way in life. His father, who's Siamese, runs a shop in Savannakhet. But his uncle, a certain Aprasith, is a police colonel in Bangkok. Like most Thai officers, Aprasith is full of admiration for the Japanese and actively collaborates with them. Si Mong, who travels constantly between Thailand and Laos, has come under his influence. He went to school late; he showed an astonishing zeal for learning. But all his work was of no avail to him. In a few months he did better for himself in Vientiane by licking the boots of a worthy colonel who promoted him from sergeant-major to second-lieutenant. He now believes work is pointless and the only thing that counts is intrigue. Captain Piétri thinks he's playing a double game at the expense of France. Si Mong is playing only one game, in favour of himself. He'll always serve the stronger side. Unfortunately, France is in a bad position in Asia."

Pamphone gave a roguish grin and took Ricq by the elbow:

"I know everything he does through his wife, a Sino-Laotian woman, who's in debt and occasionally comes and asks me to help her out. She's also very pleasant in bed. I'm able to give her what she lacks with her husband. Si Mong never laughs.'

"He might get his own back on you."

"Pooh! He's too ambitious and opportunist to be jealous."

It was also during this stay in Paksane that Ricq met Prince Sisang at Father Maurel's. He was impressed by the young man's intelligence and common sense but thought he already had a tendency to take too lofty a view of events.

Sisang was more interested in the political programme of the Resistance than in the number of rifles and transmitters it had at its disposal.

Like a seasoned old statesman, he assured him of his full support, promised to join the maquis when the time came, and went back to Vientiane.

At the end of January 1945 Ricq returned to the Phou-Khouay range, accompanied by Father Maurel and fifty young Christians whom the missionary had selected with the insight of a veteran recruiting-sergeant. But the priest demanded they be kept apart from Gibelin's thugs. Every morning, in the middle of the forest, he said Mass for them. The big tree-trunks were the columns of the church, the altar was a moss-covered rock.

Thon was made a corporal and Ricq adopted him as his bodyguard, much to the displeasure of Meynadier who wanted to keep him with him.

"He's the type I need," he said. "He's as strong as a horse. In two months I'll make a first-class wireless operator of him. He's quick on the uptake."

Four more teams had been parachuted into Laos. Captain Puyseguin's, the nearest, was installed north of the mountains overlooking Xieng Khouang. There was no news of them, since each team had orders to remain completely autonomous.

Gibelin was absent for a month. He went first to Saigon, then to Hanoi, and came back without any difficulty by way of Luang Prabang and Vientiane. On 7 March he turned up at the camp.

"Things don't look too good," he said.

"Communications between north and south have been cut by the American air raids. A terrible famine is raging in Tonkin as a result of the bad harvest of the tenth month of the year, further aggravated by floods. Since autumn it has caused a million deaths. The administration has fallen apart. Public services have come to a standstill. One nudge from the Japs and there'll be a complete collapse.

"Tempers are rising in the countryside and the Vietminhs are making clever use of this for their propaganda. We're going to have trouble from the Viets, but also from the Chinese and Americans. Meanwhile the Japanese have just moved an entire division into Tonkin. That's not for nothing.

"And those pro-Vichy idiots, instead of taking to the bush, are calmly waiting to be nabbed. Anyone who's pro-Vichy is a bourgeois, and the bourgeois, as everyone knows, are always taken in. They try to hang on to their possessions and in the process lose everything. A free man shouldn't have any possessions except . . ."

"Debts perhaps."

"That's another of Maurel's lies."

Gibelin shared Ricq's thatch hut. After dinner, which consisted of a bowl of rice and some boiled vegetables, Gibelin lit his pipe. He seemed embarrassed and at the same time amused:

"You know, I had an interesting encouter in Hanoi. I went and called on an old pal of mine, Prince Lam Sammay. He's the archivist at the museum. I spent the evening with him and a funny little Vietnamese girl he has just married—a bit of a tough customer, I thought. Lam Sammay was at the School of Palaeography and his wife, Loan, at the School of Oriental Languages, at the same time as you.

"We happened to talk about the bourgeoisie. She cited the case of François Ricq, a little French bourgeois, who had an exceptional gift for languages but was doomed to spend his whole life in carpet-slippers deciphering ancient manuscripts. I couldn't stick that. I told her the little bourgeois had been living barefoot in the jungle for the last month, that he had arrived by parachute, was a first-class pistol shot with either hand and could use a dagger like a professional killer.

"It's amazing: she became quite furious. I've known other women like her, who conceive an idea of a man at a given moment of their lives and refuse to modify it. But they never behave like this about someone who means nothing to them."

Gibelin gave Ricq a hearty slap on the thigh:

"Now I know you're not a virgin. That woman Loan isn't a Viet, by any chance?"

"She may be."

"I wouldn't like Lam Sammay to veer in that direction. It would be serious. He belongs to the royal family. In Laos a prince can afford to do anything, even the silliest things. People will still follow him."

Two days later, on 9 March, Ricq and Gibelin learnt of the Japanese offensive through a signal from Calcutta. The Langson garrison had been massacred, Admiral Decoux and his staff interned, the civilians imprisoned. Only a handful of troops had managed to escape and were trying to get to Laos or China.

They struck camp A at once, destroying every trace of their activity, and prepared to take refuge in the camps further off.

Each partisan had orders never to sleep without keeping a haversack beside him containing ammunition, medical supplies, a few hard rations and a couple of plastic charges. All contact with the Kha villages was forbidden.

Since there were no further developments, Gibelin and Ricq went down to Paksane again. The Japanese had not moved but were preparing to invest Vientiane. In utter disorder, the military and the French and Laotian administrators had set off in the direction of China, abandoning the population to their new masters who had not yet arrived. Captain Piétri had gone with them reluctantly. But since the Resident was a Corsican, he had obeyed. If he had been from Tours or Lorraine, he would certainly have joined the maquis. Pamphone, the *chau-muong*, had stayed behind. Guérin and his assistants went off with Ricq to blow up the bridges on the R.C.13, the only way of retarding the Japanese advance. When it came to demolishing the big metal bridge over the Nam Nhiep, Guérin insisted on placing the charges himself.

"You see why, don't you?" he had said to Ricq. "When you have a horse you are fond of, and he has to be put down, it's your duty to do the job yourself. I spent two years building this bloody bridge; it goes against the grain to blow it up."

The bridge collapsed into the river-bed, its platform cut in two by the charges.

"I wasn't going to make a bosh shot all the same," the engineer concluded.

He was grieved at having to destroy his handiwork and at the same time pleased to have acquitted himself so well with this technically perfect demolition. All the Public Works Department coolies were mobilized to cut down trees, which were then used to obstruct the road over a distance of half a dozen miles. Because of these demolitions, it was not the troops of the Japanese garrison of Vientiane that came and occupied Paksane but those from Thakhek. They had just made a name for themselves by massacring all the Europeans, men, women and children. The women and girls, even the very small girls, had first of all been raped by the Mikado's soldiers in front of the husbands and fathers who were buried alive with only their heads emerging above ground.

The Laotians were revolted. But a few Annamites, especially the houseboys, had found it an amusing spectacle.

A hundred and twenty men eventually reached the Phou-Khouay range, including thirty Europeans, Father Maurel, a dozen minor Treasury and Customs officials, some N.C.O.s of the Indo-Chinese Guards, and the Public Works Department team. Guérin had even brought with him his Annamite *cai*, or head coolie.

Pamphone waited for the Japanese to arrive on 13 April before leaving for the Phou-Khouay. He learnt how to throw grenades and fire a sub-machine-gun, then, after a week, went back down to the plain.

The *chau-muong* moved into a house belonging to some relations of his a couple of miles outside Paksane. The Laotian civil servants who had stayed behind came and visited him there regularly and he was thus able to continue to administer the region until 6 May.

No sooner were the Japanese installed in Vientiane and Luang-Prabang than they declared the independence of Laos and the end of French rule. The king had remained true to the protectorate treaty and considered himself a prisoner in his own palace, but the viceroy had gone over to the Japanese. He had immediately appointed another *chau-muong* in place of Pamphone. The man he had chosen was Si Mong.

But the Siamese halfcaste had been careful not to break off relations with his predecessor, in pursuance of that everlasting principle of Asiatic politics that decrees one should always behave to one's enemy today as though he may be one's ally tomorrow. He applied himself above all to filling his pockets. On two occasions he notified Pamphone that Japanese patrols were on the lookout for him. On the other hand, he was careful not to send him any warning when the Japanese prepared their big operation against the Phou-Khouay.

Thon served as Ricq's bodyguard each time he went down to see Pamphone in the plain. On several occasions he spent the night at Vientiane without being bothered. He brought back with him a certain Khammay, a bright young barber who had been beaten with the flat of a sword by a Japanese officer for whom he had refused to make way. This had not pleased him at all.

Khammay knew all that was going on in the town, even the names of the Vietnamese notables who consorted with the officers of the Kempetai.*

Gibelin and Ricq decided to make an example of someone. Khammay suggested teaching a good lesson to Ngoc, a rich rice merchant who lived on the bank of the river.

The job turned out badly. Khammay had gone to Ngoc's in the middle of the night armed with a club. But he stumbled over some bodies lying on the floor and woke the entire household. Women and children began rushing about in all directions; the neighbours lit their lamps. Thon, who was on watch outside, came to his comrade's help just as Ngoc, with a revolver in one hand and a torch in the other, was holding Khammay up. Surprised by his arrival, the Vietnamese turned his head. Khammay disarmed him and slit his throat with a razor.

The two men only just managed to get away in a pirogue, pursued by a Japanese patrol. Gibelin congratulated Khammay:

"Well done. After the way the Japanese behaved at Thakhek, there's no need for us to be tender-hearted. Anyone working with the Kempetai must be regarded as a traitor. Did anyone recognize you?"

* Japanese military police, equivalent to the German Gestapo.

"I don't think so."

"Would you do it again? A hundred piastres for each execution, does that suit you?"

Father Maurel intervened:

"The only time you ever think of paying, Gibelin, is either for a woman or to have someone killed. Traitors indeed! You know how many traitors there are in Paksane? Two hundred thousand, and all of them Annamites. One barber wouldn't be enough for the job. If you start executing collaborators you'll only thrust the waverers into the arms of the Japanese. And once you've started, you can't stop. Why not instead ask your little pal Khammay to bump off the Japanese major who ordered the massacre at Thakhek? I'll double the reward, out of my own pocket."

"For a thousand piastres I'll have a shot at it," Khammay calmly announced. "I know where he lives. His house is guarded only by a couple of soldiers and he gets stinking-drunk every night."

"It would have been better had we started off with him," said Ricq, "but it's no good crying over spilt milk."

Gibelin and Maurel looked at him in amazement. They had been speaking Laotian and he had understood the entire conversation in that language. His composure had impressed them. But Ricq had had to make an effort. He had a horror of blood and he pictured Ngoc, with his throat cut, in the midst of his family—a cock killed by a fox in the hen-house, and all the feathers flying about, the women's dresses stained with blood. But a sound thrashing with a stick was merely Molière comedy. War was tragedy; blood had to be shed.

Ngoc was the uncle of the Public Works Department *cai*. A week later the *cai* disappeared.

On 6 May two Japanese battalions arrived from Thailand by way of the Mekong and landed at Paksane. Pamphone at once sounded the alarm. But on the following day he announced there was no cause for panic, the Japanese were not being sent against the Phou-Khouay. They were preparing to move off towards Xien Khouang along the path bordering the river. Their mission was to cut off a small French unit who were trying to get to China through Northern Laos. Scarcely had they landed than their colonel sent some detachments in that direction to prepare the camps and requisition food. The hundred and sixty men hiding up in the Phou-Khouay had at their disposal only twenty sub-machine-guns with four magazines, a score of rifles and a couple of Brens, one of which had a broken firing-pin. This was not much with which to face a thousand well-armed Japs.

Once the alarm was over, Ricq, accompanied as usual by Thon, had gone down for the night to one of the villages on the bank of the Nam Leuk. Anxious to find out how the Khas would react if the Japanese turned up, he intended sounding out the "witch-doctor".

At four in the morning Ricq was woken by the medicine-man. He was still feeling queasy from the ritual drinking in which he had been forced to indulge in order to find out that the Khas would do nothing and would hide away in the forest.

The "witch-doctor" told him to leave at once, in his under-pants, barefoot, just as he was. The Japanese were surrounding the village, but he could still slip through the cordon by way of the torrent. As soon as it was light, this would no longer be possible.

Ricq had to warn his friends at once. Thon had disappeared. He left him to his fate and made his getaway in the dark, passing a few yards away from the soldiers of the Mikado.

By making them believe they were heading for Xieng Khouang, the Japs had set a trap and they had fallen into it.

Ricq woke Gibelin and Meynadier, who had no idea what was happening.

"We're getting out of here," the lumberman decided straight away. "It's impossible to defend the camp. What with? Three Stens and a couple of rifles. We've been had for suckers. Let's make for Camp E up in the caves. After that we'll see. Meynadier, pack up your equipment. Ricq, warn the other camps. Where's Thon?"

"When I took off, he had left the witch-doctor's hut."

"Christ, I hope he keeps his trap shut if he's caught."

"What difference would that make?"

"If the Japs discover we have no weapons, they'll set off in pursuit. We're done for. More often than not they confine themselves to blocking all the exits, then they wait."

"What for?"

"For us to die of hunger."

Pamphone managed to join them nevertheless.

Thon turned up at the caves at dawn next day. He could barely walk; his legs were bruised and lacerated from the blows he had received, his body marked with cigarette burns. He had been tortured throughout the day but had not said a word. In the night he had even mustered enough strength to escape by killing a sentry.

"How did you manage it?" Ricq asked him, as he dabbed his wounds with mercurochrome.

"I didn't know one could hate people to the point of being unable to feel their blows any longer. Am I going to be made a sergeant now? The Public Works Department *cai* is with them. They burnt me with lighted cigarettes. It hurt terribly, worse than when they stuck daggers into my legs. Then they tied me up to a tree. But I managed to struggle free. When the sentry had his back turned, I struck him, as you taught me to, with the edge of my hand. His neck cracked."

The Japanese blocked all the tracks and exits. On several occasions the partisans tried to find a breach in the cordon, but this merely drew the enemy's fire. One of these attempts cost them three dead and four wounded. Guérin was to die inhaling his own stench of decay.

Meynadier managed to get through to Calcutta. Throughout Indo-China the Japanese were attacking the resistance groups, all of whose positions were known to them. There had been large-scale treachery.

Force 136 could do nothing about it, not even risk an aircraft to drop them arms, ammunition and supplies. It would have been caught in the Japanese machine-gun fire.

"What did they teach you to do in this sort of situation?" Gibelin asked Ricq.

"Split up into small groups of three or four and try to break through the cordon."

"Yes, but the Japs know all our tracks, thanks to that bloody little *cai*. And it's impossible to cut new ones through this jungle. It takes four hours to advance one mile.

"I hope my Hos aren't wrong. Our last chance of getting out of this mess is to take the opium smugglers' track which climbs up into the Meo country of Tran-Ninh. It starts from this range apparently."

Gibelin forthwith issued a series of orders which astonished Ricq; he forbade anyone to carry more than a twenty-pound load. Nothing but concentrated food, medical supplies and personal weapons. These were to be carried in Kha baskets made of light fibre. No rice—this was too heavy. So were mosquito-nets. No change of clothing, and no boots or shoes. The wireless transmitter was divided up into four forty-pound loads.

"What's more," Gibelin added, "if I wasn't afraid of shocking my friend Ricq and the few regulars who are with us, I'd chuck out all arms and ammunition except for a few shotguns.

"Arms can always be dropped to us later, but we've only got one life. To save it, we've got to be as nimble as monkeys."

One of the men who had been wounded in the stomach died, which spared them the nasty business of abandoning him. The others, like the newly promoted Corporal Thon, were able to walk. At dawn the long column headed due north in the wake of the Hos through the jungle which the undergrowth, thorny bushes, bamboos and sheer cliffs rendered impenetrable.

"Those bloody old Hos!" Gibelin exclaimed. "If they weren't in the same plight as ourselves, they'd never have divulged their secret to a hundred and sixty people, including five Customs officials. Bang goes their entire livelihood."

Hacking their way forward, the Hos advanced a few hundred yards, then retraced their steps and started off in another direction. Finally one of them gave a signal. Behind a tangle of black bamboos there was a sort of trench which here and there turned into a tunnel. Snakes went slithering along the ground or hung from the trees, their necks distended with fury. The track came to an end half a mile further on in front of a stream. They followed this for three hundred yards to where a second track started, concealed once again by the undergrowth. It brought them straight up against the side of a cliff.

Meynadier, who had collapsed on the ground with his load beside him, lit a cigarette:

"I don't see where we go from here."

One of the Hos shinned up a tree. Thinking their guide was trying to get his bearings, Ricq waited for him down below.

"You're meant to follow him," Gibelin shouted.

At a height of forty-five feet, the tree trunk was prolonged by a big branch, a sort of slippery catwalk leading to a ledge carved out of the rock. The ledge spiralled upwards round the rocky outcrop until it reached the summit which overlooked a dark sea of forest.

The mountains opposite were gashed open, red earth pouring from their sides like blood. The rock was damp and slippery; there were many falls.

The exhausting march continued along further tracks cluttered with roots, tree-trunks and stones. The Hos went trotting forward without ever looking back, their baggy black trousers flapping against their bare calves.

"Hang on, hang on, they're not keeping up in the rear."

Twenty times the column had to halt and wait for the laggards.

When night fell, there was a nip in the air.

"No fires," Gibelin ordered.

They shivered all night, huddled together, their feet aching and swollen. There was no water and their throats were parched.

Next day they plunged once more into the jungle, moving along further glaucous tunnels, and towards one o'clock in the afternoon came to a halt on the edge of an icy torrent flowing over a bed of sand and pebbles.

The Hos went off to reconnoitre and came back three hours later. They then started climbing up an outcrop of rock even steeper than the one before. Streaming with sweat, they emerged onto a denuded shelf on which a few rotting posts still stood. The wind was icy-cold.

This was the site of a former Kha village. An epidemic had broken out here and the witch-doctor had accused the *phis* of having caused it. The entire population had fled.

Gibelin gave permission for fires to be lit. But the sodden green wood did not give out much heat.

At midnight a thick mist rose from the valley, blotting out the trees below them and then the men themselves, who were unable to see more than ten feet in any direction.

They waited until nine in the morning before starting off again, but it was only after two hours' marching that their cramped and aching muscles could function without giving rise to a stream of oaths.

In the evening they reached a poky little village of thatched houses rising from a quagmire in which pigs wallowed. Its inhabitants, hirsute natives with leathery skin and feverish eyes, eked out a meagre living from a sparse forest which they had burnt down in order to plant rice and vegetables.

After a lengthy palaver the Khas agreed to sell a few chickens and allow the white men to rest in their dark and dingy hovels. They also brought out some haunches of smoked venison, but the meat smelled so high that only the other Khas accompanying the column ventured to taste it.

On the following day a thin rain started to fall. Black clouds scudded across the pale sky.

The partisans made themselves raincoats out of some leafy branches; the white men followed their example.

They finally followed a river running with pink-coloured mud. One of the Customs officials and two Treasury employees spoke of giving up.

"As you like," Gibelin told them. "But where will you go? If you stay here you'll die."

They threw away their baskets and went on.

"How far is the next village?" Ricq enquired.

"The time it takes to cook five pans of rice," said an old man, pointing vaguely ahead.

On the fourth night, having encountered no village, they pitched camp in some caves where they were able to heat some water and dissolve some cubes of concentrated soup in it.

The trackers killed a couple of wild boar, but the meat was so tough that each mouthful had to be chewed for several minutes before it could be swallowed. By then it tasted filthy. Three of the Europeans went down with fever. They shivered all night. The fever lifted in the morning, leaving them weak and light-headed.

"Jungle fever," Gibelin said to Ricq. "How are you feeling?"

"I'll manage, so will Meynadier. I was right about him. He keeps swearing and cursing God and all the saints, but he's carrying his forty pounds. He won't entrust anyone else with his set. What about the others?"

"They can't do anything else but follow. Tomorrow will be an even more difficult lap. We'll have to climb to over seven thousand feet. One of the most astonishing landscapes in the world!"

"Did you already know this Ho track?"

"I've done the trip once before, accompanying some worthy opium merchants, just to see what it was like. Besides, damn it all, I had financed the operation. I was going to be made bankrupt."

Father Maurel, who had exchanged his cassock for a tattered shirt and drill trousers, came up to inform them that one of his Christians had injured his foot on a splinter of bamboo.

"No question of abandoning him," he said. "What are we going to do? His foot is suppurating. I opened the wound with a knife and stuffed it full of sulphonamides."

"Make him a stretcher," Gibelin advised, "and find some volunteers to carry him."

"I'd find fifty at once, all fifty of my Christians. But I'd like to make a suggestion: we white men, those of us who can still stand upright, must take it in turns with the Laotians to carry the stretcher. I know, the Laotians are less tired than we are. But the point is to show them we are all in this together, irrespective of the colour of our skin, that we are waging the same war and have the same end in view: the liberation of Laos."

"There, Father, you're going too far. What the hell have our worthy Laotians got to do with our squabble with the Japs? One invader chasing another one out. They've seen so many pass through!"

"All the more reason for carrying the stretcher."

"All right, then, we shall. We've given the Japs the slip and there's no need to hurry. If we had had them on our heels I should have given orders for the injured man to be abandoned. To-morrow we'll reach the slopes of the Muon-Nghone. We'll stay there three or four days to recover our strength. There's clear water and any amount of game. You'll see fir trees, just as in France. The Meos used to be encamped up there, but Pamphone says they've now left."

"Because of the *phis*?"

"No, the Meos don't believe in the *phis*. They just felt like leaving. So nothing could stop them."

The sun rose and Ricq ordered some salt tablets to be issued. There was still no water. They went on climbing for six hours, along flinty paths and across large slabs of rock, stumbling over roots, falling down and picking themselves up again, light-headed with fatigue. The stretcher swayed above their heads, carried for the most part at arm's length because of the narrowness of the path.

The stretcher-bearers had to take it in turns every hundred yards. Ricq, Gibelin and Father Maurel had set the example. Meynadier insisted on doing likewise. The contagion spread to the flabby, idle Customs officers who were puffing like seals, to the junior civil servants who only a few days earlier had felt so superior to their yellow-skinned colleagues, to the old re-enlisted sergeants who used to beat up their houseboys or *congaies* when they got drunk. They all vied with one another to carry the injured man.

The *chau-muong*, harnessed to the makeshift stretcher next to Ricq, was a far cry from the elegant Paksane official. He had turned out tough and courageous and invariably even-tempered, occasionally breaking into song with his Laotians when the going was particularly bad.

Ricq reflected: it's with men like Pamphone that the new Laos must be created after the war. Not for a moment did he imagine that he would be the one to attempt, albeit in vain, to create this new country and that Pamphone would be murdered for having believed in him because they had struggled together until they were sick from fatigue to save the life of a little Laotian whimpering pitiably at every jolt.

The landscape altered. The winding tracks gave way to paths covered in thick moss. They saw squirrels nibbling the pine kernels and they gathered wild mulberries. The air was bracing and smelt of resin; sunbeams flickered between the trees.

In front of them there now rose a solid wall of blue granite with waterfalls flowing from it, silver ribbons that splashed onto the black slabs of rock, forming at their foot a thick spray in which the colours of the rainbow shimmered.

"Halt," Gibelin cried. "We're in paradise. The proof is, there's no one here."

He led Ricq up to the foot of the waterfalls.

"It was here," he said, "that Ma Yuan placed some bronze drums like the ones you saw at the medicine-man's at Phou-Khouay.

"You hear the roar of the water? Imagine a bronze drum under each of these falls. The Chinese Annals—a splendid collection of legends—say that a general in the Han dynasty, Ma Yuan, was entrusted by the emperor with the task of defending the marches of China, Laos, Tonkin, Burma and Northern Thailand against the rebel highlanders. But he had no soldiers to give him. The Son of Heaven needed what soldiers he had to conquer other territories to the north and the east.

"Ma Yuan then had the brain-wave of placing bronze drums in all the waterfalls. The water made the metal roar and thunder. The highlanders fancied they were hearing the innumerable armies of the emperor and spent years and years up in their mountains without daring to come down into the valleys.

"But one day, at last, the Khas—for that's who they were—tumbled to this subterfuge and took the drums away.

"I prefer this explanation to all the others, even though it's certainly false . . . as all the others are."

Some big fires were lit, over which haunches of meat were placed to roast. The temperature stood at zero and the ragged men huddled close to the flames, scorching their chests while their backs remained frozen.

On the following day Meynadier set up his transmitter and got through to Calcutta. He gave their latest map reference and informed them that the group was short of everything: food, ammunition, medical supplies, but above all clean clothes and blankets. In reply he received the following astonishing signal:

"On no account attempt guerilla action against the Japanese. You are the last wireless transmitter in the whole of Indo-China. British offensive from Burma postponed. Move north towards Xieng-Khouang. Find suitable dropping-zone. We shall parachute you all you need as soon as you have signalled your position. Try to establish contact with the Puyseguin group of whom we have had no news since 9 March. Congratulations to Major Antoine Gibelin, Captain Francois Ricq, Second-Lieutenant Maurel and Sergeant-Major Meynadier on their promotion. Repeat; you are the last transmitter still operating in Indo-China. Good luck."

"I would have preferred a bottle of whisky and some cigars," said Gibelin after reading this signal. "These promotions are like bad jokes. We are merely the leaders of a band of ragged vagabonds who have set out on some sort of pilgrimage or other. No need for badges of rank to lead them. With Maurel, we're now saddled with the oldest second-lieutenant in the French Army. Move up north. Where to, Christ Almighty? We have to rely on villages for our supplies."

Pamphone raised his head:

"I've heard of a basin surrounded by mountains two days' march from here. It's called Nouei-Phou Lak. Your Hos are bound to know it. It's one of the big centres for contraband opium. One of my friends who was at the administration college with me has retired there. He's a village headman. His name is Chouc. He's a Thai-Neua. Chouc left the service when he realized he would never be a *chau-muong*."

"Why not?"

"We Laotians, or Thai Laos, are jealous of our privileges as the dominant race. We keep the best appointments for ourselves, that's to say the appointments that bestow most prestige and bring in most money. In the Kingdom of the Million Elephants, the two are always interconnected. That's yet another thing that'll have to be changed if we want to live in peace later on.

"Chouc will welcome us with open arms, I'm certain. He loves

France. He's also on good terms with the Meos and speaks their language."

Gibelin Force set off once more; this was now the unit's official name, the name that appeared in the files and on the maps.

The hundred and fifty-four men, leaning on branches they had cut down, bowed under the weight of their baskets, nibbling grass to ward off hunger, shivering with fever or cold, had resumed their pilgrimage.

The little Christian had died, and also one of the Treasury officials who had been laid low by an attack of fever. They were buried at the foot of the waterfalls after Second-Lieutenant Maurel, hollow-chested and in tatters, had said a final prayer over them.

They were placed in the same grave, side by side, and under the same cross, to which was pinned a sheet of paper torn from a note-book:

"Pierre Loiselier and Bak Kham, who died for France and for Laos."

The day afterwards, the wind snatched the piece of paper away and blew the cross down.

Three days later the group came upon a basin surrounded by blue mountains.

Down below, on the edge of the river, was a large village inhabited by the Thai-Neua; and half way up the slope another Kha village, built on terraces, with pointed-roofed rice-granaries. Right up at the top stood some isolated Meo huts surrounded by big fields of poppies in bloom.

The basin shimmered with light, not the vitrous light of the lowland plains, but bright and sparkling, and as invigorating as running water.

"Now I know," said Gibelin. "This is where the tomb of Don Quixote is to be found."

Colonel Sato Kamasaki waited a week with his two battalions in front of the Phou-Khouay range. Then, since nothing happened, he sent out patrols. The forest was empty. So he returned to Paksane.

Major Homitono, the garrison commander, had had his throat slit. The murderer had crept into his billet at dead of night. Colonel Kamasaki gave the deceased a ceremonial funeral according to the Shinto rites. He delivered his eulogy to the assembled troops, although at Thakhek the major had behaved like an absolute Mongol.

But a veil had to be drawn over that unfortunate affair, so as not to tarnish the honour of the imperial army.

[4]

Chanda

THE morning of Tuesday, 19 July, was exceptionally quiet in Vientiane. The ministers, generals and ambassadors were still at Luang-Prabang in consultation with the king. The Coordination patrols went on their rounds in a slumbering town. The price of rice rose by several kips and the dollar dropped a few points. The journalists who had not been able to find seats on the official plane spent the day playing cards and discussing the situation. They maintained the international "suspense", however, with a series of mysterious and vaguely-worded cables.

Nate Hart, of Associated Press, who had been informed by the American Ambassador, was the only one who was able to point to a hardening of the Neutralists in the Plain of Jars. He cited the action of Colonel Thong Dy's Russian tanks against a Vietminh battalion which was trying to cut their line of withdrawal. But the officer in charge of censorship saw fit to improve on this piece of news and redrafted the American correspondent's cable to read: "Colonel Thong Dy's tanks have routed two Vietminh regiments who were attempting to check their victorious advance towards

o

Muong Pham." Convinced he had thus done his duty by Laos, he locked up his office.

A tornado ravaged the district of Pakse, bringing down the trees and telegraph posts and blowing the high-roofed Kha houses off their stilts. In the forest it put to flight a big herd of wild buffalo led by an enormous male whom the witch-doctors had made into a god.

A delayed-action grenade exploded in Joachim Mattei's car a few minutes before he was due to drive off in it. Mattei took no legal action but he packed his bags. He knew he was no longer protected, that his life was not worth a kip, and he went to ground in the house of the Chinese ex-General Yong, his partner in an opium den. Yong behaved perfectly but informed the Coordination. He was told he could keep his lodger on condition he took the first plane to Bangkok in three days' time. He was also requested to find a new partner, and for this purpose he was introduced to Captain Seuam, a former officer of Chanda's, who had joined the bands of General Si Mong. When Mattei asked Yong to settle up their partnership accounts, the Chinaman pointed out with extreme politeness that life was worth more than a few hundred thousand kips. Mattei did not press the matter any further and gratefully accepted the excellent luncheon his former partner provided. Then he went up to his room to have a siesta.

Joachim Mattei had come out to Laos in 1953. He had always lived in one of the two hotels, the Bungalow or the Constellation. Once a year he turned up wearing all his medals—there were many of them—at the reception given by the French Embassy for all French residents on July 14.

Mattei carefully steered clear of intrigues; he belonged to no particular set and never meddled in politics. He was known to have only one friend: Picarle, a former G.C.M.A. warrant officer, who was now living with the Meos. Officially, he was an Air Transport Company employee. The Narcotics Bureau had shown an interest in him and had him followed for months, with no result. Mattei was tall and thin, with fine dark eyes. He always wore well-cut suits, grey ties and suede shoes. Every now and then he would disappear for a few days. These absences never lasted more than a week.

Mattei hung his clothes carefully over the back of a chair and lay down under the mosquito-net with his hands behind his head. His expulsion from Laos, he felt, was connected with the *putsch*. The one man who could have saved his bacon was himself in prison. This was Ricq. At Saigon, Mattei had been a great help to the French special services, who had got him into Laos when he had had a spot of bother. They had sent him to Ricq.

Ricq had received him with his customary gentleness and warned him:

"Laos isn't Vietnam; the business you're interested in is not in the hands of little Corsican or Chinese gangs, it's controlled entirely by the men in power. I suppose you know the ones you have to contact.

"You will be tolerated only if you're nothing more than a *compradore*, a middleman. You have a fine war record as an Air Force lieutenant. You accepted all the missions no one else wanted. Pity you should have been reduced to doing this job."

Mattei had shrugged his shoulders with a depressed rather than a boastful gesture. Surely Ricq must know that there were certain commitments from which it was impossible to escape?

"If I could be of any help to you at any time, Major?"

"I may need you one of these days. You may as well know, however, that I shan't in return facilitate your business as they do in Saigon, even though the buying and selling of opium is perfectly legal in Laos."

When Ricq had asked him for help, Mattei had given it, landing agents behind the enemy lines in a Piper-Cub, going right up to the Chinese border to rescue some maquis chiefs who were being chased by the Viets. He would sometimes bring back a few kilos of opium "to cover the costs".

Only once had Ricq thanked him:

"Mattei, I don't know many men with your coolness and courage. If you should ever need me, I'll help you."

He had shaken him by the hand; they had never met again...

When the Coordination had taken control of Vientiane,

Mattei had worked with General Si Mong's men. Now they did not want anything more to do with him. If he did not manage to remain in Bangkok, he knew he was done for. He was not allowed into Phnom-Penh, Hong Kong, Singapore or Tokyo. He would not even be able to cross the airport boundaries.

Duffault and Sebastiani would never allow him to come back to France. In the Far East, he was useful to them and so they had spared him. In France, he would be a nuisance and they would have him bumped off. A sordid end: a petty killer would wait for him in a doorway and shoot him in the back.

Si Mong was as powerful in Bangkok as in Vientiane. His uncle Aprasith controlled the police. He could have had him assassinated, like Nutcracker two days before the *putsch*, but he had preferred to force him back to Bangkok and France where others would deal with him. Si Mong no longer covered his costs with Air Transport now that Colonel Cosgrove's special forces transported the Meos' opium themselves. So he had decided to wind up the company. The grotesque incident of the Nakom-Phanom radar had accelerated his decision and cost the life of Desnoyers whom everyone called Nutcracker.

Mattei had flown the Piper up to Xieng Khouang as usual. He had had great difficulty in collecting two tons of opium, even with the help of the *chau-muong*, a customer and partner of Si Mong's. The Meos of Phay Tong refused to play any longer and, had it not been for Picarle, he would have come back empty-handed.

He had ferried the load back to Vientiane in three journeys. The raw opium, wrapped in banana leaves, had been packed in some zinc-lined wooden tea-chests.

Mattei had helped Nutcracker to load the cases onto the Junkers. Trembling in every strut, the three-engined plane had flown off, as it did twice a month after the poppy harvest.

Nutcracker had taken the usual route, outside all the air corridors, and landed on a small aerodrome twenty-five miles from the Thai capital. A truck, escorted by a police jeep, was due to come to fetch the consignment of "tea". Nutcracker would get five hundred dollars, which would enable him to live quite pleasantly until his next trip. He would fly back to Vientiane the same day and by the same route.

In exchange, and under cover of some technical aid or other, Aprasith would send his nephew money, arms, rice, information and some experts in intelligence, torture and assassination who were worth any the Viets could produce.

To reassure the Thais, who were alarmed by the discomfiture of the South-Vietnamese, the Americans had just given them a splendid radar which had been set up on the other side of the Mekong at Nakom-Phanom. The inauguration took place that very day, in the presence of the king, who had brought along all his Japanese cameras; the queen, who was extremely pretty; the ministers, who had no power whatsoever; the generals, who had far too much; the ambassadors, who clucked away among them selves like a lot of old women; and the journalists, who were bored stiff. There were fanfares and speeches, followed by the American and Thai national anthems. The king cut the ribbon. An American colonel suggested giving a demonstration and switched on the radar. To everyone's stupefaction, an unknown aircraft appeared on the screen, flying outside all the air corridors. Orders were given to the jet fighters to take off, as though that old crate droning along at ninety miles an hour might have been carrying the atomic bomb. Marshal Aprasith came to his senses too late. He had forgotten this was the day for the delivery of the "tea". Escorted by half a dozen Sabres, a very bewildered Nut-cracker landed on the airfield next to the radar. Some troops rushed up to open the cases and found the opium. The journalists made a dash for the telephones, the American officers slapped one another on the back, the king looked flabbergasted, the ministers laughed up their sleeves. Aprasith was furious. But he could only congratulate the Yanks on the exceptional quality of their radar. The opium was seized and placed under seal. Nut-cracker was hauled off in handcuffs to Police Headquarters and put in a cell. The French Ambassador asked Vientiane for instructions.

"Let them work it out themselves," said Pinsolle, who was fully aware of this contraband traffic.

Two hours later Police Headquarters issued a communiqué

stating that the cargo of the unknown aircraft was indeed tea, intended for a friendly neighbouring country. The cases had been seized all the same, pending an official enquiry. But the plane and its pilot had been allowed to leave.

Mattei had warned Nutcracker to keep his trap shut. But it was too late. The whole of South-East Asia knew all about his misadventure. With a limp cigar clenched between his teeth, Nutcracker had held a press conference at the Constellation bar:

"Fancy those bloody Yanks doing that to me, an honest commercial pilot! A radar as big as a block of flats, jets buzzing all round me at five hundred miles an hour and firing short bursts just in front or just behind me, an absolute swarm of hornets round my old crate, and my left-hand engine spluttering as usual. As soon as I land, a gun is stuck in my back. Then those maniacs start opening the cases. 'It's tea,' I bellowed. But they don't understand. A young flatfoot who fancies himself as a sheriff sniffs a packet and screams, 'Opium!'. Then he snaps the handcuffs on me. Well, there's yet another lad who'll end up somewhere near the Malay Peninsula with nothing to do but control the traffic of the wild duck.

"I let him have his way. A higher-ranking officer then whisks me off before the journalists have time to take any pictures. At the police station they're quick on the uptake. I'm released and I get my Junkers back. I delivered the goods all the same. So why wasn't I paid for it this time? Can anyone tell me that?"

He was paid that very evening.

Nutcracker had drunk a dozen brandy-and-sodas and driven home in a bicycle-rickshaw. A man was waiting for him, sitting in the old armchair out on the verandah. As Nutcracker came in, he rose to his feet, brought out a pistol equipped with a silencer and fired two shots into the pilot's head. After making sure he was dead, he sauntered out to the jeep that was waiting for him.

Next day's coup d'état had put this incident out of everyone's mind. The consul had crossed off one of the names on his list of French residents and Mattei had discreetly set about giving Marcel Desnoyers a decent burial. There had been no question of an inquest or autopsy.

Father Maurel had blessed the corpse and taken it to the European cemetery where, amidst the coarse grass, the soldiers rotted away under wooden crosses, the administrators and businessmen under stone slabs cracked and pitted by the rain.

Mattei had waited, making no changes in his daily routine. Then the warning had arrived—by hand-grenade.

He had thought of flying off in the Piper and landing somewhere near Picarle's Meos. The Americans might have engaged him to instruct and lead their maquis.

The Piper was no longer on the airstrip and the Junkers was burning itself out at the end of the runway. An accident . . . a mechanic had carelessly chucked away a cigarette stub. A Coordination sentry was on guard outside the lean-to which served as the Air Transport office. Mattei had gone round to the Air France agency to get his ticket for Bangkok. A seat was already reserved in his name.

A heavy downpour slashed at the giant flamboyants in the garden, plucking and scattering the scarlet flowers. The atmosphere was stifling. Mattei got up and went down to the opium den.

Flore, Cléach's mistress, lay on a bunk smoking. Her Chinese skirt was hitched up, revealing her long legs. Mattei lay down opposite her. On two or three occasions he had slept with the Eurasian girl, before she had gone off to live with Gibelin. She reminded him of that other half-caste woman he had known in Hanoi. The latter had cost him his career; she had even urged him to swindle Duffauly and Sébastiani out of a million piastres.

Flore was just as mercenary and heartless, but less intelligent and less dangerous because she smoked and because opium encourages indifference.

Everyone said that Gibelin had put Flore onto it, in order to keep her with him. He was quite capable of it.

Before he left Saigon, a friend had given Mattei the following advice:

"In Laos there's a fellow you'd better not rub up the wrong way. His name is Gibelin. He's mad; he has a gang, the worst sort of all, consisting of his old resistance pals. He can do as he likes up there; no matter what he does, they'll never let him down. If he's running a racket, keep out of it. If he has a girl, don't go anywhere near her. Take it easy and wait. Some day or other the racket will flop and the girl will walk out on him. Then you can help yourself."

Yet Gibelin had been found in the Mekong with his wrists and ankles tied together with wire. Mattei had not taken up with Flore again, because he admired courage and felt that Gibelin, though mad, was courageous. He had never done any deals with him, because Gibelin talked too much.

"How are you?" Flore asked Mattei.

"Fine."

"Don't you ever get bored?"

"Never."

"How do you manage it? Here, come and lie down next to me."

"Don't you think it's too hot as it is?"

"Have a pipe. You won't feel the heat any more."

"No."

Flore hitched her skirt higher and, in the manner of a little Rue Catinat tart, said:

"You'll give me a nice little present, boss?"

Then she burst out laughing.

He went off, because he desired the girl.

"Good-night."

But he no longer knew where to go.

Before becoming a consul, Pierre Prestelot, an ex-administrator in the French Colonial Service, had worked as private secretary to the last governors and high-commissioners of Black Africa.

A few days before his arrival in Vientiane, he ran into Ricq in a corridor in the embassy. He had introduced himself, overflowing with cordiality:

"I'm Prestelot, the new French Consul. Monsieur Ricq, I presume . . . of the French School of Far-Eastern Studies. I was at the French Institute of Black Africa. You're at home in Asia, I'm in exile."

"Why did you leave Africa?" Ricq had asked.

"Africa didn't want me any longer! Every time I was appointed to a post, it was merely to pack my bags, leave the premises, hand over the keys and receive the first insults. Those newly created gentlemen, the Negro president-kings of our Africa, immediately found the residences of the former governors were not grand enough for them. They asked me to summon architects from Paris to draw up plans for their future palaces. They demanded new cars, preferably Mercedeses and Chryslers. French models weren't good enough. On the other hand, they didn't mind if the champagne came from France. They also wanted a national anthem and a flag. I did what I could to satisfy their demands. I have three national anthems and two flags to my credit. I liked my black kings. Unfortunately, they always asked me to move elsewhere. Yet I couldn't have been more punctilious about addressing them as 'Your Majesty, your Excellency, etc.'

"I embarrassed them; I only realised this afterwards. I had seen them arrive with their shabby suits, their down-at-heel shoes, their briefcases containing nothing but old newspapers. I didn't care, but they couldn't forget it. And that's why your humble servant Pierre Prestelot is embarking at the age of thirty-six on a consular career in the Far East in which he has never before set foot."

Pierre Prestelot's tie was askew, the pockets of his suit sagged, and he was shod in espadrilles. Within a few months his tie was impeccably knotted, his shirts were as white as snow, and elegant tropical suits had replaced his old drill trousers and shapeless jackets. The dressier he became, the further did Prestelot withdraw from Ricq.

He soon found himself at home among the diplomats in this rarified but aseptic air-bubble, in the centre of this magic circle in which even imbeciles have every privilege. He was to be seen at every cocktail party, every reception, but never set foot outside Vientiane. On several occasions the date of his marriage to a pretty Camp Kennedy secretary had been announced.

Pinsolle would explain, half in fun, half in anger:

"I asked for Prestelot because I'd been told he was intelligent and hadn't been to the Sciences Politiques or the Ecole d'Administration. He was already riddled with snobbery at birth."

The consul entertained him, however, with all the gossip he

reported on the foreign and diplomatic colony. Since he did his job competently, Pinsolle had put up with him.

Cléach, on the other hand, loathed Prestelot, who reciprocated the feeling. Cléach always behaved like a lout in front of the consul, who would then become exaggeratedly refined, each of them trying to think of some dirty trick to play on the other.

"I might have a go at that American girl of his," Cléach used to say to himself.

"I might," Prestelot reflected, "force Cléach to change the money he receives through the embassy at the official rate, which would reduce his salary by half."

For the last two days the whole foreign and diplomatic colony had their eyes rivetted on one single person. That "insignificant little Ricq" had suddenly turned out to be a master spy. That grubby little scholar was a romantic figure, his life was fraught with mystery and danger.

Hidden meanings were attributed to his tritest remarks, reasons of higher policy to his liaison with a Laotian *phousao*. When it was known that Prestelot had permission to visit him in prison, he had been asked to four different cocktail-parties straight away. Life was so boring in the embassies and legations of Vientiane during the rainy season.

In the car in which he was being driven to Xien Nip Camp, Prestelot pondered on the problems entailed by this interview. How should he address Ricq? As 'Colonel'? As 'Monsieur le Chef de Mission Détaché par la Présidence du Conseil'? He couldn't very well call him 'my dear fellow', a regulation form of address for a diplomat confronted with a dim little ethnologist. It would be out of order, maybe even dangerous.

Was it Ricq who kept an eye on the embassy staff and reported to Paris on their activities?

How typical of the Fifth Republic to have a discreet informer in the background! The régime was suffering from spy mania.

The consul was asked to wait first at the guard post, then in a staff office and finally he was taken to the prison. To be on the safe side, Prestelot had brought a bottle of whisky, some cigarettes and chocolate with him in his briefcase. Ricq was such an unassuming character that he didn't even know what his tastes were.

Ricq was sitting at a little table, diligently writing in his exercise book.

After feeding on so many memories during the night, the fever had lifted of its own accord in the morning, leaving him exhausted but clear-headed. Clean-shaven, he looked no more than forty, although he was six or seven years older. Prestelot had noticed this in the consulate files.

A Coordination captain was sitting on the bed. Ricq asked him to leave and the captain went out without a word of protest. The consul was amazed. He had prepared a speech full of double meaning, being certain that a guard would be present during their meeting.

Ricq got up and shook hands:

"Don't worry, Monsieur le Consul, there's no microphone concealed in the walls. The Laotians haven't reached that stage yet. They're so artless, so careless and so unmechanically-minded, they would probably have asked me to help them install it. Captain Khammay who is responsible for safeguarding me is . . . an old acquaintance."

"He called me 'Monsieur le Consul', so I must address him as 'Colonel'," Prestelot reflected as he brought the whisky, cigarettes and chocolate out of his briefcase and looked round for somewhere to sit.

"On the bed," Ricq suggested.

"Colonel," the consul began . . .

"Please, my dear fellow. You've always called me Ricq before. Aren't we almost colleagues?"

"His Excellency Monsieur Pinsolle, who seems to be taking a great interest in you, sends you his . . . best regards. At the moment he's at Luang-Prabang, with the king."

Ricq whistled through his teeth in wonder:

"Sends me his kind regards . . . Do you read Saint-Simon in your spare time? Have you abandoned Islam and its brotherhoods, André Matswa, the Bakongos and Laris, Poto-Poto and the 'black Brazzavilles'?"

The consul tried to remember:

"I've never talked to him about the Laris or the Bakongos . . . Matswa, yes, but without mentioning his Christian name. Where has he got all this information? He's had my file in his hands. What's more, he's making fun of me."

"What's happening?" Ricq enquired.

"Captain Chanda still hasn't got to the Plain of Jars, where the Communists are advancing without even having to fire a shot. It has been decided to evacuate Captain Meynadier and the six other French advisers who are still at the Neutralist command post. An International Commission plane will take off tomorrow at dawn. It will try to land on the airstrip and bring them back."

"Where's Chanda?"

"Not very far off, they say, up in the mountains overlooking the plateau with one of Colonel Cosgrove's maquis."

"Meynadier and his men must join Chanda straight away. Tell Captain Lalo to get a message off to him immediately. Monsieur Pinsolle will agree."

"Yes, but what about the Military Mission? General Molliergues is jealous of his prerogatives. Officially, Meynadier and his team come under him. I can't get in touch with Monsieur Pinsolle. He won't be back till this afternoon."

The consul was discovering a new Ricq; a short while ago he had been ironical, now he was self-assured. He sat up more stiffly on the edge of the bed.

Ricq had taken two American cigarettes and crumbled them up to fill his pipe. Then, looking Prestelot straight in the eye, he said:

"I shall have to get out of here very quickly, by official means or otherwise."

"I think . . ."

"Remind Prince Sisang of a promise he made me."

"It's thought that the best you can hope for is expulsion."

"Then let them get a move on. From Bangkok I could always join Chanda before Colonel Cosgrove has him completely entangled in his net.

"If you're the least bit interested in this country, my dear Consul, you ought to know that we must at all costs prevent its being split into two camps: the right wing and the Communists.

If that happened there would be no further reason for Laos not to become another South-Vietnam. Laos is not cut out for war. You don't put on a tragedy in a music-hall. General de Gaulle's policy would be jeopardized straight away throughout South-East Asia."

Prestelot grew progressively more reassured as the danger revealed its true face and his apprehensions were confirmed.

Ricq was indeed an Elysée man. It was obvious. A F.F.I. veteran, with all that this implies. Just as well he had not thrown in his lot with that madman Meynadier who was said to be O.A.S.

"I'll deliver the message."

"I'd also like a closer watch to be kept on my fiancée, Mademoiselle Ven. If you see Cléach, please thank him for all he's done for her and for me. I don't think you like Cléach, do you, Monsieur le Consul? You're wrong. When I saw you land at Vientiane in the same sort of clothes as Cléach and I wear, I thought we could all three become friends."

"Is there anything you need?" Prestelot stiffly enquired.

All these kind regards were beginning to irritate him and he did not take kindly to advice or reproof.

"Money, for instance?"

"It's not money that'll get me out of here. There's been too much fuss made about my arrest. I'd like you to bring me a red leather photograph-frame, which you'll find in my house. On one side there's a reproduction of a drawing: my brother tied to the execution post. On the other, Antoine Gibelin in his bush hat: executed by the Coordination. Ask Ven for it. Could you also deliver a personal message to Colonel Cosgrove? Tell him it's now too late for him to do what I was trying to do with Chanda. He can only fail . . . as I have."

"An article about you has appeared in the *New York Times*. It mentions your real activities. 'Colonel Ricq, General de Gaulle's man in South-East Asia, has just been arrested in Laos . . .' I'm quoting from memory."

"I'm blown, and dear old Cos is finishing me off."

Prestelot was fascinated; he was only discovering the role and the importance of this agent on the day he was defeated, that's to say uncovered.

"You're always talking about gambling, Ricq. Does that mean you regard politics merely as a big poker game between adversaries abiding by the same rules?"

Ricq raised his voice:

"There aren't any rules. I've lost everything. So has Cos. The winners are to be found among the most tenacious, the most cruel, the most merciless, those who tell the most lies and pursue the most long-term policies, those who attack and those who defend themselves. The Communists have got the better of us. Laos was merely an abscess on the anchorage, while they were attacking elsewhere. My error, and Cos's, was not to have realized this. We were obsessed by the rumbling of the bronze drums. We didn't find the weapons we should have used against them. Captain Meynadier wanted us to adopt the same methods. He's wrong. Yet he's a good lad."

"When he drinks . . .

Ricq shrugged his shoulders:

"He sometimes has a good excuse for doing so. I believe he once called you a 'poor wretch'. He had heard you had served in Algeria in the same parachute regiment. He had had a lot of worry that evening, mostly through my fault. And I wasn't there to help him. Instead of having a drink with him, as he asked, because he thought you were a comrade, you invited him to dinner, as Saint Simon would say . . . but for the following week. What he failed to find in you he found in Cléach, that antimilitarist who used to sign petitions against the war in Algeria. Cléach and Meynadier once came to blows in the Constellation but they went home together tight as ticks. Now, whenever Meynadier comes to Vientiane, he stays at Cléach's. When Cléach's broke, he shares his pay with him. But Meynadier doesn't sleep with Flore, who would ask for nothing better. He must be very unhappy today. He, too, is seeing all he has built up being destroyed."

Ricq suddenly calmed down:

"I'm sorry about meddling in what doesn't concern me. I've had an attack of fever. I'm being left in the lurch and abandoned. We would have made a good team with Meynadier in the Plain of Jars, both of us watching Chanda's soldiers taking to their heels and our last illusions collapsing."

Sweating, smelling like a billy-goat, Prestelot got up, so red in the face that his freckles could no longer be seen. He was ready to leap into a plane and go off to fight side by side with Meynadier in the ranks of the Neutralist army, a few thousand men whose only remaining leaders were a French captain, a lieutenant and four paratroop N.C.O.s.

At five o'clock in the afternoon the plane bringing the pilgrims back from Luang-Prabang landed in pouring rain on the Vattay airstrip. In the little lobby of the airport a minister (though no one knew any longer what his ministerial functions were) read out a sybilline statement to the journalists.

It transpired that everything was going both as well and as badly as possible in the Kingdom of the Million Elephants. Prince Sisang and General Si Mong appeared to have made up their quarrel. There had been no *putsch* on 18 July. Prince Sisang was still President, and the General remained Vice-President, War Minister and Minister of the Interior.

On the other hand, the Communist threat was increasing hour by hour. The country was in danger and Laos intended appealing to the United Nations.

Cléach rushed up to Pinsolle:

"What's happening?" he asked him.

"Everything's turning out for the best, of course, but everything's going badly as usual. I'm in a hurry, my dear fellow. Come and see me this evening."

Pinsolle leapt into his car. An hour later, after changing his clothes, he summoned Prestelot.

"Come on, old boy, get it off your chest. How did Ricq strike you?"

"To tell you the truth, rather excited, sir."

"Have another glass of this excellent brandy which I get direct from Charentes. It will help you explain yourself better. Excited? I've never seen Ricq excited."

"He'd just had an attack of fever. By way of comfort, I brought him nothing but bad news; the collapse of his Neutralist friends, the withdrawal of our mission attached to them.

"He asked me to deliver a message to the Plain of Jars ordering Captain Meynadier and his team to rejoin Chanda at all costs, even if he was with the American maquis. With your permission, of course. But all the same he wanted us to go over the head of General Molliergues. At all events it's too late. I called in at the Military Mission. The Muong Pham command post is off the air."

"I should never have given my permission, for two reasons. It's no good attempting the impossible: the American special services controlling those maquis would never have allowed us to force their hand. Furthermore, it's pointless to fall out with men whom we are liable to need one day. Why annoy that worthy general, who's as touchy as he is stubborn? He regards everything Ricq does, the way he lives, what he says and thinks, as tantamount to treason. General Molliergues is only happy when surrounded by traitors. To satisfy his mania, he invents them for himself. I think this ugly business will soon be settled to everyone's satisfaction."

Prestelot was amazed.

"What can this old stringbean be concocting now?" he said to himself. "They're already saying that in Luang-Prabang, while the king was nibbling his lettuce, the situation was reversed several times thanks to him."

"Are you wool-gathering?" Pinsolle asked him. "What else?"

"Ricq wanted to rejoin Chanda by way of Thailand after being expelled, or if needs be, escaping from prison."

"Sheer childishness!"

"Even at Xien Nip he still has friends. The captain guarding him is one of them."

"Ricq has no need to escape. This evening he'll be released. He won't even be expelled. He's too indispensable,"

Prestelot could not resist asking:

"Indispensable for what?"

"In order to destroy Chanda and his myth, my dear fellow."

"Everyone now says, sir, that it was Ricq who made Chanda what he is, that he's both his director of conscience . . . and also his cousin by alliance since that girl he lives with is the niece of the father of our busy little captain. Ricq seemed obsessed by the question of friendship. He kept harping on this sentiment, with an obstinacy that I'd call born of despair. I'm sorry, this is only my personal impression of course . . . but I don't see him betraying a friend. In fact, he would even sacrifice himself for him."

"Ricq is an agent, my dear fellow, a senior one perhaps, and with great responsibilities, but all the same he's just an agent. An agent carries out the orders he's given. He serves his country and isn't allowed to have personal sentiments. Ricq is like that. Twenty years of this job hardens a man, even if he has kept his choirboy looks. It's quite normal he should have a momentary twinge of conscience. But you'll see, it'll soon be over."

"Are you sure, sir? He also asked me to deliver a message to Colonel Cosgrove; he alluded vaguely to the noise of the bronze drums. The rambling remarks of a tired man."

"He'll get over it. Are you going to the Indians' cocktail-party? The Indians always seem to be in mourning for some recently lost illusion. I find them depressing and sententious. And they've just lost Nehru, the man behind the disastrous policy of co-existence with China. It's too much for me. Give my regards to that pretty American girl with whom you're seen more and more frequently. What's her name, now?"

"Marion Sullivan. I intended introducing her to you officially in a few days as my fiancée. We'd like to get married on 8 August . . ."

"Congratulations. I've been married twice. Bring her along to dinner one of these days. I'll open one of my tins of duck liver. I hope Marion doesn't drink Coca-Cola or milk with partridge or patés?"

"I don't think so."

"You'd better look out. Women come out with plenty of surprises once they've got the ring on their finger. Before getting engaged to her for keeps, get to know her tastes. My first wife used to drink tea at meals and my second only liked boiled mutton. Love can't withstand that sort of thing. Good-night, my dear Consul. And don't repeat what I've told you about Chanda."

Prestelot thought he would find another opportunity to ask the ambassador to be his witness. He had just enough time to change before going to fetch Marion at Camp Kennedy. She did not like being kept waiting.

Marion often used to talk about the attentions that were a woman's due but never about a woman's duties. But she was pretty and lively and showed decision, determination and efficiency in everything. She also had fits of extremely naive emotion and a temperament that only asked to be aroused.

She would make an excellent wife for a consul and future ambassador.

When he saw her again, looking radiant, he no longer had the slightest wish to "botch" his career by running off and playing soldiers with Meynadier. When she asked after Ricq, he merely replied:

"He's a little tired."

Xavier Pinsolle settled down in an armchair, with his feet on a stool and a tray of drinks within reach. He lit a cigar with infinite care, deriving a gluttonous pleasure from prolonging the wait for that divine pleasure, the first puff of a well prepared Havana.

He was disturbed by what Prestelot had told him. Just when he had managed to restore the situation, was Ricq going to slip between his fingers?

Under the mocking eye of the king, Prince Sisang and General Si Mong had publicly made up their quarrel in face of the Communist menace, and secretly come to an agreement to combat another menace—the menace with which the American secret services were burdening Laos.

Pinsolle had been the instigator of that second agreement.

The Laotian government was anxious about Colonel Cosgrove's activity. The Meo maquis had slipped entirely out of the control of the Vientiane government now that they were being supplied direct from Thailand. Their leader, Phay Tong, had even opened a sort of embassy in Bangkok.

The Meos might some day demand their independence. If every minority behaved like them, the country would be split up into twenty states which would no longer be adjacent but superimposed. It would even be the first time in history that such an aberration had ever been seen: a state in the form of a block of flats. Forty storeys, one storey for every race, and at the very top, on the roof garden, the Meos growing their poppies.

Pinsolle had given the prince and the general a terrifying description of what Laos would be like then. Sisang had realised the danger at once. Si Mong had taken a little longer. National sentiment had never disturbed his sleep. But, for fear of seeing the opium slip out of his hands if the Meos became independent, he had decided yet again to change sides. He had also been impelled by other considerations. The Americans, he knew, did not want to have anything more to do with him. For the same reason, they had had enough of all the would-be generals in Saigon who were scheming to assume power.

Pinsolle had cited Chanda's case. The little captain was the only obstruction to a genuine reconciliation between the two tendencies, the right wing and the Neutralists.

What did he represent today? His best troops had gone over to the Communists with Colonel Thon. The others had disbanded.

Chanda, if the rumour was correct, had just thrown himself into the arms of the American secret services. The C.I.A. was liable to use him to bring together several very diverse elements: Neutralists, minorities, soldiers of fortune. . . . If he managed to control Chanda as directly as he had the Meo maquis, Cosgrove would find himself at the head of a mercenary army inside the country. He might, for example, start raiding North-Vietnam, using Laos as a base. Therefore Chanda had to be annihilated before he became dangerous. The only man who could do this was the man who had created him: Ricq. Screwing up his eyes, the Thai halfcaste had murmured:

"In other words, Your Excellency, since Colonel Cosgrove has picked up Chanda, you're giving us Ricq to destroy him."

He had turned to Sisang:

"What do you think, Your Highness? I could apologise to Monsieur Ricq and, without even telling a lie, lay the blame for his arrest on my subordinates."

Sisang had merely grunted. Since the *putsch* he was no longer in Laos. He seemed pleased all the same that Ricq should be released without his having to make an effort to keep his promise.

Pinsolle had been unable to resist indulging in a bit of leg-pulling that would have delighted Gibelin. When the general asked him how he should approach Ricq, he had advised him to invite him to dinner.

"But he's in prison."

"All the more reason, my dear General."

"He believes I wanted to have him killed."

"Come now, Ricq is much too sensible and knows you far too well to believe you capable of such . . . clumsiness. There has been no *putsch*, we all agree, therefore Ricq has never been to prison. Send him a message at Xien Nip."

"You think so?"

"Absolutely."

But what if Ricq refused? Pinsolle knew it was General Si Mong who had caused the downfall of the Neutralist movement, who had given the orders for Gibelin to be killed and for Ricq to be put out of the way. Si Mong was nothing but a grasping gang leader. His morals, his habits, his cynicism were such that even the Americans were horrified. Might they not go so far as to liquidate Si Mong in order to back Chanda and boost him with dollars?

Morality and politics never went hand in hand. Against the new Asia of the Communists, one could only defend oneself by using, for lack of time, the old Asia. But it was rotten to the core. The Neutralists had tried to assume the best of both sides, the valour of the Communists, the liberty and respect for the individual of the Western world. A synthesis suggested by Ricq, captivating but impossible. Ricq had stayed too long in the same country. He had grown roots here as though it was his real motherland, making friendships and falling into habits of which he would never be able to break himself. It was a great mistake. He should have been replaced earlier. But who would have been prepared to lead this unobtrusive, exhausting, dangerous life? No one knew Laos as well as he did. All on his own, he had achieved such results that France, a secondary power, still retained a leading rôle here. This desperate need to cling to friendship, however, was the sign of a drowning man. Ricq might make a serious mistake, such as following his own heart and indulging for the last time in the romanticism of his youth.

Why was the world run by old men? There was a very good reason. As they grew old, men dried up. The sap trickled out of their hearts and their loins. They thought only of themselves. Their gestures were calculated, they were liable to commit fewer blunders. Generosity, tenderness, loyalty to friends and to the noble and heroic idea of life one conceives at the age of twenty—all these disappeared. Pride alone might destroy great insensitive old men, but never heart. Pride was a disease of their age, like gout or prostatitis.

Pinsolle felt uneasy. He remembered a man under whom he had served for a long time and for whom he still felt affection. But he could not show his feelings without endangering his career. The man had been highly successful without ever ceasing to be a student. He had been one of the leaders of the Resistance, a minister and then Prime Minister, but without ever having been able entirely to suppress the affectionate, unruly, mischievous child he had been, the needy student, the indigent professor writing his articles and correcting the proofs at a café table.

He had had his qualms of conscience, but only when everything had been lost, when the cause of Algeria had become indefensible . . . because one cannot run counter to certain currents of history, because those who wanted to defend Algeria had mismanaged it or were thinking of other things. . . .

Reverting to the age of twenty, he had committed the blunders a mature man ought to have avoided. He was to be seen embarking, in despair, on a pointless crusade that was lost in advance.

At the age of sixty he had departed for a long and painful exile. His behaviour had appeared so idiotic to his friends that they had not dared to defend him, as they ought to have done, by explaining what was mad but also what was noble in his behaviour.

Pinsolle had also kept silent. He had stifled a few pangs by doubling his intake of alcohol. Was Ricq going to embark on an equally extravagant adventure, carried away by his better nature? Pinsolle felt he might. He got up and drafted the telegram which could still save him: "Request immediate recall of Lieutenant-

Colonel Ricq, even if he is released, even if he is allowed by the Laotian government to resume his former activities."

The ambassador thought of his cosy apartment on the Seine embankment, the thick carpets, the ancient ornaments on which no customs duty had ever been paid, the cellar full of wine and brandy, the countless books, the first editions, and Julie, his old governess, who looked after it with such care. In his mind's eye he was back there, looking at the Seine flowing past from his armchair by the window. It was autumn. The crowds rustled in the streets like the last red and golden leaves on the trees. The light at five o'clock in the afternoon assumed a quality that was unique in the world, the colour of antiques and old bindings.

A scratch at the door. Julie brought him in the *Monde* and the strong tea he liked, a tea grown on the high plateaux of India, with blood-red glints in it.

"I'll lend Ricq my apartment," he decided, "for as long as it takes him to get Laos out of his system through the charm and fascination of Paris . . . until he finds another appointment, as military attaché in a big embassy. He's now cut out to hold an official position with an iron collar round his neck which will force him to stand up straight. He'll be subjected to inept rites that will dry up his sap. If I come to Paris, I'll stay at an hotel. With a heavy heart, I'll walk past my windows but without ever going upstairs."

Pinsolle was too clear-headed not to know that he was not making this sacrifice for Ricq, but for someone else—the exile. It was by way of reparation . . . for he had become adult and incapable of folly. Adults still make sacrifices but they never sacrifice themselves.

Pinsolle suffered from his solitude like a sick person who has no one to call to his bedside except a nurse paid by the week.

Who in Vientiane could become his friend? Pierre Prestelot? His teeth had grown too quickly. The type of nurse whose reward is a good report. His councillor, Saint-Urcize? Washed out, devoid of imagination and impulse, a man of empty gestures . . . Cléach? But the journalist wouldn't understand. He would despise him from the height of his self-sufficient youthfulness. Who then?

There was only Ricq, half way between Cléach and himself, Ricq whom, all sentiment apart, he had to sacrifice to this mixture of improvisation, prevarication, lies and vague interests which constituted a policy.

Without Ricq, all his plans went down the drain. Laos might be dragged into the war in Vietnam and this time become a real battlefield. It would be a pity for this country, and also for Pinsolle's career.

The ambassador tore up his telegram. Ricq would remain in Laos for as long as it took to put an end to Captain Chanda and Colonel Cosgrove.

At six o'clock in the evening a soldier brought Ricq, in his prison, an invitation to dinner. The card, engraved with the Laos coat-of-arms—the double head of a white elephant—was inscribed on one side in French, on the other in Laotian:

"General Si Mong, Vice-President, Minister of National Defence and Minister of the Interior, requests the pleasure of the company of Monsieur François Ricq at a dinner which will be given in his residence on 20 July 1964 at 9 p.m. Lounge suit."

Ricq turned the card over again and again in amazement, trying to make out what this change in Si Mong's attitude and this vulgar joke could mean. Lounge suit indeed! Why not a dinner jacket?

Was the general going to say to him, as he had to Sisang: "It's a mistake. The officers who arrested you have been punished. How could you ever have thought I wanted to have you killed? What an idea! A regrettable move on the part of one of my subordinates. I just wanted to make sure you were safe. Let's have a drink, let's have dinner together . . . and talk of the good old days."

At eight o'clock Khammay came to fetch Ricq.

"You see, everything's all right," he said delightedly. "*Bo penh nhang*. After dinner you'll go home, you'll find your *phousao* and enjoy yourself with her, *bo penh nhang*. Prince Sisang held a press conference at the aerodrome to say that all's well now. The French soldiers who were at the Plain of Jars are coming back before they have their throats slit. *Bo penh nhang*."

"What about Chanda?"

"*Bo penh nhang* for him as well. He's with the Americans. He's eating corned beef and sausages. He'll be given lots of dollars."

"Who'll be at this dinner?"

"You'll be alone with the general."

"No, I shan't be alone. There'll also be Pamphone and Gibelin whom Si Mong arranged to be killed, and all the others who were with us and who died fighting against the Japs and the Viets: Father Séraire, hanged; Sergeant Crette, disembowelled with bayonets; and Sanakhom, whose head was carried around in the streets of Vientiane.

"At that time Si Mong was giving information to the Japanese; then he worked for the Viets, after that with us, and now with the Americans . . . Always for money. I would never be able to dine alone with him. There would also be my brother sitting beside me—my brother whom the Japanese of Europe, the Germans, shot after torturing him."

"Did he talk?" Khammay enquired with the interest a technician always shows in such matters.

"No," said Ricq, blushing.

"Then your Germans weren't up to much. Why do you carry all those dead men around with you? The dead keep to themselves and the living shift for themselves. The dead have departed to the village where the cock never crows, but we others are woken by the cock every morning. Are you putting your shoes on?"

"What if I went barefoot? We were barefoot when Antoine Gibelin and I slipped into Si Mong's house through the window and dragged him out on the end of a rope."

"You were barefoot, but you had carbines and grenades. You no longer have a carbine and Gibelin's in his village for keeps."

Regretfully, Ricq tied his shoe laces. He felt extremely tired and was unable to find a refuge in fever. After a final glance round what had been his prison for three days, he followed Khammay outside. In the courtyard he took a deep breath, but the air also smelt of mildew. Khammay made him get into the back of a jeep. On the next seat sat an armed guard, and the driver carried a pistol. So he was not yet free. The car drove through Vientiane. By bending down, Ricq was able to see the brightly-lit shops, the even brighter lights of the Constellation, some bonzes ambling along under their umbrellas, a couple of women laughing and, in the distance, the unfinished concrete monument that General Si Mong had had erected to his glory.

This monument had also brought him in a great deal of money. Every merchant in the town must have coughed up, and Si Mong had pocketed almost the whole sum.

The jeep drew up on a patch of gravel. An armoured car escort was on guard. Some soldiers sat leaning against the wheels of the vehicles, playing cards by the light of some little oil lamps they had made for themselves. Flanked by Khammay and the armed escort, Ricq climbed the steps to the front door. He was shown into a long narrow room furnished in the worst possible Chinese taste: low tables with corkscrew legs, chunky vases topped by red silk lamp-shades shaped like pagodas, coloured prints of buxom women with great bovine eyes.

Ricq collapsed into an armchair. The soldier sat down opposite him, his submachine-gun on his knees, and Khammay slipped behind a bar carved from an enormous piece of teak. Only Gibelin could have discovered a tree like that. The wood must have come from one of his timber yards. They had been looted after his death.

The captain gleefully examined the bottles cluttering the bar, picking them up and reading out the labels: Haig, Old Forester . . .

"What would you like? Now that the Coordination controls the sale of alcohol, one can at last get a drink at the general's. Or maybe you'd rather have tea?"

"Not tonight. Whisky, neat and without ice. Whisky helps to send the dead back to their village."

Si Mong kept them waiting. He was meanwhile receiving the head of the Sureté, Oukharon.

"How's Soumboun?" he enquired.

Oukharon assumed a satisfied air:

"He's in poor shape, very poor shape indeed."

"And Mattei?"

"He's taken his ticket for Bangkok, but no further. He wants to stay there."

"Tell Bangkok to deal with him. What about Khammay?"

"Khammay has all his wits about him, sir. He's well liked at the Coordination."

"I must make some gesture to prove my good-will to those stupid Americans. Khammay will serve the purpose perfectly. He's become the symbol of the extortionate officer. I've known others who have stolen larger sums, but none of them has ever had the silly idea of building himself a swimming-pool. At the same time I'll be pleasing Sisang.

"Besides, he's played me one or two tricks for which I fully intend to make him pay; he took part in a *putsch* without notifying me and refused to carry out one of my orders. This *putsch* has been useful to me and if that order had been carried out I should have been in trouble, but he needn't know this."

"If we arrest Khammay, he'll talk."

"To whom? To you, who'll interrogate him; to his judges, to whom I'll promise his mortal remains. The swimming-pool will be nationalised . . . for the students."

"When the fruit's ripe, sir, I'll shake the tree. We're going to defend virtue and legality by arresting Khammay. Why not?"

Oukharon withdrew to make place for Li Jon, the Chinese who dealt with the businesses controlled by Si Mong: rice, gold and opium. He collected the taxes on pig-slaughtering as well as on the import of taxi-girls and spirits, on the opium dens and brothels, the fresh vegetables sold in the market and the luxury groceries imported from France for the foreigners.

Li Jon opened a big ledger and began to read. The taxes were coming in with difficulty; the merchants needed a lot of persuading. Once again, some examples would have to be made. Si Mong did not bat an eyelid. Li Jon went back to the Banque Nationale du Commerce to replace the ledger in a safe. The bank also belonged to Si Mong.

Then the general went and listened behind a partition to what Khammay and Ricq were saying.

"Why did you stop Soumboun killing me?" Ricq asked.

Khammay shrugged his shoulders and his sly face broke into a grin:

"You were a good boss during the war. You've never forgotten those who fought with you. You got me into the police. I knew you wouldn't stay in prison very long. Soumboun was incapable of thinking things out and foreseeing who tomorrow would be rich or poor, powerful or weak. He only believed in whatever stared him in the face. You know what has happened to him? He was stabbed during the night. He's in hospital. He's in very poor shape.

"A prince is always a prince, even when he's put in prison. Only an utter madman would strike him."

"But then only an utter madman would arrest him, Khammay."

Khammay turned round and sprang to his feet. The general had just come in, tussore trousers stretched tight over his little paunch, pearls by way of cuff-links, a hand-painted tie on his white silk shirt, and a fan in his hand.

He greeted Ricq in the Laotian manner, pressing the palms of his hands together. His wide grin revealed two gold teeth.

The general dismissed Khammay and the soldier with a wave of his fan, then apologized to Ricq:

"There are people who wish me harm: I always have to have protection. Yet all I desire is the welfare of the Laotian people."

With his glass of whisky resting on his paunch, Si Mong appeared to be working out in his mind how to bring about the welfare of the Laotian people. "A people," he had said one day at a dinner in Bangkok, "who must be kept firmly in hand, because they are born disobedient, who must be forced to fight, because they are not courageous, to work because they are idle, to respect their leaders because they are not respectful."

"You don't like me, Monsieur Ricq. You go around saying I'm a racketeer, that I'm prepared to sell out to the highest bidder and that I never keep my word."

Ricq was taken aback by the abruptness of the onslaught. Usually Si Mong preferred lengthy circumlocutions punctuated by an occasional acid remark. He had a curious adenoidal voice —a voice with a faulty register, an elocution teacher would have said. It was throaty and rose to a squeak when it cracked.

"We've known each other for twenty years, Monsieur Ricq. You've always tried to find a bad side to my actions. You've never asked yourself if I mightn't have had good reasons for behaving as I have. You've only listened to what Antoine Gibelin told you, because he was your friend. Gibelin wasn't anyone's friend . . ."

"I don't believe you."

"Gibelin hated people who raised themselves above the rest through their own intelligence, courage and industry. In France you call that sort of person an anarchist. Gibelin wanted to go on living in a country where no law existed because he couldn't put up with any law."

"He had his own attitude to life. It may have shocked some people but no one could accuse him of trying to impose it on others."

"Gibelin hated law and order whereas I, Si Mong, a former civil servant on the colonial strength, a French officer, a former *chau-muong* of Paksane and *uopalath* of Muong Kadouk, have always served law and order. I followed Pétain and Admiral Decoux because they were the men who represented law and order, wisdom and authority. I wasn't the only one. All three of our princes were with me in the Marshal's cadet corps and training camps. One of them later became a Communist and the other two fought against the Communists. It was the future Communist, Sammay, who was the most fervent Pétainist of the three. We used to sing: "Marshal, we're prepared . . ."

He started humming the Vichy anthem but could not remember the tune properly.

"Stripped to the waist, in shorts and sandals, mixing freely with our white comrades, we saluted the two flags, French and Laotian. It was the first time they had floated together. We had a sense of discipline and respect. 'Work, Family, Country'. That was also the motto of Confucius. France was adopting the same moral precepts as we Asiatics.

"Gibelin was furious because he hated all moral precepts. He took to the bush with a gang of ragamuffins. Like jackals, they used to prowl round the villages, stealing rice, women and alcohol.

"You came and joined him, dropped by parachute from India. You then set to work with your submachine-guns and high explosive. You said you had come to fight against the Japanese but you accused the loyal civil servants, both French and Laotian, of being traitors."

"I agree about Decoux, we may have made a few mistakes about him. But the Japanese? Neither Gibelin nor I reproached you for having loyally served the French administration, but for having placed yourself in the service of the Kempetai."

"The French weren't strong enough to oppose the Japanese. Those like you who took to the bush caused reprisals against the villages. By appearing to help the Japanese, by deceiving them, I was actually preserving law and order, the peace and security of the population.

"You people were like the Vietnamese Communists. All they thought of was hoisting the red flag, you the tricolor. Where was the Laotian flag? The Japanese were the only ones who tolerated it. The day of independence had arrived and we could not put up with a government which would have been controlled by your gangs. It consisted above all of adventurers, men who had followed you and indulged in your sort of warfare because they had nothing to lose. You flung the notables into prison. You listened only to Pamphone, who gave you a false idea of our country, or to that man you met at Nouei-Phou Lak who wasn't even a Laotian."

"After the Japanese, General, you served the Viets, the Thais, the Americans . . ."

"I've always hated the Viets, even when I pretended to be working for them. It was merely the better to betray them. I gave you proof of this: the list of all their arms stores, all their leaders in Vientiane. If I hadn't thought of betraying them, I wouldn't have drawn up that list. If the Viets had found it on me, they would have killed me. You mentioned Thailand just now. The French Indo-Chinese Federation had fallen apart and Laos could not live on her own.

"What did we have in common with the Cambodians and the

Vietnamese? But the Thais were the same race as ourselves; they spoke more or less the same language. Why not recreate a Thai federation? The Laotians would have kept their autonomy within this federation and we would have been considered a great nation. One of my uncles was actually head of the Thai army. I was in a good position to bring about this union. As for the Americans, we needed them to defend ourselves. You French wouldn't give us anything any longer, but sheltered behind the Geneva Agreements. You had lost the war in Indo-China at Dien Bien Phu.

"But the Americans are dangerous; they're like spoilt children who insist on having their own way. They learn about history and morals from strip-cartoons and Western adventure stories."

"It took you some time to realize that. Why did you have Gibelin killed? He saved your life in 1945; in 1946 he got you back into the administration."

"When my troops recaptured Vientiane, some officers saw Gibelin directing the mortar fire against them and his trucks bringing in machine-gun ammunition from the bush. He was getting it from the Viets.

"In spite of Prince Sisang's influence, Chanda meant disorder in the streets, demonstrations, Communist agents creeping in everywhere. There was no longer any discipline in the army. Chanda, a mere captain, gave orders to the colonels, the generals and even the ministers; it was he who received the ambassadors. A band of paratroopers held the reins of government. This could please no one but Gibelin. When he saw that my troops, the regular royal army, were going to drive these hot-heads into the jungle, he fought on their side. When my officers arrested him he was foaming with rage. He insulted them; he even struck one of them. But we were no longer a French colony, Gibelin was no longer king of Vientiane as he had been in 1945. He had been a king for three days, which he spent massacring all his friends. People say he was done to death slowly. I don't know anything about that. When I was notified it was too late. I might perhaps have given orders to kill him, but decently. A former associate . . . who ruined me, moreover. You were also at Vientiane. But you kept quiet and no one bothered you. Under your influence, however, Monsieur Ricq, the French services made a serious mistake in urging Chanda on. They unleashed civil war in Laos."

"What proof do you have that the French were behind Chanda?"

"I had all Gibelin's papers searched to find certain bills, and evidence of French interference. Gibelin never had your sense of security. Don't worry, there was only a black notebook which wasn't of the slightest interest, apart from proving Gibelin was mad. I'll give it to you presently."

"Let's go in and eat. I've arranged a French-style meal for you. I would have liked my friend Colonel Andelot to be with us this evening. We graduated together from the Ecole de Guerre. But there are certain things we have to discuss which couldn't possibly interest him. Tomorrow you'll be able to see Prince Sisang and your ambassador. They will both confirm that this time we're in complete agreement."

As usual Si Mong was combining truth with falsehood. In 1945 already Pamphone used to say of him that he was a complicated character who had at the same time a yearning for power and money, a desire to appear munificent and even a certain love for his country—just as a gangster can love the town he exploits and terrorizes. Pamphone found an excuse for everyone. Ricq was now convinced that human beings, in spite of all the contradictions in their make-up, always followed the dominant trait in their character. As they grew older, they gave into it more and more.

In Si Mong's case it was love of gain, combined with the fear of suddenly finding himself once more as poor and deprived as on the day he was born in the shop at Thakhek, among the bags of dried shrimps and jars of ginger. He did everything to insure against this, but the insurance never seemed adequate.

What agreement could have been reached between Si Mong, the guttersnipe consumed by the fear of "missing something"; Prince Sisang, an indifferent man, a stranger, who only wanted the opportunity to escape from this hornets' nest; and Pinsolle, the crafty, nosey aesthete? The ambassador laboured under no delusions about the Laotians or the value of the policy that France was following in this part of the world without means, without precise instructions. There was his career to consider, of course.

What did Si Mong want exactly?

"To Si Mong, there are always three kinds of truth," Gibelin used to say, "the first for the general public and international opinion, the second for his henchmen, the third for himself. The first appeals to fine principles and fine sentiments, the second is combined with self-interest, the third is limited to a brutal and specific avidity, such as controlling a racket or doing a big deal. Si Mong's only real truth is that of the Chinese shopkeeper."

The table was laid with a white cloth embroidered with flowers. The glasses were pure crystal, but the plates of coarse earthenware. There was wine, but also brandy in the Chinese manner, and bowls for the soup. The servants wore white jackets and uniform trousers; they were barefoot.

"The Americans don't know anything about Asia," Si Mong went on, tucking his napkin into the neck of his shirt. "Even Colonel Cosgrove. Otherwise he would never have done what he has with the Meos."

"The first kind of truth, for the benefit of public opinion," Ricq reflected. "Cos threatens the integrity of the Laotian country by promoting the separatist tendencies of a minority. Now for the second truth, for the benefit of the Coordination bands: the dollars going to the Meos are deducted from the American aid, therefore Si Mong and his men lose them.

"Finally, the third kind of truth: the one that matters to Si Mong personally: his opium monopoly is menaced now that Cos delivers it direct from Xieng Khouang to buyers in Bangkok. Half of his income will disappear. If he has no money, Si Mong will have no more soldiers and will find himself delivered defenceless to his enemies.

"Therefore the nuisance—in this case Colonel Cosgrove—must be eliminated. Si Mong is forgetting one essential factor, however —the rapid deterioration of the situation in South-East Asia: the countryside of Annam and Eastern and Southern Cochin-China in the hands of the Viets, Cambodia veering towards

China, the Americans' lassitude with this war. He's making the same mistake as Cosgrove and myself. He still believes Laos is the centre of the world. The Communists' bronze drums prevent him from hearing the guns thundering at the gates of Saigon."

The general leant back in his chair, a fake Renaissance chair, heavily studded and covered in green velvet for which he must have paid through the nose. The big birds of prey always get diddled by the crows and magpies.

"I believe," he went on, "we'll be able to persuade the American Ambassador to wind up Colonel Cosgrove's mission. It merely needs a few articles in the press showing how the C.I.A. agents are themselves organizing a drug racket and using their aircraft to transport the stuff. One of these aircraft might, for instance, be seized at Bangkok. American public opinion is very hostile to dope-peddlers.

"Yet here we have an American government organization indulging in this very racket. What a loss of face! Taking advantage of the scandal, the French Military Mission might be able to resume its activities and be responsible again for the training of the Laotian army, while we get rid of the instructors and advisers from Washington. You'll see, the Americans will go on giving us money just the same."

"A vicious but crafty beast," Ricq said to himself. "For this sort of dirty work, Si Mong doesn't need me. So what is he after?"

Some leathery old steaks and potatoes fried in pork fat were served.

"Ah, France!" the general sighed. "When I was at the Ecole de Guerre, I used to eat every day in a little restaurant in the Avenue de la Tour-Maubourg. They used to have sausages and lentils and chips that smelt as good as these.

"A little wine? Let's drink to the health of dear old Colonel Cosgrove. Do you know he cheats when he plays poker? No one will be surprised to find him involved in a dirty deal. He'll be replaced by another colonel who won't know the country at all. Getting rid of Cosgrove presents an additional difficulty since yesterday. Do you know that Captain Chanda is now in the Meo maquis with part of his men? The least seasoned ones. Chanda in the hands of the C.I.A. is a feather in Cosgrove's cap all the same, and a personal rebuff for you. The Neutralist soldiers were reputed to be the best and the most honest. On the military plane, their value to-day is nil, since they no longer have Colonel Thon's parachute battalions with them or the leadership of the French advisers.

"Mistakenly, Chanda is regarded by a certain section of international opinion as the symbol of the unity of Laos. If he joins forces with Cosgrove, the latter can no longer be accused of running a separatist movement—unless, of course, all his troops abandon Chanda and he is reduced to being a petty adventurer without rifles. Officers like Satou, Lom, Ham and Dong-Ly have stuck by him only because they were ordered to do so by you. I too have some of Chanda's men on my pay-roll and I know what's going on. We could reintegrate these officers, in a higher rank, into the royal army. They're Laotians, therefore they don't like the Meos and the Meos don't like them. They are Neutralists, therefore they have certain grounds for complaint against the Americans. If you consider it necessary, we could offer them a few advantages in kind."

"Those men hate you, General, even more than the Meos and the Americans."

"Why bring my name into this operation? Prince Sisang's, yours and Captain Meynadier's will be enough.

"Colonel Thon wasn't a Communist when he served as your bodyguard. He's even a Christian. Why did he go over to the Viets? Here's the explanation you might give to Chanda's officers and men who still can't understand his desertion—it was because Thon discovered that for a long time already Chanda had been in the pay of the Americans, because Chanda is a Kha and dreams of making the Khas into what Phay Dong is making the Meos, a nation within a nation. He can't do this without the support of Colonel Cosgrove's services who are backing the minorities in Laos as well as South-Vietnam."

"For a long time, and you know it, Chanda hasn't thought of himself as a Kha but as a Laotian. He's only half-Kha anyway, just as you're half-Thai. In his case it was his mother, in yours your father."

"Now look, it's only a question of finding some suitable means of eliminating Chanda . . . for reasons of higher policy. Prince Sisang and the representative of France are agreed on this point."

"Monsieur Pinsolle may have misunderstood where our interests lie. Prince Sisang has never forgiven Chanda for receiving the Soviet Ambassador in his place. He still bears him a grudge because his pride was hurt. But you're the one who has most reason for getting your own back. You're hated, Chanda is loved."

"Chanda has dropped you in favour of the Americans. You too have an old score to pay off."

"You're always talking about paying off old scores, General. You had Gibelin killed because he made you lose face a couple of times. You hate me for the same reason. You now want to get rid of Chanda, or rather you want me to get rid of him for you. You also want Cos out of the way because he interferes with some of your rackets."

Ricq flung his napkin down on the table.

"I'm tired. I'd like to go home."

"I'm afraid that's not possible. You'd immediately warn Chanda through the Maha Son or one of his bonzes. Prince Sisang agrees with me. Either you accept my suggestion or you only leave Xien Nip to take a plane straight back to France. I don't think Mademoiselle Ven would be able to follow you . . . even if she says she wants to."

"Keep Ven out of this."

"Secret Service agents who disobey orders are severely punished in France. Without your rank, in that country you no longer know, what will you do? You'll be one of those lost soldiers who trail about the streets of Paris, who've been thrown out because they rated their friends higher than discipline, the promises they made to some harkis or settlers higher than their oath of loyalty to the government. Who was it said, 'One doesn't carry one's country away with one on the soles of one's shoes'?"

"Danton. But I'm a Frenchman."

"No, you're not. Laos is your fatherland. You've become Laotian. Look at the way you hold your fork—like a Laotian who's used to eating with his fingers. If you leave this country you'll be an exile everywhere. Chanda's done for, he's just a pawn who'll topple off the board at the flick of a finger. One little flick . . . like that . . . and the thing's done."

"Chanda is my friend. I want to be driven back to Xien Nip."

"Your plane for France leaves in three days' time. You'll be taken to the airport by the military police. The French Consul will hand you your ticket and passport, as though you were an undesirable or a dope-peddler who's being thrown out and for whom the police are waiting at another aerodrome, ready to slip on the handcuffs. There's another solution open to you. Turn traitor. The Americans pay a high price for specialists."

"Gibelin was too naive and tender-hearted. He didn't slit your throat."

"Three days—two days and three nights to be exact—that's all the time you have left to think it over.

"Gibelin wasn't naive. We did many a good deal together. Four tons of opium ditched from an aircraft into the sea off Nha Trang, in fifty-kilo bundles wrapped in waterproof sheeting and attached to cork floats. Some junks came to pick them up. Ten dollars the kilo at Xieng Khouang, a hundred dollars at Nha Trang—quite a tidy sum. The pilot was Desnoyers. I suppose you've heard he had an accident? Yet he had been in Laos a long time. But this normally discreet man suddenly started talking. A pity."

"There's still Mattei."

"When a limb is diseased, in Europe they cut it off; in Asia, they kill the man. There are so many men!

"Look, as a bonus I'll spare Mattei's life for you if we manage to come to an agreement. He'll leave Bangkok safe and sound. I know all about him, Ricq: he used to work for me, because of the money, and he cost me a great deal. For you he used to work because of the honour, and he did it for nothing. How on earth do you get round all these people?"

"I appeal to their better nature, you to their worst."

"Do you know the Laotian proverb: 'You must fish in the mud if you want to catch an eel'? Your friend Gibelin often used to quote it."

"I want to go back to Xien Nip."

"Let me show you out to your jeep. You are still my guest. Remind me to give you that black notebook. I believe that when you've thought it over, when your anger has abated—you conceal your anger extremely well, incidentally, just like an Asiatic—you'll send me word, through our friend Khammay, that you agree to abide by the orders of your government. In Asia, all men of a certain standing want to become kings. Like them, Ricq, you've dreamt of being a king of clandestinity and secrecy. A pity you won't taste my wine. A present from General Molliergues, who must have put it down on his expense account. I'd like to know if it was good or not, but I haven't a trained palate."

"I'm a Laotian, nor have I."

"Prince Sisang, who's an expert in these matters, claims it's slightly sour. But Sisang is a Frenchman. If things go badly, he'll always have his estates in Dordogne. Poor old Si Mong will have nothing. He has no bank account, either in France or Switzerland. Who inherited Gibelin's money, do you know? He had a lot of money in Switzerland, didn't he?"

"I did. He had a thousand francs."

The jeep drove once more through Vientiane. Hard, glittering stars had appeared in the sky. As they drove through the Vietnamese quarter, where Cléach lived, Ricq leant towards Khammay and, so that the driver and guard should not understand, said in French:

"Let me escape."

"You could have gone home this evening. You didn't want to. Ven was waiting for you. You're now under close arrest. No one is allowed to talk to you any longer. I'm gambling my career, my life, all that I've earned. What do you give me in exchange, you who one day will leave Laos?"

"Resumption of our life in the bush . . . barefoot . . ."

"My feet hurt. Be quiet."

"Remember."

"I have a wife and children, a beautiful house. You have nothing but a *phousao*. Chanda is finished. He'll be made a general. He'll drive around in a Mercedes like all the other generals and steal money from the Americans as they do."

"Just one hour at Cléach's."

"Because Ven is living at Cléach's. You're now like all the others. Your friends are done for; our country's going to be dragged into a war or else handed over to the Communists. What do you want to do? See Ven? I've always believed men were all alike, that they were neither better nor worse than one another and that they all did the same thing at one moment or other of their lives. They chose what belonged to them: their wife, their house, their lands, their money. It's stronger than the rest: ideals, friends, memories. They used to tell me: that may be true for everyone else, but not for Ricq. Today it is true, even for you. You might have asked me to let you escape so that you might join Chanda or the Communists. But no, you only want to see Ven."

"She's all I have left, Khammay."

"Then you have nothing left. Ven isn't your wife, you have no children by her. She's just a *phousao*. She knows she'll be unhappy in any other country but Laos. You speak our language perfectly, you live the way we do. But you're not a Laotian."

"If I have to leave, Ven will follow me."

"Ven may love you perhaps, but less than her village, less than bathing in the river with her girl friends. She already followed you to Vientiane. It was a great sacrifice. Did you know she used to cry in secret? Phila, her servant, told me. In France, where will Ven go to the pagoda? There are no bonzes to whom to donate her basket of rice. It's a cold climate. I spent six months in France; I was wretched there. I have orders to stay with you all night. If you like we'll play cards."

"I don't know any card games."

"That's true, you don't know how to do anything other men do. The dead are still close to you. I know of a bonze who drives the dead away. He's deaf, dumb and blind, but there are secrets he knows. I'll send a soldier to fetch him. He'll burn some herbs, he'll touch your head, and you'll be cured."

"What if I tried to escape?"

"I'd knock you out; you're out of your mind. No one wants to kill you now."

"Remember . . . Paksane."

"That was long ago. Now I'm old and you're old too. But I've grown sensible; you're still mad. That reminds me, you still owe me the thousand piastres you promised me if I killed the Japanese major. A thousand piastres of 1945 add up to quite a lot of kips in 1964. I wouldn't have dared ask the Captain Ricq I used to know. But now you've become like me. You think first of all of a woman. I was only joking, of course."

"I don't think you're being very wise, Khammay. The man who slit the Japanese major's throat, the skinny little penniless barber, would have known better. Your money has blinded you. You're done for as well, Khammay."

"What on earth are you talking about?"

"Think it out. You were with Soumboun when you arrested Prince Sisang without orders from Si Mong. You disobeyed. In order to show he has not been bypassed by his men, the general is bound to make an example. Of course he won't tackle the majors and colonels who have soldiers behind them. Soumboun is already dead or about to die. And you, Khammay, have made yourself extremely conspicuous with all that money you spent on your house, your swimming-pool and on girl friends. I owe you a thousand piastres and my life. In exchange, I'm saving yours. Get out of Vientiane. I want to see Ven; it's true, I do love her. But I'm not worried; she won't leave me. I'll tell you a secret; she's expecting a child by me. You come with me. We'll go back to Xieng Khouang. I know a man who'll fly us up there. We'll join Chanda. We'll start again afresh."

"I don't believe you. I've always been loyal to Si Mong. I also know a lot about him. You've just made this all up to persuade me to let you escape. Everyone knows how crafty you are. You were once an upright, honest man but now the *phis* are devouring your brain. If you go on like this, you'll be like Colonel Thon, like that French warrant officer who's with the Meos. When the Viets have no further use for Thon, when the Meos have no further use for Picarle, they'll kill them."

Ricq found he was grasping Gibelin's black notebook in his hand.

As they drove past the police post, while Khammay was

parleying with the sentries, he opened it. By the light of the lamp he was able to read, among a number of quotations, accounts and girls' names, a sentence translated from Pali:

"Table companions are easily found, companions in death are rare."

He went on thumbing through it. There were thirty or so pages of smaller handwriting, accompanied by sketches, maps, footnotes and marginal comments. It was a sort of diary, sometimes straightforward, at other times incoherent, in which Ricq's name kept appearing on every page.

Khammay stayed for half an hour in the prison with Ricq. He appeared to be lost in thought as he paced to and fro, pausing only to spit on the floor from time to time.

"I'm going out for a bit," he said suddenly.

"You're worried. What about your orders? You're not meant to leave me."

"I'll come back tomorrow morning. Tell me if you've changed your mind."

"You'll realise, from the way your friends receive you, if I was simply trying to frighten you. I don't feel like sleeping. Ask them to leave the light on."

"The generator stops at midnight. You want to read that notebook Si Mong gave you, don't you? I'll leave you my torch. I'll go and see Ven tomorrow and let you know how she is. I promised her you would be released this evening. She will have waited for you all night. But you're no longer in danger since you have given her a child."

Ricq lay down on the bed and opened the notebook. He came across the quotation from Unanmuno with which Gibelin had greeted him on the Paksane dropping-zone and in which the word "enormity" was underlined three times, the legend about the bronze drums from the Chinese Annals, some Laotian love poems which were often obscene, still more figures, and then:

11 November 1944

I am taking to the maquis with three thousand piastres I have borrowed from Guérin of the Public Works Department and twenty chaps, my team from the Upper Mekong Forestry Company. I haven't paid them for three months.

Contacted Calcutta on Captain Piétri's set, using the call signal that M. gave me.

They promise me arms, money, and to parachute a team into me: an officer and a N.C.O. wireless operator.

6 December 1944

It's Little Ricq. Gentle, well behaved, a boy scout who in nine months has been taught to kill, blow up roads, live in the jungle. I put on my act for his benefit. He reacts partly in the way I always thought he would, partly according to the act I put on.

Ricq wants order, even amidst all this disorder.

He'll be a companion who's easy to live with. He is astonished and enchanted by everything.

Christmas 1944

Three poor wretches in a thatch hut, eaten alive by the mosquitoes and leeches, tried to recall the Christmases of their childhood. Meynadier was a scullion in Antibes, Ricq used to go to Mass. I said nothing. From the age of fifteen I used to spend Christmas night out hunting. I hoped to kill a white elephant. I am leaving Ricq to organize the Phou-Khouay camps on the lines he has been taught in India. Clandestine camps interconnected by camouflaged tracks. An arduous and pointless task. On my side, I have taken certain precautions by sending my Hos on a reconnaissace to see if the opium track is still practicable. If the Japs come after us right into the forest, we'll use it. But the Japanese will never come as far as that.

7 March 1945

Back from a trip to Tonkin, Annam and Cochin-China for the D.G.E.R. Bad impression. The Communists are organizing everywhere, creating committees, infiltrating the nationalist movements. What is it I don't like about them, I who am neither a colonialist nor a racialist? They are boring, convinced of what they expound, and in their own way colonialists and racialists. If they're successful, Laos is in for a bad time.

When Ricq was a student at the School of Oriental Languages, he had a fling with a Tonkinese girl who is now Lam Sammay's wife. She is ugly and intelligent. I had always thought Little Ricq was a virgin.

9 March

Japanese offensive. All the French massacred, arrested or in flight. What on earth are the Japs up to, since they know they are done for? Their aim is to destroy the prestige of the Whites in Asia and of the French colonizers in Indo-China. It's Ho Chi-Minh's Communists—half-whites like the Japanese—who are going to reap the benefit.

20 May

Six months ago I was on the verge of bankruptcy. Here I am today at the head of a unit bearing my name. We have the only wireless set in Indo-China that's still operating. All the rest have closed down.

Ricq amazes me more and more. I'm trying to find his weak point. Too credulous, perhaps. I'm the one who gets things moving but he's the one they follow. Too modest also to realize this.

From the Mekong plain to the Meo country it was an exhausting march. We climbed to nine thousand feet, barefoot and in rags.

Result: On leaving we were a column of refugees on the run. Today we are an army. Father Maurel still watches me out of the corner of his eye, never knowing what trick I'll be playing on him next.

This bloody priest is a born leader. For thirty years now he has been indulging in the most difficult sort of propaganda—trying to impose the virtues of an antipathetic god. He made us carry the stretcher of one of his injured Christians. When the man died, he had him buried in the same grave and under the same cross as a Frenchman, a poor little clerk who had been carried off by fever. These two gestures sealed the union between the white and yellow members of our unit. Pamphone has surprised me as well. I had regarded him as a softy, a playboy without too many scruples as to how to obtain money. Is he trying to impress Ricq?

1 June

We have settled next to a Thai Neua village, Nouei-Phou Lak, commanded by a certain Chouc, a friend of Pamphone's. Chouc embarrasses me when he talks about France, in which he has never set foot. He makes it out to be a marvellous country, such as children dream of. Who was the idiot who said that man lives on bread? He lives on myths and conceives his own personal paradise.

We too are living in a dream world in this village which has preserved its customs, rites and superstitions. Noudeng, Chouc's wife, is pregnant. On the witch-doctor's orders, she has stopped eating the larvae of bees, tamarinds and aubergines, for fear of making the child turbulent. She has stopped using cosmetics, to prevent it from growing up proud; she avoids stepping over a bullock's tether, for fear of its being greedy, or sitting on the bottom step of the house so as not to retard the birth. When she bathes at the end of the day she must turn towards the setting sun and comb her hair with the tail of an eel. Thus, when the child emerges from her belly, it will slip out as easily as a snake. Noudeng is very beautiful. I hope she gives birth to a girl who takes after her. Chouc, of course, wants a boy. He already has a nephew, Chanda, who follows Ricq everywhere like a dog and longs to carry a rifle. He's frightened of the other Whites.

Slightly darker than most Thais, short, lean-faced, Chanda has the vitality of an animal. He knows all the tracks in the forest, the lairs and habits of every wild beast; he goes out hunting by himself, using a bow and arrows. But he is scared of the *phis* and secretly makes sacrifices to them.

Pamphone tells me his father, Chouc's brother, married a Kha. From the Khas, Chanda has inherited their timidity, their reserve and that touch of melancholy which they are never able to shed. The melancholy of an ancient race driven out by the invaders who have come from the north in successive waves.

Pamphone is growing fat and sleek again. He's found a *phousao* who feeds him like a fighting cock. I have to make do with an occasional roll in the hay with a girl of no particular interest.

What makes a girl interesting? The fact that she disturbs you and is desired by others? Making love is a boring business; playing at love is fascinating.

There's a path leading from Nouei-Phou Lak to Xieng Khouang. The Japanese who have spread all over Laos are liable to approach from that direction. The village can no longer provide for over a hundred men with ravenous appetites.

2 June

Chouc advises me to go up to the Meos to buy some cattle. He knows them and speaks their language fairly well. But the Meos will only be paid in gold leaf or silver ingots. I've asked Calcutta for some. What on earth will they make of such a request?

4 June

The silver ingots and gold leaf have arrived without a word or comment. The British of Force 136 aren't surprised by anything in this war. Ricq has engaged little Chanda as his bodyguard and also Paul Thon, a young Christian with the air of a gorilla, whom Father Maurel has lent him. The three of them live in a hut they have built on the edge of the river. What they do at night? Do they sing hymns or tell their beads?

6 June

Neither. Ricq teaches Chanda to read and write in French; Thon to write in Laotian. Chouc corrects the exercises.

Touching? No, not to my mind. Exasperating rather, this mixture of youth club, boy scout camp and evening class. I'm all for everything nice and higgledy-piggledy.

Ricq absolutely insists on coming with us to the Meos. He's curious about every aspect of that country, the races who live up there, the dialects they speak. Chouc, being a lowlander, distrusts the Meos. I, on the contrary, have a deep affection for them. The only law they respect is their own pleasure; they are drunk with liberty.

If I weren't Antoine Gibelin, I should like to be a Meo.

Ricq doesn't understand that liberty is like alcohol, hunting or women. To appreciate it properly, you have to over-indulge in it.

15 June

We went up to the Meos and came down again, bringing back with us a dozen shaggy ponies—vicious, bad-tempered but indestructible little beasts—also some pigs, chickens, corn and paddy. Establishing contact with them was difficult, even though Chouc had sent them a message notifying them of our arrival.

They appeared on the edge of a steep pass, outlined against the crags behind a curtain of mist. There were about twenty of them, dressed in indigo cotton clothes, short jackets and baggy trousers revealing their huge calves. They all brandished ancient home-made rifles, consisting of a long tube, without stock or sights, but equipped with a wooden grip on which to rest the right cheek when firing. They make their powder out of charcoal and saltpetre. Their bullets are old rusty nails or bits of iron. Like sixteenth-century arquebusiers, each of these men had a coil of lighted touchwood round his wrist—hardly a sign of friendship. There were three children with them. Meo children carry little rifles which seem to grow in proportion to their own rate of growth. They are handed down like old clothes from elder to younger brother.

I also know from my Hos that they have other rifles hidden away underneath their huts—modern ones which the Japanese have sold to them.

It could hardly be a worse moment for visiting them—in the middle of the opium harvest, when all sorts of brigands swoop down on the mountains.

Chouc goes forward to meet them. How different he is, with his fine features, fair skin, tall stature, supple gait, elegant gestures, from these thickset little mountaineers with their pigtails, their silver collars round their necks, filthy-dirty, arrogant and suspicious. The Thais of the Haute Région and the Laotians of the valleys have shamelessly exploited the Meos' credulity and simplicity. They used to buy their opium in exchange for worthless rubbish or even promises which they never kept. Eventually the Meos became furious and massacred a rapacious merchant, a dishonest civil servant. The Thais and Laotians immediately rushed to the French saying those savages had attacked them without reason and that they refused to pay their taxes. This was enough for several repressive columns to be sent against them—usually in vain, for by then the Meos had decamped.

The Meos don't hold with laws, because laws always act against them. For thousands of years they have been placed in the dock by other races.

The discussion drags on between Chouc and the man who appears to be the Meo chief. Eventually they signal to us that we can pass through.

The Meos climb every slope vertically, even the steepest ones. Their tracks have no twists and turnings. We have a hard time following them in the icy mist. Suddenly we find ourselves above the clouds. These peaks, black or white, emerge like islands in an ocean of milk. The Meos live at a height varying between four thousand and four thousand five hundred feet, all the way along the frontier of China, at Cao Bang, Phong Saly, Sam Neua, Luang Prabang, but mostly on this plateau of Tran Ninh on which we are now installed. No one has ever been able to take a census of them. Father Maurel claims there are between a hundred and fifty and two hundred thousand Meos in Laos. But they have no national or even tribal sentiment and don't care if they are a mere handful or a million. The French missionaries, ethnologists and administrators have divided them into three groups, according to the costume worn by their women: the white, black and flowered Meos.

The Meos scarcely ever come down below three thousand feet, and never for a long time. Those from Chen Keng-Khai, when they're short of salt, come and fetch it from the Muong Sen Valley where there are a few shops belonging to Chinese merchants. They start off at sunset, arrive at the Chinamen's at midnight and load their salt as quickly as possible so as to be back in their highlands by sunrise.

The Meos don't mind the cold and wear hardly any clothes in a temperature bordering on zero. On the other hand, they hate the heat. They never wash. Those who have come to meet us are particularly filthy.

We come within sight of a village, a few low huts in the middle of some poppy fields. Some women are working there, their baskets on their backs, holding in their hands the little trident with which they scratch the capsule of the flower to extract the sap. The poppies are sown in October and the sap is harvested, depending on the height or the region, between April and May. The harvest here is coming to an end.

The Meos produce the best opium in the whole of South-East

Asia, approximately forty tons of it, which serves to supply the clandestine traffic of the drug. The Indo-China Excise Office has to whistle to obtain even a few pounds of it.

We get a closer view of the women. They have flattened faces, and wear pleated skirts and thick leggings which make them waddle as they walk, but they are covered in gold and silver jewellery.

I once asked a Meo chieftain from Xieng Khouang why he gave so many jewels to his women. He replied:

"I cover them in stuff that clinks—like that I always know where they are. When they want to slip off at night to another man, I can hear them."

The Meo girls start sleeping with the boys from the neighbouring huts at a very early age. Infidelity is a commonplace in every household. The marriage ceremony must be the simplest in the world: when a man finds a woman he likes he takes her to live with him. If he's rich and can feed them, he has several wives. If he's poor, he has only one; if he's full of beans, he can make free with his neighbour's.

These Meo women may be easy, but how dirty they are! One of them with a turban wound round her head has a pretty smile and looks at us, the hussy, with an interest she makes no attempt to conceal.

We are shown into one of the huts which, built right on the ground, is only a provisional habitation. Everyone lives, men and beasts alike, in complete promiscuity. The pigs and hens squabble with the dogs and children over the food. The horses have their mangers inside the huts, and their hind-quarters protruding outside. They are entitled also to take part in the communal life. The pigs are equipped with huge wooden collars to prevent them from destroying the crops. But it never enters a Meo's head to confine or shackle anything, either animal or human. He thinks that, like himself, animals that are locked up die.

We are given biscuits made of maize, meat sprinkled with spicy herbs and rice spirit. Then we get down to business with an old man with a shaven pate, a distrustful expression and the features of a Red Indian chief. He can find us what we need but first of all he wants the gold and silver. I bring out my gold leaf. We come to an agreement, but the old fellow makes no attempt to conceal the fact that our presence at Nouei-Phou Lak is unwelcome because we are going to make trouble for the country. He hopes by selling us some horses to see the last of us.

The old man then offers us some opium.

To a Meo, opium-smoking is a manly pastime, as puffing a cigar or a pipe is to us. The women are not allowed to smoke because they must be kept in their place, that's to say beneath the men. There are no addicts amongst them. No doctor has been able to explain this anomaly to me. Ricq refuses to taste the stuff. So does Pamphone. Few Laotians smoke opium, whereas they all deal in it.

Chouc and I lie down opposite the old man, who prepares the pipes. The opium is first-class, with a faint taste of violets.

I could never become an addict. The opium-addict's world is cloistered and silent and regulated by a strict time-table: the moment for one's pipe which one can't afford to miss, the unbearable restlessness brought about by any change in this routine. Opium rejects fresh air, sunshine, fantasy, it makes one tolerant and wise, morose and disillusioned. It's the most subtle snare I know, but to begin with it gives the impression of freedom.

Using Chouc as an intermediary, Ricq squats at my feet and questions the old man on the origin of his people. Flattered, the old boy tries to tell him what he remembers. He mentions a certain snow-capped mountain, the Himalatan, reputed to be the cradle of his race, and also the country in which long periods of daylight are followed by long periods of darkness, like the polar region.

Ricq leaps to his feet with enthusiasm:

"I read a book of Forrest's in India. He says this country is situated in the basin of the Ienissei River, which flows into the Arctic Ocean. The Meos, according to him, belong to a Jong tribe who were the first inhabitants of China. Coming from the extreme north, driven back into the mountains by other invaders, they made their way down to Indo-China, gradually crossing the whole of the continent of Asia. In the Ienissei, the Russians before the war accurately identified a little tribe speaking Tibeto-Mongol who could have been related to the Meo family."

Good old Ricq! He won't rob a temple, he won't sell arms or drugs, but he'll study the history of a people by pursuing them into the deepest valley, up to the highest peak, before the great tide of Communism engulfs them completely.

According to a more simple version, the Meos come from Kouei Cheou, or Yunnan, from where they were driven out between 1820 and 1840. They were seen to arrive in small groups at the beginning of the nineteenth century. They travelled only along the highest ridges, bringing with them their wives, children, ponies, shaggy dogs and poppy seeds. My father told me that in 1912 one of his friends, the French Resident in Xieng Khouang, Barthélemy, suggested to his superiors that all the Meos should be expelled from Indo-China. These "hot-heads", he said, were burning down the forests to plant their rice in the ashes. No one could ever establish contact with them and it was impossible to make them pay their taxes. They also manufactured their own alcohol and sold their opium direct to the Chinese merchants of Yunnan instead of going through the Excise Office.

To a good official, these practices were intolerable. To Barthélemy's successors, so were mine. Poor Meos! At the start of the rainy season they are plagued with disease—jungle typhus and dysentery. They die young and are given to committing suicide when they're bored. Sometimes, in the dry season, the Meo abandons his family and, with his arquebus over his shoulder, wanders off along the ridges, merely to see what's going on elsewhere. This tireless marcher thus covers hundreds of miles. When he's hungry or thirsty, he enters the first Meo hut he sees. He eats, then sets off again. The Meo is a man of few words and respects the whims and fancies of the individual. At the end of two or three months he comes home again without a word of explanation.

Happy Meos! Hardly any religion—just a crude form of Shamanism—and opium which, according to them, cures all the evils of the world, including the worst of all, the one that especially attacks free men: boredom. The old boy has become more talkative since being questioned about his ancestors.

I try to find out what's going on in the mountains. The Meos appear to be divided, but they all consider there are too many intruders these days. The Japanese have approached them through the Thais in their service. They offer them a rifle for every five pounds of opium.

The old man asks me if I'm interested. For a rifle, what would a Meo not do! But that's the very thing I am unable to give them. If they have rifles they'll immediately attack the valley people. They have plenty of old scores to settle with them! We are backing the Laotians, their king, their delightfully corrupt administration. We are not permitted to make use of the minorities. But these minorities constitute two thirds of the population and they're the most dangerous.

The old man talks a great deal of a certain Phay Tong, a Meo who lives in the heights overlooking the Plain of Jars. The French are said to have given him some rifles. In the north there is only the Puyseguin group, unless it has been wiped out.

We sleep in the huts. They stink and there isn't a moment's peace what with all these animals living inside and the ponies which keep stamping and champing, their heads forming a living frieze in place of a wall. The Meos are pleased to see the last of us. No rifles, no Meos.

17 June

Chouc has just had a daughter. He has christened her Ven. Father Maurel, half seriously, half in jest, suggested she be brought up as a Christian since her father was so fond of France. Ricq would be god-father.

Chouc got out of this rather well:

"All religions are equally good. Why not stick to the one we already have? In Laos we follow Buddha."

"And what if you lived in France, Chouc?"

"I'd christen my daughter Françoise, after Ricq."

We attended the rites that accompany a birth among the Thai Neuas. Chouc himself does not believe in them, but he insists on their being observed so that the village might continue to live in peace.

As soon as Noudeng felt the first birth pangs, he sent for Mo-Sado, the male midwife, the man who has the power to force locked doors. A candle was lit next to the silver cup containing the offerings.

The Mo-Sado did nothing but insult the child until it began to emerge. When it was born he hastened to tie round its neck, and also round the mother's neck, the pieces of black and white cotton which will protect them against the evil spirits. The old grandmother then picked up the winnowing-basket, held it over the flame and, standing on the threshold of the door, drove away the Pai *phis*, the djinns who make off with children.

"Kou-Kou, you Pai *phis* who are able to assume the aspect of night birds, those birds that give a deep-throated cry. Kou-Kou, be off! From now on this child belongs to us."

Under Ven's mattress she slipped a needle, since the child was a girl. A boy would have been entitled to a dagger.

Chouc picked up the little girl and dangled her feet on the ground, uttering this ritual formula:

"Stamp the earth, stamp the grass. Here is your comb, here is your mirror"—he handed her a comb and a sliver of broken looking-glass—"you have trodden the earth, you are a human creature."

Then he turned to Ricq:

"If you like, you can be godfather according to the Buddha of the Christians. You will give her presents when she is grown up. Take her in your arms, but don't drop her."

20 June

I have tried to explain to Second-Lieutenant Maurel that I often used to make up stories but never told lies. He doesn't believe me. We are still waiting for another transmitter; we are short of weapons.

3 July

A man has turned up, exhausted, down-at-heel, emaciated, bearded, more filthy than the Meos. It's a certain Masson, a Force 136 lieutenant who was on the same course in India as Ricq. He belongs to the Puyseguin team. I don't know how he heard that our set was still working, but he has marched more than seventy miles over mountain paths, through zones infested by Japs and the bands of robbers—Meos, Annamites and Thais—in their service, to send a signal to Calcutta. Their transmitter has not been working for two months.

Masson's hand shakes as he writes down his message on the signal pad that Meynadier passes to him:

"Captain Puyseguin has gone mad. He's arming the Meos and launching them against the valley Laotians on the grounds that the latter have consorted with some Japs and are lacking in moral fibre.

"The Meos went down the Xieng Khouang and looted the shops. Puyseguin violently rejects all advice and warnings from the other members of his group. For the last month he has been living apart with a young Meo chieftain called Phay Tong. He refuses all contact with the Europeans parachuted with him, communicates with them by means of written messages, and talks of hauling anyone who tries to thwart him before a court martial —probably a Meo court martial. Several Chinese and Laotian merchants have been murdered. We don't know which way to turn and are in danger of being denounced to the Japanese. Request Captain Puyseguin be recalled before we are obliged to kill him."

Masson turned to Ricq:

"You knew him, didn't you? Brutal, violent, arrogant, but a very good officer. At the end of January six of us dropped into the Plain of Jars. A garrison lieutenant had come to pick us up in a car. Puyseguin straight away started cursing him:

" 'We don't want to have anything to do with Vichy collaborators and traitors'."

The lieutenant prepared to drive off, leaving them in the lurch with the parachutes and containers. Luckily he was a good fellow. Masson managed to argue him round and he drove them to an abandoned military camp. But he refused to do anything more for them.

Puyseguin decided to live in a separate hut and mess there on his own.

By this time the lieutenant realized the captain was not quite right in the head. Then the written orders started coming in: "Lieutenant Masson will proceed to Phou Ngan with two men and establish contact with the local population. He will report the result to me in writing."

For all his sexual appetite, Puyseguin now declined to have anything more to do with women since they might undermine his strength, which he owed to his mission. He cooked for himself, all alone, a mile away from the others, numb with cold on his solitary peak. He looked after his horse himself and played endless games of patience while the wind whistled and howled outside. He resolutely set about learning Meo. One fine day he appeared in front of his group, wearing a Meo silver collar round his neck and dressed like a Meo, barefoot in the frozen mud. He had even shaved his skull and started to grow a pigtail.

"I have decided," he said, "to arm the Meos of Tran-Ninh and turn them into an army with which to drive out the Japanese. They are warriors; the Laotians are a lot of milksops."

Another day he told them:

"I'm drafting a memorandum to General de Gaulle's government asking them to grant the Meos their well deserved independence."

Puyseguin was to be seen everywhere, now on foot, now on his horse, clambering up the steepest slopes, visiting the most inaccessible villages, issuing weapons from the parachute drops.

The major in command of the Xien Khouang district confided his apprehensions to Masson. He suggested getting in touch with Calcutta by wireless. It was too late; the Japanese had moved in. The major was bayoneted. Puyseguin became more and more crazy. He took a Meo woman and married her according to a rite that did not exist and which he invented himself. The two officers and the N.C.O.s in his team, after an anxious conference, decided to ask Calcutta to recall him. Their situation was intolerable. The Japanese, informed by the inhabitants of Xieng Khouang, were on their tracks. Phay-Tong's bands were showing signs of restlessness now that Puyseguin had promised them independence. Masson drafted the signal for Calcutta, but in the middle of the night Puyseguin and his Meos came and seized the transmitter. Fortunately the sergeant operator managed to put it out of action by removing the crystals. From then on they were prisoners. Masson heard that we had just moved to this sector. He escaped and made his way to us. The reply to his signal arrived from Calcutta a few hours later:

"We are asking Major Antoine Gibelin to investigate and take the necessary action."

8 July

What a business! Masson and I took five days to reach Puyseguin's camp. We arrived just in time. The group, consisting of five Europeans and a score of Vietnamese and Thais, were preparing to attack their leader who, on his side, was protected by about fifty Meos. I did my best to pacify these madmen, for they really were all mad. They distrusted one another, slept with their revolvers beside them and spent their time compiling mysterious files.

Meos have a soft spot for creatures like Puyseguin, especially when they give them rifles. I send for Phay Tong, a foxy young fellow who's trying to find his feet and wants to become chief of Tran-Ninh.

We have tea together and smoke a few pipes of opium. I casually remark that I have a hundred and sixty men nearby, well-armed with mortars and machine-guns, that I'm expecting five hundred more, that I'll be receiving any amount of arms by parachute and that I'm willing to issue them to men who are wise enough not to use them inconsiderately.

Phay Tong agrees to hand Puyseguin over to me. He brings him back in fetters on a horse. I have him released. He stands stiffly to attention in front of me, with his three months' growth of beard, and makes this astonishing request:

"I cannot tolerate being relieved of my command in such circumstances, on the strength of some base rumours emanating from an ambitious go-getter who wants to usurp my place. I insist on justifying myself before the highest authorities."

I tell him the nearest French mission, the M5, is in China, at Kunming, the capital of Yunnan, nearly five hundred miles away.

"I shall go on foot as far as the frontier, sir. From there I'm bound to find some means of transport. I shall report back."

Since I don't know what to do with such a hot-head and since it's impossible, after all, to keep him locked up in a hut from which he could escape by thrusting his shoulders through one of the walls, and since it's equally impossible to tie him to a stake like a goat or have him guarded by a sentry whom he is quite capable of strangling, I give him permission to leave for whatever destination he chooses. I let him have some money, food, a couple of horses, a guide, and off he goes.

Before starting off along the path which is to take him through Muong Sin up to the Chinese border and the mountains of Yunnan, he warns me:

"Look out for Ricq, sir. He's a British agent. In India he was detailed to keep us under observation during the course. I've already put in my report about it."

I put Lieutenant Masson in command of the group and came back with the guide Phay Tong gave me, relieved at escaping from that atmosphere of hatred and insanity, that crowd of unhinged wretches. A marvellous trip along blue ridges, bare slopes, and paths that defy the laws of gravity.

By holding all the passes, the Meos could check any invaders coming from the north. They would still need a personal reason for fighting against them. I can see only one: the defence of their two assets—opium, which is current throughout the world, and liberty which will soon be current nowhere.

Puyseguin wanted to create a Meo army and a Meo nation. Was he a madman or a forerunner?

I live like my guide, stopping wherever there happens to be a village, eating and drinking without saying where I'm going or what I'm doing. The cold and the mist chill me; the sun warms me up again. I am not particularly pleased to get back to Nouei-Phou Lak, where I find my soldiers busy training.

22 July

We have been close to death, a most disagreeable death—decapitation with a sabre. The Meos from the highlands of Nouei-Phou Lak betrayed us to the Kempetai in exchange for a few rifles.

On 14 July, assembled round a post on which our flag had been hoisted, we were going through the motions of a parade to celebrate the band of merry drunkards and raving fishwives who seized the Bastille. The 14 July, the feast of disorder and improvisation, is dear to my heart. All of a sudden we saw a sorry-looking convoy arrive—ten officers, a dozen N.C.O.s, six administrators, a police commissioner and a doctor, who had escaped from the concentration camp of Hoa Binh and made their way up here by way of Xieng Khouang. They had no arms or medical supplies. For three months they had been living on wild berries, herbs, sometimes on the charity of the *nha-ques* or mountaineers. Consumed by dysentery, malaria, ticks, leeches, they had been reduced to mere skeletons with swollen tongues and blubbery lips. They were incapable of moving a yard further. Collapsing onto a mound of earth, they burst into tears and couldn't stop crying. They were crying over themselves, over the tattered flag fluttering on the mast. Above all, they were crying from exhaustion. We moved them into the village. The doctor mustered enough strength to say:

"Not too much food; it would kill us. Quinine and a little rice water."

The Japanese who are on their tracks can't be far off. We send a detachment down the Xieng Khouang track with orders to make a noise and withdraw as soon as they see the enemy. But we hadn't thought of the Meos.

The main part of our group, consisting of a hundred and thirty men, our most precious piece of equipment—the transmitter—and Meynadier are sent into the forest with the Khas. Father Maurel who speaks their language is in command of them. Twenty of us, the most agile or those who have some notion of medicine, remain behind to look after the sick.

On 18 July, at five in the morning, guided by the Meos, two Japanese companies emerged from the mountains. Ricq had gone off on reconnaissance with Chanda and Thon. They saw them and with a machine-gun managed to hold up their advance for a few minutes. Ricq later told me that Chanda stood upright, firing the gun from his hip, while Thon crouched behind a tree a little further off, throwing hand-grenades. Thanks to them, we had time to escape, stark naked or in our underclothes, from the huts on the edge of the river where we had put the survivors from Hoa Binh.

Impossible to take them with us. How can they be made to run when they can no longer even walk? The doctor gives me a little wave. He is under no delusion as to how the Japanese respect the Geneva conventions.

"Good luck," he manages to say.

The others whimper or are so exhausted that they don't wake up.

Ricq on my right continues to fire short bursts from the machine-gun. I know he has only three magazines. I see him cross the river and make for the cover of the forest. With my fellows, I follow suit. But I run into three Japs wearing their ridiculous peaked caps and brandishing their long-barrelled rifles with bayonets fixed. I mow them down with a submachine-gun. One of my partisans is wounded in the leg; he can no longer keep up. I am forced to train my gun on his companions who want to carry him. Sheer madness! We manage to reassemble on a limestone spur overlooking the village. The Japs are not following us. They have a dozen dead and wounded and feel that's enough.

Concealed behind some rocks, we watch what goes on down there through our field-glasses. The Japs haul the sick out of the huts and finish them off with their bayonets. The partisan who was wounded in the leg and Josserand, a Customs man whose legs had given out, are dragged on to the village square. An officer in spectacles furiously fires a bullet into the back of the wounded man's neck. Then he draws his sabre and hands it to the soldier behind him. Four Japs force Josserand to his knees. The executioner takes three blows to cut off his head.

"Do you think you can hit him?" Ricq asks me. "My hands are shaking too much." And he hands me a rifle.

The range is about eight hundred yards. I rest the rifle on a boulder, hold my breath, clench my teeth and aim for the man's stomach. The target at that spot is larger and if I hit him the swine will suffer hell before dying. I fire once, twice. The Jap officer whirls round and falls, clutching his guts. Ricq squeezes my shoulder:

"Thanks, Antoine."

All that remains now is to decamp at full speed. We are light and in training. The Japanese are heavy and encumbered with their kit.

16 August 1945

The Japanese surrender is imminent. We have been waiting

since 6 August, when the atomic bomb was dropped on Hiroshima. The military are behaving like wild beasts; the civilians are clinking glasses.

I've given orders for the whole group to head back for the plain, this time along the tracks; our baggage is to be carried in carts. I want to be the first to enter Vientiane. It's the rainy season. We march, soaked to the skin, without ever being able to get dry. The Viets are very active; they have formed liberation committees everywhere and the Japanese are handing over their weapons to them. The Laotians as usual are acquiescent. *Bo penh nhang*! Ricq says it would be unwise to attack Vientiane and suggests installing ourselves in the vicinity of Paksane where we still have many friends. Always this mania of his for the small clan, the carefully organized operation, always this lack of folly!

Paksane: one street, a few concrete shanties, a Customs post. Fancy risking one's life in order to recapture Paksane! I assemble the group in a tornado which uproots the trees and swells the torrents. I have to shout to make myself heard. How should I start off? "Soldiers, comrades-in-arms . . . ?" That sounds idiotic. "My friends . . . ?" Like hell! Well then?

"You lot of ragamuffins, you've chosen of your own accord to fight on our side. Captain Ricq and I are now asking you to choose where and how to go on fighting. Ricq is going down to Paksane. Those who come with me will take another route, to Vientiane, where no one is expecting us. Paksane is your home, your wives and children and houses are there. I think you'll be warmly welcomed. Make your choice."

Fifty partisans form up on my side—the veterans of the timber company—then Meynadier, after a moment's hesitation. Father Maurel's Christians, the Khas, Chouc, Pamphone and all the ones who come from Paksane join Ricq who seems surprised and embarrassed. He never thought that one day we should have to part company. If he ever marries it will be for life; he already doesn't care for divorces.

2 September

The Japanese surrender is now official.

We halt to share out the arms and ammunition between the two groups. I've asked Calcutta to send me fifty sub machine-guns and a hundred sets of equipment. Meynadier brings me the reply:

"Impossible to arrange drop because of adverse weather conditions, postpone your operation."

I don't believe it. The Force 136 pilots drop anything, in any weather, anywhere. I send another signal to say I am pushing on towards Vientiane. In reply to this, I receive the following message:

"You are ordered to abandon occupation of Vientiane."

Vientiane is situated north of the 16th parallel. According to the Potsdam Agreements, the Japanese are to surrender to the Chinese troops coming from the north, the 93rd and 2nd Divisions, and no one else. The Americans are backing this view wholeheartedly, they are supporting the viceroy, who has proclaimed the independence of Laos, and want to prevent the return of the French, so they're keeping a close watch on all Force 136 aircraft.

"You're out of luck," Ricq says to me. "Believe me, it's better this way. We'll send out small patrols around Paksane. We'll infiltrate some agents. Pamphone, from the outside, will resume the administration of the town. When the fruit is ripe, we'll hoist the French and Laotian flags. We could establish another base in the Phou-Khouay or lower down."

His plans are sensible, but I don't give a damn for sense. I seize him by the shoulders:

"For me the tomb of Don Quixote is now in Vientiane, not in Paksane. I've always dreamt of moving into the Residency, from which I was thrown out before the war because I'd come to a reception to which I wasn't invited. Think, too, of the hundred and forty-three French civilians taken prisoner whose lives hang in the balance. Eleven thousand Annamites would like to see them dead. I can save them by a surprise attack."

Ricq says this would only lead to their being massacred.

"We're parting company, Little Ricq. I'm choosing folly, you're taking the sensible line. You now have a second wireless transmitter; you're your own boss. I, Gibelin, reject the Potsdam Agreements."

Ricq thinks I'm fighting neither for my own country nor for

Laos but just to amuse myself, to bring off a fine scoop and be the first to enter Vientiane. The tomb of Don Quixote is empty—I know—and there are men under me for whom I'm responsible. I gave them the choice, however, between remaining good little soldiers and committing an 'enormity'. Fifty are on my side—a very high proportion.

Next morning Ricq came and embraced me. Good old Ricq. I feel sure he longed to follow me, but he's far too serious-minded. Besides, there were his orders to consider, not to mention those damned Potsdam Agreements signed by criminals who don't even know where Laos is on the map.

4 September

The last Japanese have left Vientiane. They're pulling out towards Paksane on carts piled high with loot, on bicycles and motor-bikes. I've placed my men in ambush on both sides of the road. I halt the Japs by firing a few bursts of Sten in the air. Their commander won't see reason. He claims we are merely partisans and not recognized as regular troops by the Allies. He even becomes insolent and demands to be let through. I give him a good clout in the face. I take his sword and break it across my knee. We search the carts and retrieve a dozen rifles carefully hidden under some mats.

I requisition two motor-bikes and eighteen bicycles, then drive those cruel, arrogant little men off with a few kicks in the arse.

Thanks to them, we have lost Asia for ever.

5 September

Twenty tramps, soaked to the skin, equipped with a strange variety of weapons including even shot-guns, entered the capital of Laos pedalling their Japanese bikes. Meynadier and I had gone ahead on our motor-bikes, which kept breaking down. We had left forty partisans behind. They had neither arms nor bicycles. We arrive at the Residency and I have the French Flag hoisted. The news spreads: "The French are here; they have taken the town." Crowds gather in the street, crowds of Laotians only. They cheer us discreetly, far too discreetly. The whole lot of them are trembling with fear.

I have a glass of beer, the first in six months. In the empty offices I look through the open drawers spewing their contents on to the floor. I don't find as much as the helmet or even the buckler of Don Quixote but only a few Japanese magazines with photographs of naked girls. For my liking, their legs are too short. The Laotians melt away, the streets become deserted. The rain has soaked the flag. It hangs like a limp rag.

7 September

Things are going very badly. The merchants have received instructions not to sell us food under pain of death. Last night three of my partisans disappeared. They had their throats cut. Their heads are now being carried round the Annamite quarter and I can't do a thing about it. I am cut off in the Residency; I can't communicate with anyone. Impossible to get news of the French prisoners, let alone have them released. The Japanese have handed them over to the Viets.

This morning two sentries were killed, and the forty partisans who were to join us were unable to get through. Demonstrations and red flags. The town belongs to the Annamites, who parade outside our windows demanding independence and the departure of the colonialists.

We are especially short of grenades to calm down this brawling mob.

Meynadier has found a pack of cards. We play belote for one piastre a point. At this game, at least, I win.

An American captain calls on us, impeccably turned out, gloves in hand, distinguished-looking, with a crew cut and thin lips. There's nothing of the cowboy about him, he's the very model of the old-school cavalry officer. He is unarmed.

I fling down my cards and he introduces himself in a French that betrays a barely perceptible accent:

"Captain Cosgrove Tibbet, liaison officer attached to the Armistice Commission and responsible for seeing that the armistice is kept."

I in my turn introduce myself as the commander of A Group of the Resistance Forces.

He smiles as he peers at my togs, my feet shod in espadrilles and my badges of rank cut from an old sardine tin.

"Major, I've come to ask you to quit these premises at once. I hold myself responsible for your security and that of—" he hesitates—"your partisans, until you have left Vientiane."

I tell him to go and take a running jump at himself. His voice becomes curt:

"If you don't leave tonight, the hundred and forty-three Frenchmen in detention are liable to be killed. The Residency will be attacked by a thousand armed men. We wouldn't be able to do anything for you. According to the terms of the Potsdam Agreements, you shouldn't be in this town at all."

I insist:

"Laos is a French protectorate."

"No longer. The American Government is preparing to recognize her independence which has been proclaimed by the viceroy, head of the Lao Issara movement."

Here's the first Allied officer I meet, ordering me to move out of the town I have just taken!

Cosgrove has arranged for a truce which ends at ten o'clock tonight. He is going to call again at eight o'clock for my reply. If it is negative, he will cross the river and leave me alone to face the music. He salutes, marches out and climbs into a jeep. It's the first time I have ever seen this vehicle. While we were struggling on foot along the mountain tracks, other men were waging war in jeeps. I send off one of my Hos to find out what's happening. Disguised as a Chinese, he can move about freely anywhere. He confirms that the American wasn't bluffing.

A thousand well armed Vietnamese, to whom the Japanese have handed over a hundred and fifty rifles and four machine-guns, are preparing to attack us. The viceroy, who owes his present position to France, is already completely in the hands of the Viets, whose representatives in Vientiane are Prince Lam Sammay and his wife Loan. The prince wears riding boots, a bandolier and a cap adorned with a red star. How can such a clever fellow appear in public in such a ridiculous uniform? Intellectuals can't resist confusing war with theatricals.

A young Vietnamese rests his bike against the railings, walks across the garden and brings me a message from Prince Sammay on notepaper headed "Laos Liberation Committee". The wording on the other hand is anything but official:

"Antoine, bugger off if you don't want the French prisoners, yourself and your band of brigands to be massacred tonight. I shall no longer be able to repress the popular anger against the imperialists. Laos is independent; adventurers of your sort have no business here any longer."

Signed: "The Laotian People's Commissar with the Armies."

I try to give a piastre tip to the *ba-con* who brought the message. The boy disdainfully replies:

"I don't take money from colonialists."

At eight o'clock Cosgrove is back. I can't even defend myself without endangering the lives of a hundred and forty cowardly little Frenchmen with their panic-stricken wives and snotty-nosed brats. I accept his conditions.

Surrounded by a jeering mob, we drive out along the Paksane road. I refuse to shake hands with Cosgrove. He shrugs his shoulders and goes off to continue his dirty work elsewhere. I find my forty men chatting merrily around the fires they have lit to dry themselves. For the first time in my bloody life I feel like crying. I've botched my 'enormity'.

25 September

I've rejoined Ricq. He captured Paksane, lost it, then captured it again. He stayed on there in spite of the Japanese, the Americans, the Viets and the Chinese, thanks to the help of the local population, thanks especially to his composure and the enthusiasm he was able to inspire in his band of choirboys and jungle savages.

I see I am already drafting the text of his mention in despatches.

Ricq had advanced towards Paksane with Father Maurel, Chouc, Pamphone and a score of men. Two thousand Japanese who had come from Thakhek, Xieng Khouang and Vientiane were already occupying the town. Nothing can be done to dislodge them. They stick to the conventions of the armistice and refuse to recognize the groups of Franco-Laotian partisans. The Japs destroy everything they can't take away with them and which we need so badly, such as trucks, explosives, ammunition. They set fire to the petrol dumps, they throw their supplies of rice into the Mekong, when the whole population is starving. The soldiers give or sell their weapons to the Viets or to racketeers who have crossed the river to join in the free-for-all.

On 13 September Ricq, through his agents, spreads the rumour round Paksane that the Chinese are arriving. The two hundred Japanese still in the town are so terrified that they build rafts to get away as quickly as possible by river.

According to a pre-arranged plan, the Viets were to assume power as soon as they left. They are taken by surprise and are still busy conferring together when Ricq, in a torrential downpour, moves his partisans into the town. He himself takes over the Customs building and hoists the flag.

He has only two machine-guns, both of which are out of use, a few submachine-guns and some muskets with eight rounds per man.

The Viets are ten times more numerous, they have four times more arms, but they dare not move until the reinforcements they are expecting from Thakhek and Vientiane arrive. When their chief, a certain Nguyen Van Tho, at last receives these reinforcements, he announced he will attack unless Ricq and his partisans move out.

Ricq does indeed move out, with the blessing of that splendid fellow Cosgrove who once again has insolently come and offered his services. According to an agreement they have made with him, the partisans in Thailand will likewise be disarmed forthwith. But Ricq is so gentle, so naive, that Cosgrove's suspicions aren't aroused. Ricq crosses the Mekong late in the afternoon and that night receives a drop of arms. At dawn he seizes some Thai pirogues, recrosses the Mekong and rejoins the rest of the group waiting for him a mile or so north of the town.

The Viets have hoisted the red flag and are celebrating their victory.

This ceremony is attended by our friend Si Mong, who is now *chau-muong*. Ricq falls upon them. In five minutes thirty Viets bite the dust. The rest take to their heels, abandoning their weapons. Father Maurel moves back into his church, which had been transformed into a propaganda centre, and celebrates a Te Deum in front of the portraits of Marx, Lenin and Ho-Chi-Minh. What I tried to do at Vientiane, Ricq succeeded in doing at Paksane.

I rejoin them, having left a mere handful of agents in the capital and, five miles outside it, a small armed group with orders to lie low and avoid engaging the enemy.

Khammay informs us that Si Mong is hiding out in the house of an old Chinese woman. I bring a rope with me, which is all we need to deal with the swine. He doesn't even defend himself but, backing up against a wall, stars at us with the eyes of a madman. Pamphone goes up to him and slaps him three times across the face.

"I saved your life, Your Excellency," Si Mong whimpers.

"So, as you see, I'm not taking yours. But it's you who betrayed the Phou-Khouay camps to the Japanese. Gibelin and Ricq are going to kill you—they haven't the same reasons as myself for showing you indulgence."

Si Mong is in such a hurry to talk that he splutters:

"I know what the Viets are going to do, I know where their hide-outs and ammunition depots are. I know the names of all the Laotians working for them. I'll tell you everything if you spare my life, even the place where the American captain meets Nguyen Van Tho. I've always liked the French. I only wanted to avoid the Japanese and Vietminh reprisals."

I pick up the rope, tie his wrists together and drag him out of the house.

A crowd has gathered and greets its glorious *chau-muong* by throwing stones and spitting on him. Si Mong is so wild with rage that he almost recovers his courage. He would like to bite and hit back.

Having arrived at the Customs building, we untie him. Ricq takes him into his office and interrogates him for the rest of the day.

Next morning we arrested the whole of the local Vietminh network and seized four arms depots.

We were just in time. Some units of the 93rd Division coming from Yunnan were manifesting the intention of moving into Paksane. They were a band of looters who were out for what they could get now that there was no longer any danger. They were good for nothing except pillaging, killing, raping and burning. The British had driven them out of Burma at gun point.

Cosgrove had organized a very clever plot to get rid of us. The Viets and the Lao-Issara were to let the Chinese in, while the French were to be interned, massacred or driven into the jungle. The Chinese flag was to be hoisted alongside the National Front flag—an emblem of bright red relieved by a single blue star.

Consternation of the Chinese general on disembarking from his launch. He expects to find friends, he sees only Frenchmen; he expects to see the Chinese and Vietminh flags, he sees only ours.

In a trench nearby there are a hundred men with three machine-guns and two mortars.

"The forward elements of my battalion," Ricq calmly tells him with his customary formality.

We have no shells for the mortars, no ammunition for the machine-guns.

The Chinaman gives an angry scowl. He confers with a few popinjays on his staff, then re-embarks uttering threats.

"Tomorrow," he says, "you'll see a regiment arrive. Our men will land even if you oppose them by force."

28 September

There are now ten thousand Chinese soldiers in Laos, equipped with the most up-to-date American weapons which they luckily don't know how to use but which they sell. There are two thousand well armed Viets. There are five hundred French and Laotians all told, armed with ancient pop-guns.

I have just received orders to re-occupy Vientiane. I must steal a march on the glorious warriors of the 93rd Division who are preparing to occupy the capital. They are pinching everything, even door-frames. This time I make careful plans for my re-entry.

30 September

Inevitably, I bump up against the Chinese. So far there are only fourteen of them, who have slipped in before I could. They were made to parade under the triumphant arches erected by the Vietnamese and they believe they are masters of the town. Their colonel asks me to lay down my arms. I tell him, with all the oriental courtesy I can muster, to go and take a running jump at himself. He goes off to notify Chiang Kai-shek (through the Americans' transmitter) of this fresh French aggression against China. Next day there are forty Chinese. They try to take over the police. I grapple with them like a good fellow. There are now a hundred and fifty of them.

At Luang-Prabang, the king who was in favour of us is deposed. The Vietnamese are becoming insolent again and provoking my wretched men.

The Chinese and Americans are urging them on. I have the official appointment of Town Major (with a strength of fifty men) and Resident, but no civil servant has called on me. I have some notices put up, they are immediately torn down. An American colonel, accompanied by the inevitable Cosgrove and the chief of staff of the Chinese division, comes and lectures me about the San Francisco Conference which proclaims "the principle of independence for the colonies after the war with the exception of those that have not yet reached a sufficient degree of evolution to govern themselves". In the latter case, the colonel adds, they will have to be guided by a great power.

I ask him if France is still a great power.

Cosgrove replies for him:

"I don't think so. But she still has some lovely museums."

A hundred more Chinese arrive as reinforcements. I move my forty fellows out of the town and remain in the Residency with Meynadier and three men. Meynadier never feels at ease unless everything is going very badly.

30 September

I have just been arrested, I have just been released again.

Transported on Chinese barges, supplied with arms by the Americans, the Viets attacked Ricq at Paksane and arrested Pamphone, Si Mong and three of his men. Ricq withdrew during the night, then came back. Pamphone was liberated just as he and Si Mong were being led off to be shot.

But a Chinese merchant got killed by a stray bullet. The general in command of the Vientiane division claims this was a prearranged massacre. He produces some faked photographs. In reprisal, I am locked up in the Xien Nip barracks.

I was released with apologies so exaggerated as to be downright insulting. On my way back to town, a Viet who was waiting for me tossed a grenade into my car. It was an old French grenade and the firing-pin had been eaten away by rust. Stop press: the Chinese are also having trouble with the Communists. The Viet flags are disappearing from the Vietnamese quarter. I see the possibility of playing a trump card and invite the stalwarts of the 93rd Division to a great banquet.

15 October

My little scheme seems to be working.

15 November

It actually worked too well. I am now in Saigon Hospital with two bullets in my legs and another in my shoulder. This time it was Lam Sammay who organized the attempt on my life. I had succeeded in alienating the Chinese completely from the Viets. Then I had driven off along the Paksane road to meet Ricq and let him know my plans. Major Ports, of Force 136, accompanied me with a couple of bodyguards.

Ports was just telling me how Cosgrove had allowed Lieutenant de Belza to be killed, when we came under fire from three machine-guns concealed behind a bush. Ports was wounded in the head, one of my guards had his leg shattered. I felt the sting and impact of the bullets. The driver took fright, skidded, and the car overturned. We took cover in a ditch while the Viets set fire to the car. We waited for help for four hours. My wounds hurt like hell. Luckily Ports had a bottle of whisky with him. The alcohol served to bathe our wounds and raise our morale.

The war is over for me. Ricq is taking my place in Vientiane.

Two days ago I was decorated in hospital with the Légion d'Honneur. Colonel Durozel, the head of the D.G.E.R., then asked me to soldier on with them. He did not appreciate my initiative when, despite his orders, I seized Vientiane. But since then I've redeemed myself by opposing the Chinese and Viet-minhs. No, I shan't stay on. The timber I've stored since the war is worth a fortune today and I'm only disinterested when I am my own master.

I advised him to take on Ricq instead, a fellow who is unlikely to commit "enormities". As for me, I'm going to start life afresh.

Leclerc's regiments are moving up towards Tonkin, setting fire to villages and looting the shops. A new war has just begun. I don't want anything to do with it.

The light went out in the prison. Ricq closed his eyes.

On 25 April 1946 the troops of the expeditionary corps had again recaptured Vientiane, and the viceroy had fled to Thailand.

By September Laos had been completely liberated, and the Vietminhs driven back to the Than Hoa.

But already, for the last two months, Captain Ricq had become a humble ethnologist, attached to the French School of Far-Eastern Studies and living in a thatch hut. He had not even been invited to the reception given in the presence of the king to celebrate the victory.

But Prince Phoum Sanakon was President, and Pamphone was Minister of National Defence. Lieutenant Si Mong had rejoined the army and, after a six-month course in France, had come back a captain.

Chouc had gone back to Nouei-Phou Lak without anyone having thought of recommending him for a decoration. Sergeants Thon and Chanda were on a parachute course in Saigon.

Antoine Gibelin was selling teak in order to buy himself girls. Every now and then he would come and call on his old friend.

In the silence of the hut they would allot positions of command to the men they considered the best, the only men they knew because they had fought on their side.

The Resident and the military commander were the only two who knew what Ricq's duties were. They resented taking advice from him and several times requested his recall either because he was doing nothing or else because he was doing too much or because he refused to put pressure on his Laotian friends.

The government that had emerged from the resistance proved a failure.

Prince Sanakon was constantly drunk, and his ministers slavishly took their orders from the French. Pamphone, who was denied both soldiers and funds, handed in his resignation.

Ricq suggested going to Bangkok and fetching back the only man with sufficient prestige and following to become a real head of state: Prince Sisang.

Six months after he had become President, Sisang sent for him and said:

"Laos is a country without cohesion and is liable to fall apart. We must restore peace at all costs. My cousin, Prince Lam Sammay, isn't a Communist. The Laotians can't stand the Vietnamese, no matter what their political opinion. The day Sammay is with us again, the rebellion will come to an end. He is the Laotian guarantor of this Vietnamese rebellion. If I try to establish contact with him I'll only arouse suspicion. You won't. Your work as an ethnologist might justifiably take you to Sam Neua. It's strange how quickly everyone has forgotten the valiant little Captain Ricq."

"What shall I say to him?"

"Nothing has been done so far about education. I need a good minister to deal with it. Colonel Durozel promised me I could always count on you."

Footsteps in the corridor outside: it was Khammay coming back, lighting his way with a torch.

"Mattei's Piper-cub has vanished," he said, "and the Junkers has caught fire. Mattei is hiding out in Uncle Yong's opium den. General Si Mong has seen to everything. You'd better accept his conditions."

"What about Ven?"

"I didn't have time to go and see her."

"What about your friends?"

"They're all away. Soumboun is dead. He was given a transfusion from the wrong blood-group to replace what he had lost."

The doctor had been caught out in front of everyone. He had bowed his head, but with his hand in his pocket he could feel the hundred thousand kips he had received..

[5]

The Plain of Jars

THE 20 July 1964 was an unremarkable day except for the heat. Vientiane was transformed into a steam room, and the three evening showers did nothing to cool the atmosphere.

Several streets were flooded and two huts washed away.

On the edge of the river, the big event was neither the *putsch* nor the change of district leader, but the 500-lb *paboeuk* caught by That, a fisherman. It was the biggest that had been seen for years. The *paboeuk* is a sort of huge catfish which in Cambodia is so fat that it is only good for making oil. But after mounting the rapids of the Mekong, it arrives at Vientiane with a firm and delicate flesh. The fisherman would have liked to sell his catch in the market, but he was obliged to give a *boun* to celebrate his remarkable exploit. The party, in spite of the curfew, went on until late at night.

Wanting to make the most of his fish, That ate so much that he was sick. A witch-doctor had to be called in who was also a palmist, sorcerer, fortune-teller, shawl vendor and police informer. He made That drink a decoction of herbs that he had rubbed on a whetstone to reduce them to a powder. For this he charged thirty kips. That's mother-in-law, the aged and cantankerous Me Fa Lom, rushed round to the neighbours saying her son-in-law had been punished for having insulted the water *phis* and Phrom, the mother-crow. Instead of throttling the *paboeuk,* the king of fishes, with a piece of rope, had he not disembowelled it with a knife? Just what you might expect from a creature like That who respected neither local custom nor his elders.

In the course of this party no one remembered that one year earlier, to the cheers of the population, Captain Chanda was seizing Vientiane with a battalion of paratroops.

Before flying up to the Plain of Jars, Cléach thought he had better send his agency a summing-up of the main coups d'état that had either steeped in blood or merely animated Laotian political life since 1955. Out of an exaggerated sense of the dramatic, in a country in which all is comedy, the term "coup d'état" had often been bestowed on a change of ministry or an electoral swing brought about under the pressure of certain elements who had at their disposal either foreign currency or arms of foreign manufacture; the last three had occurred between July 1963 and July 1964. Only one was to leave a gory memory.

On 20 July 1963 Captain Chanda and his battalion of paratroops seized the town of Vientiane, bringing Prince Sisang back to power. One man killed, six wounded. The War Minister, General Si Mong, head of the so-called right-wing faction, who had the backing of the Americans and Thais, took refuge at Savannakhet, in the south.

On 22 December 1963 General Si Mong recaptured Vientiane from Captain Chanda's paratroops after shelling the town from the Thai bank of the river.

Prince Sisang fled to France. 300 dead, 1200 wounded.

On 6 April 1964, as a result of the repeated reverses of the Royal Laotian Army, on the one hand against the Neutralists who had taken refuge in the Plain of Jars and on the other against the Communists who had infiltrated up to the outskirts of the large towns, the ambassadors of the powers interested in the fate of Laos intervened in their turn. They forced General Si Mong to make up his quarrel with the Neutralists and to hand over the reins of office to Prince Sisang who once again found himself President. This intervention came to be known as the "Ambassadors' *putsch*".

Then came the "half-cock coup d'état", of which there were no traces to be seen today since ministers and generals had apparently resumed their previous appointments. Ricq alone was still in prison.

Cléach looked at Flore asleep on the bed. The noise of the typewriter had not woken her. Under the mosquito-net, she looked like a lovely poisonous flower in a hot-house.

The old Citroen was difficult to start. At the window of the pent-house above Uncle Yong's opium den, Mattei's unshaven face appeared.

"What the hell is he doing there?" Cléach asked himself. "Generally speaking, pimps don't go to brothels, nor do dope-peddlers frequent opium dens . . . except to rake in the cash . . ."

Cléach had had great difficulty in getting a seat on the white International Commission aircraft. Luckily the pilot, Hubert Péningaud, was a friend of his. Long before Cléach, before Gibelin even, Flore had honoured Péningaud for a few weeks with her favours. Those are the sort of memories which create a bond between two men when they have not yet turned the women they have shared into a symbol, a statue or a private property. Just before take-off Péningaud hid Cléach in the cockpit. The two Indian officers escorting the aircraft had nevertheless noticed his presence. But Cléach had promised to stand them a Chinese dinner, a jaunt to a night-club and a couple of girls they could afterwards take home with them. The Indians had allowed themselves to be won over by these fine promises which the journalist knew he was unable to keep. His funds were low and the Thai, Vietnamese and Chinese tarts could not bear the Indians, to whom they referred among themselves as "white Negroes". The plane, a Dakota which had been through the whole of the Indo-China war, took off in pouring rain.

"Put the intercom helmet on," Péningaud yelled at Cléach. "Can you hear me? If it wasn't in order to pick up Meynadier and his little pals, I'd never come out in such weather. The airstrip on the Plain of Jars may be held by the Viets at this moment. It's the same old situation as during the Indo-China war. When there was any danger, the military pilots took refuge behind their regulations and the civilians went in their place."

"The French Military Mission in Laos doesn't have a plane."

"They ought to have sent for one, considering all the money they're spending on the Negroes."

Péningaud was often deliberately difficult; he would then contradict himself still more frequently and be astounded when this was pointed out.

He was fifty-six years old, with grey locks plastered to his forehead by his helmet and a face that looked devoured by disease. In fact he was in the best of health, but would certainly have failed most flying and navigational tests. Short-sighted as a mole, he never looked at his instruments but relied on his instinct.

"Meynadier must be pretty fed up," Cléach remarked.

"You can say that again. He must be furious at leaving his bloody paradise, as Gibelin used to call it. You know that on the Plain of Jars he's the big boss! He makes such a nuisance of himself that the Laotians let him have his own way. Officially, he was sent to Muong Pham to teach fellows who've been fighting for ten years how to handle a gun. Adviser, my arse! Luckily he's up there, otherwise the whole Neutralist army would have buggered off long ago."

The pilot turned to the wireless operator, a big man from Rouen who sat crouched over his set, and asked:

"Bernardin, are you in contact with the Plain of Jars?"

Bernadin replied in his thick burr:

"No, skipper. There's no answer from Muong Pham. From here, we should have got through to them already."

"The Viets must be closing in on Chanda's command post. Meynadier's been forced to pack his traps."

Tossed about by the gusts of wind, the plane kept dropping in the air pockets and bouncing up again.

Péningaud twisted round in his seat and, through the cabin door, saw the two Indian officers vomiting into paper bags. Satisfied, he closed the door again.

"At least we shan't be bothered by those two. You know, Cléach, I'm only meant to be carrying out a reconnaissance. No question of landing. Once again I'm going to be forced to make up some story or other about a break-down. What whoppers that fellow Meynadier has made me tell! One day I brought him some plastic explosive which one of his pals had pinched from Camp Kennedy. Plastic in this lovely white aircraft, which is only entitled to carry wounded and medical supplies! Enough to get me the sack. And you know who I had sitting on those cases? That one-armed fellow from the Red Cross. I told him they contained serum; that's why they were marked fragile. I had tried to paint out the word 'Explosives', but it was still quite visible.

"You know the one about the International Commission?"

Cléach, who had heard the joke the very first day he arrived, resignedly prepared to listen to it for the tenth, the twentieth time:

"A Pole, an Indian and a Canadian were up on the Plain of Jars in a neutralized zone where no one was supposed to be. A Communist tank suddenly appeared twenty yards off. The Canadian seized the Pole by the sleeve:

" 'Hi, Poniatowski, just look at that Viet tank! It's heading straight for us'.

"The Pole looked and shook his head:

" 'I don't see anything'.

"The Canadian then called out to the Indian who was a few yards behind him:

" 'I say, Brahma, you at least see that tank, don't you?'

"The Indian made the gesture of counting out banknotes:

" 'How much will you give me for seeing it, Laffleur?'

"Ha-ha-ha!"

The wireless operator leant towards Péningaud.

"I've picked up something. It comes from Muong Pham. But the reception's rotten."

"Try to decipher it, you nitwit!"

A few minutes later the operator handed over a sheet of paper. After reading it Péningaud passed it on to Cléach:

"Sporadic mortar fire on the airfield. Visibility good. Get a move on, the Viets are coming."

"Mortar fire," Péningaud growled. "Shall we land all the same?"

"Why ask me? You know perfectly well you will. His Lordship has a reputation to keep up; he never leaves his pals in the lurch."

"Go and warn the Indians," the pilot told Bernardin. "They believe anything you tell them, maybe because you're as black as they are. What a bunch of racialists! Spin them the usual yarn about a breakdown. A radiator-hose has burst; impossible to get back to Vientiane. So we have to land to do repairs on the spot. Tie them into their seats."

The sky was clearing. The heavy black clouds had dissolved, revealing grey mountains and streams swollen with pinkish water.

The plane buzzed over a bare crag.

"We're in Meo country," Péningaud announced. "Look, just above the Yanks' maquis, into which you're so keen on sticking your dirty nose, eh, Cléach? Admittedly, there must be a lot of funny business going on, with all that opium lying about. . . . Look at those little fellows galloping about on their ponies, and further on, over there, some smoke.

"Christ Almighty, helicopters! They look like 'Bananas'. And next to them a Sikorski. There's a gun firing down there . . . those two flashes on your left. Muong Pham's right between those two peaks. Fasten your belt, we're going to dive. Who was the silly idiot who said one couldn't do aerobatics in a Dakota? It's absolutely made for the job."

The plane taxied over the grass, throwing up a cloud of spray. A man leapt into the aircraft, his poncho glistening in the rain. It was Captain Meynadier:

"Péningaud, you silly bugger, get this plane parked properly. Move her to the end of the runway, otherwise, with all this stuff dropping round us, you won't have a plane any longer. Like the rest of us, you'll have to get back to Vientiane on foot. Unless you prefer the Viet re-education camps. Hellow, Cléach. We've been missing you. Even you won't be able to make more of a muddle than there is already."

His emaciated face was streaming with water and his red beret was no more than a rag.

The two Indian officers showed signs of apprehension.

"What . . . what . . . what is it?" they asked.

"I'll deal with them," said Meynadier.

The plane started moving again. A shell fell thirty yards away.

The Indians kept repeating:

"What is it?"

In broken English, Meynadier explained:

"It's the others, the Viets, the Pathet Lao, the Communists, the Chinese; they're not respecting the cease-fire. They're firing on the International Commission plane. What a scandal! I'll have to draft a long report with fifty copies, which the fifty recipients will chuck into their waste-paper baskets, because no one gives a damn about what's going on up here. While the repairs are being done, come into our dug-out. We'll make you a hot toddy. It's a visit you mustn't miss: the Muong Pham Command Post. After this we're closing down. . . ."

Having recovered his moral and physical composure, one of the International Commission officers protested, waving his bamboo swagger-stick:

"Unforgivable . . . this break-down. We're allotted an obsolete aircraft . . . the importance of our mission . . ."

Péningaud, who was emerging from the cockpit, lost his temper. He refused to let anyone insult his Dakota:

"If you're not satisfied, why don't you provide your own planes and pilots? Your old crates are eaten away by termites. If you lean on them they crumble apart."

Péningaud did not even pause to have a look at the engine which he claimed had broken down, but followed everyone into the dug-out.

At the end of the runway, on a hummock of earth and damp, moss-covered rocks, stood an ancient post consisting of some flooded trenches and three blockhouses covered in corrugated iron sheeting and protected by sand-bags. They surrounded a slightly larger central dug-out, from which a long aerial projected. This was the Muong Pham command post. A petrol stove made from a jerrycan gave out a feeble heat which did nothing to dispel the icy draughts. A boy stood over it, boiling some water in a ration tin.

Recovering their former resignation, the two Indians huddled together as they waited for the toddy, for death or maybe for nothing.

"What's the situation?" Cléach asked Meynadier.

The captain lost his temper:

"Did you come here to see me or make a nuisance of yourself?"

"Both. Where's your pal Chanda?"

"In the first place, he's no longer my pal; he's a skunk. He's up there with the Yanks. How's Ricq?"

"Still in jug. But I think he'll soon be out."

"I was afraid they might bump him off. They've tried hard enough."

"So you, too, knew what his real job was."

"I've known Ricq since 1944. We were on the same course with Force 136 in India, we were parachuted together into Laos. At the time of Dien Bien Phu I helped him organise the maquis bands in the north, which came to be known as the G.C.M.A.s.

"When I made a fool of myself in Algeria, he was the one who saved my bacon by getting me posted back to Laos to work with him again. Ricq was my boss, the only man I acknowledged as such—yes, Lieutenant-Colonel Ricq of the S.D.E.C.E., of Nouei-Phou Lak, of Paksane, the Thai maquis and Chanda's *putsch*. Si Mong used to be his houseboy and he made Sisang into a president. Will that help to fill your paper, you little newshawk?"

"You've deceived me good and proper. And what about you, the great warlord?

"Only two companies left, barely two hundred paratroopers. In a couple of hours the Viets will be here."

"That's all that remains of the Neutralist army? What about the battalion of Russian tanks? There was a lot of talk in Vientiane yesterday about their victorious counter-attack."

"Colonel Thong Dy, who was in command of them, didn't spare them or himself. Yet he was very keen on his lovely P.T.76s. Tanks that can move through water, plough through mud. For two pins they'd grow wings and fly. Thong didn't want them touched. He kicked up a hell of a fuss when I wanted to try one out.

"Thong Dy's battalion got surrounded yesterday afternoon in

the Nam Salat basin. Thong tried to get through to us. I went out with a battalion to retrieve him. We took up a position above the Xieng-Khouang road on the few crags that were not yet occupied by the Viets.

"Through my field-glasses I saw the tanks advance. Two of them were blown up by mines. A third was knocked out by an artillery barrage. When they were almost on top of them, the Viets demolished the lovely Russian tanks with rudimentary but damned efficient Chinese bazookas. Remember this date, Cléach—on 19 July 1964, at four o'clock in the afternoon, some Chinese bazookas destroyed several Soviet tanks. So far it's only material that has been engaged. But soon it will be men. What was there to stop a Soviet adviser being in one of those tanks and a Chinese adviser firing a bazooka at it, eh?

"Colonel Thong Dy is *tay*, that's to say dead, blown to smithereens in his lovely command tank, because his best friend, that swine Thon, deserted and joined the Reds with two battalions of paratroops . . . troops I had trained myself, who had been through this very pair of hands. They followed him from sheer habit. They didn't even know where they were going.

"The remaining tanks turned round and fell straight into the trap. Then they surrendered."

"Even after Thon and his two battalions went over to the Communists . . ."

"Not 'went over', 'deserted', as I said."

"Chanda still had ten battalions left, that's to say six thousand men. Where have they got to?"

"Those battalions were merely companies. The six thousand men had never been more than three thousand. They all took to their heels and made for the mountains. After Thon's treachery, the position had become impossible. I got through to Chanda by wireless at seven o'clock this morning on the wavelength of the Americans, the ones with the Meo maquis. Chanda himself ordered me to get his chaps out immediately and leave the stores and artillery behind. Some Meo guides would be waiting for them at the foot of the mountains. I asked him whether I was supposed to join him as well.

"He was silent for a moment, then I heard him talking to someone next to him. In the end he replied:

" 'I'm sorry, Meynadier. Frenchmen aren't wanted up here. Forgive me'.

"First it was Thon, and now here was Chanda leaving me in the lurch. It was under my instruction that Chanda fired his first rifle shot, when we were at Nouie-Phou Lak. Until then he only knew how to use a bow and arrows. At Saigon I put him through his first parachute jump. When he came to France with Thon on a training course, they both used to spend their leave at our place in Antibes, where my father is about the only hotel-keeper who in the summer doesn't dish up fish soup out of a tin. On 20 July, when Chanda organised his *putsch*, he was lucky enough to have me behind him; otherwise he would have botched the whole business.

"Exactly a year ago today. Funny sort of anniversary! Ricq in jug, Gibelin murdered, Thon with the Viets, Chanda with the Yanks, and me all alone up here in the shit.

"Three days ago it was even worse, with all the women and children those Coordination swine had landed on the airfield. You should have seen that wretched herd rushing about in the rain. Mortar shells kept falling right amongst them. Sheer butchery. You know Lieutenant Vallières? He's anything but a milksop, yet he was blubbing his heart out."

Meynadier looked at his watch:

"Twelve o'clock. They've been marching for five hours. But it will take them ten to reach the foot of the mountains. Now it's our turn to pull out. As soon as I heard the sound of the plane, I gave orders for my two companies to withdraw. They'll soon be here."

"You speak of those men as though they were yours. You don't belong to the Laotian army, and they don't belong to the French."

"You're right. Officially, I'm only an adviser . . . like Vallières, like Lutz, like Jourdin . . . like those twenty thousand American advisers fighting in South Vietnam. What exactly is an adviser these days? A white man leading native troops who, on their own, are incapable of fighting or looking after themselves. I don't know why the South Vietnamese and the American advisers are fighting, whether it's for the pay or to defend their country against the

Communists. But those two companies of Laotian paratroops are fighting for me, and for no other reason. They refused to follow Thon who was their colonel. When he came and saw them that night, the officers told him: 'Yes, we'll go over to the Viets with you, but only if you have a note signed by Captain Meynadier, giving his consent'. Nothing about Chanda, you hear, just Meynadier."

"What are you going to do with them?"

"They're going to join Chanda all the same. They're the last two hundred paratroops he has. Two of my warrant officers, Mérot and Lutz, will accompany them up to the Meos. Then the Americans will bring my two fellows back to Vientiane. I hope they'll have time to have a look at what's going on up there. Like me, they're on good terms with Picarle, the oldest lost soldier in the French army . . . since 1955. I'm fascinated by those Meos. They do sweet bugger-all. Yet they're brave lads, well trained and armed to the teeth."

"You're leaving behind the stores, the guns, the trucks, the bulldozers?"

"Have you got room in the plane for them?

"Every army in the world is overflowing with material. What's lacking is the men; but they're only lacking on our side. After all, Chanda may be right to have gone over to the Yanks, and Thon to the Communists. We can't do anything more for them except preach at them and make promises."

There was a sound of shuffling feet outside, a clatter of arms, a rustle of branches, words of command and muffled cries. Meynadier went out. Cléach followed him, for he knew his friend had to do what he disliked most in the world: tell a lie.

A dozen Laotian officers, Lieutenant Vallières and the four French warrant officers, all soaking wet, haggard with fatigue, filthy dirty and covered in mud, crowded round Meynadier.

"This is the situation," he said. "We can't hold Muong Pham, the Plain of Jars and the Tran Ninh Plateau on our own. It would need two divisions. So we're going to take to the mountains. Chanda is waiting for us up there. Lutz and Mérot, you'll each take a company. Compass bearing 30 degrees south. Radio silence.

You'll pull out by sections . . . As soon as the Viets show up, you fire and clear out at once. We've got to check their advance, not fight against them. Watch out for the ammunition. Don't waste it. Further drops are out of the question . . ."

"And you, Captain," asked a Laotian lieutenant, "what are you going to do?"

Meynadier growled:

"Apart from the two warrant officers mentioned, all the rest are flying out with me at once. We take off in three minutes' time."

"It's not true!" Vallières exclaimed. "We're not going to leave our paratroopers in the lurch just when things are as bad as they can be. You're not going to do that, Meynadier?"

"Who said anything about leaving them in the lurch? The Mission is scouring Vientiane for tents, blankets, ammunition and men. There must be three or four hundred fellows wandering about the town without leave. The whole lot will be booted back here. We'll recreate a battalion . . ."

There was a sob in his voice . . .

"Regiments, a new army."

His voice broke.

"We'll start all over again, we'll take Vientiane, make peace, go back home and have a *boun* every night till the end of our days."

Cléach seized Meynadier by the arm:

"Steady on, old boy."

Dragging their feet, the two companies set off again. Standing on the hummock of mud, Meynadier saluted them as they went past, his face streaming with rain or maybe tears.

When they had all disappeared, swallowed up by the mist and the rain, he picked up his carbine, removed the breech and flung it into the stream flowing at the foot of the hummock.

"You do the same," he said to Vallières and the three other warrant officers. "No weapons allowed on the C.I.C. plane. Weapons can be found anywhere; the whole world's full of them. All that remains now is to lower the curtain. What do you say, Cléach? Let's get going."

Péningaud had to go "all out" to get his plane off the water-logged runway.

The first Viets to appear on the airstrip belonged to the Hanoi Officer-Cadet Training Centre, who had been sent to Laos to gain practical experience of warfare. They were disciplined units who carried out the orders they were given to the letter.

So they did not fire on the white International Commission aircraft. The Laotians or Pathet Lao minorities could not have resisted such a target.

At Vientiane the group of French "advisers" assembled at the villa they had been allotted near the embassy, opposite the French P.X. where sardines, wine and camemberts were available. Without even changing his clothes, Captain Meynadier went off to report to General Molliergues, the head of the Military Mission. He was surly and brief:

"Sir, hostilities have come to an end in the Plain of Jars. The shooting has stopped. The last Russian tanks, after Colonel Thong Dy's death, surrendered. The Communists collected a mass of material in perfect condition, enough to arm a division: five batteries of 105 guns, two batteries of 155, mortars, trucks, jeeps, wireless sets, hutments, tents, blankets, food supplies, three bulldozers, four electric generators, not to mention Colonel Thong Dy's L.T.76s which are among the finest tanks in the world. Two parachute battalions, the 1st and the 3rd, that's to say about a thousand men with their weapons and equipment, went over to the Viets with Colonel Thon. A further two thousand soldiers have deserted, gone home or been taken prisoner. That's all, sir."

General Molliergues took off his steel-rimmed spectacles and wiped them. The lenses were misted over by the damp. Without them, he looked helpless and pathetic, blinking his little red eyes. He put his spectacles on again and at once reverted to the colourless, spiritless man he was, who inspired neither respect nor affection and attracted even no attention.

The general, who wanted further details, invited Meynadier to dinner. But the captain dodged this, pleading fatigue as an excuse.

"I absolutely understand," Molliergues said ironically. "These last days have been extremely hard. What you want now is a little peace and quiet, a 'break', as you paratroopers say. Just a word of advice, however . . . Don't meddle in Ricq's business. At any price. We're already in enough trouble on that score. Have a good night's sleep and tomorrow draft me a detailed report on the final incidents. Of course, you will only mention your official role as an adviser and instructor. No point in stating that your subordinates and yourself also saw fit to play at soldiers."

Meynadier saluted, but the tone in which he said, "Very good, sir," was an insult and at the same time a mis-statement.

Then he went round to see Cléach. He could not have sat through a tête-à-tête dinner with the general without venting his feelings, still less could he have spent all evening with Vallières and the warrant officers. He could well imagine their unvoiced reproach and exaggerated thoughtfulness.

The journalist was not at home, but on the table he had left a copy of the cable he had just sent off.

Cléach made no mention of the French "advisers" or their true role.

The captain took off his soaking, mud-stained clothes to have a shower. Flore came in, swaying her hips, with some whisky and some ice. He took the whisky and quietly said:

"Flore, you make me sick. You can't see a pair of trousers without getting ideas. You can't bear the thought of two men getting on well together and so you try to come between them. Get out of here until Cléach is back."

"Why are you angry with me?"

"I'm not angry, I just don't want you in here. Since I'm not made of wood, I want you to leave this room. Have you seen Ven?"

"Ven is staying here because she's frightened. Ven is so silly. She's either in tears or changing her clothes. But anyway, who said I want to sleep with you? I don't find you attractive. But I know your secret: you'd like to have Ven. You've actually wanted her for some time. Ricq's in prison and there's no danger of your giving her a baby. She already has one in her belly. Maybe it's Ricq's . . . maybe someone else's . . ."

"You're stupid as well as being a slut. I've known Ven ever since she was born. Her father, Chouc, who's also a friend, wanted to call her Françoise because Ricq's name was François. Ricq took her in his arms. He was so moved that he dropped her. I picked her up. Ven is part of my family, the only family I still have."

When Cléach came back he found Meynadier lying on a bed and Flore in the kitchen sulking.

"What shall we do?" he asked. "Treat ourselves to a Chinese dinner? Get roaring-drunk?"

"No," said Meynadier. "You know I've never smoked opium? I munched some once to get rid of a stomach-ache because I had nothing else handy. Gibelin suggested it. Opium's not very popular with the paratroopers. Just a way of dodging the issue.

"Today's the anniversary of Chanda's *putsch.* Just imagine, I too believed all the nonsense I was told by that little fellow whose parents used to wander about the mountains half naked. Everything's collapsed, there's nothing left. I must try and find something to do, otherwise I'm going to burst and commit some gigantic folly.

"Ricq's in prison. With a friend, you share your rations when you're hungry, your water-bottle when you're thirsty. With Ricq, I shared a dream. You see, knowing he's in jug makes my blood boil; I can't stop thinking about how to get him out. It would be child's play to capture a prison. But a camp like Xien Nip is a different proposition altogether. Let's go round to your Chinese general. But leave Flore at home. She won't understand what I have to say to you . . . Oh, what the hell, you may as well bring her along . . . What the devil does it matter now!"

"When Flore smokes she doesn't hear anything, she just sucks her thumb like a baby. She takes refuge in a strange paradise. Maybe her paradise is merely a cocoon, a cradle or a womb."

Cléach and Meynadier lay stretched out on the bunk. Flore, lying on her back and staring at the smoke-stained ceiling, was already in her cocoon.

Between them stood the tray: in the centre, the little oil lamp with its glass shade, the needles, the copper bowl containing the liquid opium, the long bamboo pipe with the seven precious stones to protect the smoker against the seven obsessions. Yong, the owner of the den, affable, indifferent and emaciated, brought them some China tea which was almost colourless but whose merits could only be appreciated, like the drug itself, through years of education. Just a gesture of courtesy.

Then he withdrew, a flickering shadow, an indefinite shape in the deep penumbra of the den, impregnated with the heady, pungent, oily smell of the Xieng Khouang opium. An assistant took his place—either his daughter or his wife, no one quite knew which. She wore trousers and a little black jacket, her hair was cut short, her face was deathly-pale and expressionless, and a tiny artificial diamond glittered in the lobe of one ear.

She rolled the pellets with her slender fingers and held them over the flame without moving a single feature of her face. When the pellet was ready she tapped the bamboo pipe with the needle to attract the smoker's attention.

His first pipe had made Meynadier cough. The disagreeable smell nauseated him. But he had persevered, learning how to inhale and retain in his lungs the thick smoke that smelt at the same time of earth, decaying vegetation, a freshly dug ditch in a garden. After his sixth pipe he felt a great sense of peace. His brain grew clearer. For the first time he understood that the men opposing him and his aims were not necessarily dirty dogs impelled by the desire to do him harm and that their conception of the world, of life and politics, might be no less valid than his own.

Cléach poured him out some tea; he had difficulty in picking up the cup, so clumsy had his movements become. But he succeeded in talking effortlessly about things he usually kept to himself:

"I've never been able to judge my life and actions so clearly. I thought I had ideas, but all I had was affection or dislike for such and such a chief or such and such a comrade . . ."

Mattei came in, wearing a tie and impeccably creased trousers, bending his tall frame to pass under the beams. His only concession to the heat was a folded handkerchief with which he wiped his brow. Aggressively, Cléach asked him:

"I thought you liked being alone in the evening?"

"Not this evening. I'm frightened of being alone."

The Corsican spoke in a tone of utter despair that surprised the journalist.

"Sit down," Meynadier said to him, "or lie down and have a drink. You're reputed to be a racketeer and a pimp; you're not allowed into any civilized country. But the men of the G.C.M.A.s, especially those of Laos, remember you as the coolest pilot they've ever known. You've come just at the right moment: we're talking about the old days. Ricq's no longer here to tell us to shut up; he's in jug. Gibelin's missing as well."

Cléach propped himself up on one elbow:

"So Mattei belonged to your network?"

"Network indeed! You've been reading too many spy stories. We were merely a few decent fellows, Laotian and French, united behind Ricq. We trusted one another. We had known one another for a long time and we wanted to get this country out of the mess she was in. Behind Ricq, not Gibelin.

"Antoine Gibelin might have remained the boss. But he had pulled out because he couldn't do the same thing for long, because he was no longer interested in all this Laotian nonsense, in which politics, family ties, commerce and sex are involved. He said Laos could no longer be saved."

"Then why did he get himself killed while helping Chanda's Neutralists?"

"Laos may have been lost, but Gibelin couldn't do without her, just as Flore can't do without her dope. Neutralism did at least mean a year or two's respite. When Gibelin was killed he didn't have a cent left. No one would have risked lending him money except old friends like Ricq, like myself, to help him live decently. Only he needed such a devil of a lot! To spend on girls, to overawe those idiots in the bars with those incredible yarns of his. His real adventures were far more fascinating, but he was shy of mentioning them. Girls! They weren't much use to him any more. In the end this outstanding, intelligent, cynical fellow used to resort to the same drugs as the elderly Chinese use in order to make love: powdered stag horn, *giseng* root. Real quack remedies. Father Maurel liked him very much and never stopped telling him off;

'Take some holy water, Antoine, it will cost you far less and do you as much good'.

"Didn't Flore ever mention this to you?

"I think I'm going to have another pipe, with a big cup of tea to take the taste away. I can't stomach this smell of earth and roots."

"You'll be sick."

"I'd like to be sick, I'd like to have a raging fever for two weeks. Then, when I woke up, I'd find it had all been a nightmare. No Chanda, no Gibelin, no Ricq, no 13th May and Public Safety Committees, no *putsch*, no O.A.S., no de Gaulle, no Si Mong, no Dien Bien Phu, no Yanks. Nothing: just a pitch-black tunnel and, right at the end, Meynadier smoking opium because he has nothing more to defend, not even Laos. . . .

"I'd left Laos in November 1946. Ricq was already a civilian again. I went back to France without knowing exactly what I was going to do. After three months' leave in Antibes with my old man I realised I would never again put up with his tirades and the restaurant business. In Indo-China I used to long for France; in France I longed again for Indo-China. I re-enlisted for three years. In 1948 I found myself a warrant officer in a parachute battalion. A year later I became a second-lieutenant, commissioned in the field. In 1950 I was back in France and became a regular. In 1953 I was a lieutenant in a mobile group operating in Tonkin. One didn't have to be a genius to see that the way we were fighting, with tanks against mosquitoes, was bound to turn out badly. The mobile group never moved off the main roads, leaving the Viets free to wander about wherever they wanted, spreading their bloody propaganda. What we had learnt with the British in Force 136 and from our own experience in the maquis, all was forgotten. One fine day, when we were dying of heat under cover of a corrugated iron roof, I was summoned to Hanoi Headquarters. I was received by an extremely cordial colonel. The colonels of Hanoi and Saigon were always cordial towards officers who were just back from the paddyfields. I told him my life story. He questioned me about my first spell in Laos and my training as a wireless operator and commando in India. He wrote down all my answers.

I tried to fathom what all this was about. All of a sudden he asked me whether I would like to work again with Major Ricq. He specified 'a hazardous assignment which might one day prove interesting. You can refuse, of course, and believe me, it won't be held against you. If you accept you'll be attached to the D.G.E.R. because it's the special services who are mounting the operation'. That colonel's lack of enthusiasm and the happy memories I had of Laos and Ricq, and especially of Gibelin, prompted me to accept.

"When, in 1945, I had to choose between Gibelin and Ricq, it was the former I chose, because he was exuberant and colourful. Gibelin was forty-two at that time, Ricq twenty-six, three years older than myself."

"What if you had to make the same choice now?" Cléach asked.

"I should have chosen Ricq."

"I was posted to Saigon. Ricq introduced me to General Durozel, the master spy. Not a very inspiring fellow—cold, detached, thin-lipped, and at the same time exaggeratedly polite. The style that's now much in favour in Uncle Charles' army. There's a man who must have done well for himself. What's more, he was a Polytechnician!"

Cléach interjected:

"But also a Republican. General Durozel had just been pensioned off. A dozen lines this morning in the A.F.P despatch. He had been given his third star and appointed to more important duties. He must have had no illusions, after pursuing that career so long, and forthwith handed in his resignation. He was allowed to leave, much to everyone's relief. What sort of terms was he on with Ricq?"

"Very good, I believe. Whenever he had anything to say, Durozel used to turn to Ricq the whole time, as though he needed his approval.

"He told me: 'We have decided to fight the Communists with their own weapons, by action against their rear lines. It will be a difficult and expensive job. My friend Major Ricq, on the other hand, claims he can do it with very few means. We're going to let him try out his cheap experiment in Laos. You'll help him. Meanwhile we shall pursue our own attempt in Tonkin and the Haute

Région with more substantial means. Naturally, I hope Ricq is right but I don't think so. Waging that sort of war without money demands men of exceptional quality and motives as compelling as those of the early Christians, the early Communists or the genuine resistance workers. You alone will appear in your true colours, Lieutenant Meynadier. Major Ricq will stick to his ethnologist cover story and clandestine role'.

"Ricq was in civilian clothes. He looked like a little clerk with his shabby suit, his tie askew, his cracked and badly polished shoes. But his face and hands were tanned by the sun and rain and he had the loose-limbed gait of a man who was used to the jungle.

"Ricq asked me out to dinner at a fashionable restaurant. He must have made some last-minute enquiries and been sent to the most expensive and flashy establishment. I felt embarrassed at addressing him again by the familiar '*tu*'. He was no longer the same man. I had to remind myself that I had fought beside him, that we had shared the same handful of rice. He drank nothing but tea and ate very little, but kept puffing away at his pipe. I asked him what had become of Gibelin. He told me he was still in Laos where he had resumed his commercial activities.

"Friendship is like an electric current. I felt it seeping back after the initial hesitation. While the people at the other tables were discussing the rate of exchange of the piastre, the rubber market and the price of rice, I gave him an account of my war in Tonkin—the villages that were bombed without anyone checking beforehand to see if there were any Viets in them, the blunders of the staff officers who were trying to fight the Rif War or Leclerc's campaign all over again. I also told him about the myth which was taking shape among the paratroops. He, in his turn, flew off the handle for a moment—unusual for him, because I know few men who have so much self-control. Even in India or at Paksane, he never let himself go.

"Ricq had gone back to France for only one week, to settle some family business. Since then he had never left Indo-China. The exemplary life of a secret agent disguised as an ethnologist! For seven years he had directed the French special services in Laos, the Haute Région and on the Chinese border. But he had also become a genuine ethnologist. That's Ricq all over. He studied the minorities, learnt their languages. At the same time he delved into their history and customs to discover the best means of impelling them, when the time came, to fight against their enemies of the moment: the Viets. He was well acquainted with their doctrines, their methods and their senior commanders. He was even in touch with some of them and had recruited several agents from among the battalions operating in Laos against us.

"Ricq used to send his reports to Paris or Saigon Headquarters. At Saigon they were thrown into the wastepaper-basket, in Paris only Durozel took any interest in them.

"He also had some articles published in the bulletin of the French School of Far-Eastern Studies—a thingamijig for specialists and pedants.

"The famous 'Ricq network' which the American papers are now so full of—what did it amount to? A few Frenchmen who helped him voluntarily, like Mattei and Father Maurel, and also Gibelin, of course, but only when he felt like it. Sometimes the Ministry of the Associated States or the War Ministry used to send him an officer, an administrator or a specialist to assist him on some specific assignment so as to avoid his coming out into the open. Then the fellow would go back home and Ricq would stay on.

"His entire organization was based on Laotians, not one of whom worked for money but sometimes for marginal benefits —promotion, for instance, which he obtained for them through his contacts. The two mainstays of his team were Sisang and Pamphone—the former, wavering, capable, always prepared to dash off to France when he didn't like the look of things, always equally prepared to come back; the latter, less intelligent, less brillant, but staunch, hard-working and absolutely devoted to Ricq. When Pamphone was Minister of the Interior, Ricq used to lodge his friends with the police; when he was Minister for War, he made Chanda and Thon lieutenants.

"Unfortunately Si Mong, when he felt his hour had come, arranged for Pamphone to be killed.

"Ricq had studied Pali and made many friends among the Buddhists. He had found a perfect excuse for visiting the monasteries and travelling about the country in all weathers: the quest for a manuscript of the *Ramayana*. He never acted the part of an intelligence agent. He was never to be seen taking notes or distributing arms or money. He would move into a village or a pagoda and lead the same life as the Laotians, whom he encouraged to talk.

"In Vientiane he lived in a cosy little hut and did his own housework. He spent his pay on helping people here and there. Ricq, I'm certain, hasn't saved a penny. He was even more prodigal than Gibelin, but he sometimes gave the impression of behaving like a dotty old maid and being very tight-fisted.

"His aim was to make Laos into a nation. It was an even greater enormity than any Gibelin had attempted or envisaged.

"The French government had entrusted him with an initial mission: to urge Laos to adhere to the French Union that had just been created with such a song and dance. The French government hoped Vietnam and Cambodia would follow suit. Ricq had put his finger on the error. Laos was to appear in the eyes of the world as an independent nation, even though the French discreetly continued to administer her. It was therefore sheer madness to make her still depend on the Ministry of the Associated States which was based on Paris.

"He obeyed his orders all the same, banking on his personal prestige, his contacts, Sisang and Pamphone, but also on the veterans of the resistance networks, on the religious leaders like the Maha Som, on the Khas, the Thais and the Meos, to whom he had demonstrated that only the presence of France would ensure their liberty. He had convinced them that the Viets were dangerous because they were Vietnamese in search of new territories in which to settle. France alone could prevent them from doing this. Ricq's task was like a torn cloth that had to be mended anew every day.

"But ranged against him there was Si Mong, then a major, later a colonel and eventually a general. Ricq had done his utmost to obstruct his promotion. Unfortunately Si Mong had found some influential protectors in Headquarters and among the French administrators.

"He knew how to organize a parade, click his heels, captivate our military representatives by talking the whole time about 'smashing the Viets', without ever taking command of a battalion or a regiment. He would have been quite incapable of it.

"Already, in 1953, he had plenty of funds at his disposal, sent from Thailand where his uncle, Marshal Aprasith, the man the Americans were backing, had assumed power.

"Ricq worked on a basis of friendship. Si Mong distributed presents to those he needed, he was thus able to make them indebted to him and compromise them. After that he held them in his power.

"In October 1952 the Viets launched their big offensive against Laos, which had just joined the French Union. We were in honour bound to defend her. Then came Na San. Ricq found himself personally involved in this fighting, but he wanted to direct it in his own way.

"Ricq at that time wanted the maquis bands to fend for themselves by enlisting the help of the local population. He asked us to wage a paupers' war.

"He had installed the training camp at Nouei-Phou Lak, right up in the mountains. Fifty partisans, all told, led by Chanda and Thon, both of them paratroop second-lieutenants, and four French warrant officers, including Picarle who is now with the Meos. Chouc was in charge of supplies and recruitment. Ven was then eight years old and kept getting in our way. Ricq sent her off to the convent at Thakhek and paid for her board and lodging.

"An airstrip had been built near the camp. Mattei came and landed there every week in his Piper, and Pamphone visited us several times. For three or four days he would live like us, take part in our training and, as in the old maquis days, we all called one another '*tu*'. He brought Gibelin along. Gibelin refused to dabble in politics any more, but he kept talking politics, which was the best way of getting on the wrong side of the French authorities, both civil and military. As usual he was in financial straits and would have gone to any lengths to get money. He was still the same Gibelin, prematurely aged perhaps, worn out by the debauched life he led, but indestructible and better acquainted with Laos than anyone in the world.

"Ricq had decided to use only small groups of five or six men, each equipped with a transmitter. He recruited on the spot the partisans he might need for a raid or sabotage operation. He insisted on our respecting the customs of the various ethnic groups among whom we were to live, without trying to impose our regulations on them and so turn them into regulars. He was forthwith reproached for lack of efficiency because he did not obtain immediate and spectacular successes. Ricq isn't a liar. He never tried to build up a minor skirmish into a full-scale battle or transform the occupation of a village into a victory.

"Each team was assigned a particular mission, with the Khas, the Thai Neua, the Pou Thais or the Lus, that's to say among the minorities who were already, or were liable to find themselves, in zones occupied by the Vietminh.

"But he refused to recruit the Meos. He had lost confidence in them ever since some of them had betrayed us to the Japanese. He felt they were lacking in cohesion and national sense. Gibelin, who was always well informed on what was happening in their part of the world, corrected this error. And with good reason!

"He was running an opium racket.

"Being back with us at Nouei-Phou Lak had dispelled his former bar-room torpor and lassitude. He became once more the man he had been. Since Ricq chose to reject the Meos, he went out of his way to prove, on the contrary, that without them we could achieve nothing.

"The Meos, according to him, had the best reason for fighting against the Communists. They wanted to defend what to them made life worth living: liberty in its most exaggerated form. The Viets, in the zones in which they had seized control, had tried to force these nomadic highlanders to settle in a fixed spot. They had deluged them with propaganda, obliging them to attend meetings, form committees and respect the laws of hygiene. The Meos had rebelled against the gloomy, finnicky little men from the deltas.

" 'Just imagine,' Gibelin said to Ricq, 'the Viets want to force the Meos to wash. That's utterly impossible. The time has come to set all these highlands ablaze, from Yunnan to Tran-Ninh'.

" 'Go ahead and do it,' Ricq retorted, as though issuing a challenge.

"Gibelin took over a team commanded by Picarle and disappeared with them into the mountains on the other side of the clouds. He came back a month later saying everything was going very well.

"In less than a year there were maquis groups swarming all over North Laos and the Haute Région. They denied the Vietminh divisions the higher passes and defiles. The Meos helped us because they felt the French were less of a nuisance than the Viets.

"Then came Dien Bien Phu. We repeated all the blunders of Na San by going to ground in an entrenched camp instead of engaging in maquis activity. We wanted to save Laos, but we were going to lose the whole of Indo-China.

"At the beginning of 1954, the 316th Vietminh Division advanced once more on Luang-Prabang. Utter panic. An entrenched camp was created in the Plain of Jars. Legionaries were brought in to dig the trenches. We others were behind the Viet lines, myself on the Tonkin border, near Dien Bien Phu; Chanda and Thon in the mountains dominating Lai Chau, Picarle at Phong Saly.

"But I must tell you a story showing how Ricq influenced opinion without ever coming out into the open. He had discovered an old blind bonze at Luang-Prabang of whom no one had ever taken the slightest notice. All of a sudden this bonze started uttering phrophecies, saying the Viets would never take Luang Prabang, the holy city. The credulous Laotians acted accordingly. Instead of yielding, as they usually did, to the invader, they started filling sand-bags. The 316th Division turned about, but in order to attack Dien Bien Phu. It was Ricq, of course, who had activated the old blind bonze. He was pulling a number of other strings as well. He had engineered the desertion of an entire Pathet Lao army concert party which he had come across while looking for his *Ramayana*. He, a white man, had simply extolled the pleasures of Laotian life. Straight away they had all gone back to their villages.

"When, at the end of April 1954, it was known that Dien Bien Phu was lost, I received orders to make my way down to the entrenched camp to try and pick up any escapers. An attempt had been made to send out a rescue column from Luang-Prabang: men in jungle boots and with heavy equipment. Ricq could hardly bear it. But headquarters had curtly asked him to mind his own business. I arrived with my Thai partisans to within five miles of the entrenched camp. From a ridge I witnessed the final bombardment of Isabelle. I waited three days, playing hide-and-seek with the Viets. No one showed up. But two of my Thais reported a long column of French prisoners heading in the direction of Thanh Hoa.

"Meanwhile Chanda was in the process of taking Lai Chau, the capital of the Thai country, alone with thirty partisans. Thon, who was wounded, had been evacuated a month earlier and it was you, Mattei, in your Piper, our only aircraft, who had come to pick him up."

"I remember," said Mattei, "he had a nasty wound in the leg. When we had to bend him double to get him into the plane, Thon was bellowing for all he was worth. On our way back we received five bullets through the wings and fuselage. Those were the days."

Meynadier gulped down a cup of tea and went on without caring if anyone was listening to him or not:

"The capture of Lai Chau, when we had lost Dien Bien Phu, was the most absurd and extraordinary adventure of that war. The maquis had been ordered to attack all the Viet supply lines so as to relieve the entrenched camp. Chanda was then two hundred miles from his base, sixty miles north of Dien Bien Phu as the crow flies. He had been holding the mountain for three months and his transmitter was no longer working. He made his way down to the Clayeau Pass. There was no one there. He pressed on in the direction of Lai Chau, the key town of the Haute Région. There were fifty or so Viets there, holding conferences and self-examination sessions and hanging up streamers. All the rest were at Dien Bien Phu. Chanda surprised them during the siesta hour. Thanks to him, while the Viet flag was being hoisted on General de Castries command post at Gono, the tricolour went up at Lai Chau. No one knew this.*

* The true-life hero of this outstanding feat of arms was a man by the real name of Ly Seo Nang. He is at present living in New Caledonia with all his family.

"It wasn't so easy to pull it down either. Chanda had got a firm grip on the town and wouldn't let go.

"Once again Mattei swooped over the crags held by the Viets and dropped him a message. Ricq was in the plane."

"We would have landed," said Mattei, "but we had only just enough fuel to get back; and the Viets were moving up."

"Well, after holding Lai Chau for four days, Chanda withdrew on foot, losing no more than a third of his men. Two months on the march. I too came back on foot, but I left my wounded behind.

"Chanda's quite a fellow, at least he used to be."

Mattei interrupted Meynadier's long monologue. He was familiar with the state of mind of the neophyte smoker who in a toneless voice keeps talking without stopping:

"I can tell you another G.C.M.A. story, about Sergeant-Major Picarle who was with a group of Meos north-east of Phong Saly, opposite Muong Ou Thay, in Vietnamese territory. We knew the Viets, who had crossed through Communist China, were going to take Phong Saly from the rear. They were out to liquidate that particular group of partisans. Ricq came and saw me:

" 'I have a difficult proposition for you: I want you to pick up a French warrant officer behind the Viet lines. I was the one who involved him in this adventure; I'm responsible for him. I've been ordered to abandon him because he has already once refused to pull back in accordance with the armistice conventions. I can't get hold of a plane. If we have an accident, it's just too bad. But neither of us has a widow to weep over us. We have one chance in two of getting back alive, hardly more . . . and you won't get anything out of it except my personal gratitude'.

"I agreed, because Ricq is a hell of a fellow and never talks nonsense. It was difficult, far more difficult than he thought. I touched down on a crag without coming to grief. A miracle. There were four seats in the Piper. Ricq and I already occupied two of them.

"We saw Picarle arrive, with a long feather stuck in his bush hat and a Meo silver collar round his neck, as filthy dirty as the thirty men with him. Ricq repeated the information he had already been given by wireless, namely that the game was up, the armistice had been signed at Geneva and that he had come to fetch him back. I remember Picarle's beady little eyes and every word he said. They're the sort of words that aren't easily forgotten:

" 'I can't do it. I'm staying with my lads. Either we'll manage to make our way back to Laos on foot or the Viets will get us. But we're staying together. Orders? Whose orders? When I'm ordered to behave like a dirty swine, it's funny but my ears get blocked. Here's to our next meeting, Monsieur Ricq . . . if we ever do meet again'.

"Ricq had risked his life and his career to come and fetch him. But he didn't bat an eyelid. He merely asked Picarle what he could do for him.

" 'Give me your carbine ammunition. I only have one magazine left'.

"We left Sergeant-Major Picarle and his Meos. Four months later he turned up at Xieng Khouang, by way of the highest ridges, without having lost a single man.

"When you come across that sort of mulish obstinacy, Monsieur Cléach, it warms the cockles of your heart."

"Yes," Meynadier went on, "but we eventually lost Picarle. He got himself demobbed at Vientiane. He drew all his allowances and arrears of pay, then vanished . . . back to the Meos. Now he commands the whole Tran Ninh maquis on behalf of Colonel Cosgrove and the American secret services.

"Realizing the mistakes they had made, the Viets granted the Meos who remained in their zone a liberal charter. Merely for practical reasons.

"In us, the Meos had merely found some allies who helped them defend their way of life against the Viets. When the Viets realized that they too had to respect that way of life, they made up a lot of ground they had lost with them.

"In the midst of this disorder and confusion, a new sentiment, as yet undefined, the sentiment of belonging to a same set of people and a same race, had taken root among the Meos.

"The Viets exploited this embryo of nationalism for all they were worth. The French hadn't dared to, for fear of embarrassing their Laotian friends. Insensibly, the Meos began to drift over to the Viets, who promised them a Meo nation, until Colonel Cosgrove Tibbet, an old South-East Asia hand, undertook to make them the same promises.

"He found an ally in ex-Sergeant-Major Picarle, who by then had become an adviser to Phay Tong. Phay Tong had been alarmed to see his unstable followers going over to his rival, the pro-Viet Cheng Pou. Picarle flung him into Cosgrove's arms. Picarle hated the Communists and had never forgiven the French for having one day ordered him to abandon his partisans. Besides, there was the opium. Pursuing their new policy, the Viets not only made a point of not forbidding its cultivation, as their puritan morals would have demanded, but actually paid a high price for it . . . and proved honest in their contracts. Opium was worth its weight in gold for buying arms and ammunition, agents and accomplices.

"The Americans were compelled to follow the same course. American secret service aircraft have recently been seen smuggling opium into Bangkok, Saigon and the Philippines, while the States are waging a battle to the death against narcotics and dope-peddling.

"Each time Ricq and I tried to talk to Picarle about France, the G.C.M.A.s or our old friendship with the Meos, he would reply:

" 'France can't give us anything; she doesn't buy opium, she doesn't provide arms. France is backing the Laotains, the king of Luang-Prabang and the Vientiane government. She refuses to recognise our independence. The Americans may perhaps abandon us one day but meanwhile they're giving us arms and money, enough to enable us to remain free for some time to come'.

"Ricq did his utmost to get Picarle back. He even offered him a commission in the regular army."

Mattei nodded in agreement; it was he who had been entrusted with that mission.

"He also offered him money, but what a paltry sum! Picarle was making ten times as much with the Americans. Anyway he didn't give a damn about money."

"I thought," said Cléach, "that in your dirty secret service world, when you couldn't buy a man you liquidated him."

"That's not Ricq's method. Colonel Cosgrove had also warned him that if anything happened to Picarle some of our South Vietnam agents working under cover in the rubber plantations would straight away pay for it with their lives. He produced a list of them. It was unfortunately up to date."

"Charming way to behave!"

"In any case the Americans are deceiving themselves. Their maquis bands aren't worth a brass farthing. And it won't be the riff-raff that Chanda brought them who are going to improve the situation.

"After Dien Bien Phu, Ricq had a difficult time.

"The Laotians were fond of us, certainly, but they couldn't forgive our loss of face. It was all very well saying to them it was in order to defend them that we had taken such a hiding. It cut no ice at all. Before Dien Bien Phu, when referring to a Frenchman, they always used the word '*Than*' or 'Monsieur'. Afterwards it was '*Phu*' or '*Mo Bak*'—'that fellow', 'that lad'.

"Then Pamphone was murdered and Sisang himself was wounded. The government was throwing a party for the king's birthday, a little intimate *boum*, just the ministers, their wives and friends. It was held in Prince Sisang's villa, where the windows open out on to the garden. The guards who were meant to be on duty were in the kitchen having a party on their own.

"Someone flung a clutch of grenades through the window and skiddaddled. Pamphone, the War Minister, was killed outright, and so was his wife. Three other ministers were wounded, including Sisang who received a splinter in the throat and another in the shoulder. At the same time several garrisons rose up in arms and threw out their French instructors and advisers.

"It wasn't the Viets who were behind it; it was Si Mong, supported by the Americans and Thais. The Americans, who had refused to recognize the Geneva Agreements, had decided to take over from the French who had been defeated all over Indo-China.

"The killer was a Thai police lieutenant. The next day he was promoted to captain, but his accomplices, a couple of *samlos* he had recruited on the spot, were executed in case they talked.

"Prince Sisang went off to be treated in France; Pamphone's

body was ceremonially burnt and Si Mong took their place. Officially, he was not Prime Minister, he had to use the services of a man of straw. But he already had control of the War Ministry and the Ministry of the Interior.

"The Americans began to arrive by the plane-load. At their head was Colonel Cosgrove who had been waiting in Thailand until the coast was clear. The Yanks took over everything—the police, the army, the administration, the postal and agricultural services. The experts poured in, and so did the dollars.

"On the eve of my departure for France I had dinner with Ricq and Gibelin. In memory of Pamphone, we kept a place for him at our table. Gibelin drank even more than usual. He told us then:

" 'One day the red flag will fly over Saigon, and up to the last minute we shall go on fighting in Laos against armies that don't exist.'

"Gibelin went on to say that Ricq was one of the main culprits of this farce. Cosgrove was taking over where he left off, and the farce would go on. The best way of saving Laos was to get the hell out of it.

"I still remember how Gibelin hurled the glass he had just finished against the wall, then got up and left."

All of a sudden the blood drained from the captain's cheeks.

"My head's going round and round."

Cléach nodded:

"You've smoked too much for the first time. I warned you."

Meynadier got up and went out and vomited in the lane.

When he came back he swore:

"I'll never touch this bloody stuff again. It makes one talk too much. Now I understand why Ricq never smoked opium. This smell turns my stomach.

"There's another feature of Ricq's character I've just thought of—his readiness to lend a helping hand in an emergency. I got into some trouble in Algeria; he sent for me as instructor to the French Military Mission in Laos. It was a bit of luck for me. Had it not been for that, I should have been in jug or else in such a fix that I'd have repudiated my pals and my promises. I've repudiated myself as well, but only this morning.

"On landing at Vientiane, I found myself in the middle of an absolute shambles. The army had just assumed power again. It was our old friend Si Mong who had organised the plot. Prince Sisang had rushed off to France as usual. Prince Lam Sammay, the Commy, had just been put in jug and there was no one in command. Laos doesn't change much. There's always a shambles here. To put things right, under pressure from the ambassadors, it was decided to hold an election. A masterpiece. In Vientiane alone, the candidate backed by Si Mong won two thousand votes more than the total electorate. No one had voted for him.

"Our elections in Algeria were child's play compared to this. The place was full of Americans. They interfered in everything and flooded the country with dollars, arms, equipment, missionaries and secret agents. I no longer knew anyone, I no longer recognized anything. I was absolutely lost. Ricq and Gibelin were away. I had left Laos in 1955. What on earth had happened to this country in eight years to make it so utterly rotten?

"It was like leaving a girl in the prime of youth and beauty and coming across her again a raddled old hag.

"When I reported to General Molliergues, he told me he couldn't recall my face and that he hated officers dabbling in politics. He found my turn-out left much to be desired and wondered what an adventurer like me could be doing in an army riddled with tradition and honours like ours.

"At the time of the 13th May the poor fellow had been put in jug by his own captains.

"Molliergues posted me as instructor to a battalion of Laotian paratroops somewhere up country—'a battalion', he said, 'which has taken quite a pasting, been reduced to three hundred men and is commanded for the time being by an unknown captain called Chanda. They say he's actually a Kha, a savage, whose parents used to wander about the forest stark naked.'

"But I happened to know this Kha extremely well, and also his second-in-command, Lieutenant Thon.

"It wasn't Molliergues' idea to post me to this battalion. It was a suggestion of Ricq's, backed by an urgent order from Paris, one of those orders which made that blithering old general mad with rage.

"Three months later we seized Vientiane with Chanda's battalion.

"Christ, how my head aches! I say, Mattei, you didn't tell me what the hell you're doing in this den."

"I'm waiting for a plane. Unlike Picarle, I shan't make any difficulties about taking it. I have no sense of honour left. But the plane won't come. Goodbye."

Mattei disappeared and they went back to Cléach's house.

"Where's Ven?" Meynadier enquired.

Flore came in from her bedroom with a smile on her face:

"While we were at the opium den, she came and took her things away."

"Maybe Ricq's out of jug."

Cléach picked up the telephone and called up Captain Lalo. Ricq had not yet been released, but he was expected to leave Xien Nip at any moment.

"Ven's waiting for him at home. Do you think she loves him?" Meynadier asked suddenly.

"I don't know," Cléach replied. "She was certainly very upset by his arrest."

Flore kept playing with her shawl:

"I happen to know she doesn't love him. I heard her singing this morning. Ricq is old and ugly, he's like Gibelin. Maybe she has gone back to her village, to Nouei-Phou Lak, where she'll be warmly welcomed by her handsome *phoubao* who doesn't make her feel she needs a bath after making love."

"What about the child?" Meynadier shouted. "You forget all about the child, you little slut."

Flore pouted:

"Gibelin taught me many things about Laos.

"When a girl from a mountain village comes home with a child in her belly, and the child is a white man's and the girl's parents are minor notables, like Ven's, what do they do? They go and consult a witch-doctor or a bonze, who sells them some plants. With these plants they make a brew and give it to their daughter to drink. The child goes away, and the *phousao* goes off with the other girls to bathe in the river and joke with the boys . . . In Laos, only the town whores keep their bastards."

Meynadier leant on the table:

"Only this village happens to be Nouei-Phou Lak, and this particular girl is Ven, and the man who gave her a child happens to be Ricq."

Flore shrugged her shoulders:

"All girls are alike. As you see, you're in love with Ven, since you think she's not like the rest."

Without another word she went and lay down on the bed.

"My head's throbbing," Meynadier groaned. "Give me some aspirin and water, a whole pail of water as though for a mule."

Cléach looked at him without moving:

"You've had a good laugh, you old sod. You let me make an absolute fool of myself in front of Ricq and Gibelin. I ought to break the water jug over your head and slip you some arsenic instead of aspirin."

Meynadier was unable to sleep. He could hear all the usual nocturnal sound with painful clarity: the footsteps of a patrol, the dogs fighting round a refuse heap. The same haunting thought kept returning: Ricq is in jug. A year ago we were masters of Vientiane; it was our patrols then who used to disturb the hours of darkness.

Yet the 3rd Parachute Battalion wasn't up to much when Meynadier had taken charge of it. For a year it had been made to turn its hand to every kind of job. It was still, however, one of the few units that had any fighting quality, thanks to Chanda and Thon. The battalion had been in action in the province of Sam Neua; it had attempted a thrust towards Phong Saly, recapturing the posts which the regular army units had abandoned to the Communists without firing a shot. But the Viets did not allow themselves to be dislodged so easily as the Royal Laotian Army. After every engagement the battalion left some dead on the field. Meanwhile, at Vientiane, the officers grew fat and idle. They spent every night in bars and brothels, they squandered fortunes on dance hostesses and tarts, and dipped into the regimental funds. But the 3rd Parachute Battalion had drawn no pay for three months.

The captain likewise found this hard to stomach.

After Indo-China there had been Algeria, the 13th May, the Barricades, the *putsches* that had succeeded and failed, friends in jug, on the run, or on their uppers.

But when he found Chanda, Thon and Laos again, he had felt happy. Chanda had been promoted to captain after his exploit at Lai Chau. But for eight years he had kept the same rank, like Thon who had remained a lieutenant. Promotion was earned in the towns.

The battalion, encamped by the Nam Ma, the "horse river", had given a *boun* to welcome Meynadier.

With their hatchets, the paratroopers had built some huts and arranged garlands of flowers, finding a few chickens and a pig with great difficulty, any amount of girls and musicians with ease. They had even bought some brandy, whisky and beer on credit from the Chinese merchant.

The atmosphere was warm, the sound of the river, when the *khene* players fell silent, rose to a roar which gradually died away. The girls sat huddled together, breaking into peals of shrill laughter.

At the embassy in Vientiane, Captain Lalo had merely told Meynadier that Ricq would contact him when he needed him. Then he had resumed his stolid silence and began looking through his papers.

Meynadier had a well-established reputation as an activist, which alienated all the military who were afraid of contracting this disease though it was nothing more serious than a cold in the head.

Thon had seized the captain by the shoulder, Chanda by the arm. The three of them then went strolling along the river together while the chickens and pigs roasted over the fires.

"Where are Ricq and Gibelin?" Meynadier enquired.

It was Chanda who replied:

"We're expecting them. They should have been here by now. You know things are going very badly in Laos?"

"Worse than ever," said Thon. "You left a few days after the assassination of Pamphone and the flight of Prince Sisang. Since then Laos has never been the same; because of the dollars. In your days the ministers used to be driven around in *samlos*. On Sundays they went fishing and in the evening had a *boun* with the neighbours. Today, ministers, generals and colonels are selling themselves for a car, a villa or a handful of banknotes."

"The land," Chanda went on, "used to belong to everyone. Those who have dollars now want it for themselves. For the first time in Laos the fields round the towns are being enclosed.

"The army won't fight any longer and is badly behaved. Something serious has happened at my village, Nouei-Phou Lak. Ricq and Gibelin have gone up to see. They didn't want me to go."

The Nam Ma was punctuated by a series of rapids which spread out into broad sheets of water. Just as the sun was about to set in the river, two pirogues appeared and beached by the camp. Maynadier admired the boatmen's adroitness, the way they handled their vessels in the current, using their paddles to avoid a rock protruding from the water. He felt at home again on the edge of this river, which some men came to know yard by yard through learning how to deal like this with its shoals and rapids.

Two white men sprang from the pirogues, barefoot, wearing bush hats and vaguely military uniforms. They were Ricq and Gibelin, together again as in the good old days. They had come a long way and had been living for weeks in the jungle. Their clothes were tattered and torn. They carried American carbines on their shoulders, and the wooden handles of their hatchets protruded from their webbing haversacks. The six Laotians with them unloaded all the paraphernalia of a long trip in the forest: sacks of rice, jerrycans, cooking pots. From one of the pirogues they hauled a big dun-coloured deer they had just shot and flung it at Meynadier's feet.

"A present for you," said Gibelin, imitating the accent of the Vietnamese.

But he was making an effort to appear cheerful. Ricq also came up and shook hands, like a man expressing sympathy at a funeral.

Chanda produced some bottles of beer, which he opened with his teeth.

"Well," he asked Ricq, "is it true?"

Ricq had squatted down on his haunches and was playing with a branch of dead wood.

"Yes."

Gibelin flung his empty beer bottle away:

"I'd rather tell you myself what happened at Nouei-Phou Lak. Ricq wouldn't be able to. It concerns us all—you, Chanda, because it's your village, because Chouc was your uncle and Ven's your cousin; you, Thon, because your wife comes from there, because Chouc was a friend of yours and because you're a proper soldier who suffers when the Laotian army behaves badly. For Meynadier, for Ricq and myself, Nouei-Phou Lak was the refuge we had chosen once and for all. We used to go to Nouei-Phou Lak like men returning to the village in which they were born. I was firmly resolved not to meddle again in war or politics. Now I shan't stop until I put paid to Si Mong, even if it's the Communists who succeed him at Vientiane. Si Mong had sent a company of the Royal Army to defend Nouei-Phou Lak against the Communists. There weren't any; his real reason was to steal the Meos' opium.

"On his arrival the company commander demanded some chickens, rice and alcohol. Chouc let him have what he wanted. That's the general rule now. The army lives on plunder. Then he insisted on going up to the Meos, where he was rather badly received, not with old pop-guns, as in our days, but with automatic rifles and even machine-guns. In no time five of his men were killed and the whole company scooted off. Risking their lives for the sake of two hundred pounds of opium and a paltry bonus didn't appeal to our warriors. That evening the company commander came back to see Chouc; he was blind drunk. He accused him of having warned the Meos and, of course, of being a Communist. Just then Ven came in. She's now eighteen, Meynadier. If the nuns at Thakhek didn't teach her much about arithmetic and composition, they at least developed her sense of dress. She's the loveliest girl in the whole of Laos, just as Nouei-Phou Lak is the loveliest village. The sight of such a gorgeous girl gave that swine ideas, but he was reckoning without Chouc. When he tried to touch Ven, Chouc gave him a good hiding. He came back later, this time with twenty soldiers.

"They beat Chouc up with their rifle butts. They hit him so hard that he died under the blows. Then they seized Ven and a dozen other girls and took them away by force. In one week Ven had to submit to more men than a whore in a brothel. Ask Ricq. He's the only man she could bear to see."

"Yes," said Ricq, still playing with his piece of wood. "I found her hiding away in a corner of the hut, with a glazed look in her eyes. When I tried to touch her, she trembled. When I made an abrupt gesture, she whimpered and hid her face, her breasts or her belly. Ven made me feel ashamed of being a man. We thought of taking her back to Vientiane or Thakhek, but she refused to come."

"I went to see Si Mong," Gibelin went on. "I asked him to have the company commander court-martialled. He couldn't understand why an officer should be shot for amusing himself with a girl and beating her father to death."

"What's his name?" Chanda asked.

"Major Phouy—he was a captain but he has since been promoted. After the Meos and Khas had chased him out of the basin, he reported that he had been pursued by a Vietminh division. He even stated that Chouc and his daughter were Communist agents and had tried to assassinate him."

"I'll go and kill him. I'll make mincemeat of all his men."

"That wouldn't do any good. The evil has to be uprooted by driving out this régime and at the same time getting rid of the corruption it engenders. To prevent soldiers from behaving like this, peace must be restored. I shall do absolutely anything, I shan't stop for a moment, because of Ven's eyes that keep haunting me."

Chanda did not budge, but his face was grey and his shoulders drooped:

"I shall kill Phouy and Si Mong all the same."

Ricq outlined his plan.

With the battalion, they would seize Vientiane and bring Prince Sisang back to power. Then Sisang would ask the head of the pro-Communist faction, Prince Lam Sammay, to take part in the government, integrate his troops in the Laotian army and drop the Vietminhs.

Gibelin continued:

"We went back to the neighbourhood of Sam Neua. We saw Prince Sammay—in secret, of course. Ricq's plan is feasible. Lam Sammay has at last realized that Communism in Laos means primarily the elimination of the Laotians to the benefit of the Chinese and Vietnamese. All the rest is a lot of nonsense. Communism has no business here. Land isn't going to be divided up in a country where it already belongs to the man who cultivates it! As for creating heavy industries where there's no coal, no possible dams, no railways, no proletariate, where no one likes working . . . Or bringing tractors to places which are even inaccessible to goats, proclaiming the class struggle where no classes exist . . . The racial struggle, perhaps, at a pinch . . ."

Ricq elaborated on this:

"Lam Sammay now knows he has placed himself at the service of foreigners and that he is only acting as a screen for them. There aren't many Laotians in the Pathet Lao: two battalions, a few hundred half-hearted junior N.C.O.s. They too are discontented. If Sammy and his people found a Neutralist government in Vientiane—a government on the Indian model, for instance, led by a tolerant and receptive man like Prince Sisang—they might contemplate joining it.

"From then on the Viets would be mere invaders against whom Laos would be able to ask for help from every nation, from the Third World as well as the American bloc. All that's needed is to seize Vientiane and get Prince Sisang to come back. We have his consent. We'll reunify Laos and restore peace. The French government will encourage us if we succeed; it will leave us in the lurch if we fail. A new ambassador is going to be appointed in Vientiane. His name is Xavier Pinsolle. His instructions are to help us, but without compromising himself.

"First phase: we seize Vientiane by surprise.

"Second phase: Sisang comes back to lead the government. He gets himself recognized by every nation, whether committed or not. Paris and London will back him.

"After that, a coalition government is formed with Prince Sisang and Prince Sammay. The two Pathet Lao battalions join the national army. They'll soon stop being Communists and become *khene*-playing, girl-chasing Laotians.

"Sammay breaks publicly with the Vietminhs and demands their evacuation from the two Laotian provinces they're not controlling in the name of the Pathet Lao—Sam Neua and Phong Saly.

"If this operation succeeds in Laos, what's to prevent us from extending it to South Vietnam?"

"Pipe dreams," said Gibelin. "Even if we manage to get rid of Si Mong and punish those swine who desecrated Nouei-Phou Lak, killed Chouc and raped Ven and the other girls, it will already be something. But first we have to seize Vientiane. Do you agree, Chanda?"

"Yes, if I can get my hands on Phouy."

"What about you, Thon?"

"Yes, if I can do anything about Si Mong."

"And you, Meynadier?"

"On my return from a difficult operation in which I had had heavy losses and been wounded myself, an Algerian French girl asked me: 'You, you paratrooper captain, is Algeria your country today? You've just shed your blood for her.' I told her my country was Nouei-Phou Lak. It has just been pillaged, and you still ask me if I agree?"

The soldiers prowled round the fires, stripped to the waist. Others splashed about in the river. Some of the girls were dancing. Meynadier looked at Gibelin and Ricq—the gaunt, prematurely aged skeleton and the quiet little man whose hair was turning grey. But this time they had changed places. Gibelin had become the realist and Ricq was playing Don Quixote.

Ever since May 13, Meynadier had known that it was never difficult to capture a town. In Algiers a few parachute regiments had overthrown the Fourth Republic, with the neutrality of forty million Frenchmen. There were one million five hundred thousand

Laotians, and all of them wanted peace. A battalion should be enough to seize Vientiane. But the red prince's personality disturbed him.

Ricq had asked Meynadier to undertake the training of the battalion and prepare it for street fighting. As he left, he let him have a plan of Vientiane.

For a week Meynadier had studied the capacities of the paratroops in the battalion. In their own way, they were first-rate soldiers.

When they felt they were being hard pressed or losses were too heavy, they would split up into small groups and reassemble in the forest or the jungle, following the old guerrilla tactics. It required other qualities to seize a town. Meynadier started off by instilling in them a certain military bearing. It did not matter if in the jungle the paratroops were slovenly-dressed, went around barefoot and with chickens tied to their belts with pieces of string. But in a camp or a town this was disastrous. Thon understood him, he was a soldier. It was more difficult to convince Chanda. He was still a gang leader, open-hearted and naive; he revelled in disorder and confusion.

To obtain a certain standard of discipline, Meynadier put the paratroopers through frequent periods of physical training: cross-country runs, obstacle courses, every man on parade stripped to the waist. He went further and had their heads shaved. The 3rd Battalion began to live at the paratrooper's tempo. Suddenly reinforcements and weapons arrived. From four hundred, the battalion jumped to six hundred. On the edge of the river, christened the Mekong for the occasion, Meynadier built a rough model of Vientiane and the essential objectives: the post office, headquarters, the Assembly, the central police station, the wireless station, the electricity works, the main intersections. A few hoardings and two or three thatch huts were used for this purpose. For the first few days the paratroopers enjoyed this new game. But in the long run they got tired of going through the same motions over and over again and taking the same routes, being forbidden to smoke or to talk, having to muffle their weapons so as not to make a sound.

Chanda and Thon attended to the psychological preparation of the men. The two officers were utterly dissimilar. Thon had already grown a beard and wore his hair long. These hirsuite appendages made him look like a mangy poodle. He had sworn not to shave until they had taken Vientiane. But he was still a real officer, punctilious about regulations, never satisfied, putting his men through the same exercise over and over again. He was respected, but not loved. Chanda, on the other hand, was adored.

Chanda charmed his men with the endless stories he told them. They were full of *phis* and witch-doctors, wild animals in which the dead were reincarnated. Meynadier had never been on close terms with Chanda. He remembered him only as a funny little fellow trotting about and swinging his shoulders, with a high forehead and a long fine-featured head out of proportion to the rest of his body: he remembered also his gentle manner, his tender eyes, his smile.

He knew he was capable of wildly audacious actions, like the capture of Lai Chau. But he did not know about his superstitiousness, the magnetic influence he exercised on those round him, his mysticism, his occasional madness and lust for blood.

In the evening Chanda used to assemble all his soldiers, company by company. Sitting on the ground, he would listen to what they had to say and only at the end did he speak himself. They did not want to fight against other Laotians but would rather stand aside and let the Russians, Chinese, Americans and Vietnamese kill one another off, while they planted their rice and courted their girls.

Communist propaganda had proved effective. By making use of Prince Sammay, the Viets had led people to believe that there existed a real Laotian liberation movement, the Pathet Lao, whose aim was not to install Communism but to restore purity of morals and quietness of life.

Patiently, Chanda would explain to them that the Vietnamese wanted to seize the land, that the Pathet Laos who were with the Communists had realized this and only wanted to make peace and be among Laotians again. Among Laotians anything can always be straightened out. Everyone was agreed on this point.

For a month there was no mention of Vientiane, then, to everyone's astonishment, the battalion received new uniforms, jungle boots, the most up-to-date weapons which the Americans had just delivered, and their arrears of pay. A few days later the order arrived to make for the capital as quickly as possible. Having packed their kit, the paratroopers set off by truck.

Gibelin had just organized his most tremendous hoax at the expense of Si Mong.

Whereas Ricq had been in constant conflict with the general for years, Gibelin had become his boon companion and partner in a number of deals. The man's cynicism and crapulence were a constant delight to him.

For a long time Si Mong had wanted to become president and, subsequently, dictator. He would then no longer have to share the dollars from American aid with deputies and politicians who were infinitely greedier than soldiers. He dreamed of a military régime which would combat the Communists efficiently and at the same time be welcomed by Washington and the Pentagon.

Si Mong was likewise convinced that it needed only one battalion to seize Vientiane. It was with Gibelin that he had worked out the details of his coup d'état, with his assistance that he had drawn up the plans for occupying the town, in his presence that he had received Chanda and obtained his adherence to the scheme.

Gibelin had rolled the old robber in flour in order to fry him more thoroughly.

At Vientiane, Meynadier had been amazed at Chanda's powers of dissimulation considering he had hitherto been known as an insecure chatterbox. He was to be seen every day paying court to his "king", Si Mong. Chanda appeared to steer clear of the French and on several occasions ostentatiously avoided saluting Meynadier.

The general, in full-dress uniform, had paraded and inspected the battalion, scrutinizing each man as though he already belonged to his praetorian guard. He was accompanied by two American colonels, his two guardian angels, tall, lean and clean-cut as Olympic Games athletes in contrast to himself, short, wall-eyed and pot-bellied.

Immediately after the meeting between Chanda and Si Mong, the officers of the 3rd Parachute Battalion found themselves being cossetted by the Americans, who invited them to go on training courses in the States and study tours in Thailand.

After playing up to them all day, Chanda, Thon and the other officers would come back to Meynadier, laden with whisky and American cigarettes, happy to have played a trick not only on Si Mong but also on the Americans, whom they hated for their blunders and despised for their credulity.

"Luckily at that time we didn't have Colonel Cosgrove to cope with," Ricq was later to remark. "He would have tumbled to our little game. Cos knows the country too well . . . and the role Gibelin and I played during the initial capture of Vientiane in 1945. He also knew we had belonged to Force 136 and later to the French secret service."

Cosgrove at that time was in disgrace somewhere in Malaya or India for having demonstrated to his ambassador with icy politeness that His Excellency was an imbecile, and four of his assistants crooks, who were filling their pockets and helping themselves to the aid they were meant to be distributing.

The battalion had resumed its training: but in the town itself and with the blessing of Si Mong and his advisers. They even came and watched the men at work. On several occasions Meynadier, who was still instructor to the battalion, had caught the American officers smiling. This Frenchman, so they thought, was unwittingly preparing a coup d'état to bring to power the man whose first action would be to eliminate France from Laos. Quite a spicy situation.

For the last year the whole country had been waiting for the late king to be cremated. His worthy old corpse had meanwhile been preserved in formalin. According to one tradition, it was necessary to wait until a sandalwood tree several hundred years old was found in the forest, from which a coffin could be carved in one piece. Gibelin announced that his prospectors had come across the tree that was needed and the cremation ceremony was fixed for 20 July.

As soon as he heard the news, Ricq called a final meeting. He suggested taking Vientiane on the very day of the ceremony. This presented the most favourable conditions for the success of the enterprise. Ministers, generals, ambassadors, deputies and Si Mong himself would have taken the plane for Luang-Prabang the night before, and the capital would be empty.

He asked Meynadier to get himself confined to barracks to prove he had not left his quarters that day. On no condition should there be the slightest inkling that the French were involved in the events that were about to take place.

"Fix it somehow," he had told him. "Your friendship with the officers of the 3rd Battalion is too well known."

Meynadier had fixed it. Since his return to Vientiane he had had endless trouble with General Molliergues, who accused him of having a bad influence on the battalion he was responsible for instructing, and turning them into film-star paratroops who swaggered about the streets wearing the red beret in an aggressive manner.

He had even added:

"One would think you wanted to make *putschists* out of them. Wasn't Algeria enough for you?"

On 14 July the Mission gave a pre-luncheon party. It was more economical than a proper cocktail party and at the same time in keeping with French military tradition.

Meynadier turned up with Thon, both of them in battledress, and wearing all their medals, but shirtless and with their jacket collars unbuttoned.

The general rushed up to him:

"What the devil is the meaning of this turn-out, Meynadier? Go away at once and change. Come back properly dressed. This isn't carnival week."

The captain had snapped to attention.

"General, in this turn-out many of my comrades died in Indo-China and Algeria. It's in their memory that I'm today wearing this uniform which often served them as a shroud."

"Your comrades . . ."

The general had gone purple in the face:

"Your comrades, Captain, are a lot of riff-raff. They found

their proper place in prison . . . or as O.A.S. killers."

Ricq had tried to intervene; the general had turned on him:

"You're meant to be an ethnologist, you'd better mind your own business, which it seems you don't always do."

Gibelin, who was fairly drunk, planted himself in front of Molliergues and said:

"Call yourself a general, do you? General, my arse! There are a number of witnesses amongst us who have heard you insult an officer junior in rank to yourself, and in front of a Laotian lieutenant who is also a former French officer. My comrades may have made fools of themselves in France and Algeria, I agree. They're lost soldiers, not dishonoured soldiers. While you were hanging around ministry offices and anterooms, they were getting killed."

He clawed at Molliergues' decorations with his dirty fingernails:

"A general, and you only have the Légion d'Honneur—pretty poor show! So you'd better apologise at once, otherwise you'll get the contents of my glass in your face. May I remind you that I don't give a damn about making a scene, that your Minister was one of our men . . . and that he must therefore consider himself likewise insulted. Well, what about it?"

The general had apologised and next morning Meynadier had been confined to barracks for fifteen days . . . for being improperly dressed at an official ceremony.

During the night of 19/20 July, Chanda, Thon and the battalion company commanders had held a final meeting. They had rehearsed the operation on paper but were unable to memorise the street-plan.

Captain Meynadier was in despair. How could the coup possibly succeed? The paratroops would move off in disorder and lose their way in Vientiane. In spite of being confined to barracks, in spite of Ricq's request, he had come with them. Sitting in a Signals jeep, in which it was difficult to see him, he had taken command of the operation. The paratroops had forgotten the most important objectives: the airfield and the wireless station.

A guard post which had been alerted refused to surrender. Chanda did not want to open fire. Meynadier had ordered Thon to ignore this. One man was killed and three wounded. There was almost another casualty. Thon had lobbed three mortar shells onto General Molliergues' villa.

Fuming with rage, Meynadier had taken him to task:

"Generals, Lieutenant Thon, don't get assassinated, they get shot. Furthermore, the firing squad presents arms and the detachment goes on parade to the sound of drums."

By nine o'clock in the morning the paratroops had occupied the whole of Vientiane. Everyone thought Chanda was acting on Si Mong's orders. The paratroops had formed a revolutionary committee out of what elements they had been able to find: a few generals and colonels who were frightened to death, a Health Minister who was ill and had been forced to take to his bed, a handful of opposition deputies and policemen, some former contacts of Ricq's or Gibelin's or veterans of the anti-Japanese resistance movement.

Ricq had straight away headed for Bangkok and from there flown to Paris. He was off to fetch Prince Sisang back.

After smoking opium, Cléach always liked to lie down and rest in the warm fetid darkness rendered resonant by the drug. Indulging in day-dreams, memories that he evoked and in turn dismissed, with his eyes wide open and his limbs sluggish and numb, he would gradually yield to a feeling of amused indifference.

"When I smoke, I grow old," he reflected, "old and tolerant, therefore almost a coward. Opium is the temptation of complicity. Meynadier tried to make an accomplice of me just now. I don't mind being his friend, but I won't be his accomplice."

Flore lay beside him, breathing deeply and regularly, her body exuding a scent of vanilla and young animal.

Cléach recalled his arrival at Vientiane a few days after the town had been taken by Chanda and his parachute battalion. At that time he was unaware that behind the little captain there was Meynadier, the technician; and behind Meynadier, Ricq, the secret agent; and still further behind, Pinsolle, the ambassador, representing a country and a policy.

Cléach had arrived at a moment's notice to replace a colleague who had contracted dystentry and had had to be evacuated. The only aircraft at Bangkok that had been prepared to take him was the International Commission's. Since the coup d'état, the regular planes avoided landing at Vientiane. In the car in which he drove into town with the crew, the journalist had encountered a demonstration: several thousand men brandishing blue flags and red streamers. They were preceded by some young bonzes in saffron-coloured robes, walking along barefoot, each with a Chinese umbrella under his arm, and some older monks in cycle-rickshaws, looking self-important, self-satisfied and serene. Behind them came the mob, shouting slogans and clapping their hands.

Péningaud, the pilot, had stuck his head out of the window. After sniffing the air for some time, he had turned to Cléach and asked him in a mysterious manner:

"Is this your first trip to the Far East?"

"Yes."

"Does this demonstration mean anything to you?"

"No."

"Well, to me it stinks of Vietminh! I, Péningaud, an Aigle-Azur veteran, who for seven years piloted the old crates which did the rounds of the posts in Thai country, can't be mistaken. It takes me back ten years, to the days when the Viets used to enter the villages in Tonkin that we had just abandoned and acclaim peace among nations."

"Prince Sisang's and Captain Chanda's movement is said to be Neutralist, not Communist."

"You're telling me!"

Péningaud addressed the driver in Laotian:

"What's this circus show all about?"

"The Young Laotian Neutralist Movement, boss. They're demanding peace, neutrality, continuation of the war against General Si Mong and his traitors who have taken refuge in Savannakhet, immediate recognition, and the recall of the ambassadors of Russia, China and the Popular Republic of North Vietnam."

"Are you taking this all in, Mister Journalist?"

Cléach took a rather favourable view of these developments. He felt in sympathy with the Communists and thought that only they could save Asia from disorder and starvation. He looked at the crowd more closely.

There were many peasants carrying bags of rice on their backs; since they had brought their provisions with them, they must have come some distance—probably from the zones controlled by the Reds.

The bonzes seemed to be taking an active part in the movement. Had Buddha become a Neutralist? A few of Chanda's paratroopers, in red berets and with grenades in their belts, half-heartedly controlled the demonstrators.

"Paratroops in the service of Progressivism and Neutralism," Cléach sneered. "It could only happen in Laos."

He followed the demonstration and found himself in the festival hall where the President, Prince Sisang, was delivering a speech.

The driver, who had accompanied him, translated it for his benefit.

On the platform, Sisang, a thickset little man dressed in white and wearing a flower in his buttonhole like a stage-door Johnny, spoke with a composure and self-assurance that impressed Cléach. He promised the opening of negotiations with his cousin Prince Lam Sammay, head of the pro-Communist Pathet Lao movement, and the immediate end of the war. He gave his assurance that he had never dreamt of treating with the Savannakhet Committee which was presided over by his other cousin, Prince Phoum Sanakon, and General Si Mong. The whole crowd started booing the general, whereas it had remained silent at the mention of the prince. Sisang also gave his assurance that diplomatic relations would be re-established at any minute with the U.S.S.R. But he said nothing about China and North Vietnam. Then he ended up with a proverb which the whole audience appeared to appreciate:

"Hasty words lead to loss of confidence, hasty feet to a fall."

The situation remained static for several days, the following day being assigned to preparations for the Festival of the Waters, which marks the end of the Buddhist Lent, and the day afterwards to the celebration itself. The subsequent days were devoted to a well-earned rest after so much expenditure of energy.

The curfew was prolonged from nine in the evening to midnight. A peaceful, carefree crowd ambled down the main streets of the town and along the banks of the Mekong. In the warm night, lights glittered along the walls of the temples and in the windows of the houses—tallow candles, oil lamps in red glasses, little torches, which flared and flickered in the gentle breeze. Groups of young men went chasing after girls, brandishing delightfully obscene emblems and spraying them with water from syringes. In the Vietnamese quarter the houses were decorated with multi-coloured stars of wood and paper. Families sat huddled together in their shanties, sharing the traditional moon cake and bowing and wishing one another a thousand prosperities.

Cléach drifted along with the crowd, responding as best he could to the laughter and jokes. He came across some Americans who did not seem at all afraid of "the anger of the people", and a group of French soldiers who were looking desperately for a brothel which would allow them credit. For the first time in his life Cléach felt at ease in a foreign country. Under the door of his room in the Bungalow, he found a scribbled note:

"If you don't know what to do on your first evening in Vientiane, come and share the moon cake at Huong van Trinh's Vietnamese restaurant. Ask for Péningaud, the International Commission pilot, or Antoine Gibelin of the Upper Mekong Timber Company."

Being unfamiliar with the customs regulating the life of the local Europeans, and unwilling to offend their susceptibilities on his very first evening, Cléach put on his best suit and a tie. A *samlo*, to whom he had the greatest difficulty in making himself understood, took him to a dingy restaurant built of clay and planks but adorned with a splendid neon sign. The *ngoc* and red peppers, the soups bubbling on the hob, the meat simmering in rich sauces, exuded a warm, savoury and spicy smell.

Around the table covered in a fly-blown paper cloth sat Antoine Gibelin and Flore, the pilot Péningaud, an International Commission hostess, Meynadier with his drawling voice, and, leaning against a wall, with his knees drawn up on a bench, François Ricq, the representative of the French School of Far-Eastern Studies.

"What a bore this is going to be," was Cléach's immediate reaction. "There's nothing missing, not even the stock ethnologist. These people are obviously unaware of events and know nothing about the situation. Just look at them—transplanted petty bourgeois, a parachutist like a fish out of water, a timber merchant who looks like Pluto. Judging by his clothes, he can't be making much of a living. Luckily there's the gorgeous Eurasian girl! Whom does she belong to, I wonder?"

Gibelin handed Cléach a glass of whisky and, as though answering his unvoiced question, said:

"Flore here is my girl, old man . . . that's to say I'm paying a high rent for her at the moment. To my mind she has great qualities: she's interested in nothing but herself. The only problems she has concern her body, one of the most perfect bodies I know. She exploits it admirably for her own pleasure and her partner's. Flore will follow you or anyone else if you can double the rent. Isn't that so, Flore?"

The girl shook her head.

"No," she said, "I'm all right with you."

Then, casting a disdainful glance at Cléach, she said:

"I prefer older men, but only those who have lived a long time in Asia. Young men disgust me. Giving them a woman is like putting grilled rice in the hands of a monkey."

Ricq had smiled and some of Cléach's bias against him was dispelled. A man with a smile like that was obviously warm-hearted and ingenuous.

"What do you think of Vientiane?" Ricq asked him.

"I've seen nothing but heedless pleasure-seeking and political folklore. The country's gently drifting into the Communist orbit."

"I don't think so, Monsieur Cléach. Communism is an imported product. Those who sell it are the Vietnamese, whom everyone hates and despises. The country is merely feeling intense relief, knowing that for the first time there's a possibility of the war coming to an end. This sentiment affects Laos as a whole and the ten thousand villages in the country, even those which are now in the Communist zone.

"That's all Laos is—ten thousand villages living in total autarchy and feeding on the rice they plant. . . ."

"They plant no more than they have to for their personal needs," Gibelin interjected, stroking Flore's back. She shuddered. Was it from pleasure or disgust? Cléach hoped it was disgust, since he found the girl attractive. Ricq went on with his lecture:

". . . who feed on the chickens and pigs they raise, the fish they catch in the rivers in front of their huts, who are clothed in material woven by their wives . . . who with their own hands make the implements they need: rice baskets, nets. . . ."

"What about the elephants?" Cléach asked. "This country is called the Kingdom of the Million Elephants. Where are they all?"

"The only remaining herds belong to the king at Luang-Prabang, Prince Phoum Sanakon in the south, and Gibelin for his timber business. There are a few thousand still in freedom, led by irascible old males who suffer to the point of madness from the itch caused by parasites. That's why they bathe in certain types of mud. Ask Gibelin, he knows their habits. I like elephants. They're dying out, like the old Laos. A pity!"

"You can't be very pleased with what's happening now, since you're so in love with the past?"

"It's sometimes good that certain things should happen. You ought to meet Captain Chanda and his second-in-command, Lieutenant Thon. Interesting fellows. Thanks to them, the hitherto inert and indifferent population has recovered a semblance of enthusiasm and faith."

"Because Chanda promises them peace? I heard at Bangkok that the Laotians weren't fond of fighting because they're fervent Buddhists."

"The Laotian Buddhist is a man of peace. The bonzes deny cremation to anyone who has died a violent death, such as a soldier in action. His body has to rot in the soil and his soul remains for months attached to the decomposing body while suffering the tortures of the damned before being able to detach itself. In Laos there are no monuments erected to those who have died on the field of honour. But the bonzes, like all priests, know how to adapt their principles to the circumstances. Most of them have lined up behind Prince Sisang and Captain Chanda under the influence of one of their leaders, the Maha Son."

"Socrates," Gibelin roared, "good old Socrates . . . as queer as a coot . . . but fascinating. You won't be in any danger if you go and see him. You're not his type. Ricq is right. If one of Chanda's soldiers was killed today, he'd be entitled to cremation because he's no longer fighting for war but for peace. A subtle difference!"

That evening they all drank a great deal, with the exception of Ricq.

Péningaud once more described his Indo-China campaign; the hostess, casting melting glances at Meynadier, mentioned her fiancé who had been killed at Dien Bien Phu; the captain talked about his battles against the Vietminhs. He dismissed Ho Chi-Minh's little men with a succinct and final statement which exasperated Cléach: "They're a lot of dirty bastards." Ricq kept silent, puffing at his pipe. Flore doodled with her finger on the fly-blown cloth and Gibelin discoursed on sex in Asia:

"You've just arrived. So you have one choice to make: white or yellow. In Laos the white women are unbearable. Too few of them, therefore too sought after. They regard themselves as goddesses. What a song and dance they make just to grant you an occasional siesta! The siesta is adultery hour. I make an exception of a few grand and noble whores and a few extraordinary women who burst into bloom in Asia though in Europe they would have withered away. Out here the white woman suffers from moodiness, fits of depression, bouts of fever, attacks of megalomania, and interminable periods. When she copulates she sweats, but at least she makes love. The yellow woman hardly ever. She lends or sells you her body, her smooth, fresh, stark-naked body, her long hair, her graceful gestures, her discretion before, during and after the act, and her original purity which has never been tarnished by the slightest sense of sin. She may be faithful to you, never because of the pleasure you give her but because you're a man on whom she can rely. When she does get any pleasure from the sexual act, she almost apologises as though for a breach of politeness. But she'll despise anyone weak, she'll torture him, even if he's a good lover. You must never treat a woman from Asia as we've been taught to treat white women, seeing to their need, bestowing on them the marks of respect which out here are man's prerogative. You'd only disturb her and, by forcing her into a world that isn't her own, you'll make her lose her sense of security and balance."

"I don't agree," Ricq broke in.

Paying no attention to the interruption, Gibelin went on:

"Flore is Europe and Asia at one and the same time—Europe by virtue of the violence of her nature, her endless quest for pleasure, Asia by virtue of her indifference. Isn't that so, Flore?"

"I'm bored," she replied. "Let's go and dance at the Viengrathry or have a pipe at the Chinaman's."

"Very little for us," Ricq remarked, casting a significant glance at Meynadier.

He rose to his feet:

"Now's the moment the Laotians launch their little bamboo rafts in honour of the 'Mother of the Five Buddhas'. They're lit by oil lamps and float out into the river, bobbing up and down in the dark water. Are you coming with us, Monsieur Cléach, or would you rather listen to more speeches from Antoine in a picturesque opium-den? It's run by a former Chinese general. I don't smoke, I never have. But I think opium taken in small doses is less dangerous than alcohol. It tranquillises and doesn't overexcite. Less dangerous, too, than certain women; the local opium is first-class and doesn't cost much."

Antoine Gibelin raised his glass:

"Thanks for the lecture, Little Ricq. Flore, say thank you as well."

That night Cléach did not go on with any of them. Already exhausted by the climate and the journey, he had to get up early in the morning to call on the ambassador and send off his first cables, on which his future career depended. He recalled his editor's final words of advice:

"We have to send someone to Vientiane at once, old fellow. Your predecessor can't even wait until you arrive, he's just been evacuated to the French Hospital at Pnom-Penh. This is your first assignment abroad. You're staking your livelihood, you'll be judged by the results you obtain. So be careful what you do, very careful indeed. The French government is backing Prince Sisang. But don't compromise yourself with anyone. Bear in mind there are some words which out there don't have the same sense as they have in Europe, such as . . . treachery, extortion, Marxism, nationalism, country . . . Be careful about the girls, they're said to be dangerous; about alcohol, it sends you mad if you drink before sundown; the water, it's full of bugs; opium, it destroys your will-power; the climate, it exhausts you; and sensational news, it'll get you thrown out. Our funds are low. You'll be travelling tourist-class, on a line that makes a special price for us. Your expense account will be as small as possible. If you wear a tie and kiss a few hands, you ought to get yourself invited everywhere. Make the most of your tie and visiting cards. Well, you're now head of a branch of Agence France-Presse. How I envy you being young and going out to such a fabulous country. At the age of twenty, I should have given anything to be in your shoes. One final word of advice: you're a journalist, not an intelligence agent. You'll be expected to do the ambassador a few favours. Steer clear of the Special Service people."

Next morning Cléach called on Xavier Pinsolle, wearing a tie and his only tropical suit, which had suffered somewhat from the previous evening. The ambassador received him cordially.

"I've just arrived here myself," he said, "so I don't know much more than you do."

With his finger he flicked Cléach's tie out of his jacket.

"Take that thing off, old boy. In the evening, yes, at a pinch. Slovenly clothes or parachute uniform are the fashion out here. Roll up your sleeves and swing your shoulders. I try to, but I can't bring it off. Who have you seen since you arrived?"

"Monsier Ricq."

"A serious-minded, conscientious lad. He's been here for twenty years and knows all about the history of Laos and the tribes inhabiting the country. Speaks any amount of dialects."

"Also Captain Meynadier."

"That fellow's in the swim, as they say in Paris. He can introduce you to Chanda, whom he knows well. But he's rather suspicious of journalists. Do you know what our American friends say? That our worthy Captain Meynadier helped Chanda to carry out his coup d'état. Merely because for a month or two he had instructed his battalion. Ridiculous. In any case Captain Meynadier was confined to barracks at the time of the *putsch*. A little altercation with General Molliergues who's in command of the Mission. You'll have to call on the general. Wearing a tie. You won't get anything out of him, but he'll be flattered. Our general behaved admirably during the night of 19/20 July. Three mortar shells fell on his villa. He didn't leave the house until he was properly dressed—not in pyjamas, mind you, but properly dressed, in uniform. Everyone was waiting to see. It seems he sleeps in pink silk pyjamas. Come and lunch with me . . . without a tie . . . and have a drink this evening so that I can introduce you to Prince Sisang, our new President. Tie and jacket. Who else have you met?"

"Antoine Gibelin."

"A fascinating fellow. Beware of him as you would of the plague. He has a weakness for practical jokes and is said to indulge in every vice under the sun. Was he with Flore?"

"I found her very pretty, but . . ."

"Asinine, that's how Gibelin likes them. He behaves as though he doesn't give a damn, but he's got that girl under his skin. He can be very violent and jealous. The Corsican racketeers who deal in opium, arms and contraband have never dared get on the wrong side of him. He is said to have got rid of quite a number of characters—not very respectable ones, admittedly. His business affairs look healthy and prosperous: teak and sandalwood. He was born in Laos and has lived here all his life. He's a reserve major, with the Légion d'Honneur. One wouldn't think it. It was he and a handful of partisans who took Vientiane in 1945. But he was driven out again by the Vietminhs. He's a great chatterbox but he confines his chatter to a certain form of erotico-paraphysical delirium. He'll tell you Malraux's a ninny, but he models himself on one of his characters. A case of literary intoxication."

"What's he doing with a man like Ricq?"

"They were in charge of the same partisan group. These two utterly dissimilar men are bound together by an old friendship. Who else?"

"Péningaud, the International Commission pilot. I arrived in his plane."

"A good lad but slightly dotty. You've already got hold of the best elements in Vientiane. They're people I don't receive at the embassy, except at the official receptions to which all the French are invited. Their way of life is much too . . . shall we say . . . unusual. Believe me, I'm sorry. At least those fellows are alive. As for the rest—the worthy businessmen who belong to the local Rotary Club, the schoolmasters, the military, the technicians—most of them have brought nothing with them from France but their own pettiness. I'd like you to meet Chaptain Chanda and get an interview out of him. You've just arrived; I'd be interested to hear what you think about that restless little fellow. Our assistant military attaché, Captain Lalo, will give you all the information he has. No point in concealing from you any longer that Captain Lalo is the representative of the French Special Services. So long, my dear fellow."

Still disconcerted by this welcome and by this erratic character, who was so far from the notion he had of an ambassador, Cléach set out in pursuit of Captain Chanda. An interview with this army leader who only yesterday was still unknown would be a feather in his cap.

But Chanda was elusive as an eel and never in one place for more than a few minutes. He was not in his office at headquarters or at the Ministry of Defence. One of his officers said he was at Paksane, another that he was in the Plain of Jars, a third that he was in conference with Prince Sisang.

In the French advisers' office in the Ministry of War, Cléach came across two colonels in uniform and a third in civilian clothes. At a loose end, cut off from everyone and everything, without any advice to give, without any troops to instruct, the colonels were bored stiff. They told Cléach they had had a bellyful of this Laotian shambles.

"But where's Chanda?" the journalist enquired.

One of the colonels sneered:

"You'd better ask Captain Meynadier. Weren't you out with him last night, and also Gibelin and his tart?"

"Where can I find Meynadier?"

"Wherever Chanda is, of course."

In despair Cléach rang up the "cloak-and-dagger" Captain Lalo, who replied in his unctuous voice:

"I think your bird is out at the airfield. Have you a car?"

"No. Maybe a taxi . . ."

"Impossible to find one. You're at your hotel, you say? Then I'll send my driver round. He'll take you out there."

At the airfield Cléach ran into Meynadier standing with his hands in his pockets and gazing up at the sky which was full of grey, rain-swollen clouds.

To get into conversation with him, the journalist likewise looked up at the sky and asked:

"Is it going to rain?"

"I'm afraid so," the captain grumbled, as though blaming him personally for this. "It's always a bit of a nuisance dropping paratroops when it's raining or windy."

"Dropping paratroops?"

"Yes, of course. To welcome the new Russian Ambassador."

"First I've heard of it."

Meynadier jerked his head in the direction of a group of twenty people, the men in jackets, the women in native robes and shawls, who were waiting with flowers in their hands.

"The official government delegation. But Comrade Ambassador Alexis Serguieff won't be landing here."

"At Luang-Prabang?"

"No, at the other end of the airfield, where Captain Chanda and his men are waiting. Chanda sent one of his officers to the control tower to divert the aircraft. As this officer was carrying a sub-machine-gun, he's the one who'll be obeyed."

"Maybe I had better go and join Chanda?"

"No one's stopping you."

Meynadier turned his back on him.

Cléach had to sprint the full length of the runway to reach the spot where a company of armed paratroops and another group of girls carrying flowers were likewise waiting for the Soviet Ambassador. One of them, the prettiest of the lot, was Ven. In the background there were four officers sitting on a concrete block.

"Which of them is Chanda?" Cléach wondered, panting for breath. "The fat one with the beard? Or maybe the little fellow with the huge wrist-watch?"

Noticing that the bearded one wore a French paratroop badge, he went up to him:

"Monsieur . . . ?"

"Lieutenant Thon."

"What's happening?"

"First of all, who are you?"

"Cléach, of Agence France-Presse."

"You must be hot, aren't you? Come and sit down. The plane's late."

Lieutenant Thon made a place for him between himself and the little officer with the big wrist-watch.

"This lieutenant speaks French as well as I do," Cléach reflected, "and his accent is hardly noticeable. We no longer have an empire, there was no point to it, yet there are still fellows like this to be found. So much the better! I'm going to pick his brains."

"Lieutenant, at the airport terminal I saw an official delegation waiting for the Russian Ambassador. Are you waiting for him as well?"

Thon stretched out his hand and touched the little officer, who seemed to be day-dreaming, on the shoulder:

"Chanda, you tell him."

Chanda turned to the journalist, revealing his drawn features.

"You see, Monsieur, it was the paratroops who seized Vientiane. It's because we're here that the Russian Ambassador is now able to land on this airfield. Prince Sisang didn't want me to come. Receiving an ambassador is a matter of protocol, he said. But had it not been for us, Prince Sisang wouldn't be here either. So I held a meeting with my officers and we decided it would be us and not protocol that would welcome the representative of Russia."

"May I quote you on that?"

"See Prince Sisang first. He alone directs the policy of the country, as he'll tell you himself. I know nothing about it, it seems."

"What were the motives of your coup d'état?"

"We didn't want to continue a pointless and fratricidal war. The staff and the army were rotten to the core. An army of thirty thousand regular soldiers, twenty thousand militiamen and five thousand gendarmes, who were unable to get the better of three thousand Pathet Laos. In other words, they were unwilling to fight. It was always the same men who were sent into the jungle. The colonels and generals thought only of filling their pockets and buying cars, villas and girls. They wanted to rob the peasants of their land."

"Is the population in agreement with you?"

"The population, yes. General Si Mong hasn't dared come back from Luang-Prabang for fear of the anger of the people. He's the most corrupt man in the kingdom. He has taken refuge in Savannakhet, where he's trying to recruit an army with the money the Americans and Thais are giving him."

"An army that's not worth a straw," Thon interjected. "Give us a few planes, and with two companies I'd take Savannakhet. I'd get hold of that fat swine Si Mong and bring him back to Vientiane and string him up. But they won't give us any planes. We're going to ask the Russians for some."

"Who won't give you any?"

"Prince Sisang. All he ever thinks of is negotiating. To the French, whatever Prince Sisang says is Holy Writ."

His broad hirsute face broke into a grin which revealed the gaps in his teeth.

"I know what Holy Writ is, you see. I'm a Christian and I was baptised. My Christian name is Pierre."

A delegation of bonzes arrived, led by a gaunt man on stalk-like legs with a black umbrella under his arm—the Maha Son, whom Gibelin called Socrates. Then came a crowd of young people waving little paper flags. There were about a hundred of them.

"I now have two thousand men," Chanda went on. "When I seized this town a month ago I had only six hundred. But I still don't have a house of my own, or a car, and I stay with anyone who will put me up."

Meynadier rushed up with his beret askew.

"Well," he angrily enquired, "is Popoff arriving or isn't he? I have my crate circling round up there and using up fuel. Don't forget Thailand has cut off our petrol supplies and Cambodia can't send us any since that dirty bastard Si Mong holds the south."

"Wait a bit," Chanda replied. "Five minutes more."

Still as bad-tempered as ever, Meynadier turned on Cléach:

"And you, Mister Journalist, try not to get things too wrong. I'm acting as instructor to this battalion. The commanding officer, Captain Chanda, has asked me to arrange a training jump of two sticks. I'm carrying out his orders. But I don't meddle in politics. Got that? If I had my way, I'd greet Popoff with a few whizz-bangs."

The regular aircraft bringing His Excellency Alexis Serguieff from Pnom-Penh circled over the airfield, touched down and came to a stop on the edge of the runway. Down the steps came a man with thin hair and a lean face, wearing spectacles and a dark suit, and carrying an umbrella. He might have been a member of the British Foreign Office and a graduate of Oxford or Cambridge.

Some parachutes opened in the sky. The crowd started clapping. Ven, with downcast eyes, went up to the ambassador and presented him with a bunch of flowers. Then a hilarious soldier brought him a bottle of beer and a glass.

"You must be thirsty, aren't you?" Chanda asked him with his lovely smile. "Laos is a fine country but it's hot, especially for strangers. I'm Captain Chanda and this is my second-in-command, Lieutenant Thon."

Bewildered by this odd welcome, peering in every direction in the hope of seeing a member of his staff, Serguieff stammered:

"But . . . what about the official authorities?"

Meynadier stood sulking in a corner; he could not stomach the Russians or the Communists but he was quite pleased with the little demonstration of two sticks who had jumped well grouped. The troops were now collapsing their parachutes. Ven was still holding out her flowers, the soldier his glass and bottle of beer. The ambassador took the flowers and the bottle, and kissed Ven on the cheek. Then Chanda and Thon in their turn embraced him.

He perceived Cléach with relief, flung himself on him and, likewise embracing him, whispered in his ear:

"I don't like beer. What's going on here?"

"This is Laos, Your Excellency."

"But what about all these paratroops?"

"Laos is living in the paratroop era. I've been in this country since yesterday. Everyone here keeps saying that everything sorts itself out in the long run—*Bo penh nhang*!

"Where's my chargé d'affaires?"

"At the other end of the airfield with the officials."

"Is this a diplomatic incident?"

"Not even, just a music-hall turn."

By now Cléach was genuinely amused. He was enjoying this country which paid no attention to childish ritual and protocol. He could not resist adding:

"You know, Your Excellency, that in Laos the king, who's a disciple of Jean-Jacques Rousseau, grows his own lettuces; the president plays belote or bowls with the ambassadors. . . ."

"I only play bridge. And I don't like Jean-Jacques Rousseau at all. I wrote my thesis on him. Hateful man. Your name, Monsieur?"

"Cléach, from the Agence France-Presse."

"But where are Pravda and the Tass Agency?"

"With the officials."

"Protocol, for a diplomat, is extremely important. I'm distressed by all this. Our dear comrade Krushchev would have liked it perhaps, because he's fond of practical jokes. As for me, I'm merely surprised. . . ."

Chanda was getting impatient. He grabbed Serguieff by the sleeve in a familiar manner and led him past the chattering bonzes, laughing girls and sparse, gesticulating crowd.

An official car drove up at full speed. It was flying the Soviet flag. The ambassador climbed into it after handing his beer to Meynadier and the flowers to Cléach. Then, leaning back against the cushions, Alexis Serguieff took a handkerchief out of his pocket and wiped his face. Speaking Russian now, he said to his chargé d'affaires who had arrived the evening before:

"Really, Nicolas Ordinsky, I'm not cut out for exotic countries."

"Nor am I," sighed Nicolas, who was feeling the heat even more than the ambassador.

"Yet you'll be staying on among these clowns. I'm merely presenting my letters of credence to the king before flying back to Pnom-Penh. At least in Cambodia they have a prince to govern them, not a paratroop captain."

"They also have a prince here."

"But he doesn't govern anything. Where are we staying?"

"At the hotel. The Americans offered me one of their villas. But it was difficult to accept it."

"A pity, they're the only people who can install proper air-conditioning."

Cléach drove back to town, still in the obliging Captain Lalo's car. On the terrace of the Constellation he caught sight of Gibelin and Flore. Dismissing the driver, he walked over to their table, with his bouquet in his hand.

"Well," Gibelin enquired, "did the arrival of the Moscow eye go off all right?"

Cléach gave a brief account of the reception and the parachute display that had accompanied it. Gibelin was wreathed in smiles. Then the journalist handed his bouquet to Flore.

"With the best wishes of His Excellency Alexis Serguieff."

"Flore doesn't like flowers," Gibelin murmured.

"Yes, I do," she retorted. "Thank you, Monsieur Cléach."

After sending off his first cable, Cléach made his way on foot to the French Embassy. When he heard of all the ups and downs that had marked the arrival of his "dear colleague", Xavier Pinsolle almost choked over his roast duck.

Only one year had elapsed since then; Cléach had witnessed the succession of coups d'état and seen his nature get the better of his good resolutions. He had never tried to worm his way into local society but had found his friends among those living on the fringe of it. Was he happy or unhappy? He did not know himself.

His tongue was furred, so he picked up a bottle of water beside his bed and took a big mouthful. Turning over in her sleep, Flore had pulled the mosquito-net loose.

"Gibelin wreathed in smiles!" Cléach reflected. "And Pinsolle's allusion to his liking for practical jokes."

He put on a sarong and went into the next room where Meynadier lay on a camp bed sleeping off his opium. He shook him:

"You old bastard. . . ."

"Get out, I have a splitting head-ache. Give me some tea and some aspirin."

"First of all, I want to ask you something."

"Oh, shit!"

"No aspirin, then. You convinced me one day of the necessity of torture. The parachute display, the reception of the Soviet Ambassador at the far end of the runway—whose idea was it? Answer me, fat-head. Was it Gibelin's?"

"Yes, it was Gibelin's. He suggested it to Chanda and Thon. Those two rogues revelled in it. I couldn't do anything to stop them. Ricq was furious, Sisang even more so. The prince gave Chanda, who was master of the town, fifteen days' C.B. Absurd. Naturally Chanda didn't do his fifteen days. Can you imagine Pflimlin giving de Gaulle fifteen days' C.B. at the time of the 13th May? But from then on they began to fall out. The Communists and Si Mong's men at Savannakhet took advantage of this.

"My head's ringing like a bell . . . When you woke me I was having a nightmare. Do you know what was happening? I had just seized Vientiane in a Signals jeep. I didn't quite know what to do with the town, so I handed it over to Chanda who, not knowing what to do with it either, passed it on to the Communists, who likewise didn't know what to do with it. Si Mong was the only taker, but he was also the only one to whom it wasn't offered.'

At midday Ricq failed to receive the meal that Ven had sent in. He assumed that since he was under close arrest, she had been forbidden entry to the camp.

Khammay did not turn up either, so Ricq had to make do with

the ordinary prison rations: a ball of rice seasoned with *padek* and a mug of tea.

Night fell. He listened to the footsteps of the sentries, the noises in the courtyard, the cries of the soldiers, while wave after wave of apprehension swept over him. He tried to convince himself that Ven was faithfully waiting for him at home and that he had not been mistaken in the policy he had followed in Laos.

Ven and Laos were bound together. Laotian Neutralism—it was while talking to her that he had discovered it. In 1961 Ricq had come and taken refuge yet again in Nouei-Phou Lak. Si Mong and the American agents had made his life untenable in Vientiane. Because of the recent agreements between the French and American governments, Colonel Cosgrove was unable to get his French opposite number expelled but he did his utmost to put him in such a position that he was forced to leave the capital.

Ven was then fifteen and already had all the winning ways of an adult woman. When Ricq and Chouc made fun of her, she lost her temper.

"You're nasty old men," she would say. "Your eyes only shine when they see a rifle. You talk all day about war, partisans, Viets and murders. They don't shine when they look at me. I prefer dressing my hair in front of a mirror to listening to you two.

"When Ricq arrives, everyone in the village is frightened. They say he's gentle and kind, the best of the *Phalangs*, but that he's fated to bring war and death with him. People want to live in peace. They'd like to see the last of Ricq."

From then on Ricq began to review the situation in his mind. Laos could not be defended with artillery and machine-guns. She had no frontiers; her inhabitants were feckless. She was populated by such diverse races that at a distance of thirty miles they were unable to communicate with one another.

Gibelin was right. The only way to divert the interest of the Americans from Laos, and at the same time that of the Chinese and the Viets, was to put an end to the petty squabbles that kept occurring and to neutralize the country. This would be in France's interests. Once again she would be able to exercise a discreet influence and with a few subsidies help the government to keep alive.

Ricq spoke about this to Chouc, who was enthusiastic:

"It's a good idea of yours, because it fits in with the Laotian temperament and religion. The people are tired of all these conspiracies and these foreigners who keep telling them to fight and providing them with arms and money. You know who might help you? The bonzes. I have a friend in Vientiane, at the Vat Sisaket—the Maha Son. For a long time he has had the same idea as you."

The village gave the customary *baci* for Ricq's departure. On a big wooden tray stood a silver cup adorned with lighted candles, sticks of incense and flowers. Threads of white cotton were attached to it. Arranged round the cup were a hard-boiled egg, balls of rice, pastries, bananas, an old silver coin, a jug of spirit and some glasses.

The bonze in charge of the ceremony, the *achar*, had recited the ritual invocations addressed to Ricq, while the crowd jostled behind him.

"Come, my soul, come by the path that has just been opened, by the track that has just been cleared. Come back to us . . ."

Then everyone present had wound a thread of cotton round his wrist, to retain the thirty-two souls of the thirty-two parts of the body.

It was then Ricq had promised the people of Nouei-Phou Lak that they need never be frightened of him again, for he would not come back until he brought peace with him.

They voiced their thanks with a low murmur. Ven, with downcast eyes, handed him a flower.

Ever since that day, Ricq had connected the idea of Neutralism with Ven. Neutralism had died under the blows of the Communists and Americans, but Ven still remained. She was now the reward for twenty years of suffering, she represented renewal and revival, solace and strength.

Father Maurel visited him at eight in the evening, Khammay a few minutes later.

"Here I am again," said the missionary. "I even have a note from General Si Mong allowing me to stay with you as long as you like. Do you mind?"

"Certainly not, Father."

"You know me, Little Ricq, I'm not scheming on anyone's behalf . . . I serve a master other than yours and I don't like scheming . . . Pinsolle knows this too. However, he asked me to come and have a word with you. I'll pass on his message without giving my opinion. I say, your prison is becoming a palace."

"Will Dupont will soon be forcing them to paper the walls. I have a second bed, a mosquito-net, a bigger table, some sheets, a washbasin, a wireless set, books. But I wasn't given the meal Ven must have sent in at lunch-time. Why not?"

"I called at your house an hour ago. I wanted to talk to Ven about this marriage and tell her what the Catholic religion demands in such a case. She had gone back to her village. Phila told me. She was crying."

"It's not true, Father."

"Since your arrest she hasn't had a moment's peace. They kept coming to search the house and question her. Her neighbours were frightened and no longer behaved in the same way towards her. They told her she was a Thai, a Northerner, not a Laotian. Of course she could always stay with Cléach. But she didn't like Flore. Or else at the Mission. The poor thing couldn't bear it a moment longer; you must understand."

"Didn't she leave a message?"

"Yes, to say she was waiting for you in her hut at Nouei-Phou Lak. Ven took away with her only one dress, her jewels and a little basket."

"No one persuaded her to leave?"

"The Maha Son told her that for the time being she would be better off with her own family. I saw him too. He can't believe Chanda has gone over to the Americans with his arms and equipment, but especially the equipment. His men threw away their arms so as to be able to run more quickly. The Maha Son heard Thon's indignant voice broadcasting on Radio Hanoi from the Plain of Jars. He was denouncing Chanda's treachery, thereby diverting attention from his own."

"That's all Ven said?"

"That she was happy to be with child by you."

"Ven's all that remains to me. After all sorts of failures, I've at last discovered with her the joys of the body and the pleasure of love. That counts for a man exhausted as I am by a struggle in which he no longer believes. It counts, to wake happily in the arms of a girl who in the morning is like a flower. It counts, for a prisoner, to have a meal that has been prepared by the person whom he loves with all his remaining strength. I want to get out of here, just to be with Ven again at Nouei-Phou Lak. I don't give a damn about anything else. What's the news from South Vietnam?"

"A battalion of the South Vietnamese army wiped out, two American planes and four helicopters shot down, four advisers killed, six missing."

"You see, the mask has been discarded. No one needs Laos any longer, or her bronze drums. But I need Ven."

"You can get out of here if you like. Accept Si Mong's conditions. All this political and secret service business of yours disgusts me. I don't want to meddle in it. What's your decision? Your plane leaves in two days' time. Your seat is booked. Pinsolle is firmly resolved not to put a knife to your throat. Even if you deceive Si Mong, he won't mind. Swindling Si Mong is an honest action. As for Chanda, he no longer exists."

"It's Ven I need."

"Then take my advice, go to her at once."

"Tell Pinsolle to have me released, tell him I promise him anything he wants. In any case Si Mong will come to a sticky end within the next three days. The Americans want to liquidate him before the presidential elections."

"What will you do once you're outside?"

"I'll get Ven back, then I'll try all the same to help Chanda. But keep that to yourself."

"There's still something I have to tell you, and it requires all the friendship I feel towards you. I'm afraid you won't be able to get Ven back. Chanda has slipped out of your control completely, and you're no longer wanted in Laos. Go back to France. I'll do as much as I can, all the same, for you to get Ven back and marry her like a Christian. At certain times, prayers are a help."

"So is opium, Father, and alcohol, and anything else that leads to resignation . . . You can look at the stars and reflect that they are millions of light-years away and that nothing is of any importance."

"You'll be able to get out tomorrow morning. Pinsolle will certainly want you to stay at the embassy. Everyone in Vientiane now knows what your real activities were. There are too many people prowling round your house. It would be better for you to lie low. Come to Mass tomorrow, the early service. No one will be there."

"No, by then I'll already be in Nouei-Phou Lak."

Father Maurel banged on the door. Khammay appeared. The missionary slapped him on the back:

"Well, you old rogue, it's always nice to see you again. I think our friend has seen reason and agrees to come to terms with Si Mong. You'll be able to go home and take a dip in your lovely swimming-pool. They tell me the villa and the pool cost you twenty million kips. Is that true?"

Khammay stayed no more than a moment with Ricq. He apologized:

"I must go and report to General Si Mong. But I don't know where he is, otherwise you could leave here at once."

The captain climbed into his car and drove down the Vientiane road. He felt more and more anxious.

Tomorrow morning Ricq would be out. He would resume his little talks here and there. Soon Vientiane would see Chanda's soldiers, sergeants and officers arrive. Room would have to be made for them in the Coordination, at the expense of those who already belonged and subscribed to it.

Si Mong had got rid of fat Soumboun. There was one place free. But more were needed. A policy of virtue was going to be introduced, in order to please Chanda, the Russians and the Americans. Everyone who had taken part in the *putsch* would be in trouble. Especially poor old Khammay, who had acted thoughtlessly without taking adequate precautions. That damned swimming-pool!

The Filipino medical officer from Camp Kennedy, Dr. Ramon

Luis Rigas, had asked him several times to come and have a drink at the Viengrathry. He went there every night, entertaining everybody lavishly. Khammay was too clever to be unaware that the Filipino belonged to Colonel Cosgrove's organization. There was a rumour going round that the Americans wanted nothing more to do with Si Mong. He was too expensive for the paltry results he obtained against the Communists. Chanda would take his place. But Si Mong was not going to give up without a struggle. Khammay had divined his plan. It was worth fistfuls of kips and dollars and, even better, guarantees for the future.

At the Viengrathry, Khammay was welcomed with open arms by Ramon.

"Ricq will be released tomorrow," Khammay whispered to him.

"Let's go out for a breath of fresh air," said the doctor.

In the garden, he asked:

"Why is he being released?"

"A scheme between France, Sisang and Si Mong to make the rest of Chanda's troops desert. Afterwards they'll settle Colonel Cosgrove's hash. They claim that by promising the Meos independence the colonel is trying to split Laos apart. But General Si Mong is thinking of the opium.

"My dear captain, you've earned your evening. How can we thank you enough for the services you have just rendered?"

"I'd like to leave the country."

"When do you want to go?"

"Tomorrow morning."

"That's wise. Would you care to have a look at the Philippines? A lovely place, splendid women, the best brothels in the world. All expenses paid, of course."

"I have a house, a wife and children in Vientiane."

"We'll look after them. On your return, I think we could offer you a post in keeping with your capacities. Let's go back to those charming creatures inside who are not always too healthy, alas! Come and stay at my place tonight. Maybe you'll have more information and further details to give me."

Dr. Ramon slipped off for a few minutes to telephone Camp Kennedy. Colonel Cosgrove had not yet come back.

[6]

The Meos of Tran-Ninh

IN her letter to her sister Juliette, Muguette said:

"This country is going through a strange time, to say the least. I don't know what to make of it. On Monday, for instance, Monsieur Ricq was arrested. He used to go to church regularly, but he's a Communist. They tried to murder him in prison. On Tuesday Monsieur Ricq is no longer a Communist but a colonel. He runs an espionage network. He's even General de Gaulle's secret envoy. His arrest straight away becomes an affair of state. The Ambassador even goes off his food. Fortunately Monsieur Ricq is not murdered. He is merely going to be expelled. On Wednesday everything's topsy-turvy again. Monsieur Ricq will be released that very evening and resume his 'duties'. (I'd like to know which ones!) He will have an official office in the embassy. He will still be an agent but he will no longer be secret (in which case there'll be no point to him at all. A secret agent who works in full view of everyone can hardly furnish General de Gaulle with any useful information.)

"On Thursday everything is back where it was. He's not released, he's again going to be expelled. Really, I can't make head or tail of what's going on. Father Maurel goes around saying that Ricq is the victim of a scheme of General Si Mong's, and Monsieur Troussier claims the general is our last bulwark against Communism.

"Colonel Andelot and his wife invited me to dinner the other evening. There wasn't enough salt in the jugged hare and the tart was burnt. Madame Andelot would do better to attend to her cooking than to go off to Bangkok every week to try on new clothes. Over the coffee, the colonel said Monsieur Ricq thought he was Lawrence of Arabia. What has Arabia got to do with Laos? Meanwhile our poor Prince Sisang is having to deal with everything."

Muguette put down her pen. All these incidents had upset her. To recover her spirits, she couldn't resist the temptation of a little glass of Benedictine.

Benedictine reminded her of her husband, Monsieur Helbronn, who had always been such a gentleman. Another glass followed, then a third. Muguette went to bed in a haze, leaving her letter unfinished.

Muguette had grown up into a tall, beautiful young girl. She was marrying Prince Sisang, to the sound of the great organ of Notre-Dame. Colonel Ricq, on horseback, followed her carriage, with his sabre on his shoulder, while Cléach, who was once more a little boy, received a great clout from his mother, an old, black-clad Madame Andelot.

Up in the mountains above the Plain of Jars, Colonel Cosgrove, muffled in an outsize greatcoat, warmed his hands at the fire which the former Sergeant-Major Picarle was trying to fan into life with a piece of cardboard. But the damp wood spluttered and smoked without emitting any heat.

"I don't like this invasion of ragamuffins," said Picarle.

The veteran of the G.C.M.A. still had the same eccentric appearance as when Ricq had known him. He was wearing a bush hat adorned with a long pheasant's feather and, round his neck, a big Meo silver collar. His ankles were encased in canvas leggings, and his thick unkempt black beard accentuated his angular features. His battered hat and loose drill shirt with torn sleeves made him look like a scarecrow.

"Why not?" Cos asked.

Choking in the smoke, Picarle stretched up:

"Apart from the two companies of paratroops that were brought here by the French sergeants, the rest are a lot of boobies. What are we going to do with the women and children who are dying of hunger and cold? They're exhausted by their march. And the men? They're not soldiers; they all threw away their rifles to be able to run faster. . . . At a height of five thousand feet, they don't feel well. They're dear little townees or else peasants from the deltas. Life is too soft in the towns; rice grows all by itself in the valleys. I talked to Lutz and Pérot about it. Why did you send them off at once to Vientiane as though they had cholera?"

"I don't like Ricq's men poking their noses into my business."

"They're the sort of lads we need, however, instead of your cowboys. Apart from the paratroops, whom they kept firmly in hand, every worth-while Neutralist unit has gone over to the other side. We've got the duds, the office-boys, the malingerers, who had found an easy billet in Vientiane and haven't yet recovered from being sent into action. The N.C.O.s? Former students recruited by Chanda in a moment of over-enthusiasm. They know nothing about fighting and now want to go back home."

"Chanda's the man I want. In order to get him, I have to take the rest."

"You won't get anything more out of him, Colonel. That fellow's done for. A year ago he almost managed to persuade the Laotians he was going to get them out of the mess they were in. But what's the result? As for Prince Sisang, he cuts no ice at all.

"My old pal Phay Tong tells me no one any longer believes in what the prince did or said. He's just being kept for window-dressing. It needed a mere handful of men to throw him into jug and send Chanda packing. The nucleus of the Neutralist army, Colonel Thon's two battalions, followed their commander and went over to the Viets. The French advisers are all back in Vientiane. Gibelin has been liquidated and that little bastard Ricq, the brains of the whole scheme, is behind bars in Xien Nip Camp.

"Ask those fellows dying of cold and hunger under their drenched ground-sheets if they still believe in Neutralism. General Si Mong has won right along the line. . . ."

"Or rather, the Communists have. Si Mong is a smoke-screen, like your Meos. Because I hope you're labouring under no delusions as to them or the importance of their role."

"I wonder, Colonel. These maquis bands are costing you so much that even the Americans wouldn't fling all that money out of the window for nothing."

"If we have to fight against the Communists one day, I don't think we'd ever choose Laos as a battlefield, or this basin of the Plain of Jars. In the basin of Dien Bien Phu, which was bigger but just as badly situated, the French lost a war. The maquis bands didn't do any good. You know that as well as I do. You're a man for whom I have a high regard, Picarle. . . ."

"What are you getting at?"

"I wouldn't like to lie to you, to be obliged, like Ricq, to say to you one morning: 'Get into the plane, everything's lost'. My government will always prefer the friendship of the Laotian people to the support of a few picturesque minorities."

"There's no such thing as the Laotian people. It's a lot of eyewash!"

"You know it, so do I. But in Washington they still believe in the myth of Laos. If we have Chanda with us, if we manage to build him up sufficiently and put him in the place of Si Mong at Vientiane, I would be able to ask the C.I.A. and the Pentagon for further funds. They'll be used for rebuilding the Neutralist army and supporting your Meos. In Washington they think you're too expensive, they also think Laos isn't as important as they once believed. The war is being waged in South Vietnam."

"Don't forget, all the same, what you promised Phay Tong—independence."

"One day we shall have to reach a realistic settlement of the Indo-China problem. I don't think the fate of a few thousand highlanders can be taken into account."

"You're talking like Ricq. But at least you issue an advance warning."

"We'll save a few Meos like Phay Tong who have been useful to us. We'll keep them in reserve against the day we'll have to start all over again. Because, as you know, Picarle, in Asia everything starts all over again. Nothing is ever won, nothing lost. For all our faults, we Americans are a great nation now because we can afford to wait and start again."

"Then we'd better pack up, Colonel."

"No, not yet, I assure you. What the French Expeditionary Force lacked was perhaps funds and manpower but especially the support of their country. We in America can criticise the Indo-China war and the way it has been run. No one stops criticising it in fact. But we never attack the men who, under orders of the American government, are fighting and dying in the process of this ugly war. Your stevedores at Marseilles refused to unload the coffins of the men killed in Indo-China. That wouldn't be possible in the States. The soldiers of France took their revenge, they gave those Communist stevedores a dictator in the shape of a general as old as time."

"You're not going to say you can win the war in Indo-China thanks to American civic sense."

"Win it? No, I don't think so. But at least we may be able not to lose it the dirty way if we maintain sufficient friends for when we come back."

"The loser's always a dirty dog. That's something you ought to learn."

"Chanda in our hands represents a trump card. We thought Communism was a monolithic religion. It merely needed Stalin's disappearance for the world to realise there were still some laws superior to ideologies and religions—the laws of geo-politics, the eternal conflict between wealth and poverty.

"The Russians, in their turn, are becoming rich; they are threatened on their frontiers by the poor—the Chinese. They'll be forced to join our side. We can hardly ask them to help us support General Si Mong, a dope-peddler and racketeer, a brothel-owner who is kept in power by a gang of pimps and hired killers. There's only one man on whom we can see eye to eye: Chanda.

"Prince Sisang, I agree, is a wash-out, a puppet of the French. What young Laotian would be prepared to risk his life for Sisang? More than a thousand have died for Chanda. That counts. We don't want to go on backing men of straw, but men who have their heart in the right place, who don't fight for a handful of dollars but because they want to live as they see fit.

"In five years' or ten years' time we'll be proved right. We're going to create a new race of Americans and, to begin with, a new army—the revolutionary army adapted to subversive warfare which some people had envisaged in France. It won't consist of big healthy guys fed on milk and fruit juice, but dirty little inventive men who are never discouraged, who'll live as you do, who'll get by on a handful of rice and be able to fight on their own. They'll have their doubts and moments of anxiety, but they'll realize that a nation deserves its wealth and comfort because others in exchange are waging a hard war."

"The colonel must be feverish," Picarle reflected, "he's suffering from the sort of fever that in the rainy season sends the most hardened men off their heads for a few days.

"Only he might have chosen a more suitable moment. He'd do better to start restoring a little order in this shambles or else drink himself unconscious. Then he'd stop making a fool of himself while the fever lasted. I would never have believed it of him."

But Cos pressed on with his argument:

"We'll rid America of all her stupid taboos, her psycho-analysts, her films which always have a happy ending, her publicity racket, her matriarchs, her gangsters, her corrupt policemen and her stars with tits like cows. I wanted to tell you this before asking you to adopt American nationality and become one of the instructors of this new army."

"I'm sticking to my Meos; I don't give a damn for all the rest."

"What will your end be, Picarle? A final solitary combat on a mountain ridge with two or three men who haven't abandoned you, a heroic end which no one will know about."

"I lead my life as I see fit. You'd better approach Chanda, he's the type that enjoys being preached at.

"There's a favour I want to ask you on behalf of Phay Tong. We have two tons of opium to transport to Thailand where the buyer is due to take delivery tomorrow evening. No plane can land at Xieng Khouang or in the Plain of Jars and we've decided to do without the good offices of Si Mong."

"I don't like that kind of racket."

"The French used to do it before you, to finance the G.C.M.A.s. Others will do it after you. Phay Tong wants to maintain his market. He doesn't believe you'll stay here for ever. Your helicopters are the only aircraft that can transport the opium. We have it up in the village, packed in powdered milk cans."

"Where is the stuff to go?"

"I don't know. That doesn't concern me. But Phay Tong wants it delivered tomorrow."

"What do I get out of it in return?"

"The Phong Saly radar. It's a nuisance to the reconnaissance planes you send over China. It gives warning of them before they've crossed the frontier. Don't be difficult, Colonel. It's not the first time Special Forces have done us a favour in return for other favours."

"Si Mong may make trouble for us."

"You have him where you want him, and his uncle Aprasith as well. They come and eat the dollars out of your hand."

"I'll let you have my answer tomorrow."

"Very well, Colonel. Now there's something I have to do. Your cowboys have just played another trick on me. They went off with two hundred kilos of plastic and a dozen Meos to blow up a road which isn't used at all . . . Because in the rainy season no one can use any road; they're all under water. The Meos left your fellows in the lurch at the foot of the mountain. They had lost interest in the business. Those cowboys of yours, a lieutenant and two sergeants, are now talking about desertion and asking me to make an example. Yet again I must repeat: the Meos fight the way they like and when they like. They're neither soldiers nor mercenaries. To them, the all-holy dollar is a lump of shit. They'd much rather have big silver *sapeques* to hang round their women's necks. When you want to involve them in an operation, you have to know how to handle them. Make an example indeed! Put one of them up against the wall and shoot him, just because they got bored with playing at soldiers! Damn it all, the whole lot of them would abandon us at once and go straight over to the other side . . . providing they didn't first slit our throats. They don't give a damn for democracy and the defence of the West, for what's being plotted in Peking or the Pentagon. What they want is a little distraction and no bother from anyone else.

"No, Colonel, your army isn't ready yet. Your fellows are lacking in patience. They can't understand people who are different from them, their reasons for living, for dying, for fighting or for doing damn-all. It's not enough to give the parents a few rifles or the kids a few cans of milk and bars of candy."

Reverting abruptly to his usual domineering attitude and sarcastic tone, Cos demanded:

"Do you want me to handle this business and send those three men back to base?"

"No, Colonel. They've been with us four months. They've learnt something in that time. With new ones, we'd have to start all over again. These three at least have guts and want to fight."

Picarle picked up his carbine, wiped his smoke-blackened face and vanished into the night. Colonel Cosgrove reproached himself for having yet again appeared ridiculous in front of Picarle, a mere soldier of fortune. In his imagination he had built him up into a hero, at least his conception of a hero—a cold, deliberate and at the same time enterprising man, who never overlooked a detail though his mind was full of great projects. But Picarle was interested only in his own personal adventure. Cos lay down in the muddy grass by the fire.

Chanda, muffled in a raincoat which came down to his heels, came and sat down on a stone beside him. Resting his chin on his clasped hands, he remained deep in thought. As the fire flared up, Cos was able to see his high forehead and shaven pate.

"I felt tired," the captain eventually said, "and fell asleep with my raincoat over my head. I dreamt I had conquered the seven *phis* of the mountains and rivers. The *phis* assume every shape, every face; they are men, beasts, torrents, trees, rocks and storms in the sky. The *phi* of the Muong Lone led me up to the summit of the mountain where only vultures venture, The icy wind nipped my skin. The *phi* of the Nham Tok dragged me down into the underground caverns where the waters trickle away and vanish.

"I defeated them; my men too have recovered their confidence since I was victorious over the *phis*."

Cos felt deeply depressed. He had staked all the funds of the American secret services, he had worked out the most cunning schemes, to get hold of what he believed to be the trump card of Laotian politics. This card turned out to be a child who believed in Snow White's seven dwarfs.

Yet Ricq had achieved amazing results, thanks to Chanda. He had seized Vientiane, roused an entire nation and created the Neutralist movement, for which thousands of men had fought. Against Chanda, America had in vain spent hundreds of thousands of dollars . . . How had Ricq managed to conceal the fact that the little captain was half-crazy, a near-savage, who on the military plane was barely fit to command a company? At one time he had had thousands of men in his command, not to mention a battalion of Soviet tanks.

Chanda went on in his deliberate voice:

"Millions of men for millions of years have believed in the *phis* and still believe in them. They are the angels and demons of the Christian world. Buddha and Christ fought against the *phis*—the holy books say so. When they defeated them they became gods."

"What do you intend to do now that you've defeated your *phis*?"

"I must find some means of feeding and housing my men, equipping and arming them. I must send their families back to Vientiane with enough money to keep themselves alive. You've seen them; they have nothing but torn groundsheets to protect them from the weather and mouldy rice to eat. The Meos refuse to give them anything, except in exchange for their rifles or wrist-watches."

"And afterwards . . . ?"

"All those who went off with Thon will be obliged to obey the Vietnamese; they won't like it. I want them to know that everything's going well with me again, that the men are happy and the officers are no longer intriguing against one another. We are going to recreate an army in a camp in the plains. The Russians and Americans will give us tanks, guns and trucks . . ."

"You'll still be short of men who are willing to die for you."

"I know the sort of words that will sway the Laotians—peace, the end of privileges and extortion, power in the hands of the young . . ."

"Promises of that kind only work once. Why did you lose Colonel Thon?"

"He was envious. The whole world knew about Captain Chanda, no one had ever heard of Colonel Thon."

"Why, when you promoted your lieutenants to majors, colonels and generals, did you remain a mere captain?"

"It was Ricq's idea. I think it was a good one. No one pays any attention to yet another general in Laos. A captain who commands colonels and generals is more noticeable."

"If I send you away with your men, who will hold the heights above the Plain of Jars?"

"No one, Colonel, except your Meos, who'll stay perched on the ridges without doing anything. The Meos never once came down to help us. They even attacked one of our sections that had lost its way. They thought my men were coming to steal their opium. If the Viets send in only one battalion, they'll get through the mountains. The Communists don't want towns; they're frightened of them. If they seized Vientiane, the word would soon get around that the Pathet Laos are almost all foreign invaders, Vietnamese, Northern Thais . . ."

"What prompted you, after being an ally of the Communists, to go against them?"

"The Communists have never been trustworthy. When my troops were anywhere near them, all they thought about was creating cells and enticing them over to their side.

"But Prince Lam Sammay wanted to leave the Viets, Ricq told me. Ricq knows a great many things. That's why he has been thrown into prison and may even be killed. Ricq is my friend and the friend of the Lao people."

Cos interrupted irritably:

"Ricq, like me, is merely an agent of his government. Paris decides for him, just as Washington decides for me. I can't send you back to Vientiane. General Si Mong is master of the town, Prince Sisang is his prisoner. Is there any electric light round here?"

"Up in the Meo huts, where your medical officers have installed the infirmary."

Some naked bulbs shone down on the wounded, with their limbs shattered by the artillery and their faces gashed by the falls they had had from their stretchers. A medical officer, in a smock that was more bloodstained than a butcher's, was hacking away at the bodies laid out in front of him. The operating table was a plank resting on some trestles. When the operation was more delicate than usual, a sergeant trained an electric torch on to the table.

The colonel touched the medical officer on the shoulder.

"A nasty job, sir," said the latter, raising his head. "All the wounds are gangrenous; the casualties are exhausted. If they're not evacuated straight away, hardly one in ten will withstand the post-operation shock. I'm running out of morphine. At a pinch I could amputate the men after giving them a big mug of *choum* to drink. But what about the women and children? A kid yelling under my knife turns my stomach. Look at that one over there, with all the blood drained from his face. He's going to die in a few minutes. For Christ's sake do something."

The table was surrounded by pools of blood and piles of soiled bandages. The rain was coming in through the roof. An old Meo sat huddled in one corner against a wooden pillar, puffing at his opium pipe, indifferent to the cries and groans.

"There's no shortage of morphine, Doc," Cos remarked bitterly, "Make a search in the half-dozen houses of this village and you'll find several hundred kilos of opium, over ten kilos of morphine. Ram some opium down the throats of your casualties before operating on them."

"They're almost all hit in the guts; they'd die if I did that. It's true, we're knee-deep in opium and I have three ampoules of morphine left. Meanwhile all this dope will be smuggled into the

States to poison our young people. I'm just an ordinary guy, but this war seems meaningless to me. What the hell are we doing here?"

"You're the only one who can answer that, Doc. You're looking after the wounded. You'll save some of them. Can I use your table for a couple of minutes?"

"Go ahead. I'm going to have a drink before getting down to work again, until I collapse leaving my lancet plunged into an open belly. The flesh starts rotting straight away. Even my cigarettes stink of puss."

Squatting beside a wounded man lying on a bamboo litter, Chanda spoke to him softly in his own tongue. The man seized him by the shoulder and smiled.

Cos spread out a map on the bloodstained table. He called Chanda over and pointed to a spot behind a series of contour lines representing the mountains.

"Look. Here, thirty miles away as the crow flies, is the Nam Sounan Valley. There are some tracks leading to it. There's an old airstrip there which the Japs used to use. It can easily be made serviceable again if it isn't flooded. Here's the village of Ban Puei, a hundred huts scattered along the river bank.

"The Vientiane road has been cut by the Communists fifteen miles to the south. It's up to you to regain control of it. The Viets may have pulled out because of the rains. I can take you up to Ban Puei with two sections. You dig in and I'll send you supplies from Thailand. Meanwhile all those capable of walking will join you."

"What about the wounded, the women and children?"

"We'll bring them back to Vientiane."

"General Si Mong wouldn't allow it."

"I swear he will. I'll send you a dozen instructors with weapons. If in two months you're able to rebuild an army with these gangs of ragamuffins, we'll have another talk. If not, I'll drop you."

"Ricq would have come with us. Captain Meynadier wanted to follow me."

"We're pressed for time. We have a lot to do. We don't judge men by their dreams or hopes but by the results they achieve and which we are able to control. You're quite free to ask for help from the French. But they can't provide it.

"I've already taken the responsibility of coming and picking you up in the jungle. Stop bothering about those *phis* of yours. I'd rather no one sees you in town. It might amuse the journalists but it would obstruct some of my plans. You'd also be in danger of being assassinated. You'll have no further contact with the French Military Mission, even if Captain Meynadier comes and ferrets you out. The French want immediate peace in Indo-China. We also want a certain type of peace, but not just yet and in other conditions."

"What if I refuse?"

"You can't refuse. In exchange for your consent, you'll be entitled to American aid. We'll take charge of your men's pay, their family allowances, their training and supplies. . . ."

"In Moscow, the Russians told me . . ."

"When you asked them for ammunition for the arms they had given you, they refused it. I'm paying cash down for a couple of months. How about it?"

"Now I know, Colonel, why the Americans are unable to make themselves liked. They pay cash down, it's true, but they treat the people they pay like servants. With a heavy heart, I accept your conditions because of my men and Laos."

Cos shrugged his shoulders, ashamed all the same at having taken it out on Chanda because of Picarle. He called to the medical officer:

"Doc, your table's free. You can get on with your work. Captain Chanda, we take off at dawn for Ban Puei. First batch; thirty men—paratroopers, of course—with personal weapons and nothing else. You'll be with me in the Sikorski. It's armour-plated and equipped with rockets and a machine-gun. We'll land first, to see if the Viets are there. You need to show your soldiers you haven't lost your nerve."

"What about you?"

"With a carbine in my hands, I'm worth as much as Ricq or Meynadier."

"Once we're installed in Ban Puei, we'll give a big *boum*."

"You're crazy."

"When you arrive in a village for the first time, you have to give a party to win the respect of the inhabitants."

Picarle took a path which, according to Meo custom, went straight up hill, and crossed a pass where a number of "sons of the Dog" sat squatting round a fire, their shaggy little ponies standing untethered beside them.

They were the G.C.M.A. veterans who had marched with him from the China border. They were the only really reliable nucleus of the Plain of Jars maquis and were responsible for the defence of the camp, mounting guard on the surrounding heights. Picarle exchanged a few words with them while his pony came and nuzzled against him. Then he went on.

"Special Forces" were quartered in a bell-tent heated by a petrol stove and illuminated by the harsh glare of a hurricane lamp.

Lieutenant Hall Roche, in a white track suit, was rubbing his feet with ointment; Master-Sergeant John Sweeny was heating a can of stew he had just extracted from a ration box; and Sergeant Will Forbes was carefully cleaning his pistol after dismantling it and laying the parts out on his sleeping bag. The three Americans pretended not to notice Picarle standing in front of them and leaning on his carbine.

"What about talking it over?" he suggested.

Roche stretched out his foot and looked at it with satisfaction as though he had just modelled a masterpiece.

"Talking what over?"

He had the Canadian accent peculiar to natives of Maine, which sounded almost Burgundian. But everything else about him was uncompromisingly American: crew cut, pasty complexion, lean, muscular body, clear-cut but rather characterless features. The lieutenant resembled the two sergeants, who resembled every other young officer or warrant officer in the Marines or Rangers who had graduated from the school for subversive warfare. The lieutenant repeated:

"What do you want to talk about, old man, The weather? It's raining and it'll go on raining like this for two months. The war? We've lost the Plain of Jars. We told you a month ago: 'If we lose the Plain of Jars, we're done for. The airstrip must be held at all costs.' We still say the same thing: this position is useless. We ought to hold the heights."

"I'm not talking about that, Hall, but about what happened with those Meos of yours."

"What happened? Nothing at all happened? Isn't that so, Sergeant Sweeny?"

"Sure, Lieutenant."

"Forbes, have you heard about anything happening?"

"No, sir."

Picarle put down his carbine, took off his plumed hat and ran his hands through his tousled hair:

"Will you kindly stop behaving, all of you, like actors in an old Western film—'See anything, Joe?' 'Not a thing, Bill'. I must know what happened."

"Then it's just too bad. But we'd rather you didn't meddle in this business. Your goddam bastard Meos left us in the lurch at the foot of the mountains. It was a miracle we were able to find our way back among all those tracks criss-crossing and leading nowhere. A miracle we're not all three of us down in the plain, strung up like sausages, with our balls dangling in the air and some Viets winding a magneto to send the current through us while questioning us as to what's going on up here. The Viets are inquisitive and we fellows do our best not to give too much away. So the session drags on. Finally, since we're too knocked about to be shown to the valiant and industrious population of Laos and Vietnam, we each get a bullet through the head and our bodies are tipped into a flooded ditch.

"That's what might have happened if we hadn't had the luck of the devil. Now, Picarle, if you don't want us to settle the score ourselves, you need only make an example yourself."

"What do you mean by an example?"

"Tomorrow morning you parade your savages and call out a certain Lou Tsen and his group. They're the ones who agreed to accompany us, but not for nothing—three sacks of rice, five carbines, a thousand rounds of ammunition and ten uniforms. You make them hand over the loot. After which you have Lou Tsen shot for letting us down en route. In regulations, that's what's known as desertion in the face of the enemy. I'll be happy to carry out the execution. I'm not an old soldier like you, but I assure you my hand won't shake."

"If we do as you say, not one of us will finish the day alive. Lou and his pals are even capable of going and selling our heads to the Viets. I don't know how much yours is worth, but I've had a price of a hundred thousand kips on mine for the last two years. That counts for something, a hundred thousand kips, even to a Meo. In this sort of transaction, like opium, the Viets are honest and pay cash down! You see I'm beginning to use Yankee phrases. The Meos will return what you gave them—that's quite normal, since the contract wasn't carried out.

"But there's something I don't understand about your story, young Hall, something that amazes me in fact—the idea of going and blowing up a road which is under water. Who do you think you're fooling?"

"That's quite enough from you, Picarle. We wanted to push a couple of miles north, where there are the eight Soviet tanks, still intact, which the Viets captured from the Neutralists. They're guarded by a dozen Pathet Laos who would have taken to their heels if we had shaken them up a bit. We didn't say anything to Lou Tsen except about the road. That was the first objective. Once we had got down there, we would have put him in the picture and maybe doubled the bonus so that his fellows would continue to guide us and carry the plastic."

"You cowboys! Who was it gave you such good information about what was happening in Viet territory? I don't know how you set about it, but I know this country and its inhabitants, and also speak the language, yet I never manage to get such a lead. Maybe because they know I'm not so easily fooled. I can smell a Viet trap a mile away.

"When Lou Tsen realised what you wanted to do, he left you then and there without any further explanation. The Meos don't like explaining things. Lou considered you were sufficiently capable to find your own way back. Otherwise you were done for . . . this time or another, for the moment is bound to come when you'll have to fend for yourselves.

"You drew up a contract with him to blow up a road. He thought it was silly, but he wanted some rice, carbines and ammunition. So he undertook the job, in agreement with his men. Because, among themselves they don't give or receive orders but draw up contracts. You had talked about a road, and suddenly there you were wanting to blow up tanks. He left you after you had already crossed the road, didn't he?"

"Yes, maybe."

"When he realised you were rushing straight into the hands of the Viets who were waiting for you."

"You're fancying things, Picarle, just to find an excuse for your Meos. You're like a cuckold who still loves his wife although she's unfaithful to him. One of my uncles was like that. It was a painful sight."

"You still haven't told me who it was gave you that information about the Russian tanks."

Reluctantly, the lieutenant admitted:

"One of the fellows who arrived with the last batch of Chanda's paratroops. I made him draw me a map on a piece of paper. He told me he stayed behind after the Viets reached the airfield and had seen the tanks collected. Then he had taken to his heels."

"What language did this fellow speak?"

"French . . . fairly well."

"Then he wasn't a Meo. The Meos are incapable of learning a foreign language. It bores them. They find life is sufficiently complicated as it is and even resort to their own tongue as little as possible.

"If you don't mind, shall we go on with our little investigation? How was the fellow dressed?"

"A sort of uniform, in tatters. I'd be able to recognize him. He had a flat face and bow legs. He had lost his rifle and wanted a carbine. That's how he got into touch with us."

"He also had slanting eyes, didn't he? No point in looking for him now. He must have gone back to the Viets long ago to make his report. He had mingled with the refugees to find out what was going on. The idea occurred to him on the way to bring off a double coup, to lay a trap for you three big boobies who were sufficiently aggressive, sufficiently furious at having taken a hiding, to nibble such an obvious bait: eight brand-new tanks with no one guarding them. Think it over, cowboy. War in this country is a vicious business. Nothing is left to chance.

"Now will you give me a drink? Later on you'll explain to your two sergeants how you almost came to grief, not on account of the Meos but through your own lack of experience. Meanwhile congratulations on making your own way back and not getting nabbed in the plains."

"What would you like to drink, Picarle? There's whisky or beer."

"Beer, please. How long did your course at Fort Knox last?"

"Subversive warfare and jungle warfare, sabotage, basic language training: six months in all."

"Ten years ago I also went on a course. It lasted ten days. The instructor's name was Ricq—a dirty little bastard, incidentally. That may be why he knew his job so well. He told me: 'Picarle, never forget that once you're in the jungle you're on your own, and even with your partisans you'll still be on your own. To begin with, they'll all be watching to see where your weak point lies. During that period you must sleep with one eye open, never fall sick or at least never show it. Your partisans must feel you're never caught at a loss in a country in which you're ignorant of everything: what the tracks are like, in which direction the rivers flow, what animals inhabit it and what the customs of the various races are, their taboos and enmities. Everyone will be out to get you. The fellows on the opposite side are patient and have any amount of tricks up their sleeves'.

"Ricq also used to say: 'You must have flair—what idiots call having luck. As long as you're not bound to your partisans by personal habits, all those little things that make you get to know one another, tolerate one another, until finally you'te unable to do without one another, never ask too much of them. Above all, never let your men get bored, never leave them with nothing to do. A group of partisans isn't really fit for action until they've been together for at least six months'.

"Ricq knew what he was talking about. He had operated for almost a year against the Viets and Japs, without a penny, with a few old pop-guns. But you Yanks insist on keeping to yourselves. You don't mix and you live on canned food.

"What about that beer? Thanks.

"Now don't forget. If anyone ever again offers you a spectacular operation, come and see Picarle. A hundred to one it's a trap. But just that once it may be genuine, because it's an odd war we're fighting. In which case, of course, one shouldn't miss it."

The lieutenant scratched his throat and diffidently asked:

"Don't you ever miss your own country and friends? I saw you with those two Frenchmen who brought the paratroops up here. You looked like ants from the same ant-heap putting out feelers."

"Things have happened on which it's impossible to go back.

"I'll get Lou Tsen and his gang to return the weapons and uniforms, but we'll have to leave them the rice. They'll exchange it with the Neutralists for rifles, so everyone will be happy all round. So long, you fellows."

Picarle made his way back to the saddle where the Meos were stationed, straddled his pony and, letting the reins hang loose, rode off with his feet almost touching the ground. The sky was black and starless. He ascended and descended a number of slopes, then skirted a patch of forest until he arrived at a small shack where a light was burning. Here he dismounted, while his pony went off to take its place at the stall between two other horses. The girl who was waiting for him was young but had huge calves and a flat round face.

He went inside and warmed his hands at the flame flickering between two stones in the middle of the floor.

For a moment he thought of the big farm in Allier where he was born. It was almost like a factory with its silos, tractors and sheds. He thought of Denise who by now must have had four or five children by another man.

On Sunday afternoons they used to go for a stroll together along the banks of dark rivers flowing through rich pastureland. The smell of the fields and the freshness of the water, combined with their love, made them breathe more deeply, while they were swept by an emotion in which they mingled the memory of their childhood together with the promise of a peaceful life to come.

Picarle took off his drenched clothes and lay down on the mat beside this Meo girl who, with four horses, the shack and the poppy field, was now his sole possession.

Next morning the mist lifted, leaving shreds clinging to the black rocks. The helicopter pilots warmed up their engines and the big rotors slashed the air, then stopped. Numb with cold, Colonel Cosgrove kept stamping his feet to restore the circulation.

"Well?" Picarle asked him, leaning against the pony.

The colonel stopped stamping for a moment:

"I'll take your stuff for you, but it's the last time. How can I be sure you'll blow up the radar?"

"I want to."

"You'll need . . . ?"

"One week if you drop me by parachute with my Meos, one month if I have to get there on foot. I know the spot well, I've been there before."

"So the proposition I put to you yesterday evening doesn't tempt you at all?"

"No. It's not France I've rejected, but the life one has to lead there. America would be even worse."

The medical officer arrived with a blanket over his shoulders. He was unshaven and his eyes were bloodshot.

"What are those cans?" he asked Cosgrove, pointing to the Meos who were loading them into the helicopters.

"I made a mistake, Doc. It wasn't a few kilos of opium they had in the village, it was two tons. We're flying it out."

"To burn?"

"I'd do so if I could produce two hundred thousand dollars out of my own pocket. But then a radar situated on the China border wouldn't be blown up."

"It's a dirty job you're doing, sir. How many wounded are you having to leave behind in order to transport this muck?"

A signaller handed the colonel a message. General Walpish had just arrived at Vientiane and wanted Cosgrove to report to him at once.

Chanda's thirty paratroopers climbed into the helicopters. Their weapons were wrapped in oily rags to protect them from the damp.

"Those fellows are soldiers," said Picarle. "They don't mind being soaked to the skin themselves, but they keep their weapons dry."

Chanda and the colonel then boarded the heavy Sikorski bristling with rockets. The machine had difficulty in rising from the waterlogged surface. Behind it came the Bananas, one after another, and the swarm of heavy hornets disappeared over the mountains.

There were no more Viets in the Nam Sounan Valley. Cosgrove left Chanda and his men there and went on to Vientiane. The two Bananas with the cans of opium separated from the group, crossed the Mekong and headed for Thailand.

Dr. Ramon was waiting for Cosgrove in his office. He gave him a brief account of Khammay's revelations and General Si Mong's intentions. Ricq was going to be released at any minute. Khammay had also told him how Nutcracker, the Laos Air Transport pilot, had died and why the Junkers had caught fire and the Piper disappeared. Cosgrove drove straight to Si Mong's residence. The general was having his breakfast: a big bowl of coffee with pieces of bread and butter floating in it.

"Why am I honoured with such an early morning visit?" he asked, sucking at his bread and butter.

"You're having Ricq released?"

"The French Ambassador's remonstrances, my friend Prince Sisang is himself desirous . . . But didn't you also intervene in his favour, and in a somewhat cavalier manner for a foreigner . . . ?"

"Ricq will be expelled tomorrow. Until then he'll remain at Xien Nip."

"I've given orders for him to be released."

"Cancel those orders . . ."

"Very difficult, Colonel."

"Then the *Bangkok News* will come out tomorrow with a full account of that plane which was intercepted by radar and found to contain two tons of tea."

"The pilot has since had an accident. The plane caught fire."

"The *Bangkok News* will also describe how the accident occurred and how the Junkers of Laos Air Transport, a company of which you are the sole proprietor, caught fire on Wattay Airfield. We have a statement from Captain Khammay who, on your orders, directed the killing of the pilot and arranged for the aircraft to be destroyed. Captain Khammay flew out to the Philippines this morning. As soon as he arrives he'll hold a press conference."

Si Mong wiped his mouth with his napkin.

"You win, Colonel. I thought you only had three kings in your hand. You've produced another out of your sleeve to make four. But the game's not over yet."

He rose to his feet, picked up the telephone and called Xien Nip.

Cosgrove then drove round to the American Embassy where General Walpish, "the Christmas-tree fairy", was waiting for him.

"Well, Cos?" he asked. "Having a good time with your Meos? Let's hear what's going on up there."

Cosgrove made his report. He described the final defeat of the Neutralists in the Plain of Jars, how he had managed to pick up Chanda, and explained that the Meos would have to be used in a different manner—for instance, in commando raids to destroy targets like the Phong Saly radar.

The general nodded:

"Very interesting, all this, but only when things are a little calmer. You're forgetting the situation is rapidly deteriorating in South Vietnam. We now have whole battalions and regiments lined up against us. Every day we're losing American officers and soldiers who are paraded in front of the Vietnamese to boost their morale. Five days ago we launched the biggest airborne operation of the war: three thousand men transported in 115 helicopters escorted by twenty fighters supported by ten bombers. Result: one suspect arrested and one motorbike captured.

"Cost of the operation: two million dollars. The regular Vietcong units, as we know, come from the north along the Ho-Chi-Minh trail which runs through Laotian territory. It more or less follows the course of the Mekong, only thirty miles further east. Impossible to bomb it. It runs through forests or deep gorges which conceal it from the air. So what I want you to do is send all your Meos and this fellow Chanda and his men to blow up the convoys, lay mines and ambushes—a proper guerrilla activity.

"That's impossible, General. The Meos aren't capable of fighting except in the mountains with which they're familiar. It will take at least three months to make an army out of the Neutralists. The Ho-Chi-Minh trail isn't what you think it is—a road on which convoys can move—but a series of tracks suitable only for small units, groups, sections and columns of coolies in single file, on foot, with their arms and rice strapped on to old bicycles."

"All these guys, Meos or Neutralists, are no good to us unless they can help us when we need them. What tribes live in the forest through which the trail runs?"

"The Khas."

"Then get hold of the Khas. Arm them."

"The Communists got hold of them long ago. For the last two years the Khas have been on their side. A specialist like Ricq would tell you this."

"Ah yes, the Frenchman who's been arrested. Was it you who finished him? French-backed Neutralism, that's our enemy . . . Cos, we want you to make peace in South Vietnam. To extricate ourselves with honour, we need a few spectacular successes. Fabricate them if necessary, but do something. You're supposed to be one of the greatest experts on South-East Asia, yet you spend your time playing around with people who won't fight except on their own doorstep. As for that radar, forget it. We'll send three bombers over it and it will be demolished more thoroughly than with your commando. Get a move on, Cos. America needs you.

"I also wanted to tell you . . . er . . . er . . . There've been some nasty rumours about your using our planes to transport that stuff . . . er . . . opium, which grows up there. I know we can't fight this sort of war with choirboys . . . but after all it only needs one goddam journalist to write a story about it and we'd be in trouble, bad trouble, you especially. You realize that in a case like this we wouldn't be able to cover you, don't you? So just you go and blow up that Ho Chi-Minh trail for me."

"Dozens of tracks zig-zagging through the forest . . ."

"Our organization in Laos must produce some result, and

damn fast. In Saigon you're being accused of wasting your time on pointless intrigues. Get down to some real work."

"We could parachute a hundred wretched fellows into enemy territory. They'll be massacred before landing."

"I want a tangible result. The methods you use are your own business."

Si Mong sat for a long time with his eyes closed and his hands on his knees. Then he summoned his escort and drove out to the airfield. An hour later he landed at Bangkok. His uncle, Marshal Aprasith, had sent his big black Mercedes to meet him. The drawn curtains hid from view the occupant of the car.

By the end of the afternoon he was back. His features betrayed no expression at all, neither satisfaction nor disappointment.

A little later two officers of the Thai Military Police knocked at the door of one of the helicopter pilots who had transported the cans from the Meo maquis. Like his colleagues, he always wore civilian clothes; his permanent residence was in Bangkok and he officially belonged to a private company, Air Trading, which served as a cover for the "Special Forces" pilots.

The pilot immediately asked if he could ring up his consul.

"He's already waiting for us," one of the Thais replied with the utmost courtesy.

At police headquarters, in the presence of the consul, a colonel produced two of the cans and asked the pilot:

"These were what you transported from the Plain of Jars Meo maquis, weren't they?"

"That's right."

"And it was Colonel Cosgrove who ordered you to take them at the same time as Captain Chanda's men whom you landed at Ban Puei?"

The pilot glanced at the consul, who gave him a sign that he could answer the question.

"Yes, that's right."

"You didn't know what was in these cans?"

"No."

"After being landed, these cans were loaded on to a truck belonging to the Laotian Minorities Delegation, weren't they?"

"Yes. We always deal with the Delegation. They're responsible for the maquis supplies."

"Your name is Jonathan Chambers . . . Six months before joining Air Trading, you were still a Marine lieutenant, weren't you?"

"That's right."

"That'll be all. You're free, Monsieur. You can go back home. We apologize for having inconvenienced you."

The French Consul, Pierre Prestelot, was waiting for Ricq at the entrance to Xien Nip Camp. Pinsolle had given him instructions to bring him straight to the embassy.

Ricq appeared with an old cardboard suitcase in his hand. Just as he drew level with the guard post, a sentry rushed up. The Coordination captain accompanying him motioned him to wait, went inside the post, then came out again.

Prestelot saw Ricq gesticulating violently as he was forcibly led back into the camp.

The consul did not understand what was happening. He asked to see an officer. The latter told him there had been a misunderstanding, that Monsieur Ricq would probably be released shortly, or else this afternoon or evening when the matter had been cleared up. *Bo pen nhang.* At all events the French Embassy would be informed straight away. Prestelot reported what had happened to Pinsolle. The ambassador rang up General Si Mong. The general was away; Prince Sisang knew nothing and was under the impression that Ricq had already been released.

Pinsolle was irritated by these perpetual setbacks and at the same time relieved not to have to make use of Ricq against his wishes. Baron de Sait-Urcize, who had gone to see if there was anything Ven needed, had found the house empty. She too had disappeared.

Ricq was led back to his prison with the graffiti on the walls and the bars on the window. He was so deeply distressed that he did not ask to see anyone or even try to find an explanation for this fresh reversal of the situation. He felt exhausted, did not touch the meal he was brought, and lay down on the bed. Dozing off, he stretched out his hand; it encountered nothing but the coarse cloth of the 'biscuit', the dusty old mosquito-net, but not Ven's smooth young body.

Since that first night he had spent with her in the ruins of her hut, he had fallen into the habit of stroking her gently each time he woke up. When the moonlight fell upon the bed, he would prop himself up on one elbow and gaze at her lying rolled up in a ball, sheltered in sleep as though in a nest.

The silence of the prison was disturbed only by the faint rustle of insects, worms or termites devouring the woodwork of the camp buildings.

There were movements on the other side of the door, a sentry picking up his rifle and dragging his feet, another coming to relieve him.

The first time Ricq had watched Ven sleeping, he had hoped that the night would never end. When he had smoothed back her hair which was plastered to her forehead with sweat, she had whimpered like a child being disturbed.

Ricq had not slept with many women—only Loan, the secretary of a businessman in the Belgian Congo, a W.A.C. in India and a few whores or semi-whores. Each time he had rushed away immediately afterwards, longing to be alone, relieved at having got the chore over. He was not yet in a position to know that true love began after pleasure, when it turned to tenderness.

After the Nouei-Phou Lak tragedy, Ricq had only seen Ven again at Vientiane.

Chanda, immediately after the capture of the town, had sent for her to show her that her father had been avenged. Ricq often used to see her at ceremonies or demonstrations. Each time, he was surprised to see how different she was from the other Laotian girls. Taller and more slender than they, she had a small waist, firm little breasts. Her face with its slanting eyes, her fine head on its long neck, reminded him of the girls from the Haute Région, the red Thai or black Thai women. She was always dressed in dark colours and looked as cowed and timid as a young animal that has just been beaten. The clash or rattle of a weapon made her jump with alarm.

The pity he felt for her gradually turned to tenderness. He bought her a silver belt and some shawls. She thanked him, as usual with downcast eyes. But each time she left him, he felt disturbed and depressed.

Ricq was then engaged on maintaining a semblance of unity in the Neutralist faction.

Lam Sammay, the red prince, had at last informed him that the Pathet Lao was willing to take part in the government.

Ricq thought he had won. He came to fetch Ven at the house of some friends of her father's where she was staying and, with his eyes shining, promised her that this time Laos was going to have peace and that what had happened at Nouei-Phou Lak would never be witnessed again.

But the prince arrived accompanied by his wife Loan and two companies of Pathet Laos, among whom there were very few Laotians, to act as his bodyguard.

Ricq grew apprehensive.

There was a cordial reunion between the princes, demonstrations for peaceful co-existence, appeals for peace and reconciliation, parades in which bonzes with shaven pates mingled with paratroopers in red berets, and messages were despatched to every head of state in the world.

Ricq waited four days before calling on the red prince. He and his bodyguard had been billetted in the villas on the edge of the river. Seated on chairs, with their Russian submachine-guns on their knees, the Communist sentries mounted guard as though outside a prison. When Ricq was shown in, the prince had his wife with him. He kept lighting cigarettes and putting them out again immediately afterwards. Loan was dressed in Laotian style and wore a bun, which did not suit her at all. The passage of twenty years had produced little alteration in her appearance. Her body was still as slender, her features still as ugly; she now spoke French without an accent.

Loan greeted Ricq amiably but he felt she was still animated by the same fanaticism that had frightened and at the same time enchanted him at their first meeting in Paris.

The Central Committee of Hanoi, it was obvious, had instructed her to keep an eye on her husband. Had the Committee got wind of Lam Sammay's projects? Had it noticed his ever-increasing lassitude, his reluctance to swallow and pour out the official propaganda?

There was something unnatural about the prince's manner. He was at the same time too cordial and too aggressive. He nodded his head whenever his wife joined issue with him and when Ricq looked at him too intensely. And those cigarettes he kept lighting, those matches he kept breaking against the side of the box . . .

"Has Loan any inkling of what I'm up to?" Ricq wondered. "She has remained a Vietnamese, and so has the prince; she's a real Communist and he's a dilettante."

Loan handed Ricq a cup of tea and turned to the prince:

"Our friend here has always been frightened of me . . . even in the very distant days when we were both studying at the School of Oriental Languages. Ricq was a remarkably gifted student. But I had the impression he would end his days surrounded by dusty old books . . . Suddenly I discover he's leading a life of adventure. He is dropped by parachute from India and commands an anti-Japanese maquis group which soon turns into an anti-Communist group. You remember, Sammay, when we had Ricq and his killers on our heels? We knew we could count on no respite or pity from them. Now Ricq is busy with something else . . . scholarship, ethnography. Yes indeed, the gentle Ricq who could handle a machine-gun, grenades and a dagger so efficiently, the gang leader whom the biggest thugs used to follow without a murmur, suddenly abandons his adventurous life. He opens his books and works at the French School of Far Eastern Studies, he becomes a friend of the bonzes, a peaceful and quiet creature. Let's hear something about your research work, my dear Ricq."

"The origins of Laotian Buddhism, the Indian influences . . . A certain manuscript of the *Ramayana* which is said to exist somewhere near Sam Neua might provide evidence of those influences."

"Ah, that's why you've been reported several times travelling about the North. From love of scholarship, to find that *Ramayana*, you were willing to risk your life, Wonderful, Ricq!

"Discreet, unassuming, engaged on peaceful tasks which, by a strange coincidence, always lead him to trouble spots just as important incidents occur. You must be happy that peace has been restored and Laos is at last united. You'll be able to resume your research in complete security."

"I hope so, Your Highness."

"But maybe you don't like security? How does it feel to call me 'Your Highness'? It amuses you, doesn't it?"

"I think you deserve the title, Loan. I know the courage you've always shown when you've gone off with the prince, either into battle or into the jungle, looking after him when he was wounded or sick, never leaving him for a moment."

"That's true," Sammay agreed. "Loan has always shown the courage and tenacity peculiar to her race. She never left me."

He switched the conversation:

"You must have first-rate teachers in France, because you both speak Laotian admirably."

But Loan returned to the charge:

"When two old friends meet again, they recall the past, my dear Ricq. I seem to remember you had a brother who was extremely handsome."

"He was shot by the Germans."

"So I heard. Guess who told me? You remember Geneviève, that pretty Eurasian half-sister of Antoine Gibelin's? She had a soft spot for your brother . . . Now I'm talking like a princess, aren't I? A soft spot indeed! What I mean is, they never stopped copulating together. Hasn't your friend Gibelin heard from his sister?"

"No."

"I can give him news of her. She's living at Hanoi, maybe she's now in Laos or in the Haute Région. After the ordeals she suffered in France and in Germany, she became aware of the social injustice that reigned. She joined the Communists in Indo-China because she could no longer have any confidence in the French. Her father had made her a bastard and abandoned her. The man she had followed on his clandestine activity, another Frenchman, betrayed her to the Nazis. It was your brother. Geneviève escaped with her life because she was pretty and played the whore for the S.S. in the camp. But each time she was subjected to one of those thugs, she thought of Dan Ricq . . . She now calls herself Trai and won't speak French any more."

Ricq endeavoured to control his feelings. He had not come here to defend Dan's memory but to prevent this woman from destroying his plans.

"I know," she went on, "your brother was also tortured. But he quickly gave away the names of the members of his network, too quickly for them to be warned and to be able to disappear. I'll tell you why . . . I think you'll find this interesting, Sammay. Dan Ricq talked because he had no political faith. He indulged in resistance work out of aestheticism and a yearning for adventure. He was not inspired by any deep conviction. If Dan Ricq had been a Communist, he would have held his tongue, at least for as long as it was necessary. You see, one must always distrust men who indulge in personal adventures, especially in countries which are not their own. They don't have popular support behind them; they don't even want it. They act from pride or the need to prove to themselves that they're superior to others. There are plenty of these adventurers in Asia nowadays, some of them quite clever and courageous, who are trying to upset the course of history. But they're not very loyal to those they exploit. When they're captured, since they have no valid reason for not talking, they betray their accomplices. Because they can't ever have any friends, only accomplices."

The prince had imperceptibly changed his attitude. Ricq was going to be made to pay for his brother's behaviour. It was really too stupid, too unfair.

"Would you have held out under torture?" Loan asked him. "Are you absolutely certain?"

"Yes."

Loan got up and without the slightest embarrassment uncovered her back and shrivelled breasts. They were marked with long scars.

"Once in 1946, I was captured by one of your friends, Lieutenant Morin. He recognized me when I had taken refuge in a village. Morin wanted to know where my husband was hiding. He was in the same village, two huts away. Morin's men whipped me all night. They then rolled me in salt. I didn't tell them where Sammay was because I loved him, because he was the head of our movement and because I was a Communist . . . Another cup of tea, my dear Ricq?"

Prince Sammay accompanied Ricq to the front door. Ricq felt the whole transaction was in jeopardy.

"Will you honour your engagements, Your Highness?" he asked him again. "We have honoured ours, we have brought back Sisang and you're in Vientiane."

The prince had shirked the issue, pleading as an excuse the Savannakhet Committee which General Si Mong had formed with the help of the Thais and Americans. He had added:

"What's your friend Chanda doing? Instead of haggling over everything, he would be better commanding his paratroops. Really, the Communists are more serious-minded."

Ricq had rushed all over Vientiane looking for Ven, as though the young girl's melancholy smile was the only thing that could exorcise Loan. He was not yet aware that he had begun to love her. Being unable to find her, he spent part of the night listening to Gibelin discussing art, literature and sex in front of Flore who was bored to tears.

Ricq remembered that period as a nightmare. He became more and more involved in the intrigues, jealousies, petty spites and enmities of the little group of paratroops he had brought to power. He had used them merely as instruments; they were turning out to be men with a few ideas and a great deal of cupidity.

He tried in vain to urge Sisang to capture Savannakhet. Si Mong's men were demoralized and a victory might restore a sense of unity among the paratroops. Sisang kept saying he had not come back to Laos to shed blood.

Cléach had witnessed a skirmish from the Neutralist side and written a colourful story about it. The Savannakhet forces had come under mortar fire and promptly disbanded. In this engagement, which was reported by the whole press as a full-scale battle, there had been only one casualty—a man wounded "by a splinter of bamboo". A shell had landed twenty yards from one of Si Mong's soldiers who was relieving himself behind a hedge. General panic had ensued.

All this publicity had gone to Chanda's head.

"I am the man of Destiny," he kept telling his officers.

Always on the move, incapable of applying his mind to any specific task, he clouded the issue and was only happy when taking part in a demonstration or a parade. He neglected operations completely. Left to their own devices, his men lost their keenness. It was more and more on Thon's sturdy shoulders that everything fell. But Thon, albeit a good fighting officer, had little prestige in the eyes of his men. Thailand embarked on a blockade of Vientiane. There began to be a shortage of rice and petrol stopped arriving.

Sisang still refused to take action.

Fortunately each fresh meeting with Ven gave Ricq sufficient courage to go on spinning the webs of his schemes. The prince no longer showed the slightest initiative and acted as a mere mouthpiece of France and her policy. At one particular press conference he had held, he had waited until Monsieur de Saint-Urcize had arrived, all of a flutter, bringing the text of his statement. The American journalists had sniggered.

Ricq had drawn Pinsolle's attention to this.

"I know," the exasperated ambassador had replied, "Saint-Urcize has no more brain than a sparrow. He wasn't prepared for the sort of diplomacy we're pursuing in Laos. Sisang is relying more and more on us. He never stops ringing me up . . . and lunches with me five times a week. He likes what my cook produces".

The Savannakhet Committee was gradually reinforced until it had thirty thousand men, tanks and aircraft.

To defend Vientiane against them, Chanda had called up a thousand students who enjoyed wearing uniform but had no wish to learn how to fight.

Ricq felt Chanda slipping out of his control. He met Cosgrove in Bangkok and asked him to stop supporting Si Mong. He told him about the secret agreement he had reached with Sammay and the latter's promise to abandon the Viets and form a Neutralist government with his cousin Sisang. The Americans had no further reason to back Si Mong who, without the excuse of fighting against the Communists, was nothing more than a gangster who was out for what he could get.

The colonel had refused to listen to him.

"I shan't believe Prince Lam Sammay really wants to leave the Viets," he had said, "until we come across his corpse."

Cosgrove was certain of recapturing Vientiane without a shot being fired, in the Laotian manner. He made the gesture of counting out banknotes.

Without notifying anyone, Chanda accepted an invitation to go to Peking.

Prince Sisang once again flew into a rage at the damage the little captain kept causing to his cunningly conceived policy. Chanda's increasingly accentuated drift towards the Communists led a number of officers, secretly swayed by Si Mong's partisans, to show signs of discontent.

The blockade of Vientiane was intensified. The euphoria of the initial days gave place to anger, despair and lassitude.

The Luang-Prabang garrison went over to the rebels, and the troops at Sayaboury and Xieng Khouang followed suit. The Meo leader, Phay Tong, suddenly found arms for his maquis bands and sided with Si Mong.

Two months after the coup d'état, a series of assassinations occurred which further increased the unrest and confusion among Sisang's and Chanda's partisans. One night two men had driven up in a military jeep and knocked on the door of Kahmseng, the Minister of Information and a clandestine agent of Peking. Unsuspectingly the minister opened the door himself. He was mown down by a burst of machine-gun fire. Next morning his daughters came and washed the blood-stains off the door, then went home and locked themselves in.

The assassins were in paratroop uniform. Two days later the

bodies of two officers were fished out of the Mekong. After a summary trial, Chanda had shot them dead with his own hand even though Captain Meynadier had moved heaven and earth to stop him. The two officers had continued to insult Chanda right up to the moment he killed them. Chanda had then burst into tears before the corpses of his former comrades, and talked about shaving his skull and entering a monastery.

Impassive as ever, Thon had ordered the bodies to be removed and flung into the Mekong. He alone still maintained a high standard of discipline, but solely in his own company.

At Ban Lok Camp, on the outskirts of Vientiane, a light tank battalion which had previously joined the Neutralists now seceded. The tanks drove through the streets without firing a shot, then returned to barracks. The paratroops belonging to the units commanded by the two officers whom Chanda had shot handed Thakhek over to the rebels.

Feeling more and more apprehensive, Ricq went and saw the red prince again.

"Well, my dear fellow," said Sammay, ironically and at the same time disdainfully, for he had no time for men who failed in what they attempted, "what's the situation? This general reconciliation seems to be turning into civil war. My cousin Sisang isn't governing anything. Chanda has lost control of his men. The town is full of spies in the service of the Americans. They do whatever they like, they suborn deputies and officers. I wonder if Loan isn't right. With certain men who envisage nothing but their own little personal adventure or who attempt to safeguard a past that is dead and gone, there's never anything to be gained. It's this past that impelled me towards you. It made me believe in your wild promises. The world is now intended for serious-minded people.

"My old friend Luong Me and Colonel Singvilay, the military delegate, have just arrived from Sam Neua with new directives from the Central Committee.

"They're serious-minded people and aren't hampered by feelings of nostalgia. I believe they are fully aware of certain of your non-scholarly activities. I'd advise you to leave the country. I'm afraid that, like your brother, you wouldn't be able to hold your tongue if Singvilay's men interrogated you too brutally. Asia needs a firm hand and iron discipline, for the whole continent is in a state of anarchy. The Communists alone are capable of taming this thousand-clawed, thousand-toothed monster which Mao Tse-tung mentions in one of his poems. Good-bye."

On the following day Prince Sammay went back to Sam Neua. Loan stayed on in Vientiane. For the past week Ricq had been sharing his house with a young professor called Espèredieu who had not yet been able to find a place for his wife and two children to stay. The couple were devoted to the theatre and music. Only three days after their arrival at Vientiane, they began talking about organizing a dramatic company. The curfew, the murders, the settling of old scores, the bursts of machine-gun fire punctuating the night, the demonstrations demanding death for the traitors—none of this affected them or scared them. They had conceived an idyllic picture of Laos and were sticking to it.

Ricq promised to introduce them to Ven and to take them to Nouei-Phou Lak.

On 8 December 1963 Ricq spent part of the night at the French Embassy trying for the umpteenth time to persuade Prince Sisang to launch the troops at his disposal against the Savannakhet forces.

Sisang argued desperately. He still refused to countenance bloodshed. Pinsolle kept out of the discussion. He felt that by precipitating war, Laos would be delivered to the Communists all the sooner; by doing nothing, the same result would be achieved, only more slowly.

When Ricq got home he found his house surrounded by police and paratroops. Thon was also there, rubbing his beard furiously.

"They were after you," he said, "but it was the little professor they killed, slitting his throat with a knife so as to make less noise."

"The Savannakhet lot?"

"Maybe not."

Espèredieu's body was lying on the floor, covered in a sheet through which the blood had seeped. His wife sat huddled in a corner, biting her knuckles to prevent herself from screaming.

With a catch in her voice, she told him:

"We were in the bedroom looking at your collection of Laotian costumes. There was a knock at the door. Robert went to open it. I heard a noise, chairs and tables being overturned. The children said, 'They're burglars, daddy's going to knock them out.' There were three of them, barefoot, in black clothes. They struck at Robert with knives. One of them had put his hand over his mouth to stop him shouting. I called out, 'Robert, Robert!' and the children started crying. After that it was utter bedlam. One of the men asked me in French:

" 'He's not . . .' Then he broke off.

" 'He's not an American, this fellow?'

"I yelled:

" 'We're French, all four of us. We've only just arrived . . . My husband is a professor'.

" 'We've come to the wrong house,' the same man replied. The one who was holding Robert let go of him. He collapsed onto the floor. Then the three of them rushed off through the garden.

"It's true, he does look like an American, he's often been told so. Look, I'm still covered in his blood. Robert died at once, saying: 'Why, Isabelle, why?'."

Ricq did not have to make many enquiries to discover who the assassins were: Luong Me's men. He himself gave support to the story about the killers coming to the wrong house. They had made a tragic mistake. It was quite plausible. A week earlier a member of the American Embassy had been staying in the house next door.

On the following day Ricq went round to the Pathet Lao Delegation and asked to see Loan. He expected to be told she was away. But she was not the sort of person to shirk an issue.

Ricq put the same question to her that Robert Espèredieu had asked his wife: "Why?"

"I love my husband. I didn't want you to cause his downfall."

"You might have chosen killers who knew their job. I'm all alone. Getting killed is one of the risks of my profession. Espèredieu had a wife and two children."

"Innocent people die in air raids. Officially, the men who killed your friend were Thai agitators. These agitators, in the service of the American imperialists, wanted to create the impression that the Pathet Laos were attacking foreigners in their own homes at night. We've just drafted a communiqué to send out to the press. Would you like a copy, Ricq?"

"What a filthy trick to play, Loan! You're vicious and narrow-minded. I don't want to cause anyone's downfall. I only want to bring peace back to this wretched country. The prince knew this."

"Ricq, I've hated you ever since that first night we spent together. You're a failed adventurer, and a failure in love and politics as well. In 1964 all you have to offer is the old outworn solution of patronage, the solution of the impotent. There's no one but puppets like you left to defend the world against Communism."

She burst into a peal of laughter which culminated in a hiccough:

"That's why I feel certain we've won. Yes, I tried to have you killed. But I was wrong. You'll kill yourself one day, from sheer disgust.

"I advise you, however, not to fall into our hands. You'd take a long time to die. And you Ricqs seem to be rather on the soft side."

Loan called for a sentry and told him in Vietnamese to accompany Ricq to the garden gate, adding, as an additional insult:

"See that this dog comes to no harm, little brother."

Events succeeded one another rapidly and Ricq felt as though he was trying with his bare hands to shore up a wall of sand against the advancing tide. Everything was collapsing all round him.

The king had joined the Savannakhet Committee and General Si Mong had at last ceased to be a rebel. He strutted about with all the self-sufficiency that his new and extremely questionable legality bestowed on him. Prince Sisang still remained President since the general had not been invested by Parliament. But there was no Parliament any longer, no deputies, no ministers, nothing but a huge and disturbing game of grab.

Between Thakhek and Vientiane, Paksane still held out, occupied by two Neutralist companies commanded by Captain Thon. He had promoted himself to this rank after seeing all the other paratroop officers assuming seniority.

Si Mong confined his activities to despatching raiding parties round the town while his emissaries tried to suborn the garrison. They would come over from the Thai side of the river by pirogue. Thon would send them back swimming.

On the 12 December Thon received a message despatched in the name of Prince Sisang. It was an order to evacuate Paksane and the vicinity forthwith and to leave no troops within a perimeter of fifteen miles. Thanks to the intervention of the ambassadors, the government had reached an agreement for a cease-fire. The delegates of the three factions had decided to hold a series of meetings at Paksane which was to be turned into a neutral zone for the occasion.

The telegram had been sent from the head of state's personal office. An hour later a further telegram from Chanda arrived to confirm it. Thon bundled his men into some trucks and left the town. Immediately two of Si Mong's battalions, massed on the opposite bank of the Mekong, landed by barge and launch. They were accompanied by Siamese police commandos.

The telegrams were fakes. The officer on duty at the President's office had turned traitor. Thon realized at dawn that he had been tricked, when some fishermen came and told him. He wanted to recapture Paksane, but Chanda had already sent him an urgent summons.

He arrived for the meeting which was held at headquarters. Chanda had asked Colonel Singvilay, the Pathet Lao military delegate, to attend it. Also present was General Atharon, the Chief of Staff, who was trundled from one meeting to another without the slightest gleam of interest ever entering his rheumy eyes.

General Atharon had ceased to exist five years ago, when he had been operated on for a tumour on the brain. He was therefore carefully retained at the head of the army.

All the officers of the 3rd Parachute Regiment were there, as well as a few other unit commanders, the delegates of the Lao Neutralist Youth Movement and the Vice-President of Parliament. The President had just fled to Savannakhet. Prince Sisang dressed in white and puffing at his pipe with a set expression on his face, presided over this strange council of war.

Chanda, after asking the prince's permission, opened the proceedings. Recent events had drawn him closer to Sisang and made him more respectful. He wanted to defend Vientiane and was relying on the support of the population and young people and the help of his "good friends" Singvilay's two companies. Lean-faced, with prominent cheekbones, the Pathet Lao military delegate looked ill at ease in his civilian suit. He was fingering a note in his pocket which Luong Me, the head of the Central Committee, the man of Hanoi, had sent him a few moments before the meeting.

Chanda turned to him:

"How many days will you need to send us reinforcements? The Russians are offering us transport planes, arms, petrol, food and medical supplies and, if necessary, some medical officers. But it will take some time for them to arrive."

Prince Sisang puffed away at his pipe and watched the flies buzzing round. Singvilay rose to his feet and took the note out of his pocket. Whereas they were all expecting him to give a direct answer, he started off by reading out a tedious declaration about the Pathet Lao's desire for peace and its friendly relations with the Popular Republic of North Vietnam. Then he came to the point.

"The Central Committee of the Pathet Lao movement and the Lao Issara movement considers that in the present circumstances the town of Vientiane ought not to be defended."

After glancing round at the handful of parachute officers in combat dress who were listening to him, at the impassive prince, a stupified Chanda and General Atharon who was fast asleep, Singvilay went on:

"We don't want the population of this town to be able one day to accuse us of provoking the massacre of innocent civilians, women and children, and the destruction of private houses and public buildings, to satisfy an outworn conception of military honour. Winning a war does not mean capturing towns but winning the hearts of the population."

He had folded his note:

"By virtue of this decision, our troops will leave Vientiane in the course of today."

Followed by the two bodyguards escorting him, with their Russian submachine-guns slung across their chests, he marched out with that lithe gait peculiar to the Vietminhs. He swung his arms and assumed an impassive expression as though already resuming the habits and demeanour which were obligatory in the military monastery of Sam Neua and Dien Bien Phu.

Prince Sisang declared that in these conditions there was no further point to the meeting and ended the proceedings.

General Atharon had to be roused from his slumbers before being driven in Prince Sisang's car back to the French Embassy where Ricq was waiting for them. The general was installed in an armchair in front of a cup of coffee. He expressed his thanks after touching his breast to make sure that all his decorations were in place.

"What did the Communists say?" Pinsolle immediately asked the prince.

"They refuse to help us. I admit I'm relieved. Turning Vientiane into a second Stalingrad is not in our nature."

Pinsolle was disturbed by the casual manner in which the prince contemplated leaving his country.

Sisang had decided to go to Cambodia and wait there until France, England and Russia received the Americans' decision to disown Si Mong.

But he insisted on remaining the legal head of the government. He was forgetting, of course, that he had only come to power through a coup d'état.

"Why not declare Vientiane an open city?" Pinsolle suggested.

Sisang shrugged his shoulders.

"Vientiane has always been an open city. It only defended itself once, against the Burmese, I never understood why. Gibelin captured it with thirty men mounted on bicycles."

General Atharon was dragged from his armchair and made to sign the document, then Sisang went off.

"Is this what usually happens?" Pinsolle asked Ricq. "To me, a town that surrenders is a tragedy. I felt I was witnessing a burlesque show."

Ricq had asked for the American ambassador to be notified that the capital would not be defended. Then he had gone off to join Meynadier, Chanda and Thon in the Maha Son's cell where they had arranged to meet. He had had some difficulty in persuading the French captain to follow Prince Sisang to Cambodia. Meynadier would have preferred to take to the jungle with the paratroopers.

The monk, even in the penumbra, kept on his cheap dark spectacles, as though it would have been immodest to uncover his eyes.

"The population of Vientiane maintains full confidence in Prince Sisang, Captain Chanda and his men. But they consider that a town is not a suitable place for waging a war. Let the soldiers fight it out between themselves, but without the women and children having to suffer," the Maha Son declared.

Chanda agreed to evacuate Vientiane during the night with his troops and their families. Thon, with thirty-five paratroopers, would wait for the Savannakhet units to advance, then pull out the moment they reached the airfield.

The embassies, legations and foreign buildings had already hoisted their flags, the hospitals the Red Cross, and everyone waited. At Wattay Airfield only a couple of planes remained, both of which were out of commission. All the rest had flown off like birds before an earthquake.

Ricq had then joined Gibelin in his office. He was busy filing papers. Flore, with the tip of her tongue protruding from her mouth, was typing a letter with one finger.

Ricq had asked him when he was going to leave, for Si Mong would never forgive him for the trick he had played on him.

Gibelin wanted to wait till the following morning. He invited Ricq and Cléach to dinner and then, raising his voice, declared:

"I'll have to come to some sort of agreement with that scribbler before I'm made a cuckold and a laughing-stock."

Gibelin's Dodge was parked in the shed outside, loaded with

cases of whisky, beer and tinned food. He was planning a hunting expedition in the jungle. Maybe he would go up to Nouei-Phou Lak. When he suggested bringing Ven back with him, Ricq had blushed.

Cléach drove up at the wheel of an old Citroen. A Chinese merchant who was winding up his business had sold it to him for a hundred dollars.

"It's the first car I've ever owned," he proudly announced. "I'd like to stand you dinner but I'm flat broke."

"Where did you get the hundred dollars?" Gibelin asked.

"I went and touched Pinsolle. He gave me an advance. Pinsolle's strolling about his garden with his hands in his pockets. He's looking at his flag flying at the mast-head and he's having sandbags piled up outside his office windows. It's as though he's actually looking forward to being besieged."

Only then did Cléach turn to Flore.

"Hello."

"Hello."

Their greeting was that of two lovers.

From Gibelin's windows they could see the Mekong and the Thai bank. Cléach was tucking into a dish of *nemes* surrounded by lettuce leaves and fresh mint but paused for a moment to ask Gibelin what he thought was going to happen.

"In Laos they wage war in the Chinese fashion, you know. The stronger man declares his cards: so many guns, so many machine-guns, so many soldiers. His opponent sees he can't match this and throws in his hand. Si Mong announced he had thirty thousand men, five batteries of 105 and four tank battalions. Chanda has only three thousand men left, no tanks and no guns, so tonight he's moving out."

"Then why, on the other side of the river, in Thailand, are they massing artillery and sending out reconnaissance planes?"

Gibelin kept glancing at Flore, while still taking part in the conversation:

"Si Mong's an odd character, a mixture of highwayman, Confucian official and French bureaucrat. He has no feelings for the people.

"To him, as to his master Confucius, the people are *minn*, young blades of grass which bend in the slightest breeze, the symbol of the herd instinct and lack of personal free-will. But the people, these blades of grass, have performed an act of free-will by choosing Chanda. He must be completely bewildered."

It was a gloomy meal. Cléach had apologised and prepared to leave. He had to despatch a cable every hour to keep the world informed of the situation.

"Why don't you take Flore with you?" Gibelin had brusquely asked him. "Show some guts, my lad. I know you've slept together. You're perfectly entitled to do so, but there's no reason why you should put on an act for me. It would actually suit me down to the ground if Flore went and lived with you for a few weeks. I have no wish to take her with me where I'm going."

Flore, without a word, went off to fetch her bag and a little suitcase, then followed Cléach outside.

Gibelin waved to them from the window and turned away so as not to see them going out through the garden.

Ricq felt sorry for his friend. He knew how keen he was on Flore. She continued to pass herself off as his mistress although for some time he had been incapable of making love. But she never mentioned this. In exchange, he took her out to smoke opium.

On leaving Gibelin, Ricq had placed his hand on his shoulder: "You're the best friend I have, Antoine."

Gibelin had replied:

"A fat lot of good that does me: I'd rather be capable of sex. All right, I'm sorry, I'm a silly old fool."

At one o'clock in the morning Chanda had arrived at Ricq's in a jeep to tell him he hadn't been able to find Ven. She was to have spent the night at a girl friend's house, but they had both disappeared. He asked him to take her back to Nouei-Phou Lak. Tomorrow she would be at the pagoda as usual to give her offering to the bonzes.

Chanda had left him with these words:

"Good-bye, Ricq, I haven't lost yet, nor have the others won. You watch, the *phis* will come to my rescue. I know they will, they told me so."

Ricq was in the pagoda garden at daybreak. His heart was beating as though this was a first rendezvous. But he still believed it was anxiety that had made him get up so early. At the sound of the gongs, the bonzes assembled for the first prayer of the day. Soon afterwards they would leave the sanctuary and disdainfully beg their food from the women bowing in front of their baskets.

It was the *Nham Heng*, the dry season. There was a nip in the early-morning air. Among the flamboyants and frangipani trees, toucans, parrots, parokeets and turtle-doves kept fluttering from one branch to another.

The river was stained pink by the rising sun. Tufts of vegetation went drifting down stream, past fishermen's boats with square nets supported on bamboo poles hanging from their prows.

Ricq had seen Ven and her girl friend Phom approaching down the long avenue, carrying their little baskets and with red hibiscus flowers in their hair. They were dressed alike and both had their hair drawn back, revealing their ears. But Ven seemed to belong to a more ancient and aristocratic race.

He felt ashamed of appearing here in his old drill trousers and bush shirt, with his bare feet shod in sandals.

"I've come to fetch you," he had said to Ven. "Chanda left Vientiane last night. He wasn't able to find you. Si Mong's soldiers will soon be here."

Ven had turned pale. He had tried to reassure her.

"You're in no danger. You'll stay tonight at my place or, if you prefer, at Father Maurel's, at the mission. Tomorrow morning Gibelin will take you back to Nouei-Phou Lak. Maybe I'll come with you."

The bonzes were now coming out of the pagoda with their tin boxes and wooden begging bowls in their hands.

Ricq had seen a red flash pierce the mist which concealed the Siamese bank of the river, and heard the detonation of the shell—an American 105. The shell fell in the midst of the bonzes and women.

Si Mong was punishing the town.

Ricq had flung himself flat on the ground, pulling Ven down with him, in a welter of spilled rice, vegetables, flowers and broken baskets. Phom started running like a maniac. She covered twenty yards, then crumpled up. A second shell chipped the roof of the pagoda, a third hit a tree trunk.

Ricq held Ven tight, preventing her from getting up and running away. The bonzes' orange-coloured robes billowed and fluttered in all directions, while further flashes could be seen on the far side of the river.

Phom lay motionless, a splinter in her head; the hibiscus flower that had fallen just in front of her was the same colour as her blood. To tear Ven from her tree, Ricq had had to twist her wrist. He dragged her to his shack and told her to wait. In the French Embassy, Pinsolle sat glued to the telephone, trying alternately to get through to Government House, the Ministry of Foreign Affairs, and the post office. There was no answer from any of them.

"Glad to see you," he said to Ricq as he replaced the receiver. "We must stop this senseless massacre of an unarmed population. Cléach looked in just now. He says there are a hundred dead and wounded. What do we do in a case like this, Ricq?"

Ricq had advised him to ring up the American Embassy or Camp Kennedy.

Pinsolle had tried, but without result, so he had then sent Prestelot round. The consul came back an hour later with the news that the American Embassy refused to intervene since the Neutralists had appealed to the Russians and Prince Sisang had resigned.

The Ministry for Foreign Affairs was empty, clouds of paper drifted in the wind. A tank had opened fire on the building just as Prestelot was driving past, shattering the walls. At the Constellation the journalists were saying that seven of Si Mong's battalions were advancing from Paksane and paratroops had been dropped on Ban-Lok Camp to reinforce the tank battalion which had sided with the rebels. These paratroops belonged to the Siamese Police special commandos.

Prestelot pretended he had just noticed Ricq's presence:

"I say, Monsieur Ricq, have you come to take refuge at the embassy? Admittedly, your house is in a bad position. You can't be used to situations like this."

Pinsolle had accompanied Ricq to the front door while Prestelot strutted about in front of the window. The barrage was continuous. After the Thai artillery, the mortar shells fired by Si Mong's troops came crashing down on the shacks and empty streets. Ricq caught sight of Cléach standing by the iron gates of the Constellation and gesticulating wildly. He went over to join him.

Stone, officially a member of the British Council but in fact head of the local branch of the Intelligence Service, cool and collected in tie and white shirt, sat sipping a glass of gin. He had greeted Ricq with a nod. A mortar shell landed in the street outside; splinters whistled through the lobby of the hotel; Stone did not bat an eyelid. Since the waiter had disappeared behind the counter, he poured himself out another gin.

Ricq and Cléach had fallen flat in the sawdust on the floor among the overturned tables. The journalist raised his head and reported brisk firing from Gibelin's office. The paratroops had still not evacuated Vientiane.

A further mortar shell fell among the bicycles resting against the trees. Pieces of metal frames rained down on them.

"I'm a dirty swine," Cléach had said. "I pinched Flore from Gibelin. I wanted her; Flore felt like a change. Gibelin didn't appear to give a damn. He even seemed eager for me to take her off his hands."

"Are you man enough to deal with her? I was forgetting. At the age of twenty-seven, one still thinks one's the centre of the universe. Antoine is fifty-eight; he knows exactly where he stands."

Ricq got up, went out of the Constellation through the corridor and found his car riddled with splinters. He drove straight to the Upper Mekong Timber Company head office.

Thon and a dozen soldiers were there, bringing up mortar ammunition. Gibelin's truck had been unloaded and driven out of the wooden shed which served as a garage.

"What's happening?" Ricq asked. "Antoine, what are you doing? You should have left by now. The Luang-Prabang road is liable to be cut. The rebels have already dropped paratroops on Ban-Lok."

"I'm staying here," said Gibelin, with his hands thrust in his pockets.

"You're mad."

"Thon and I both agree we're not going to allow those swine to fire on women, children, fishermen and coolies. We're going to lead Si Mong's little men a fine song and dance."

"I forbid you . . ."

"On what grounds, Little Ricq? We're not married."

"I beg you . . ."

"That's better."

"You'll get a lot of innocent people killed."

"Not now. Whether we defend ourselves or surrender, those swine aren't going to stop firing. Thon, come over here."

Thon came up, bearded and filthy. He was wearing all his French medals on one breast of his combat dress, and, on the other, the S.A.S. parachute badge that Ricq had given him.

Gibelin placed his hand on his shoulder as though he belonged to him:

"You tell him."

Thon stood stiffly and made his report:

"Si Mong's troops have halted their advance and are encircling the town. I sent out the leaders of the Lao Youth Movement disguised as fishermen. They talked to the soldiers from Savannakhet. The advance won't be resumed until tomorrow. Tonight the guns, tanks and mortars are going to spray the town. Yet everyone knows there's no one here. Si Mong's army is stiff with Thais who landed with their American advisers."

"Colonel Cosgrove is not so blind as to have allowed the bombardment."

Gibelin shrugged his shoulders:

"Cosgrove's not in command of anything any longer. He had a row with Si Mong and has been recalled to Bangkok. The Thais are urging their protégé to teach Vientiane a good lesson and stamp out all resistance and national sentiment. A town that is beaten to its knees is willing to accept any master, even a foreigner, even a Thai."

Ricq realized how headstrong Gibelin was. He had not looked

like this, he had not shown such bitterness, when he had wanted to seize Vientiane in 1945 in spite of orders from Calcutta. He had gone off to commit his "enormity" like a man setting out on a crusade. Today he merely wanted to fight and kill, pointlessly and hopelessly.

Ricq turned to Thon, who seemed less over-excited:

"What are Chanda's orders?"

Thon retorted:

"Chanda's gone; I'm in command. Chanda indulges in politics, he presides over meetings, he has discussions with ambassadors, he goes off on jaunts to Moscow and Peking; I fight."

"Calm down, Thon. The people of Vientiane are going to suffer."

"They already have suffered. There are two things that will stick in their memory—the thirty thousand swine who smashed the town to smithereens, and the thirty-five men who defended it.

"You're now asking us to behave like cowards, you who once encouraged us to seize Vientiane. You're leaving us in the lurch. It's a good thing Gibelin, a Frenchman, is coming with us instead of you."

Ricq had argued.

"But I can't. You must understand. I'm against your operation. The destruction of a defenceless town by artillery is going to revolt the whole world. If that town defends itself, it's a very different matter. International opinion . . ."

Gibelin had interrupted harshly:

"Opinion is always faked. People are only moved by what happens to them personally. As for the rest, they listen to any old thing, providing those who flatter them leave them with a clear conscience or that feeling of security which a coward always needs."

Ricq had persisted:

"Antoine, you captured Vientiane but were driven out again. You now want your revenge. You, Thon, made a fool of yourself at Paksane, you also want your revenge."

Gibelin had wiped the sweat running down his cheeks with the back of his hand.

"Little Ricq, you're making the mistake of regarding yourself as a Machiavelli or a Messiah. I'd rather see you with a carbine in your hand."

"I obey orders, Gibelin, I'm a soldier even though I'm not in uniform."

"What am I, then?"

"An adventurer devoured by pride, as you know yourself. You were robbed of this town nineteen years ago. You were robbed of Flore today. You want to make thousands of innocent people suffer for this."

Gibelin had squared his shoulders and recovered his pride together with the detached and disdainful tone he had not managed to assume for years:

"I think I've had enough of you. Get out of here, go and join Sisang in Cambodia."

"I'm staying on to repair the damage you're about to do. I shall make arrangements for the return of Sisang and Chanda. Because they're going to return."

Gibelin had embarked on one of those longwinded speeches of his which drove every customer out of the Constellation. But each word wounded Ricq. He hauled him over the coals, and at the same time every other secret agent:

"What difference will it make if Sisang comes back or Chanda struts about on a platform again? None at all. Remember the bronze drums. The Chinese general installed them in the waterfalls of Laos to make the highlanders believe that the emperor's army was occupying the country. But it was fighting at the opposite end of Asia.

"The Chinese Communists and Vietnamese did the same thing. They placed bronze drums all over Laos, amplifying their thunder by the wireless, the press and television. They did this to lure those credulous barbarians which the white men are to them. From north to south they engineered countless trivial incidents and engagements which resulted in a minimum of casualties. They captured towns and villages from which the garrisons had fled before they were even in sight.

"With a song and dance, they organized the Pathet Lao, a

Communist movement whose existence depended solely on their support. Each time three Laotian soldiers took to their heels, the papers reported they had been driven back by a Vietminh regiment or Chinese division. Who was beating the bronze drums? Agents like Ricq, Cosgrove, Stone and that Armenian Russian who has just arrived. All your governments and the journalists you overawed fell into step with you.

"But the Communists never wanted to seize Laos. They don't give a damn about her. The French went through Na-San and Dien Bien Phu on account of this country; the Americans have spent six hundred dollars per inhabitant here—the largest sum in the world. That nonsense about the three princes? Sheer eyewash. I'm now absolutely certain the Viets knew Sammay wanted to betray them and they let him have his way—just an additional drum to take in suckers like you, Ricq.

"But in the meantime they were hard at work, undermining all resistance. While you poor innocents were playing with your drums, the Communists were devouring South Vietnam, Burma, Malaya, Singapore and Indonesia. They moved into Cambodia and took control of the bonzes and students, they even infiltrated the troops fighting against them.

"Only drunkards like myself, perhaps, or addicts like Uncle Yong, the disillusioned spy of Formosa and Chiang Kai-Shek's China, know how to remain clear-headed by blocking our ears. Personally, I don't give a damn either way. I'm merely settling old scores and, rifle in hand, defending the country I love and which I therefore regard as my own. The captain who killed Chouc and raped Ven at Nouei-Phou Lak has not yet been punished. He's in the Savannakhet army and may be a colonel by now. That's the truth. Si Mong must be made to pay for what he has done and is still doing. He won't enter Vientiane as a conqueror without losing a single man. Where's your pride, Ricq? You can't allow yourself to be diddled like this by pimps and gangsters. Be a man again, Ricq. There's no one left in the valleys of Laos. Get your rifle and come with us."

"Antoine, I can't. Yet it's so easy to pick up a carbine."

"That remains to be seen. Thon, it's time we were off. We're going to see what's happening. Goodbye, Ricq. Go and play the clown with your ambassadors."

During the afternoon Ricq had tried to get through to Cosgrove in Bangkok. The line was out of order, the American Embassy closed and sentries barred the entry to Camp Kennedy. Pinsolle had received instructions from Paris not to commit himself and to maintain the strictest neutrality. Ricq could stay where he was, but at his own risk and peril. He was advised to take refuge at the French Military Mission which would attempt to get him over the border into Cambodia.

Ricq refused to leave and went back to his own house, grieved by his altercation with Gibelin. He had forgotten about Ven whom he found waiting for him, sitting on the edge of the divan, still trembling. When she saw him, she got up and rushed towards him. Ricq was no longer alone. He had Ven to defend and comfort —Ven who was the real Laos and its ten thousand forgotten villages. It was as simple as taking up a carbine. In her faltering French, which she never managed to speak well, she had said:

"I was frightened you wouldn't come back. When will you take me to Nouei-Phou Lak?"

Ricq had suggested driving her round to Father Maurel's, or else to the convent, but she had protested:

"I want to stay with you, otherwise you'll forget you have to take me home. I'm frightened when you're not here. I don't ever want to see war or soldiers again."

Ricq had opened some cans of food but was unable to swallow anything but a cup of tea, whereas Ven ate with a hearty appetite. She had again begged him:

"Stay with me, the soldiers will come and I don't want to be alone."

At nine o'clock in the evening the bombardment had started again. The Thai artillery and Si Mong's heavy American mortars pounded the town at random. The tanks fired sporadically and furiously.

Ricq had gone out on to the veranda.

The tracer bullets, the red flashes of the guns, the orange and yellow flashes of the mortars pierced and shattered the darkness.

A flare floated down on the end of its parachute, bathing the river, pagodas and huts in a milky moonlight. Ricq kept thinking of Gibelin. From his window he was probably looking at this senseless expenditure of ammunition and recalling the days the two of them had controlled a country as big as ten French counties with a mere hundred partisans, twenty rifles and thirty rounds per man. Several fires broke out, which were fanned by the wind. The fishermen's quarter was the first to be set ablaze. The thatch roofs went up in a shower of sparks.

A river of fire flowed all the way along the Mekong, the flames drowning or casting a reflection in the dark waters.

Ricq watched Vientiane burning with the despair of a peasant witnessing the destruction of his farm and crops. He could not even make those useless gestures which at least bring comfort, such as carrying a pail of water or clutching a rifle to his breast. His hopes and efforts of the last twenty years, the dream of peace which tonight pathetically assumed Ven's features, were going up in flames with the town.

He found himself naked and defenceless, without dreams, without plans, without friends. His eyes were smarting and tears ran down his cheeks. He kept saying to himself. "This is too stupid, it's not possible." What sadistic pleasure could men derive from destroying and slaying, from harming one another and themselves?

Just then a shell from one of the tanks hurtled through the flimsy wooden walls of the shack. With a sense of relief—for he felt he was no longer a powerless spectator—Ricq leapt to his feet to save what was still left to him, the living image of all he had lost—Ven. He stumbled against her and for a moment he thought she was wounded. But she was unhurt.

A burst of heavy machine-gun fire riddled some pieces of furniture and pierced a water jug. Ricq pulled Ven behind a bed which he turned over onto its side. The young girl was terrified yet did not fully realize the extent of the danger threatening them. This frail obstacle, this shelter which merely concealed the danger, gave her a sense of security. To reassure her even more, Ricq flung his arms round her shoulders and held her tight. Insidiously, the warmth of her young body swept over him; her legs and his were closely entwined; her hair, which smelt of frangipani blossom, was plastered against his cheek. Soon nothing existed for him but this trembling body that he had to defend and protect.

If the gun fired an inch or two lower, they would both be killed, huddled in each other's arms. Anyone who came across their bodies would believe they were lovers. With a gesture of friendliness and affection, Ricq stroked the hair and face of this partner whom destiny was granting him for a few minutes or a few hours. Involuntarily he touched her breast and Ven gave a violent jerk to escape from his embrace. Ricq spoke to her gently, mingling the words he knew of her dialect with other words in Laotian. He evoked the memory of her village, the rites that had attended her birth, the memory of her father and the flower she had given him on his departure four years before; Ven then laid her head gently against his shoulder. Despite his desire, Ricq did not want to be anything more than a father or brother to her. But never before had he so desired a woman, never had he imagined that the world could be reduced to this warm, moist little creature whimpering beside him.

There was another burst and she clung still more closely to him, her belly against his breast. He stroked her skin which was as smooth and cool as the pebbles at Nouei-Phou Lak; her blouse had opened beneath his fingers like a ripe fruit. When he tried to unbutton it further, she shrank back. Ashamed of himself, he drew away from her but she clung to him again.

He had forgotten all about Laos, his fear of women, Gibelin, the guns, the fires and the pointless killing. All he wanted was to clasp this body more tightly and lose himself in it. He whispered incoherent words mingled with prayers and plaints. In spite of his desire, which by now was unbearable, he did not want the young girl without her consent. He thought of the soldiers who had raped her. Clumsily, he tried to kiss her, but she turned her head away, uttering only a little cry when he stretched out on top of her and yielding without resistance, a rag doll in his arms.

"You're nice and gentle," she told him afterwards. "You didn't hurt me like the others. Do all men want the same thing, Ricq, even you?"

Ven had spent the night pressed against him. Each time he moved or got up, she clung to his shoulder. The artillery and machine-gun had stopped firing, but he was unable to sleep, so intense was his desire for her. In the morning, despite his resolutions, despite his shame at having behaved with the young girl little better than the soldiers, he took possession of her again, burying his head in her flowing locks, his lean body against hers, striving desperately to produce a cry of pleasure from her. She was still merely gentle and consenting.

Ricq counted forty-five projectiles that had come through the house. Ven had vanished into the kitchen. With a little fan she was trying to revive a charcoal fire. Naked under one of Ricq's sarongs, with her hair flowing loose, she seemed to him even more beautiful and desirable than the night before.

He sat on a stool, watching her as she crushed some tea-leaves and searched through the shattered cupboards. Looking up, she smiled at him without the slightest embarrassment:

"What a nice house you have, Ricq, for a man who lives alone."

"Not Ricq, François."

"François, François," she repeated.

Then she burst out laughing. It was the first time he had heard her laugh and he felt as grateful to her as though she was forgiving him. Very clumsily, he seized her hand and kissed it. Gibelin's gaunt head had appeared at one of the windows, then the rest of his body as he climbed up the stairs. He was wearing his old hat and bush shirt and carried a leather game-bag to hold his ammunition. In his hand was an American carbine with specially adapted sights to enable him to fire more rapidly.

Gibelin apologized:

"I heard your quarter had taken quite a pasting. I felt worried about you, so I came along to see. Can you give me a cup of tea, since you never have any alcohol in the house?"

He glanced round the room:

"They've turned your shack into a sieve. The hospitals are full. There's a shortage of plasma and doctors. A lot of people have been badly burnt. I say, Ven, what are you doing here with Ricq?"

Ven assumed the self-important, serious tone she could never maintain for long:

"Ricq is now my *phoua*, my husband. I'm going to live with him and run his house. Then we'll both go back to Nouei-Phou Lak. I'll weave silk, he'll go out hunting and plant rice."

Gibelin could not help laughing:

"You're mad, Ven. Ricq's a white man."

"No, he's a Lao, a Kha, a Thai, anything you like, but he's not a *Phalang*."

Ricq had found his friend Gibelin again and the fires of the previous night were extinguished. His despair lifted; he felt happy. Did not Ven's body, as it brushed against him, give promise of further embraces? For thousands and thousands of nights he would watch her and listen to her as she slept.

Gibelin drank his tea in silence, his grey hair plastered against his forehead. Then he got up:

"Stay a bit longer, Antoine," said Ricq.

Gibelin shook his head.

"Impossible. I still hope to get away with it this time. But if anything happens to me, give everything I have to that slut Flore."

"Why?"

"She will have been the last girl I had. She'll have enough to live on for a few months, no more. I've been on the verge of bankruptcy for some time, as you must have guessed. The tomb of Don Quixote has been filled in and no one will feel the urge to come and commit enormities in Laos any more. At least I've had a good time."

Then he said to Ven in Laotian:

"Look after Ricq, you've found the best *Phalang* of the lot. Maybe we'll all three meet at Nouei-Phou Lak. Ven, you must find me a pretty *phousao*, as pretty as you, if possible, and we'll have a *boun* until the end of the world."

He turned to Ricq:

"*Phousaos* are like flowers that wither as soon as they're transplanted. I'm glad you've taken a wife and that she's Ven. Thanks to her, you'll see, you'll no longer hear the bronze drums. Since her birth she has been interwoven in your life. I wonder now what I was always trying to find in women. Maybe you've just found it: tenderness, memories, the living image of a country you loved and which no longer exists.

"It's time to go and give Si Mong a good hiding. So long, Little Ricq, see you tomorrow maybe, or maybe never . . ."

Gibelin picked up his carbine and disappeared.

Ricq never saw him again.

Si Mong had taken two days to capture Vientiane, with thirty thousand men against thirty-five.

Thon and Gibelin had inflicted severe losses on him—several hundred dead and wounded—and more than once his army had disbanded. The paratroops, divided into small teams of four or five equipped with a mortar or machine-gun, took cover behind the trees and walls and let the Savannakhet troops advance. They would fire three shells, a long burst, and then vanish. Immediately afterwards they would come back, then vanish again. This resistance had made Si Mong wild with rage. Despite the intervention of the Americans, he had continued to shell the town.

Ricq had taken refuge with Ven at Father Maurel's. The church and mission building were full of refugees who had arrived with their furniture, carts, bicycles, some of them with their pigs, all of them with their sacks of rice. Gibelin had appeared for a moment, black with grime and sweat, cheerful and loud-voiced, as youthful as in the days of the resistance against the Japanese.

He was drunk with noise, fatigue and brandy, and had teased the missionary about the false teeth he always refused to wear. He had looked for Ricq but had been unable to find him. A few hours later, just as Si Mong's troops were pouring into the town from all sides, Gibelin, Thon and the surviving paratroops had escaped in two trucks. Thon stood upright in the leading one, dishevelled, bearded and spattered with blood and filth, blazing away with his machine-gun. Gibelin sat at the wheel of the second vehicle, with the wounded crammed into the back.

In spite of Thon's gestures and yells, Gibelin had stopped to pick up a couple of paratroopers lying bleeding under cover of some trees, whom Si Mong's men would have finished off.

He had lost two minutes bundling them into the truck and found himself surrounded. According to one report, Gibelin had tried to fling a grenade at the soldiers as they moved in and had had his arm blown off by the explosion. He had then been finished off with a bullet in the head, on the edge of the pavement, together with all the other wounded men in the truck. Then his body had been thrown into the Mekong. According to another report, he had surrendered without defending himself. An officer had recognized him and taken him to Si Mong who had tortured him all night before having him flung next morning into the river.

Ricq had subsequently questioned Khammay about it, but Khammay knew nothing. He did not think Gibelin had been finished off on the edge of the pavement. Otherwise why was his body found strangled? Ricq's memory of the next few days was confused, his clearest recollection being the first cry of pleasure and joy that Ven had uttered in his arms. It was at Nouei-Phou Lak.

A Catholic Vietnamese, a friend of Father Maurel's, had hidden Ricq and Ven in his truck and driven them to Paksane. His brother-in-law had then taken them in an old jeep as far as the pass overlooking the Nouei-Phou Lak basin, and from there they had continued on foot. Ven was carrying her belongings in a silk handkerchief. Ricq had a revolver hidden inside his shirt, a little food in his haversack and a handful of silver coins. No one in the village knew what had happened at Vientiane and they had been well received.

Ven had taken Ricq to her hut on the edge of the river and cooked a meal for him, which he still remembered—fish stuffed with peppers and aubergines, stodgy rice and fresh vegetables.

That night, while the torrent roared outside, Ven had moaned louder and louder and finally uttered a shrill cry, digging her nails into his back. In the morning she had bathed in the river with the other *phousaos*—a thing she had not done since being raped by the soldiers. Laughing, splashing about with her friends, she had signalled to Ricq to come and join her. There had been three days of peace and quiet, three days of oblivion, and the miracle of Ven repeated every night.

Driven out of Vientiane, Chanda with the help of the Communists seized Xieng Khouang and its airfield. Forthwith some Russian aircraft flew in equipment, food supplies, arms and artillery.

Ricq had rejoined Chanda, leaving Ven at Nouei-Phou Lak. On leaving her he had felt a sense of anguish and emptiness. He needed to be conscious of her close to him, cheerful or sad, silent or talkative, never ungracious, always neat and tidy, modest and immodest at one and the same time. Ven did not understand why he had to leave her so soon to resume his work of death and conspiracy which invariably culminated in a village being burnt, people being killed or maimed, houses being destroyed.

Part of the population of Vientiane—the students and bonzes—had fled and followed Chanda. The Communists tried to take advantage of the subsequent disorder to lure the paratroops over to their side. But they had been impatient and maladroit.

Chanda had been frightened. Ricq had recalled Meynadier from Cambodia, together with a dozen officers and warrant officers, to take charge of the Neutralist troops. Si Mong had made an attempt to seize Xieng Khouang. After a brisk engagement his troops had turned tail in spite of all the equipment the Americans had given them. The paratroops had pursued them right up to the Mekong.

The Neutralist army was expanding, its ranks swollen by the volunteers who had joined Chanda. It soon numbered ten thousand men, but less than three thousand of them were capable of handling a weapon.

Thon had promoted himself to colonel and, on Meynadier's advice, assumed command of the two parachute battalions, refusing the post of chief of staff that Chanda had grudgingly offered him.

Chanda was infuriated by the prestige Thon had acquired through the fighting spirit he had shown at Vientiane; and Thon, despite himself, was increasingly jealous of the importance Chanda had suddenly assumed on the international scene. The capture of Xieng Khouang and the abject manner in which Si Mong had behaved at Vientiane had turned the little captain into a great Laotian hero.

Chanda had gone off to Moscow and the Viets had tried to take advantage of his absence to acquire control of the Neutralist army.

Ricq, Meynadier and the French advisers had prevented the Neutralists from drifting into the Communist camp. In their fury the Viets had tried to resort to force since their propaganda had been a failure. There had been a number of brisk engagements and skirmishes between patrols, which had accentuated the rupture until finally the two armies were at daggers drawn.

One fine morning Prince Sisang had landed at Xieng Khouang and declared, in front of the journalists he had brought with him in the plane, that he was still the legal head of the government and was taking over the powers previously delegated to General Atharon.

In an astrakhan hat almost as tall as himself, Chanda visited Moscow. He was applauded and appeared on television. In a solemn ceremony the Soviet Government presented him with a battalion of tanks. The battalion reached Vinh in the Plain of Jars two days before the Neutralists and the Pathet Lao had begun to confront each other.

At Vientiane, Si Mong had united all the police forces in a single organisation known as the Coordination, to which were attached some "Special Forces" wearing paratroop uniform and mainly officered by Thais. Then, after punishing the town, he had proceeded to fleece it, robbing the banks and business houses, monopolising the sale of gold and opium. Prudently, he had involved his gangs in all these operations.

Meanwhile the Neutralists had come to grips with the Communists. In the American press they in their turn were described as "the bulwark of the West against the advancing Red tide". Si Mong was dubbed a wash-out, a puppet of the Left and a crook.

In Paris this reversal of the situation was attributed to Ricq. He was made a lieutenant-colonel and he celebrated his promotion alone with Meynadier on a mountain peak, drinking a can of beer. One morning Colonel Cosgrove landed in the Plain of Jars and submitted a proposal for getting rid of Si Mong. Under pressure from the other powers, the Americans were now willing to allow Prince Sisang to return to the capital. The prince would merely have to undertake to retain Si Mong as Vice-President.

The prince agreed. In vain did Ricq advise him to consult his officers.

"My officers are here to carry out my orders," he had replied.

Thon was enraged by this. He could not countenance a government that included the head of the Neutralists and the man who had fired on the Neutralist troops.

Ricq had tried to convince him of the political necessity. Thon refused to be appeased.

On his return from Russia, Chanda hesitated for a moment but finally fell into step with the prince's policy which was also that of the Soviets. The Russians wanted a Neutralist government at Vientiane and, in the Plain of Jars, an army which would contain the thrust of the heretic Communists. For, in the Sino-Soviet quarrel, the Viets had just taken sides with the Chinese.

Accompanied by Chanda, Sisang had made his entry into Vientiane on 28 March 1964. Ricq had gone to fetch Ven from Nouei-Phou Lak. She had altered considerably. She was once again involved in the communal life of the village, participating in its activities and the comic or sordid little intrigues that constituted its existence.

On several occasions he had caught her laughing and joking with the handsome Koumane. But this had not disturbed him. Was not the young man Ven's cousin?

At Vientiane Ricq had rented a large shack and engaged a maid, Phila, to keep Ven company.

Ven occupied an important position in his life. He taught her French and took pleasure in buying her clothes, helping her choose her dresses and shawls.

When, in July, eight days before the Coordination *putsch*, she announced she was expecting a baby, he was deeply moved. He decided: "If it's a boy I'll call him Antoine Dan; if it's a girl, Ira Françoise." But he had failed to understand why Ven was in tears.

Ricq had to continue with his work all the same. But he no longer devoted himself whole-heartedly to the job, especially since receiving some strange instructions from Paris. The solitary and ill-informed man who decided on the policy to be pursued in

Indo-China was planning to go back on the Geneva Agreements. This would mean openly affronting the Americans and secretly the Russians. Now that India was faltering, France wanted to take her place in Asia and act as the leader of a somewhat ill-defined third force, at the cost of allowing Indo-China, which was in any case doomed to Asiatic Communism, to be devoured. This was the only means by which de Gaulle, the head of a nation which today was of secondary importance, would be able to play a major role on the international scene.

Pinsolle thought that this procedure was lacking in elegance but at least had the merit of not being too costly and not in any way affecting the final outcome. Whatever happened, Laos was unable to survive. History, as Nietzsche said, consisted entirely of the practical refutation of so-called moral principles.

This evening Ricq had nothing left but Ven. His longing to be with her again, to see her, touch her, inhale her, was so intense that he called her name out loud.

A sentry opened the door and asked:

"You must be thirsty, do you want some tea or beer?"

At eight o'clock in the evening General Si Mong, before going to the annual Rotary Club dinner, rang up Colonel Cosgrove. His eyes were screwed up with pleasure as he held the receiver to his ear:

"Hello, my dear Colonel, I don't know if you've been notified yet, but the cargo of one of your helicopters has been seized in Bangkok . . . cans of powdered milk containing Meo opium.

"A minor incident. The Thai government will merely make an official complaint to your embassy and the matter will be hushed up. You know, I don't like the French, but I always manage to hit it off with them. They don't behave like Sunday School teachers. If they were involved in an incident like this, it would easily be fixed."

"What are you getting at, Si Mong?"

"Virtuous America is going to take disciplinary action against the guilty party in the name of a moral code which she professes but doesn't respect. You're the guilty party. Ricq will be expelled tomorrow. I don't need him any more now that you too will be leaving South-East Asia. Your ambassador at Bangkok gave Marshal Aprasith his personal assurance. Are you coming to the Rotary Club dinner tonight?"

"Si Mong, I've been a long time in Asia and I know a man who's finished when I see one. You're finished."

"But you'll be leaving before I do."

Si Mong rang off.

The Vientiane Rotary Club held its annual dinner in the Viengrathry Restaurant, above the night-club.

In other towns, in other countries, the Rotary Club is supposedly composed of the leading citizens, successful business men, doctors and lawyers, men who consider themselves a cut above the others and who need to reassure themselves of this periodically by having a meal together. In Laos it consisted merely of men who did business, the business being either opium or arms, and who were lucky enough to survive in this extremely hazardous profession. There were also a number of political figures who indulged in politics in order to do business, and finally those who dabbled in espionage, intelligence work and profitable contraband. The honorary president was Prince Sisang; the actual president was the British agent, Malcolm Stone, always impeccably dressed, always impeccably drunk. He was a friend of every author who had written about the secret service and had consequently been mentioned in a number of books. Some of them described him as a tall, thin, cynical womaniser, others as a short, dark misogynist in search of a meaning to life and appealing to a tortuous god to still his twinges of remorse.

Stone was actually a pleasant person of medium height and with a fresh complexion, who was approaching the age of retirement. He had once been courageous and efficient but was now a disillusioned spectator, steeped in whisky, gin and Pernod, and winding up his career in this Laotian backwater. Since it was a very hot night, the men had shed their jackets but kept on their ties.

Prince Sisang, accompanied by General Si Mong, had taken his seat at the high table next to the American ambassador. The French ambassador was conspicuous by his absence. The arrival of Cléach, wearing a piece of black string in place of a tie and accompanied by Flore who looked ravishing in a tight skirt with a deep slit up the side, had caused a scandal.

Stone came over and took him by the arm:

"My dear fellow, I'd be much obliged if you'd kindly wear something that looked more like a tie and . . . er . . . to ask this charming creature with you to meet you later on in the night-club."

Nate Hart of Associated Press then butted in:

"Stone, old man, there's only one pretty girl in this room, and that's Flore. She's slept around a bit, I agree. But she's turned over a new leaf . . . not for long, I hope. Oh yes, Stone, she's slept around, but at least not like the wife of the Public Works Minister, that lovely Chinese girl who worked for a year in Mother Duk's brothel. I saw you kissing her hand just now with the unctuousness that only a gentleman like you could put into such an idiotic gesture."

"Oh, leave him alone," said Cléach, who was fond of Stone.

But the American was now in full flight:

"You want respectability in this jungle. But just take a look round. There's Franceschi, who's on your club committee and is even a foundation member; he exports opium secretly from Xieng Khouang to Marseilles on behalf of that dirty bastard Si Mong who will presently be sitting next to you since he happens to be Vice-President. You'll afterwards thank him for having come, you'll kowtow to that worthy general, who runs all the brothels and opium dens in town, not to mention a gang of hired killers, and who ordered artillery to fire on a defenceless city. Five hundred dead, thousands wounded."

"Shut up, Nate. The Rotary Club wants to forge bonds of friendship . . ."

"Look, there's Vidal. What does he do in the Shan States with the two little Beechcraft belonging to his air-taxi service? He delivers arms to the rebels, old man, and they pay him in gold or precious stones. For this racket, he has to have the consent of the Viets. But of course you know all about it, you're as thick as thieves, you two. Vidal has useful connections. Did you notice his tie? He isn't wearing one. And the girl with him? He picked her up at Pnom-Penh, at Mother Jo's."

With his big grubby paw Nate Hart seized Stone by the sleeve of his white shirt and made him turn round:

"Look over there. Police informers, stool-pigeons and secret agents. Your colleague Justified of the C.I.A. is representing his boss, Colonel Cosgrove. Cos must have given you some excuse for not attending this dinner, because he's up to one of his dirty tricks in the Plain of Jars. Captain Lalo is likewise representing his boss, Colonel Ricq, who is now in jug after spreading the Neutralist virus throughout South-East Asia.

"I hope, Stone, you're not going to turn this Rotary Club, which is the most fascinating one in the world—this collection of pimps, crooks, dope-peddlers and cloak-and-dagger men—into one of those boring organizations which exist in their thousands in America, England and France. You don't want it to become a sort of youth club to which you can't bring anyone except your lawful wedded wife? Out of the twelve lawful wedded wives who are here this evening, there are only three who sleep with their husbands. Four of them at least spend their evenings smoking opium, one's a lesbian and the remainder think they're Antinea."

Stone tried to stem this flow of words:

"I was only telling your colleague Cléach that his tie . . . Prince Sisang isn't a crook or racketeer, he's respected throughout the world, and he's with us tonight."

"Look at the bruise he still has on his cheek. A little gangster in uniform beat him up in his own house because he wasn't flexible enough for his boss Si Mong. Now he's toeing the line. That's what used to happen in Chicago in the days of Al Capone. Look, there's Comte Leoni, first secretary at the Italian embassy, stroking the Chinese waitress's buttocks. After dinner he'll ask her to go home with him. She'll accept, she always does—for two thousand kips. Too expensive, in my opinion. As flat-chested as an ironing-board! Let's go and have a gin, Stone, before we start this goddam dinner. You can give this old spy a lead or two, can't you Cléach?"

Stone pretended to lose his temper:

"To hell with you, Nate. I have to attend to our guest, Jacob Flayelle, the rice expert from U.N.E.S.C.O. He's going to give a talk on the remarkable results he has achieved from his new methods of cultivation."

"They've been a complete failure here, Stone. The fellow's leaving in disgust. The Laotians want the rice to grow all by itself or for America to provide it. Come and have a little gin. It must be half an hour since you had your last drink. Your eyes are watering . . ."

Stone looked sheepish. This damned American knew he was pining for a drink. But he clung desperately to his urge for respectability which kept returning like a twinge of heartburn. This evening he meant to behave properly, to show he could control himself, that he wasn't finished as certain people in the British Embassy claimed. But he was now in urgent need of a drink. He tried to stifle his yearning with good resolutions but soon was unable to think of anything but an excuse for yielding to it.

He followed Flore and the two journalists, assuming the part of a busy man reluctantly looking for a stray guest. His act deceived no one.

He even bumped right into Jacob Flayelle.

"I'll be back in a moment, old boy . . . Just a moment. I can't find that fellow Henderson, our treasurer."

With great relief, he gulped down two big glasses of gin diluted with a splash of tonic water.

Straight away he reverted to the amiable man who was popular with everyone. He even found that the piece of string Cléach was wearing as a tie showed a certain casual elegance. Nothing seemed urgent any longer. Life was what it was and no one could do anything about it. He leant forward on his stool so as to inhale the scent of Flore. At Mandalay he had known and loved—or at least desired enormously—a native girl who exuded the same warm effluvia. It had cost him his post as consul general, for his wife had asked for a divorce. He had then toyed with the idea of disappearing or embarking on some wild adventure such as joining the Foreign Legion. Some friends had cured him with gin and whisky. Since then his life, while ceasing to be respectable, had become more fascinating.

Reeling slightly, he made his way up the stairs. No one showed the slightest surprise. Laos made people tolerant or indifferent to the vices of others.

Stone thumped the bell cheerfully and, supporting himself with one hand on the table, embarked on his address of welcome in French which everyone applauded without listening to it. He kept confusing names and professions and giggled to himself over these obscure jokes.

Far away in the mountains of Tran-Ninh, a Meo by the name of Ma Yu, who had left home six months before, returned to his village. No one put any questions to him. If he had gone away, it was because he had felt like it; if he had come back, it was likewise because he had felt like it. His wife cooked him some pancakes which he ate in silence. But he seemed surprised that his son, who was only fifteen, owned a magnificent rifle with a hundred rounds of ammunition. Yu took the weapon and sent the boy off to get another one from the white men who were not French and who made much less fuss and bother about providing arms.

In his prison Ricq kept calling out for Ven.

[7]

The Bangkok Plane

THE truck had refused to take Ven any further and she had continued on foot, taking her sandals off so as to walk more quickly.

She no longer knew what had impelled her to flee from Vientiane: the badgering of Si Mong's policemen, Ricq's return which she longed for yet dreaded? Or simply an irresistible urge to take refuge at Nouei-Phou Lak and postpone the decisions she had to take? Would she keep the child? Would she marry Ricq? If he was forced to leave Laos, would she follow him?

If she kept the child, Koumane would not want her, but she no longer knew if she wanted him.

If her father Chouc had still been alive he would have given her the right advice.

"François Ricq," he used to say, "is one of those white men who have chosen us. They secretly hope to mingle their blood with ours. Even though they're rejected by their own fellow-countrymen, they nevertheless remain white and we remain yellow; the two bloods don't mix."

Nouei-Phou Lak came into sight, bristling with little red flags.

The whole population was assembled in front of a bamboo platform on which a man was speaking through a megaphone.

Ven did not understand what it was all about. She started running but was soon out of breath and had to stop. Ricq's child made her ache all over; Ricq's child was trying to hold her back.

She drew closer to the crowd. No one turned round.

The men and women were sitting together on the ground, guarded by soldiers wearing wicker helmets and carrying Russian sub-machine-guns slung across their chests.

She now realized: the Communists had occupied the village. It was not a man speaking on the platform, but a woman in soldier's uniform with an expressive face and close-cropped hair. She was old, she must have been at least forty.

The woman was speaking in Laotian, but with a strong Vietnamese accent:

"The white imperialists have lied to you. They are the cause of all your misfortunes. But the worst of the lot were the ones you thought were the best, who came to live among you, who spoke your language but slept with your women. They said they were your friends in order to deceive you all the more and involve you in hazards and bloodshed. They brought with them war, suffering, hunger and death. Today you are free, thanks to the popular army and its beloved leaders Prince Sammay and our big brother Ho Chi-Minh. You will enjoy peace from now on. Long live President Ho and Prince Sammay, long live the glorious soldiers of the Pathet Lao and the Democratic Republic of Vietnam."

The soldiers cheered and the crowd followed suit half-heartedly.

"Louder, louder," the woman exhorted them.

When she was satisfied with their reaction, she climbed down from the platform and stopped in front of Ven.

"Don't be frightened, little sister. You're Ven, aren't you? The daughter of Chouc, the village headman who was assassinated by the lackeys of Si Mong, the cousin of Captain Chanda who has just become their ally, the whore of the French spy Ricq. But you're not to blame, you were deceived. The soldiers raped you, and then you were raped by the agitator Ricq, their boss."

"It's not true," Ven screamed. "Let me go. I love Ricq,

I'm going to marry him. It's his child I'm carrying."

"White men don't marry *phousaos*. They merely amuse themselves with them, then go off and enjoy the company of white women whom they excite with their glamorous adventures."

"The others may, but not Ricq. Ask anyone who knew him in the village."

"I know Ricq better than they do, and white men better than you do. I have the same father as Antoine Gibelin; he was a white man. My mother was a pretty *phousao*, like you, whom he abandoned.

"I too loved a white man. To help him I risked my life; he was Ricq's brother, Dan. Another coward and agitator. He betrayed me to the Germans. Like you, little sister, I was raped by the soldiers, but for months and months on end. It was in a concentration camp."

"Let me go."

"Where to? We are everywhere now. We're going to re-educate you. You'll tell the people of Nouei-Phou Lak how you were deceived. You'll describe the cunning, the cruelty, the ignominy of the imperialists and those who serve them. The people will then decide what you must do about the child. Maybe they will want you to keep it. We'll send Ricq photographs of the child. If he sends planes to bomb us, the bombs will fall on his own offspring."

Ven felt the trap closing round her. She screamed:

"Ricq, Ricq."

Trai calmly slapped her in the face. Her sobs died down. The Vietminh woman took her by the hand:

"Come along, little sister."

At eight o'clock in the morning of Saturday, 23 July, Ricq arrived at Wattay Airfield with his little cardboard suitcase in his hand. He was escorted by a Coordination officer and four guards.

Prestelot came over to him and handed him an air ticket and his passport:

"I'm awfully sorry, Monsieur Ricq. The ambassador would have liked to come out to the airport to say goodbye. But he has just been summoned by Prince Sisang who has put forward a suggestion for an international conference uniting the three factions . . . and the three princes. It will be held in Paris."

Ricq said to himself: "They're going to be able to escape, all three of them: the blue, the white and the red prince. They're going to find their paradise in France.

"But I'm not escaping, I'm going back to an unknown prison, without Ven. I shall wander through its huge corridors crammed with houses and people. But I'll have nothing to say to them."

Prestelot handed him an envelope. It contained a short note from Pinsolle and a key:

"My dear François Ricq,

Si Mong has changed his mind once again; for all his promises, he refuses to release you. The final reflex of a drowning fly! I've notified Paris of your splendid conduct. Unfortunately your chief and friend, General Durozel, has just been allowed to benefit from the retirement to which he was entitled. His successor, I believe, will know how to make the most of your capacities and remarkable knowledge of South-East Asia . . ."

(A good reference, Ricq reflected.)

". . . I have an apartment in Paris. I'd like you to regard it as your own. The address is 17, Quai Voltaire. My housekeeper will look after you. I've already notified her. Yours ever . . .

"P.S. Do be careful of the two Tang horses; they're very fragile. And mind my Tabriz carpet when you smoke your pipe."

Ricq now knew the number of his prison cell in France.

In front of him, lined up as though for a final parade, stood Meynadier in his red beret and camouflage uniform, Father Maurel in his mudstained cassock, Cléach who kept shifting from one foot to another, Mattei with his raincoat buttoned up to the neck and a black briefcase in his hand, and Flore who was yawning.

Father Maurel came forward:

"I've come to embrace you, little Ricq."

"What about Ven?"

"I told you I'll get her, but it won't be easy. Radio Hanoi

announced this morning that the Viets had occupied Nouei-Phou Lak."

Meynadier seized him by the shoulders:

"I'm leaving the army. I'm getting out in a couple of weeks. Without you and without Nouei-Phou Lak, this country is no longer my home. Let's buy a boat between us. At sea, you're still a free man. We'll sail all over the world until we grow too old and die. We'll call the boat the *Nouei-Phou Lak*. To while away the time, we'll have a bronze drum on board. We'll hang Gibelin's portrait up in the cabin and sit under the stars dreaming of all sorts of enormities. Embrace me, Colonel."

Cléach shook his hand with deep emotion:

"Thank you, Ricq."

"What for?"

"For being what you are."

A jeep drew up and Colonel Cosgrove Tibbet climbed out of it. He took Ricq aside.

"Are you happy, Cos?" Ricq asked him, without any bitterness. "You've won."

"Neither of us has won, we've both lost. I don't know what the end of a secret agent is in France, but I'll tell you what mine will be. I've been recalled to America. Si Mong put paid to me: a nasty silly little trick about some opium seized in Bangkok.

"For days and days I'll wander about the corridors of the Pentagon in Washington, asking to be debriefed and for an opportunity to defend myself. No one will listen to me because there's a smell of opium clinging to me, and another more pungent and at the same time indefinable odour—our defeat in Asia. One day I'll get fed up with wearing out the carpets and waiting outside the offices of generals whose doors are always closed to me. I'll bury myself somewhere in the depths of America, alone with a girl.

"Up in the mountains Picarle's Meos will be getting massacred, and down in the plains Si Mong will be stuffing himself with our dollars until the moment he too takes off.

"Good-bye, Ricq. Both of us are going to have a lot of sleepless nights thinking of those we have involved in war and death as a result of our activities. For a long time we've been accomplices without knowing it, and also friends."

Cosgrove patted him on the shoulder and very stiffly, in his cream-coloured uniform, climbed back into the jeep.

"We're travelling together," said Mattei.

Bowing his head, Ricq made his way towards the plane. A gust of warm rain swept the runway, glueing his shabby old drill suit to his bony frame. It was a forlorn grey silhouette, a prematurely aged and exhausted man, that stumbled up the steps of the aircraft.

Mattei gave him a helping hand:

"Are you tired, Colonel?"

"I'm so tired I'd like to die."

"Well, what shall we do?" asked Flore. "I'm hungry. Let's go and have a bowl of Chinese soup . . ."